SILVER AND GOLD

DAVID SAKMYSTER

WWW.DRAGONMOONPRESS.COM

Silver and Gold

ISBN 10 1-896944-98-1 Print Edition
ISBN 13 978-1-896944-98-2

Dragon Moon Press is an Imprint of Hades Publications Inc.
P.O. Box 1714, Calgary, Alberta, T2P 2L7, Canada

Printed and bound in Canada or the United States
www.dragonmoonpress.com
www.sakmyster.com

Silver and Gold

DAVID SAKMYSTER

To Shar + Denny,

My favorite fans!

thanks - and see you on Library Thing!

Love,

Dave Sakmyster

8/09

Dragon Moon

WWW.DRAGONMOONPRESS.COM
WWW.SAKMYSTER.COM

Acknowledgments

AS ALWAYS, UNENDING GRATITUDE GOES out to my parents for encouraging my imagination from such an early age; and to my wife—my first and most trusted reader—whose excitement over this project propelled me over some difficult hurdles. Thanks also go to my wonderful editor, Gabrielle Harbowy, and to everyone at Dragon Moon Press for taking on this novel, set in part just a little north of their neck of the woods.

FINALLY, WHILE ACKNOWLEDGING THE OBVIOUS influence of my boyhood fascination with the character of Yukon Cornelius in Rudolph the Red Nosed Reindeer, I am indebted to the good people at Classic Media, Inc. for allowing me to forge my own vision, and in no way have I intended to tread on the development of their own much-beloved character.

"Silver and gold are not the only coin; virtue too passes current all over the world."
-Euripides

Prologue: The Present - November, 1906

THE HUNTER

LEAVING A TRAIL OF PAW prints beside the large, determined man-tracks, the husky padded through the frosted snowdrifts. It cautiously approached the edge of the cliff where the man stood, his hands at his side, observing the kaleidoscopic light show in the night sky.

With its tail down, wagging in anticipation as it neared, the dog gave a whine and brought its muzzle to the man's hand. It sniffed deeply at the bare skin, the callused fingers and rough flesh toughened by years in the harshest elements. It caught the scent of licorice from one of those sticks the man was so fond of chewing.

"Easy, Dunder," the man said, his voice cutting through the arctic silence. Unable to lower his gaze from the luminescent scenery, he felt humbled that after all these years, this snow-covered realm continued to affect him so powerfully. Below, reflections of the shimmering Northern Lights glittered like flakes of gold along the great ice-coated river.

As he stroked the dog behind its ears, the man traced the river's path, following as it sliced through the valley, winding toward the mountains hunkered beneath the constellations like shrouded behemoths. The mighty Yukon: the sacred and storied river that traversed this arctic realm, spilling from glaciers and lakes and merging with countless tributaries. Including, farther south, the grand Teslin River—a three-hundred-and-ninety-mile driving force that the natives in their Tutchone language called the Delin Chu: the river after which he had been named.

Delin Wetherwax sighed, and continued rubbing the husky beneath its chin. Delin's beard was a respectable length, if a bit ragged, and descended halfway down the front of his emerald green coat. His golden hair, salted with grey, tumbled in curls from a faded blue hat. Twin Colt Dragoon revolvers of polished gold and inlaid silver rested in holsters on his belt, above canvas pants and bearskin boots.

He took a deep breath, as if he could force into his soul the utter stillness and complete calm pictured before him. The shadows grew and the silence deepened. The iron weathervane atop the nearby cabin stood as motionless as the other dogs, six of them still tethered to a sled a short distance away.

Suddenly, something shattered the silence, savage as an ax-blow; a sound at first so alien that the man hardly recognized it. But, trained for years to heed the slightest danger, Delin reacted immediately and reached for his revolvers.

Dunder was facing the shadow-fettered woods, and a low growl emanated from its throat. It was this sound that set the clifftop in motion. Delin sprinted even as the form burst from the woods. An instant before the bulk of white fur, immense arms and cruel talons tore past the vanguard of freshly-chopped trees, he fired twice and shouted a command to the dogs.

"*Ugiarpok!*" Just one word, an ancient Inupiaq verb, and Dunder and the other untethered husky—the one named Blitzen—tore from their stances and raced to attack.

Through the twin clouds of powder bursts, the Dragoons' blasts echoing in his ears, Delin bounded to the sled. Unsure if either shot had struck the rampaging beast, he shouted another command to the sled dogs, already in motion and heeding his unspoken request. The sound of snarls and yelps intensified as Delin leaped onto the approaching sled's runner boards. He perched, precariously unbalanced, as he slipped one revolver back in its holster and gripped the handlebar with his free hand.

The sled completed a sharp arc, then raced at the creature beset by the dogs. In the weak polar light the monster's hide almost looked blue, but the fur was pockmarked with blood, and crude holes had been torn from its flesh; its face was a mask of pain and savagery. Some weapon other than his had done this, Delin realized with a start, and pulled back on the lashings, slowing his approach.

He took aim again. This was one of the largest Sesquats he had ever seen, easily over fifteen feet tall, and its immensity brought him back to a tragic night over twenty years ago when even the smallest of these beasts had dwarfed him. Grimacing with the resurging memory of kerosene fires and scalding flesh, he fired once, then again, taking care not to hit Dunder or Blitzen. He slid through the great puffs of smoke and saw fresh wounds in the creature's torso.

In the next heartbeat, as Dunder came down from a lunging attack, a great white fist slammed into the dog. The yelp pierced Delin's heart, and he had to turn away rather than watch the dog's shattered body tumble over the ice.

He aimed again and pulled out the other pistol as the sled came around, within thirty feet now. As Delin sighted, both arms outstretched, he scanned the creature's hide. *It's not the one*, he thought, failing to see the distinctive scarring he had been looking for. The Sesquats were dwindling in number since his childhood, in no part thanks to him, but he was still surprised by their resiliency; *and still he sought that one, hoping to have one more chance against it...*

Wrapped around the beast's right leg was a tangled mess of black netting. Startled as he was by this observation, Delin didn't see the two hunters emerge from the woods.

When he finally caught their movements, it was too late. The first hunter, taller and bulkier, his parka bulging with extra supplies, charged ahead with a rifle. Before he could shoot, the creature leapt at him. Astonishingly swift, the beast tore through the man, leaving a severed leg rooted in the snow as the rest of the hunter flopped into the air and sailed over the cliff.

The rifle finally went off just as the hunter dropped from view, and the gunshot drowned out his final scream. Blitzen raced forward and snapped, taking a chunk from the monster's calf just as the other hunter got off a shot that sailed wide.

Delin blasted away with two more rounds, then tucked both revolvers away and lashed out with the whip, bearing the sled down to the lone hunter.

The Sesquat staggered back with twin impacts that only momentarily hindered it before it snarled and prepared to leap. Delin tugged hard on the gangline and cranked the handlebars, banking the sled and kicking up clouds of icy wake.

He sailed just past the Sesquat's lunging grasp, leaned over the side and reached out to the speedily-approaching hunter. His big grip caught him at the shoulder, and lifted the surprisingly light man off the snow. Delin managed to use the sled's momentum on a slight turn to flip the hunter through the air and deposit him on the empty flat bed.

With the howls of the pursuing beast in his ears, he shouted "Mush!" and they flew down the hill toward the woods and the path the dogs knew well.

Delin looked back and tried to see through the shadows beyond the hunter's hood, but couldn't make out a face. He was about to call out when the barrel of the hunter's rifle suddenly loomed in his face.

"Duck!" the hunter shouted, and Delin moved to the side an instant before the fiery cloud burst from the nozzle. Something screeched at his back just as the sled rocked to the side, teetered, then righted itself. Delin glanced back, and as the trees, frozen branches and boulders flew past in a blur, he saw the Sesquat rocking with obvious pain. Blood spurted from just below its throat. But it came on, pursuing relentlessly, hurtling fallen branches and throwing itself forward with immense leaps, gaining back the distance it had lost.

Sensing the pursuit, the dogs raced even faster, careening through the snow flattened from yesterday's trail-making, and they sped down the path as it grew steeper and steeper. Delin slipped an arm under the tow-wire to secure himself to the sled, then withdrew his own rifle from its side attachment. He shouted to the hunter, "Keep firing and slow it down!"

Delin cocked the barrel and balanced on the left runner board, giving the hunter a clear shot around him. Sighting along the barrel, he aimed in the opposite direction from the creature, forward and down the side of the cliff.

"What the hell are you doing?" the hunter yelled, in a surprisingly high-pitched tone.

"Just fire!" Delin shouted, and then aimed, trying to recognize the landmarks. In a few hundred yards the path up ahead would bank sharply left and turn around in a great 'U', working its way down the cliff. At one spot after that turn, a group of miners had broken camp during the spring, excited with a substantial find. They had left all their belongings perched on the side of the cliff and had raced back to Dawson to convert their wealth and head home to Kansas. After their departure, Delin had been slowly taking their supplies; up until now, he'd had no use for the three barrels of gunpowder left behind.

Even in the thick snowdrifts, those barrels peeked out from their perch high above the sled path. If he could get a clean shot, at just the right moment...

Something whizzed past his cheek and acrid smoke stung at his eyes. Another howl from the creature, and Delin swore he felt its foul breath blow away the sulfuric gunsmoke. He risked a glance, and wished he didn't. The Sesquat seemed unfazed, even energized, as it leapt from moon-dusted tree to tree, merging with the deep pockets of darkness then bursting out like a white streak of lightning.

Delin cursed, but calmly extended his left hand only, gripping the rifle. He held his breath and fired—just as the hunter got off another round. The Sesquat bounded onto the path just ten yards back and lunged at them, only to be caught by both shells in the stomach. It somersaulted backwards, snarled, but then jumped up again, pursuing.

"Impossible..." the hunter said, but Delin ignored him, turned around, cocked the chamber and sighted. The frosted trees hurled by like the flaps of moving picture frames he had witnessed once in Juneau, and a certain calm settled over his heart. His vision cleared and the darkness receded as if the moon had just tripled in size. There in his sights glinted the metal post from the old miners' camp, and just to the right—the rounded outline of the top barrel.

Delin pulled the trigger, then cursed when he observed the burst of snow just to the barrel's side. "Ah... missed it!"

The sled started to turn, and the terrain got bumpier as it descended. He sighted again, even as he heard the monster gaining on them. From just to his right came the horrifying CLICK of the hunter's empty magazine.

A gap in the trees appeared, and Delin focused. His finger clenched and the gun recoiled. Without looking at the result, he swiveled on the runner board, arched backward and turned. The Sesquat crashed through a low-hanging branch, shattering it in a cloud of dust and ice, and appeared right on top of them.

The rifle tumbled from Delin's hand, and in one fluid movement he now clenched both revolvers, bringing them together before his face. He fired. Again and again. Two more times, through the great clouds of smoke, the Dragoons spat out their fury, until finally, reluctantly, they were spent.

Holstering the weapons, satisfied that the beast was delayed if not destroyed, he turned and helped steer the sled. Only then did he follow the hunter's line of sight, and only then did he recognize the roaring sound echoing off the mountains. And only then did he notice the gushing black smoke, the fire shooting into the sky, the tons of ice and earth, exploding tree trunks and incinerated supplies.

He also noticed with growing dread that the avalanche, tumbling in a wave of relentless devastation, now bore down on the path ahead—closer and faster than he had anticipated.

"MUSH!" He lashed with the whip over the hunter's head. The dogs leaned into their task, aided by the steep angling and smooth trail. The wave of ice pressed on, smothering trees and gathering mass as it rolled ahead, cutting a swath fifty feet wide. A howling resumed behind them, and Delin heard the thunderous tread of the Sesquat as it gained.

The sled raced into the forefront of the avalanche, and to Delin it seemed as if he flew into a mass of churning thunderclouds, strangely beautiful in its relentless approach. He gaped up at the avalanche and it seemed time stood still…

And then they were airborne, dogsled and humans serenely coasting ahead of the advancing force.

They emerged, bursting through with just a bump. Delin looked back,seeing only a wall of white, and for a brief instant, the look of shock and pain as the wall of death slammed into the Sesquat. The avalanche carried it over the side, rending the body into shattered fragments, pulverizing muscle and bone on the way over the cliff, and then tumbling hundreds of feet to the rocks below.

"Whoa!" Delin shouted, bringing up the rope and working the handles from side to side. The dogs slowed and tried to halt their speeding descent. But the hunter suddenly sat up and leapt off the sled, shouting. "NO!"

Delin reached for the parka, but it slipped through his grasp. The hunter landed awkwardly on his dismount, screamed and went down. In a second Delin was there, leaping off the runner board and reaching for him.

The hood had been shaken free, and an astonishing face, grimacing in obvious pain, winced up at him. Delin reeled in shock. The hunter had pale, high cheekbones set in a narrow face, auburn hair, naturally curly but in knots and clumps after what must have been weeks in the arctic elements.

"A woman?"

She groaned and rubbed her ankle. "You have no idea what you just did!"

Delin blinked at her, then looked at the aftermath of the avalanche, where the last few icy rocks tumbled over the edge. "Seems to me, ma'am, that I saved your life. I'm truly sorry, however, that I couldn't aid your companion in time."

Something behind the woman's eyes went dark, and she looked down. "I'm sorry for Nathan, too. He was a guide I hired back in Dawson, but he knew the risks." She staggered to her feet and tried to put some pressure on the hurt ankle. She seemed desperate to reach the edge and look over.

"Risks?" Delin asked, suddenly recalling the net tangled up in the creature's leg. "You mean—no, I don't believe you were actually out here to hunt..."

"The *Sesquat*? Yes." The woman winced with every step. "We've been tracking it for three weeks, at considerable expense, traveling to this godforsaken place to investigate the rumors, and then return with one *intact*, if possible."

"Intact? Ma'am, you are lucky *your* condition still befits that description."

She glanced back at him, narrowing her eyes as if he had just shocked her with his vocabulary. "And who might you be?"

Delin stood up stiffly and spread out his arms. "Why, I'm sure my fame precedes me. I am none other than Delin Wetherwax, prospector in these parts and many others, and—"

"Yes, I've heard of you. Miners in Dawson City told me you live out here all alone. The more suspicious among them think you've got some kind of pact with the Sesquat creature."

"History, perhaps, but never any love lost between us." Delin's voice faltered at first as if biting down on a painful memory, then recovered. "But if you truly are out here on some sort of ill-advised zoological mission, I can scarcely believe you made it this long without being killed."

The woman leaned against a tree and looked down the twilight-speckled hill, where only a cloud of dust rose from the depths. "I'm not from the zoo."

"Oh, no? Then..."

"I'm here with a team of specialists. The others are compiling a geological survey of Alaska, while I volunteered to seek out this evolutionary throwback we'd heard about, and to bring one back for study, if possible." She glared at him. "We're from the Smithsonian Institution. I doubt you've heard of it."

Delin put a hand to his forehead and groaned. "I wish I could say that were true, ma'am. Unfortunately your Institution and the Wetherwax family have had... run-ins."

She looked up in surprise. "Who?"

"A man named Hall, a naturalist."

"William Healy Hall? You've met him?"

Delin nodded. "I was only fourteen at the time, but he traveled with my father and me up the Tanana River." He led her by the arm to the waiting sled. "Now, I have got to get back to my cabin and see about my dogs. And I must say that your ankle will need some attention."

"I'm fine."

"Suit yourself, ma'am." Delin backed away, hands in the air. "But I must tell you, unless you're awful clever at geography and can navigate by the stars, and unless you have supplies for at least a week, you may want to think about coming with me."

She narrowed her eyes, weighing some sort of response, while staring uneasily over the frozen landscape.

"Of course," said Delin, "if you're serious about locating another such creature, you're sure to be in luck. They're drawn to weak prey, and after a couple days out here alone..."

She swallowed. "Wait—how many of those things are there?"

Delin sighed. “They are very scarce, almost extinct, but they’re not just in these regions. I believe you’ll find references to them in many parts of the world, especially at high altitudes. In Asia they are called Yeti, or the Abominable Snowmen. They go by *Sesquat* to the Salishan tribes. The Athabascans call them *Arulataq*—which means ‘creature who makes a bellowing cry.’ In Tlingit they are known as *Kustaka*. Then, there’s what the Russian trappers called them—the *Almastay*.”

He sighed and looked away, wistfully. “And there is at least one more that I know of, one I’ve been tracking for years.”

“Any chance you’ll find it soon?”

“Why? So you can study it, stuff it and put it in your museum?”

The woman grunted. She tried to walk past Delin, only to wince again and go down, reaching instinctively for him as she fell. Delin caught her in his arms, and their cold faces were but inches apart, their breath steaming together in clouds.

After a moment of awkward silence, she angrily pushed free. “They warned me of other things about you as well, in Dawson.”

“Fools!” Delin proclaimed, with a slight grin. “They’re just sore that I don’t go and spend my hard-earned gold in their taverns and toss my wealth upon their vaudeville stages.”

“Nevertheless,” the woman said, “might I just be permitted to go my way?”

“Of course,” Delin said with a bow.

She looked ahead at the treacherous path and recalled the days spent meandering in the dark. The chill deepened, the stars burned boldly and the curtain-like aurora shimmered overhead. “Okay,” she said, relenting. “We’ll go to your cabin to get some supplies, and then you’ll take me on your sled into town, for which I will pay you an adequate sum.”

Delin shook his head and pointed through a crop of trees to the east. “I’m not going anywhere for the next week. Front’s coming in. The dogs know it, the birds and bears know it. The very land expects it.” He sighed. “When you chased that thing into my clearing earlier I was preparing for the storm, weighing the time left and readying my supplies.”

The woman stared at the starlit sky just above the backdrop of the towering mountains. “A blizzard? Is this a joke you prospectors like to play on visitors?"

"No joke, ma'am. Miss—what can I call you? This anonymity grows tiresome."

She narrowed her eyes and pulled the hood over her face. Without extending a hand, she limped to the dogsled and called back, "Griffith. Eloise Griffith."

Grinning, Delin followed and helped her get settled on the sled, seated amid his supplies. "Eloise, from the Greek 'Helios'—god of the sun." He winked at her. "Ironic, that you should find your way here to this land in its time of near-perpetual darkness."

Eloise regarded him as if he were some strange creature in her zoology ward. "Can we just get someplace warm, quickly?"

"Very well," Delin said. He strode up to the lead dog, and after whispering something in its ear, the sled lurched forward, beginning the long trip up the winding trail. "I'll see you at the cabin. They can't pull two of us up the hill, so I'll head up alone on the direct route and meet you at the top."

Eloise looked around nervously, jostling with the lurching of the sled. "But..."

"At the top," Delin shouted, slinging a pack over his shoulder and then bounding into the shadows.

Nearly thirty minutes later, about the same time Eloise mercifully lost feeling in her feet, the dogs began yelping, and for a moment she feared her wish had been granted and another Sesquat had found her. In moments, however, the canopy of spruces thinned and shafts of pale green light pierced through. Mesmerized, Eloise stared overhead, immune by now to the jostling of the sled over the ice-crinkled terrain.

The shimmering aurora cast furtive glances through the eaves, playing a game of first-sight, and the dogs seemed caught up in the sport, rushing to burst free of the forest and bark up in wonder at the magical vision.

But when the sled finally emerged onto the clearing with an abruptness that shocked her, Eloise stared in wonder not at the celestial light show, but at the scene on the ice ahead, at the man kneeling beside two roughly-hewn graves, piled over lovingly with hard-packed snow.

All at once the sled slowed to a graceful crawl and the team let out soft whimpers, reverently approaching the site. Eloise propped herself up, and when the sled came to a stop, she stepped off gingerly. Leaning on the rifle butt and limping, her boots crunched thunderous echoes across the polar stillness.

Delin's hat and gloves lay beside a pickax stuck in the ice. His blond curls were matted with frozen sweat and stuck to his face while his beard swirled in an unnatural wind; his eyes glistened with an oddly-tinted hue, absorbing the reflections from the cosmic spectator above.

Eloise stood and stared, wobbling slightly but ignoring the subdued pain and tingling from her feet. All the way up the hill she had practiced what she would say at this moment, prepared to show her fury and demand restitution. He had set her back months, and perhaps made her success impossible. Bad enough the others scoffed at her hunt for this legendary creature. She had argued that the Smithsonian should present just such anomalies to the cultured world, to illustrate how much of nature was still unknown and, perhaps, unconquerable.

She had meant to prove the others wrong, and while they were out drawing maps and analyzing old rocks, she would come back with something truly astonishing—something to make old Darwin himself scratch his head in wonder.

But then this man, this wild mountain prospector, had rushed in and knocked the prize from her grasp. Granted, she had underestimated the strength of the creature, but once she knew its habits and its territory, she could have returned with a team of trappers and brought it back—perhaps alive.

If not for Delin. It had been right there for her—a chance at fame, success and immortality of a sort. Right in her grasp, and despite those who second-guessed her, despite her own fears, and despite the advice of the doctors about the nameless illness which often sapped her strength and held her back... Despite all that, she knew she still had a chance to make something grand of whatever life she had left.

If not for Delin. In her mittens, her hands were clenched into fists, and in her heart her anger was still seething, but as she limped closer, a different emotion took over.

He was crying. She saw it at once—the tears sliding partially down his face before freezing and clinging like stalactites from his cheekbones. Delin let a bare hand settle on each mound. "Rest well, my friends." The words carried over the cliff like melancholy notes plucked from violin strings.

Eloise checked her anger and resisted a fierce chill that flared up her body from her toes. Her voice cracked, and she said the only thing she could think of: "What were their names?"

A thin smile tugged at Delin's mustache, curling to the right side of his face. He wiped away frozen tears as he stood. "Dunder and Blitzen! The pride of my team!"

From behind her, Eloise heard the other dogs give soft whines, as if acknowledging their own farewells. She blinked at Delin, then frowned, remembering something. "Do you know you named your dogs…after reindeer in a poem?"

"By Clement Clarke Moore!" Delin said, eyes wide. "'A Visit From Saint Nicholas.'" He stared at her, surprised that she recognized it. "My father used to read it to me when I was little. It was one of my first Christmas gifts."

"My grandfather read it to me," Eloise said. "He even had the original printing, with Thomas Nast's illustrations, from New York's *Troy Sentinel*, I think it was—in 1824."

"1822," Delin corrected. "Wish I could have seen those illustrations. Do you know that Dunder and Blitzen are Dutch for..."

"Thunder and Lightning! Yes," she said, "my grandfather was Dutch, and he just loved that poem, and the whole Saint Nicholas idea. I got three pieces of Dutch chocolate every Christmas Day."

Delin smiled. "It was hard to get chocolate up here, although we could always count on traders carrying soft Dutch treats like licorice candies or root sticks—which are my favorite, by the way, but most times I just received gold nuggets."

Eloise started to laugh, but then decided she wasn't sure if he was joking. "So were your parents Dutch as well, or...?"

"My father was," he said, walking past her to pick up his hat and gloves, and the pickax, which he promptly began to toss in the air and catch as he walked. "Wetherwax is derived from *Weiderwacht*, which means loosely, one who watches over a meadow, or a field."

Eloise gave him a sideways look. "So I imagine you fancy this entire arctic land to be your stewardship?"

Delin ignored the question, returning instead to the earlier topic. "My mother wasn't Dutch, however, but Russian nobility."

Eloise struggled to move after him. The chill was spreading, but now she felt hot—a sweat had broken out under her hood, and her neck itched. Delin's revelation was still sinking in, and she opened her mouth to express her disbelief when her rifle point slid on the ice. Her ankle turned and something cracked as she fell with a scream.

Delin was there in a moment, catching her before she landed face-first on the ice. He turned her and gently laid her on her back. She bit her lip and struggled against the numbing pain. She sensed a tugging at her foot, then she saw her boot come off and heard a gasp.

"Miss Griffith. I'm sorry, but you're in desperate shape."

Eloise shook her head. "I'm fine. Just help me up."

"No. Listen, these feet of yours are very near frostbitten. You let them get wet, and out here, that's a mistake that might be your last. I've seen more men than I could count come up here on two feet, only to leave with none."

"Really? I don't feel anything."

"That's the problem," he countered. "And on top of the frostbite, your ankle's broken. That's easy enough to fix. I'm going to set the bone now. Expect a little pain, but then we must get you inside and care for those feet. Are you ready?"

"No!"

"Good," Delin said and made a motion. Something snapped, the sound echoing off the distant peaks and roaring into Eloise's brain, along with a searing agony that flared through her numbness and throttled her senses.

She collapsed, mercifully unconscious.

When she awoke, she thought she was back in her childhood bedroom in Washington, D.C. Her grandfather must have just left her, because she was thinking about reindeer and hoping to get some chocolate in the morning from Saint Nicholas. She lay under thick blankets, some of them unusually furry, like the pelt of a polar bear. Her legs and feet felt odd, tingling, but not unpleasant.

She blinked, and as her eyes adjusted she noticed with some alarm that the items on the walls were not hers. True, there was the

Clement Moore poem, hanging in a frame on the wall beside the bed, but over there, to the right of the stove grinning its red-hot grin and pouring out heat, stood a bookshelf littered with heavy tomes. Books too thick for her to read at such an early age.

Eloise blinked again, and reality started coming back to her, even as she thought she heard the muted barking of dogs outside. She sat up in bed, propped up on her elbows, and noticed that she was dressed in clothes that seemed far too big for her—a huge nightshirt on top of several layers of undergarments. She continued to scrutinize the walls and shelves about the log cabin interior as the roof and walls shook in a rising wind. A heavy storm howled outside above the din of the barking dogs.

A wooden table occupied the center of the room and stood on a rug of stitched-together bear pelts. Just below the stove, beside a stack of perfectly chopped firewood, stood a pickax, a short-handled shovel, a cooking pot, some utensils, a teapot and four cloth sacks bulging with unidentified contents. On the left wall hung a rifle of the sort Eloise recalled seeing in very old tintype photographs, carried by the men serving in the Civil War. Below the rifle, on a mahogany end table, rested an open cherry wood box; within, two revolvers reclined on a velvet interior. They glinted with gold engravings and sparkled with a silver finish.

On another series of shelves built into the wall were other unusual items: a long bladed knife with a half-moon design carved into its hilt. Next to this, a small bird-headed totem pole on a stand. The highest shelf held a trophy in the shape of a vase. A time-worn tintype hung above it, presenting the image of a grinning young boy on a dogsled holding up the trophy.

Other photographs called to her from under a set of caribou antlers. Eloise strained to make out the images there, but could only see in one—a dual-image stereograph—what looked like two well-dressed men standing and shaking hands, while in the background, enormous mountainside factories worked heaps of ore.

Small kerosene lamps rested on the wall in copper sconces, and native tapestries decorated the remaining blank spaces. A dreamcatcher descended from the ceiling—and spun in a sudden gust.

The door blew open, then shut just as suddenly. Snowflakes cascaded across Eloise's vision, fluttering like butterflies and scattering playfully.

"Ah! Good, you're awake. Have you had some tea yet?"

Eloise blinked at the visitor. Still struggling with the shock of disassociation, she could only shake her head.

"Just as well, it's still steeping," he said. In a flash, he was out of his coat, and it was hanging on a hook on the door, along with his gloves and hat. He kicked off his boots, sending them into a corner, then reached for the teapot and two cups from behind the stove.

"Ancient Tlingit remedy, steeped in the bark of Echinacea root soaked in mint leaves." He grinned at her, and huge snowflakes tumbled from his mustache and plunged from his beard.

She took the cup in trembling hands and sipped at the steaming brew as Delin pulled up a chair, turned it backwards and sat facing her, drinking from his own cup. The dogs had quieted down, but the storm increased its pitch, howling as it slammed against the walls and tried to pry its way inside.

Delin cocked his head. "Storm got here a little early by my reckoning, but not much."

Eloise took another sip, relishing the sensation of warmth spreading through her body. "How long was I out?"

"Six hours. Sorry for the ankle, but it had to be done."

"Can I walk?"

"Not without a crutch. Probably two or three weeks before you should put serious weight on it. But I'm no doctor."

Eloise let her eyes glance over to the bookshelf again. "Are you sure? Seems you have books on everything over there."

Delin smiled. "Relics from old friends. Something to pass the time and dispel the loneliness."

Eloise regarded him again in the flickering firelight. Steam issued from his mouth when he talked, and the air still felt chilled, but it was nothing like the days and nights she had spent outside with her guide, tracking their quarry. "Thank you," she whispered.

Delin raised an eyebrow. "Sorry?"

"You heard me. Thank you. For the ankle. For saving my feet. And my life. I can still feel them—my feet. That's a good sign, right?"

"Tingly and itchy?"

She nodded.

"Good. I've also had your feet soaking in a special warm mixture for several hours."

"Another native recipe?"

"Of course."

"How did you learn all this?" Eloise asked. "Wait—don't tell me, besides your Russian descent, you're also part Eskimo?"

Delin shook his head. "No, but I lived with a Tlingit tribe for many years. You don't believe me, do you?"

Eloise shrugged. "Prospectors are prone to exaggeration." She narrowed her eyes at him, risking a little playfulness. "Maybe you think to impress me with such claims?"

Delin lowered his head. "Miss Griffith. If I aimed to impress you I'd have you take a look in any of those four sacks over there."

She looked at the stuffed bags. "What's in there, the diggings you'll wash in the spring for a few flakes?"

Delin smiled in the dancing scarlet light. "Not quite." He folded his arms and seemed to be judging her, looking into her soul, gauging her motivations. His smile faded.

"No," he said after a moment, and in a note of complete sincerity. "I don't think someone like you would be dazzled by the results of my 'diggings', as you correctly put it."

"Oh? And you think you know me so well already?"

"Maybe." He turned and rummaged around in some jars on the table, then faced her, grinning and holding two pencil-sized objects. "Licorice stick?" he offered.

"Huh? No, I'll stay with the tea for now."

"Suit yourself," he said, gnawing into one and closing his eyes. "Mmmm. Love these things!"

Eloise laughed. "Interesting. So—you think you know me? How many women exactly have you met out here?"

She couldn't quite tell, but it seemed his cheeks reddened suddenly, and when he looked away, the licorice stick dangled from his bushy mustache. "Point made," he said. "But still, you might find something here of greater interest than mere rocks plucked from the earth."

"And what would that be?" Eloise asked, taking another sip. She suddenly realized that this man she had just insulted about his lack of experience with women had recently undressed her, bathed her feet and cared for her while she was helpless.

Delin leaned back, tilting in the chair so he could toss another log into the stove. The fire crackled as he turned to her. "I know how you valued the poem read to you by your grandfather, and I can sense the magic you felt, the anticipation when the stairs creaked as he climbed up to your room with a book in his hands. Your little heart would leap as you waited under the blankets for your bedtime tale."

Eloise choked down the knot in her throat. Her eyes glazed over, and she looked beyond Delin's shoulder to the firelight.

"I think," said her rescuer, "that you might like a story."

Her fingers trembled again, and without offering, she felt Delin gently take the cup away from her. The wind slammed against the cabin again in a renewed strike, but then, spent, retreated while a calm silence surrounded them.

"Yes," she whispered, without really hearing the word. Something else worked through her mind—an idea blossoming into a purpose. Her quarry may have escaped, and her initial mission may have been lost, but there could be salvage here after all. William Hall wrote volumes about the conditions, the people and the wildlife up here. That author, Jack London, had his own success.

She regarded this giant of a man, mythical already in her mind by his heroics on the cliff and his compassion thereafter. Intrigued by the artifacts in his cabin and fascinated by the hints of his heritage, she began compiling the elements of a grand story. Something to present upon her return, something beyond a mere carcass of flesh and fur: the living words of a man who embodied the spirit of this frozen world, a man who had battled elements as well as beasts the rest of us could not comprehend. And if the items here in his cabin were any indication, this tale might be astounding in its own right, yet deeply personal.

"Wait." She lifted a hand, focusing now on her plan. "I do want a story, you are right about that. But I want to know about all this," she waved her hand around the cabin, then pointed to the sacks by the stove. "As well as that."

Delin opened his mouth, then closed it. His heavy black sweater appeared to itch him suddenly. He stood up and started pacing the floor. "It will take some time."

Eloise shrugged, then motioned to the door with her head. "As you said, the storm's here. Do you have enough supplies, food and tea for two?"

Delin nodded. "I'm always prepared for guests, or folks that just plain get lost."

"And do you also share stories with them?"

"I do. But never such a tale. Pieces of it, yes, but for what you are asking, I have to be much more thorough." He twirled his mustache, then scooped up the pickax on his renewed pacing. Unconsciously, he started flipping and catching it as he walked and spoke to her.

He shot her a sideways look. "I assume you'll also be wanting a complete perspective on the great Rushes of history, the gold and silver strikes that lured hundreds of thousands of men into the harshest of conditions."

Eloise choked on her building excitement, envisioning sweeping storylines held together by the personal revelations of a man's history. "Yes," she whispered. "All of that."

The wind whistled its intention to remain for the telling as well. Several of the dogs whined, and the cabin creaked.

"Very well, then," Delin announced, catching the pickax. He set it down, then went about lighting more lamps. "I will start the tale here in the Arctic, when I was just a little tyke, and I'll work in the rest—the good bits about how my father got up here in the first place, how I was born and learned the trade, and all the rest. You'll have to be patient, though. Think you can do that?"

Eloise glanced around the cabin again, listening to the storm raging outside. She shrugged and was about to respond when Delin said, "We're going to start with me, of course, but I assure you, I'll get to the part about how California fell into America's hands after the Mexican War—and how a pair of down-on-their-luck soldiers deserted their posts and made their fortunes in the hills of San Francisco; and how my father's best friend quickly lost his soul, how Benjamin Quitch forged an empire on the broken backs of honest men, how he sent my father out into the hills again and again to find the next great strikes, only so that Quitch could then level mountains and pry apart the land in order to slake his thirst."

"Hold on," interrupted Eloise, excitedly, her eyes blazing, heart hammering in her chest. "First, bring me some more tea. Oh—and a pencil and a notebook from my pack." She smiled and settled back against the pillows. Snuggling under the blankets, she waited for his creaking footfalls and the start of the story.

BOOK ONE

"They went to Ophir and took four hundred and twenty talents of gold from there, and brought it to King Solomon."
—1 Kings v. 28

"There is thy gold;
worse poison to men's souls."
—William Shakespeare

Chapter 1: Alaska - 1875

LEARNING THE TRADE

He brought the tip of the pick to his mouth, closed his eyes and let the taste linger on his tongue, just as Papa had taught him. The thin flakes didn't feel gritty like the ones he had tried this morning. These were softer and yielded to the press of his teeth; they danced across his taste buds with a sweetness like the birch syrup Mama smothered over flapjacks on Christmas morning.

The wind coming in from the north brought the hint of a chill, a sign of things to come, but the sun still clung to its warm perch on this late September day. Towering spruces swayed listlessly in the breeze while leaves fluttered across the sky, twisting and swooping like carrion birds. In the creek, the shallow water flowed around Delin's boots hesitantly, as if withholding its strength to endure the impending months of ice.

He scampered out of the water, holding a rock as large as his head in one hand and his little pickax in the other. The tool was last year's Christmas gift from his father, specially-made for his little hands. With a huge grin, holding the wet rock high so that its quartz streaks glittered in the sun, Delin leapt onto the grass and bounded up the hill, shouting.

"Papa, look!"

While he raced alongside the winding creek and darted around willow bushes, he thought about the teachings from Kreaga, the Medicine Man, who maintained that the Creator gave every child a gift, a special talent. With that talent came a lifelong responsibility to develop the gift and put it to use helping others.

He liked to think that this—prospecting and finding gold—could be his special gift.

Around another row of willow bushes and up a hill he came upon his father, holding his rifle, on one knee beside a large rock. Joshua held out a hand, and Delin stopped short. He saw that his father eyed a section of the forest ahead. Delin crouched low and waited for additional signals—just as they had practiced many times before.

Joshua motioned him closer with his hand.

"I'm here," Delin whispered, after creeping to within feet. He set the rock down. "Found something," he whispered.

"Good boy," Joshua whispered, never taking his eyes off one clump of trees. "Now, get ready. Something's out there."

"Is it a Sesquat?"

"Might be."

Delin heard a rustling, and what sounded like a snort. Funny—he didn't smell the nasty stench his father had described, and that high-pitched sound wasn't there either.

"You know what to do, right, son?"

"Yessir," Delin whispered back. "Get myself into the water, fast as can be!"

"And why do you do that?"

Delin tried to grin, but fear held him back, and he noticed his knees were shaking. "Sesquats don't like the water."

"Exactly. Now, if I can't slow it down or scare it off, I'll be jumping in there with you. So don't be afraid."

"I'm not!" insisted Delin as he gripped the pickax handle so fiercely his knuckles turned white. His shiny blond hair whipped across his eyes and tickled his nose, and thick curls bounced on the back of his neck. He shivered in his loose-fitting dark blue parka—a size too big, even for him. It had been passed down from his half-brother Mikhail only last year.

"Now, get ready." Joshua tensed, seeing the trees shake. A branch snapped, and a dark shape pushed through the foliage. "Say a prayer, son, and God will keep us safe."

"Yes, Papa," Delin whispered, peering over his father's shoulder, along the sight-line of the rifle. A head appeared, a rough mass of fur and teeth, then a shoulder and an arm.

His father aimed and held his breath...

"Wait!" Delin shouted, reaching for his papa's arm. "Just a bear!"

Joshua squinted, then let out a deep breath as the rest of the grizzly emerged, snorting and pawing at the ground. It was enormous, to be sure, but nothing to be frightened about.

"Ah, good thing, too," Joshua remarked, standing up slowly. "Or that Sesquat would have gotten a face-full of lead!"

As the bear wandered off, Delin scooped up the rock again and held it up like a sacrificial offering. "Look what I found! Real gold, I'm sure!"

Joshua took the stone, hefted it in his hands, then tossed it up and down before placing his tongue on its surface. "Where did you find this?"

"Creek bed, over there!" Delin pointed to the ridge. "Lots more too, I bet!"

Joshua dropped to one knee, set his hands on Delin's shoulders and looked into his son's eyes. "Relax, boy. I know you're excited..."

"Let me prospect some more! I can find as much as we can carry. We can load up the sleds once snow comes."

Joshua took a deep breath and raised his face to the sun, letting the warmth play across his skin and bathe in his eyes. "Listen to me, son." He squeezed the boy's shoulders tighter and drew him close. "You may be right—I'm sure you've got the gift as I had it. You're making me mighty proud, but there's another thing that comes with that gift. It's called sensibility. And humility, don't forget about that."

"But..."

"Now hear me. You made a good find, a couple pounds worth in here, I'd say—enough to keep our whole village and the Long House supplied with kerosene and other necessities all winter long. We don't need more right now."

Delin frowned and squinted in the direction of the hill. "But... we could get so much more. And—"

"And do what with it, exactly?" Joshua asked, his smile fading, his expression serious.

Delin shrugged. "Don't know. Just... get things. For Mom, and Mikhail and the elders, or for the dogs?"

Joshua smiled and rubbed Delin's head. "It's good that you think of others. But they have what they need already."

"Okay," Delin muttered, pouting. "But someone else will just take it instead."

Joshua stood and gazed over the hill at the crisscrossing rivers and creeks spreading into the valley—this place the Chilkat tribes called the Thron-diuck, meaning hammer-water—so named because they would hammer sticks supporting salmon-catching nets into the riverbeds during the spawning period.

"Yes," he said, "I think you're right. But that's another reason to be happy with what we have. Think, son—if we sled into Eagle City with sacks bulging with gold, how long do you think it will take before this place is swarming with desperate men? How long before the hills are turned to mud, the trees leveled and the mountains blasted away?"

Delin's mouth hung open.

Joshua continued staring into the hazy distance of the future. "How long before there are more thieves than honest miners, more gambling tables than rockers, and more brothels than trees?"

"Not long, I guess," Delin said, kicking at the earth while he took the rock back from his father.

"That's right," Joshua said. "You mind those stories I tell you of how it was back in California."

"And Comstock, in Nevada!" Delin said, excited. He loved the night-time stories, especially the ones about the early days. Of his father's adventures. Of men like Papa's old friend, Benjamin Quitch—who started off like everyone else, but then let evil and greed ruin his soul.

Joshua rubbed his son's back and pushed him forward as they started up the hill. "And remember this—if and when God wills it, then your find down there will draw in the next great rush of humanity, and it will force the development of this untouched land. But not until then."

Delin blinked, and for an instant, as he glanced in the direction of his discovery, he imagined a vast multitude trudging through waist-high snow. A veritable army shivering in the wild, overmatched by the elements, outmaneuvered by the mountains and the weather and neglected by the sun. In that one instant he envisioned a far off time, and saw to his surprise that an older version of himself stood weeping in the midst of that endless stampede, staring back at him across the years, with frost in his beard and icicles on his cheeks.

Delin snapped out of the vision and saw sunlight tickling the grass fields and shining off the white-capped mountains.

Joshua walked beside him. "I'll let you take one or two more rocks, if you can find them before dusk—then we have to go. We have a three week trip ahead of us, and I don't want to be one day late, or your mother will let the medicine men boil both of us alive."

Delin grinned as he put his rock into his pack. He started to run to the spot where he had found it—when Joshua caught his arm.

"I want to tell you one more thing." His father knelt in front of him again. His eyes were stern, and his grip fierce. "I've found a lot of gold in my day, and I've won great wealth..."

Delin beamed. "Like you did in that card game with Samuel Colt!"

Joshua's expression darkened. "No, son. What I'm telling you is that gold—these rocks you find in the streams or those flakes you pluck from the pans—they're not truly valuable."

Delin frowned, clearly confused.

"Let me explain this to you—the only treasures I've ever valued were ones that were given to me." Joshua took a deep breath, then continued. "This gold cross around my neck—as you know, a gift to me from the woman I loved before your mother."

Delin nodded. He'd often heard the tragic tale of Caroline, and he'd seen the sadness in his papa's eyes when he spoke of her. He knew the bond shared now between his parents was far more special, but every so often, usually late at night when Delin pretended to be asleep, he would notice his father holding that cross and looking up at the stars.

"The second thing is really a pair of things..."

"Your Dragoons!" Delin guessed. "Colt's special revolvers."

"Yes, given to me out of respect by their maker. And then, in turn, given by me to my best friend." Joshua sighed, as if struggling still with that decision. "And finally, there is the love of your mother. Given freely and warmly—and it is worth more to me than anything you could prospect out here in a million years."

Delin smiled, and the rock in his hand felt suddenly much lighter.

"Now," said Joshua. "Go and do what you have to do, and then let's head home."

Delin gave his papa a fierce hug that surprised them both, then he dashed down the hill. He pulled the pickax from his belt and tossed it so it spun end-over-end as he ran. Finally, he gripped it with both hands and jumped into the waist-high creek.

Joshua shook his head and laughed to himself. He set the rifle down and sat on a soft, flat spot of grass. With a heavy sigh, he prepared to watch his child's youthful exuberance. He pulled out a piece of cured porkfat and chewed it slowly, watching the trees carefully and keeping the rifle within reach. He had promised Mirna that nothing would happen to the boy out here—it was the only way he could convince her to let Delin to come. That, plus the desperate need she saw in his eyes—the urgency of spending this time with his son.

Joshua smiled again as the cry of "Awwww, shucks!" echoed from below, amidst heavy splashing. A few minutes later, and the same phrase shouted out again.

He took another bite, still grinning as he gazed at the descending sun. And he made a little personal wager—one that he knew he'd win: that his son would win the race against darkness, that the boy would shout a cry of "Eureka"—the Greek for "I have found it!"—before the sun could sneak behind the mountains.

Thoughts of such cries echoing off distant hills brought back unbidden memories, and as Joshua often did out here in the lonely wastes, usually while Delin slept, he remembered—and he thought back on days warmer, and more innocent.

Chapter 2: San Francisco - May 9, 1848

DESERTION AND DESTINY

ON THE PROW OF THE warship Providence, two men stood smoking pipes and looking out over the land that stretched in hills and plains on to the snow-capped Sierras. Their captains' uniforms, starched and pressed, fit snugly, and the medals on each man's lapels twinkled in the spring sun.

"What do you think, Joshua?" the taller man asked. He went capless, and his thick black hair whipped in the bay breeze. A finely-trimmed mustache and beard framed his rugged jawline and came to a point an inch below his square chin. His eyes were hooded and cold, as if reflecting visions distant and bleak.

The shorter man, an officer's cap tightly pressed over a head of newly-cropped red hair, took a long puff on his carved pipe. His eyes were blue and soft, but they held a hint of sadness. He reached into his coat, under his shirt, and touched the gold chain and cross around his neck. He opened his eyes, and tightly squeezed the heavy charm. It had been a parting gift from Caroline—the gold cross, plus the silver dagger at his belt. He had protested at its obvious value, but she merely smiled and quoted Wordsworth, as she often did: "Every gift of noble origin is breathed upon by hope's perpetual breath." Both gifts had served him well in the War, and they had pulled him out from the Devil's fiery grasp more times than he could recount.

Joshua didn't answer his friend, although he could guess at the intent of the question. Joshua Wetherwax and Benjamin Quitch had signed on together back in Virginia two years ago, but now—with the Treaty of Guadalupe officially ending the Mexican War—they had a decision to make.

Quitch cleared his throat. “Speechless, Joshua? Or does the magnificence of our newly-won land take your breath away?”

Joshua blinked, and his focus shifted—from the vision of his beloved whispering her love on a hot night buzzing with fireflies—to the scene before him now: the few small settlements, the decrepit windmill, and the trading post at this isolated port. His gaze followed the lone dirt path winding toward the hills. Further back, the majestic Sierra Mountains seemed painted onto the perfect blue sky.

Joshua shrugged. “It is beautiful. God’s glory in its finest, but it came at great cost.”

Benjamin Quitch made a coughing sound. “Hardly. The Mexican strongholds fell like canvas tents under our assaults. When the tables were turned and it wasn’t a thousand to one against us like at the Alamo, they didn’t stand a chance.”

“Still, they were proud, and fought remarkably.”

Quitch shrugged and appeared not to hear him. He had taken out his pistol, and was disassembling it on the railing.

Joshua looked over at him. Deciding to postpone discussion about their future, he pointed at the gun. “You really should trade that in for a new model Colt.”

Quitch shot him a dark look. “Never. These Walkers killed more Mexicans than half the canons on this ship.”

“And maimed quite a few Americans, too.” Joshua shook his head. “They have a dangerous misfire percentage, a defect Sam Colt fixed with his next models, and...”

“Yes, yes. Your beloved Dragoons. Not as powerful, that’s how he did it. Lower the powder content and shorten the barrel. Too conservative.”

Joshua sighed, stroking the heavy, black iron pistols at his belt. “You’re taking a needless chance.”

“It’s mine to take. Besides, I have to believe I’m fated for greater things. A powerful destiny is calling to me, Joshua, and it won’t be thwarted by something as insignificant as a defective pistol.”

“If you say so.” Joshua looked out over the water, toward some sort of commotion on the shore.

“Listen,” Quitch said, having reassembled the pieces. “We

can either wait out this tour and sail back to Virginia with the Providence, or—and listen to me here—we can ask for a drop off in New Orleans. Or Atlanta. Somewhere we can start fresh."

Joshua jerked his attention back to his friend. "What? No, not possible. You know I have to return to Caroline. She just wrote to me last week, and it sounds like her father is softening; accepting my position and his daughter's affections."

Quitch rolled his eyes. "What do I keep telling you? Too much water under that bridge. You'll never be what they want, and to come between a woman like that and her rich daddy? Joshua, there are other beauties out there who will croon for a man in a captain's uniform."

"With little else? My father was a Dutch shoemaker until he died in the cholera epidemic. You and I worked as loaders on the docks." Joshua looked away, back to the shore where now a small crowd had gathered outside the trading post. One man seemed to be waving hysterically and pointing back to the mountains.

Joshua took another breath from his pipe. "No, good friend. The Lord has it in mind for me to return, to keep my pledge to Caroline. I'll go to her, and I'll have the land from the government, and..."

"And what? The seventy-five dollars we are promised at the end of another six months? You've read the same newspapers as I have. You know inflation is ravaging the country. When six dollars barely buys a bag of flour, what will seventy-five get you?" He cocked the Walker Colt and spun the chamber, sighting along the edge. "So you'll have a nice plot of land. But without money to build anything on it, you'll be forced to sell it for whatever you can get."

Quitch nudged Joshua in the arm. "Unless, that is, you think her daddy will build you a nice mansion as a dowry!"

He went on laughing, but Joshua wasn't listening. By now, two soldiers in a rowboat were madly paddling back to the Providence; on the shore, men were racing in and out of the trading post, loading up supplies on wagons and saddling up. Joshua frowned. It even looked like the proprietor was outfitting his own horse and closing up the shop. The rest of the small seaport was equally buzzing: people were running about, and others were making for the hills.

"Joshua? Are you paying any heed?" Quitch groaned, then finally noticed the men scrambling back on board. "What the hell do you suppose got into them?"

Quitch and Joshua strode to the gangplank to meet the returning soldiers, who almost ran down their commanders.

"Sirs!" they shouted at once, seeing who stood before them.

"What's the rush?" Quitch barked. The private, out of breath, glanced at his partner.

"Captain Quitch, sir. Captain Wetherwax. We—that is, Private Andersen and myself, sir. We request leave, sir!"

"Leave?" Joshua asked. "For how long?"

The men shifted uncomfortably, but didn't answer.

"Why?" asked Quitch, narrowing his eyes and looking past the men, for the first time noticing the commotion on the shore.

Both privates hesitated, then spoke at once: "Gold, Sir!"

Quitch gripped Joshua's arm. "Gold, you say? Where?"

"Not far," said Andersen. "Place over the hills along the American River. A mill there's owned by someone named Sutter. Couple of his people pulled some nuggets right from the ground. Man named Sam Brannan just came running into town for pans and shovels and bags, and said there was so much lying right on the ground he couldn't carry it all!"

Joshua frowned. He had heard these sorts of tales before. Wild rumors of mythical lands literally paved with gold, causing stampedes of men who came away disillusioned and angry. "Have you seen any of this gold for yourself?"

"Yes, sir! He let us touch a rock, and it was pure. Heavy and soft, just like it's 'sposed to be."

Joshua was still unconvinced, but Quitch waved the men on. "You boys get back to your quarters, and we'll discuss this. Speak of it to no one."

The men ran off, nodding and saluting. Quitch put his hands on his hips and stared at the shore. Joshua joined him and breathed in the pure air. It seemed for just an instant that the vision ahead flickered, and he imagined an incredible transition: a harbor teeming with masts, a huge armada of desperation unloading armies of humanity to race across the hills with picks and shovels. And with them came the reek of animals, raw sewage, fires, disease and death.

Joshua blinked away the image, chiding himself for always anticipating the worst. Life was in God's hands, and it wasn't up to Joshua to predict the future. Although, if what transpired just now on the shore was any indication, things could get bad soon. He anticipated that the army might be staying on here, after all—if there was any truth to this story.

"Joshua?" Quitch turned to him with a grin under those calculating eyes. "Remember that destiny I was talking about?"

Seeing a flicker of unfathomable greed behind Quitch's expression, Joshua opened his mouth to speak, but a series of splashes broke his concentration.

They spun and saw something blue hurtle over the side. Then another, and another. Men were leaping from the railing, diving into the bay with just sacks of clothes tied to their backs. They struck the water and swam like madmen to the shore.

Just then, Commander Jones roared out from the Officer's quarters with a security detail. He slammed the door and ordered his team to stand along the rail. "This madness ends now!" Jones shouted, addressing the remaining soldiers. "I've just heard the rumor that has you all in a jiff. And I'm giving a direct order—no one leaves his post. No one deserts this crew! We are soldiers of the United States!"

He spun around, noticing Joshua and Quitch for the first time. "You. Captains Wetherwax and Quitch. Organize a search party, get a boat and retrieve those deserters!"

Joshua swallowed. But he and Quitch answered, "Yes, sir."

The sun stabbed at his eyes, and Joshua squinted, but stood up straight and saluted. He noticed that beside him, Quitch was giving him a wink as he made his own salute.

After a day's sail, Joshua, Quitch and seven other soldiers arrived at the American River. They had with them nine horses, all their rifles and pistols, plus food and supplies. Joshua had only suggested Quitch bring enough for a week, but the bags seemed much heavier when he got around to inspecting them. The crew seemed jumpy, and perked up every time they sailed past some diggers on the riverbank.

Dark clouds massed over the hills like troops patiently waiting for replacements. Joshua steered downriver, taking them past Sutter's Fort with its lonely mills and empty farmhouses. Several prospectors along the way had told them that John Sutter had experienced his worst fears: besides the desertion of his workers, Sutter had his land claim rejected by the Army contingent in Monterey. With no title to this area and its newfound wealth, he was helpless to stop the flow of gold rushers coming to pick the land clean.

Joshua and Quitch watched the men pouring like ants over the hills, perching themselves on free spots beside the river and staking their claims. Joshua gazed ahead at the bare land, hills and trees. It was hard to imagine all this overrun with tents and cabins, stores and roads, the ground teeming with miners and their sluice boxes, rockers, pans, picks and shovels.

But it would happen. He knew the tales were already multiplying, taken up by other ships in the harbor, then scattered with the wind. Newspaper stories would follow, whether or not sufficient wealth truly existed here. Then would come the hordes of gold-seekers, merchants, gamblers and swindlers.

Joshua sighed and re-examined the hastily-scrawled map they had brought with them. The American River was just one of several branches piling into the Sacramento; the Joaquin River further south had dozens of branching streams, each of those rolling down from hills three hundred to fifteen hundred feet high.

Joshua rolled up the map and continued to steer ahead. He felt the breeze on his face turn cooler as the sun ducked behind a charcoal-bellied cloud. The deserters might have made it to this river, where the stories began, but he supposed it was equally possible they stopped to pan at other streams and found the luck there just as good.

"Thinking it's futile?" Quitch asked, suddenly appearing at his side. He had his Walker revolver out again, polishing it as he set one smooth black boot on the stern. He waved to a couple prospectors beside the low hanging branches of an oak tree. They glared back at him, as if jealously guarding their stake.

Joshua eased the prow around some driftwood. "I am beginning to think the Lord does not smile on this endeavor."

Quitch nodded. "You see? You're starting to understand. There are greater things calling to us than duty. We may find these men, but what then? Who are we to deny them their chance? The land we all fought for is prepared to reward us, and yet our commander holds us back?"

"We gave our word. Our oath to serve."

"We also gave our lives and our flesh." Quitch patted him on the back. "We owe nothing more."

Joshua lowered his head as darkness glided across the hills and bisected the river in their path. A few sprinkles of rain kissed his face as the wind picked up. "We're docking," he said, steering to shore. "Tether us to that tree and we'll wait out the weather."

As the preparations were made, the dark clouds expanded, and Joshua stood alone on the prow, gazing upriver. The prospectors continued working, singly or in twos and threes. Some had makeshift sifters and pans, others just a jackknife or a spoon. Every now and then a shout of joy would echo off the hills, and men would flock to new sites.

The splashing of horses and men drowned out his thoughts, but Joshua continued to stare, even as the rain fell—at first in a light drizzle, then a complete downpour. The soldiers dragged the perishable supplies and weapons to a thicket of oak trees while others rummaged through their packs. Joshua ignored the scraping of metal, the splashing, and other scraping sounds.

Instead, he held tightly to the gold cross about his neck. Rainwater rolled off his face, soaking his thick red hair and beard; it drenched his uniform. Yet still the cross glittered in an unseen light; and as he held it out superimposed over the river, his vision transcended the vast leagues of this continent, all the way to the far ocean, back to a farm in Virginia and a third story window in a white-pillared mansion where Caroline sat and stared dreamily out over the hills.

Joshua closed his eyes, oblivious to the storm. He knew what was coming, knew the temptation he faced. He knew his own men, and he knew Quitch. This was no capture mission and it never had been, despite Joshua's best intentions.

They had supplies, horses, a boat, and guns. They were better equipped than anyone else out here; and they were months ahead of the major influx, the masses that would come to scoop up whatever hadn't been claimed. They were given a chance, just by luck and happenstance.

Or maybe, as Quitch insisted, it was destiny.

He turned, and opened his eyes.

Quitch was standing there before him, with the men in a

semicircle behind; they were all soaked to the bone, but grinning from ear to ear. In both hands Quitch held an iron pan, and down in its belly, flicked free from brownish mud and bits of sand, sparkled tiny flecks of gold.

Rain streamed from his cap and shadows swam behind his eyes. "Still going to round up the deserters?"

Joshua glanced sideways at the men around Quitch. A few had their hands on their guns, watching him closely. Joshua struggled to breathe. The cross seemed to burn his skin and the chain felt so heavy; images of Caroline swirled in his mind while the buzzing of fireflies droned in his skull.

His lips parted. And the word bubbled free from his throat in a blast of lightning—freezing the instant for all of time.

Chapter 3: September, 1849

LUCK AND FORTUNE

San Francisco had become unrecognizable in just a short year. A transition had been conjured out of some primordial urban nightmare, redesigning the rolling hills and gentle slopes. Dirt roads and thick mud trenches crisscrossed the turbulent mass of wood and brick structures in strangely geometric patterns. Ships of every size littered the harbor, their rotting masts poised in surrender.

Horses and mules carried overburdened wagons up the hills, some getting stuck in the deep mud, others falling and breaking bones under the weight. Men everywhere rushed about, hauling supplies, haggling with merchants, trading for overvalued goods, and arranging for locals to transport their heavy loads.

"They're calling themselves the Forty-Niners," Quitch said, following the struggles of one team. "And I hear they've taken to calling us Sourdoughs!"

"It fits," Joshua said, and his stomach grumbled as if insulted. "Other than bacon, that's all most of us eat."

Quitch kicked his horse and picked up the pace. "All the more reason, then, to get settled in—so we can change our gold and enjoy the finest meal of our lives!"

For once, Joshua was in agreement. He took his eyes off the Forty-Niners, who appeared dejected: this final leg of the journey, one through deep gulches and winding mule paths, was nothing like what was promised back home.

"Montgomery Street!" Quitch shouted, turning the horse and heading along a rugged path beside jerry-built houses, their slapboard walls still under construction. Rotting hulls of old brigs and tugboats camped on mud banks just twenty yards away, while seagulls careened around the shore, overwhelmed by the extent of civilization.

"Inside," Quitch said, dismounting at one ramshackle building, its roof tilted and the beams already sinking in the mud. He took two heavy sacks from the horse's saddlebags, then dragged them across the threshold.

"Are you sure about this?" Joshua asked, untying his own bags of gold dust and nuggets.

"Trust me," Quitch said, groaning. "You've been alone in the mountains too long. Until the Federals finish building their Mint here, these guys are offering the best exchange rate."

Inside, two well-dressed men sat behind a polished oak counter. The walls were bare and the floor caked with mud, but from the ceiling hung a chandelier, glittering with precious glass.

"Benjamin Quitch!" the bald man on the left announced. "Always good to deal with you in person. Not that we mind the thugs you send every other week, but they tend to be rather feisty when drunk."

The heavier man, sweat dotting his forehead, added, "Which is all the time!"

Quitch shrugged. "My apologies. Johansen and Milsberg. Allow me to introduce my partner, Joshua Wetherwax."

After dragging the bags in, Joshua reached his hand over the counter.

"Great to meet the legend!" shouted Milsberg. "Heard all sorts of stories. They say you caught a fish on the Yuba River, slit it open and found two ounces of gold in its gut."

"Well..." said Joshua, scratching at his red beard and feeling uncomfortable in his sweat-soaked shirt.

"And another time you followed a goat into the hills by Mad Mule Gulch and discovered a vein forty feet long!"

"Pure exaggeration," Joshua said.

Quitch tossed one sack on the counter. "Completely. It was only thirty-five feet long, but to Joshua's credit, he found that one's motherlode just the next day."

Milsberg squinted at Joshua. "So how do you do it?"

Joshua lifted one of his bags to the counter. "Got a nose for it, I suppose." He fidgeted for a moment, then added, "And the good Lord occasionally shows me the way."

"Hah!" Milsberg took out a large set of scales and reached into Joshua's bag. "Modesty and religion? Benjamin, the company you keep seems to be improving."

Quitch shot his partner a gleeful look. "Oh, give it time and his soul will be as damned as everyone else's around here." He ignored the glare from Joshua, and changed the subject. "Now, my good men, I know you'll need to do your tests and grind out the impurities and such, but we have some fine eating and carousing to do, so if you please—would you supply us with a modest advance, say 80% of estimated value?"

The proprietors glanced at each other, then nodded. "Very well. Visit the Parker Hotel just down the road in the Square—our vouchers'll be honored there. Tell 'em we sent you."

His partner added, "I hear there are some high rollers staying at the Hotel this week."

Quitch leaned forward. "Tell me more."

"Bankers, financiers, and new politicians. Come to invest and get in with the right people, if I hear right."

"And you told these men…?"

"I dropped a name or two."

"One of them being?"

Johansen smiled. "Yours, of course. Go to the Parker. Ask for a man by the name of Brannan."

"He's the one who started this whole thing," Milsberg added. "Never picked up a shovel, though—just bought up supplies and land, then sold them to the newcomers for ten times as much. There's another man, English fellow by the name of Norton, come here with several hundred thousand to invest."

His partner nodded. "They'll be glad to speak to you over some brandy. Perhaps some gambling, or if you prefer…a little 'entertainment' upstairs after?"

Quitch grinned. After dividing up the vouchers, forty-eight thousand dollars worth—an amount that seemed almost inconsequential suddenly to Quitch—he whispered to Joshua.

"Come, let's get suites at the Parker and clean ourselves up. It seems we've been offered a second date with Destiny."

Two hours later, Joshua stepped into the main hall of the Parker Hotel Casino. He was freshly scrubbed, his hair washed and beard trimmed, and he had dressed in a clean shirt and suit while his boots had been polished. When he set foot into the first of several great halls in the casino, his senses were overwhelmed. Through a haze of cigar and pipe smoke, under dimmed chandeliers, a sea of black top hats mingled with dusty sombreros, Chinese ponytails and uneven miner's caps. Gorgeous women in tight-fitting gowns skittered by. Music from harps and violins danced across the gilded walls while a sea of men wagered at tables.

Joshua stumbled forward, eyes bulging in amazement. He tried, unsuccessfully, to look natural. Someone offered him a drink, which he consumed in one gulp. Apricot brandy.

He walked into another hall, which looked just like the previous one. He felt the chain around his neck digging in. It had been a year since he had cleaned it, and finally, just before coming down from his room, he had polished it once again. The reflections off the smooth gold sent aching vibrations through his heart, and his longing for Caroline surged. On the way down those stairs, he had decided that after this trip he would collect his earnings and buy passage home. He had earned enough to be comfortable. To raise a family, to enjoy the beautiful Virginia fields, and to coax a living from the land instead of ravaging it for its treasures.

"Joshua!" shouted the voice that once again tore him from this dream. "I hardly recognize you!"

Joshua offered a weak grin to Quitch as his friend craned his neck to watch a pair of Asian beauties go. "Listen," he said, throwing his arm around Joshua's shoulder. It was clear from his breath that he'd had more than a few drinks already while he waited. "They're at the far table—don't look now."

"Who?"

"Sam Brannan is the one all in black. Thick beard and mustache, the smallest at the table. Man next to him is the financier, Norton, and I don't know the other. But the man with his back to us, turning right now, ordering a drink, is..."

Joshua gasped and pulled away. "Samuel Colt!" He had seen the man's photograph during the War. General Walker had posed with the inventor and had passed the image around to his men.

Quitch raced after him, spilling his brandy in his haste to catch up, but Joshua got to the table first. The players were all holding up their cards before their faces, and an enormous pile of coins rested in the center.

"Fold," said Brannan, slapping down his cards, disgusted. Norton did the same, and the last man likewise bowed out.

Colt slapped his cards face down and laughed, scooping up the center pile. "Too easy! Really, gentlemen, you must try harder or I will be forced to find other—oh, hello, sir!"

Joshua stood at his side, amazed first by the fact that Colt had just won—from what Joshua could see, with only a pair of twos—and secondly, dumbfounded as to what to say. Quitch appeared suddenly, extending his hand across the table.

"Mr. Brannan. It is a pleasure to make your acquaintance." He bowed and lifted his hat. "I am Benjamin Quitch, and this is my partner, Joshua Wetherwax."

Sam Brannan rose, smiling. "Ah, excellent to run into you gentlemen. I hear we may have some business to discuss?"

Quitch grinned. "The business of profit, sir, and a lot of it—if we work together."

"We shall see," Brannan said, sizing up Quitch with a reserved eye. His attention then fell to Joshua, and he frowned. "You're the one with the gift, are you not?"

Joshua still stared at Colt, grinning. "What?"

Quitch nudged him in the ribs.

"The gift of Sight," Brannan said, leaning forward, cold dark eyes finally drawing Joshua's out.

Joshua squirmed. "I hear they say something like that, but..." He felt uncomfortable suddenly, standing so near the small fortune that Colt had just won. Joshua's suitcoat had opened, and the Dragoon he kept in his waist pocket drew a whistle from its creator.

"Is that one of mine?" Colt asked in a deep voice with a smile that tweaked the edges of his burly mustache. His chest inflated like a barrel and his bow-tie barely fit about his neck, but he grinned and held out a hand, which Joshua promptly and fiercely shook.

"An honor, sir, to meet you in person." Joshua struggled with the words. How to explain the sudden feeling of connection to one who had created a device at once so terrifying yet comforting? "Without your Dragoons, Mr. Colt, I fear I would have been prematurely called to my Maker on many occasions."

"Glad they came in handy," Colt said, and slapped Joshua on the back. Joshua was about to mention something to Colt about the Walker Model and Quitch's reliance on it despite the documented misfire problem, but Colt shouted out suddenly: "Hey, Brannan, where you goin'?"

The two men at the head of the table stopped and Quitch, beside Brannan, spread his arms. "My apologies. Mr. Brannan and I have some plans to make."

Brannan nodded, finishing a brandy. "This may take some time. Norton and my man Crocker here can finish the game for me. Can't do any worse than I've done the past six hours."

Colt frowned. "No fun playing with just three. You, Wetherwax. You in?"

Joshua swallowed hard, then backed up, raising his hands. "Mr. Colt, I really must decline. Gambling... it's not..."

Quitch leaned in and pulled Joshua away. "Just a moment, please. A word with my partner." He dragged Joshua back to the bar, snatching a drink from a passing waitress as they walked.

"Listen," he whispered, downing the brandy. "It's time to drop this Sunday School attitude. We're a continent away from your values, your morals and your God. If you haven't noticed, it's a different world out here. Get in that game and keep those men occupied while I arrange our fortunes."

Joshua looked back to the table. "We're already rich, Benjamin. We—"

"Have to dream in larger doses, my friend. The easy pickings are gone, swept clean by eighty thousand grimy hands. The future is in vast operations, funded by immense capital from men like Brannan."

"Then he will do it without the likes of us."

"Not if we move in now. Convince him that we have the leverage he needs. What do you think I've been doing these past few months? Grabbing land, earning the trust of the men. Securing political power. It's all about power, Joshua. Power. I've been dreaming lately. Dreaming of entire mountainsides leveled by huge blasts of water. Roaring explosions shaking the gold free from its age-old prisons. Enormous wheels churning up the rocks from incredible depths as we process in hours what would normally take years."

Joshua felt dizzy and tried to pull away.

"Go back in there!" Quitch hissed. "And play!"

Joshua nodded, and backed away.

"And don't lose it all too quickly!" Arm in arm, Quitch and Brannon followed a trio of brunettes into a room behind the counter, and shut the door.

Joshua smoothed his coat and approached the table through a haze of walnut-scented smoke. His neck felt strained, as if weighted down by a stone that felt heavier with each step. But he pulled the chair back, nodded to the men, and had a seat.

"The game," Colt said with a huge smile, "is poker. Nothing wild. Five hundred dollar minimum."

The next time Joshua checked his pocketwatch it was twenty minutes until midnight. His hat was on the floor, his jacket around the back of his chair. Three empty glasses stood on end beside a stack of coins and vouchers so high he had to peek over them to see the heavy-set, thick-bearded Mr. Norton.

At first, the casino manager had come by and drawn a quarter of Joshua's sum, in medium and large denomination chips. Within an hour, Joshua had fearfully drawn another quarter. The men around him licked their lips and craned their necks like hungry vultures. They preyed on his ignorance of the nuances of the game at first, but after about the fifth shot of brandy, he caught on.

And he began to win. Small hands at first, then larger and larger takes as he perfected some bluffs, then fell into a run of amazing luck. Soon he was raising the stakes, calling at five-thousand-dollar increments, increasingly forcing Norton and the man named Crocker to fold.

Colt matched him, call for call, and lost more than he won. As blasphemous as it seemed, Joshua felt as though God Himself were standing beside him. Drink followed drink. The men paused twenty minutes for a sumptuous steak and potato dinner, topped with gravy and carrots. It was a meal unlike Joshua had had since his last dinner at Caroline's mansion, but he barely tasted it, intent only on gaining some nourishment and getting back into the game.

At times, onlookers gathered, whispering at the incredible stakes being waged. It was nearly four-thirty in the morning, but no one could tell as there were no windows, only a constant pale light bathing the room.

Soon, Joshua had amassed over two hundred thousand dollars. His hair hung over his eyes, and his lips were numb with uncounted shots of brandy, but his wits were sharper than ever. He felt as if he were back in the War, aware of his mortality with every step.

At last, a wearied Colt called for the porter. He asked for one more voucher. Norton and Crocker bowed out and sat a few feet away, still entranced by the game.

Joshua made to rise. "I'm sorry, Mr. Colt, but I cannot, in good conscience, let you proceed. In fact, my spate of luck here has shamed me, and I aim to give some of my gains back. To you, to this hotel..."

Colt slammed his palm down. "Son. Do not utter another word. You will do me no charity but to stay in this game until I am through."

The porter returned, carrying a polished wooden case in his gloved hands. He set this reverently before Colt, who turned the box and opened its lid.

Joshua squinted through the smoke but couldn't see beyond the box lid—until Colt leaned in, slid the case forward and turned it. "My greatest creations," Colt said with deliberate pacing. "Treasures that may have special interest only for one such as yourself."

Joshua froze. Inside lay two of the finest items he had ever seen in his life, outshining the beauty of anything extracted in the mines—anything, save perhaps for the loveliness of Caroline's eyes.

"A pair of First Model Dragoons," Samuel Colt announced in a reverent whisper. "Inlaid with gold trim and silver etchings. The same Texas Ranger battle scene, but minted entirely out of silver. Polished ivory handle with solid gold etchings. Crafted by Tiffany, Young and Ellis in New York, one of a set of three."

Joshua swallowed and could not take his eyes off the revolvers nestled in their bed of red velvet. "The other two sets," said Colt, "are destined for very special people. One is on its way to the

Russian Czar. The other I sent today by steamship to the Sultan of Turkey."

Joshua slowly shook his head. "Sir, the third of the set. It must remain with you..."

Colt eased the lid shut. "That was my plan, young Wetherwax. And it is still my intention to take these with me to my grave." He leaned back, took a sip of whiskey and folded his arms. "What do we say? One more round? These Dragoons for say, twenty-five thousand? One hand, no raises."

Joshua found himself nodding before he could even think it through, and moments later, when an eighth of his wealth disappeared, he could not believe the extent of his greed. He felt the light dim, and a presence seemed to leave his side.

His shoulders sagged; his throat burned. But, eyes on the closed case beside Colt's elbow, Joshua played another hand, determined to get those Dragoons back in the pot.

"Do you still want to quit?" Colt asked with a grin, when Joshua had gone through two more hands, again at twenty-five thousand each.

He shook his head, and raised the pot to forty thousand.

Colt took it. As he took the next hand.

Norton and Crocker came back in. At more modest levels, the four players wagered on into the morning.

Joshua stopped drinking, and as he sobered up and the headache came, he continued to lose. The music stopped altogether, and people no longer milled about to watch. His skin was drenched in sweat and he constantly looked over his dwindling pile of winnings.

Finally, around ten thirty in the morning, Quitch appeared at his side. "Not doing too bad," he said, noting that Joshua had about fifty thousand in vouchers and coins. "Doubled your money. Must say I'm impressed."

Joshua gave him a glare, and continued with the deal.

"Fine," said Quitch. "You're busy. I'll tell you of our new business arrangements at a later time. Meanwhile... Yes, I think I'll take a trip upstairs with these interesting ladies."

Joshua grunted and looked up after he lost the hand, only to note Quitch ascending the stairs with the two Oriental beauties from last night. He was about to return his attention to the game when something caught his eye. At the top of the stairs, at the balcony leading to the girls' suites, he thought he saw an image that couldn't be: a blonde-haired beauty, ensconced in an all-lace dress, wearing gloves and with her hair tied in ribbons. She spun around quickly and departed, leading Quitch ahead of the other girls into the shadowy room beyond.

But in just that moment, Joshua's heart had cracked. She bore an uncanny resemblance to Caroline, or perhaps his mind had camouflaged the girl in his love's guise, a further reminder of his folly, his desertion. His disgraceful selfishness.

He hung his head, close to tears. Numb, he collected the five cards before him, and turned them over. Ace, ace, ace, two, seven. A grin tugged at his lips. He glanced at the empty balcony, shook off the plaguing memory, and weighed his options.

"Raise," he said at once, smiling, when it came to him. Let them think he was bluffing. He quickly counted what he had left, and pushed it all to the center of the table. "Thirty-four thousand."

Norton and Crocker swore at once and tossed down their cards. Colt, however, wore an unreadable expression. Joshua thought he might have seen a tiny smirk as the man calmly counted out the coins and sent them forward.

"Let's see 'em," Colt said.

"Three aces," Joshua said, grinning, his body perking up, excitement coming back. Seventy-nine thousand in winnings after starting with only twenty-four wasn't bad at all. Quite respectable, and hell—enough that maybe he didn't need to go back to the mines after all. He could walk right out of there, head high, and buy passage on the next steamer to the East Coast.

But that vision evaporated the instant Colt's hand slapped the table and spread out his cards. Four threes, all in a row.

Joshua slumped in his chair, his energy gone, his dreams shattered. His mouth hung open and all he could hear were the muffled whispers of pity.

"Well, now," said Colt. He called for another bottle of whiskey and two glasses. "Fair is fair, and I seem to recall you once allowed me to remain in the game for one more hand."

Joshua nodded weakly. He was barely listening. In his mind's eye an empty swing rocked slowly beside a garden amidst the aimless buzzing of fireflies.

"Being a good sport, and recognizing a brilliant opponent—not to mention a valiant soldier and connoisseur of fine weaponry—I offer you a similar chance."

Joshua blinked out of his dream. "Excuse me?"

Colt leaned in. "Have you something of value you would wager on one final hand?"

Joshua started to shake his head, but then remembered he had one thing. He withdrew it slowly from its strap at his belt, and he laid it gently on the table. Reverently, he took the dagger out from its sheath of silver. He doubted it was worth more than two thousand, but it was all he had. A porter approached, prepared to value the item if asked.

Colt waved him away. "Most impressive. A gift?"

Joshua nodded. "From one who means more to me than anything I've lost tonight."

Colt regarded him intently, then slid the dagger back in its sheath. "Yet you're willing to part with it?"

Joshua hung his head. His throat croaked. "I... am no longer worthy to hold it."

"I don't know about that, son." Colt raised his eyebrows. He stretched, cracked his knuckles, then poured two drinks. "But I accept. One last hand, then—one straight draw, no calls. Same odds: thirty-four thousand to your dagger." He raised his glass in the air. "To you, worthy foe, and to a night not soon forgotten, whatever the outcome of this hand."

Joshua took up his glass, swirled the brown liquid, then raised it, taking a deep breath. He met Colt's eyes, nodded, and chinked glasses. "Well played," he said, and drank it down.

All five cards were soon laid out face down before him. He peeked under the first. A six. Then came a seven. Next, a four. All three cards were hearts. Joshua held his breath, tasting the whiskey in every cell of his body. He reached under his shirt and found the cross. Feeling unworthy, he squeezed it anyway, saying a silent prayer.

The next card was the five of hearts.

He glanced up and wished he hadn't. Colt was grinning, the five cards splayed out before his chin like a fan. His eyes darted back and forth across them as if he were savoring the sight of a delicious meal.

Joshua forced his lungs to take in a deep breath. He felt the weight of the dagger, just beyond the last card, it's tip aiming towards his heart. Just give me this one, he prayed. And I promise I'll leave with the next ship. I'll devote myself to you, God, and to Caroline. Just this card...

He peeked under the final card, and his breath escaped in a rush.

Colt set down his hand, but when Joshua looked up, the big man's grin was already dissipating. He had seen Joshua's smile, and it was unlike any he had seen before. "You got it, don't you?" Colt asked, even as he set down his hand: two aces and three tens. A full house.

Joshua flipped over the cards one by one. Everyone gathered around, and it took several seconds for them to process the order and to see the hand for what it was.

"Straight Flush," Joshua whispered. "Three through seven."

Colt clapped his hands together and roared, "Outstanding!" He stood and lifted Joshua to his feet, shaking his hand. "Well, I must say, Mr. Wetherwax, I have had enough. I think we both walk away from here better than when we entered."

Joshua grinned, releasing the hand only reluctantly, as if saying farewell to a good friend. As he turned to collect his winnings, a thin man in a blue suit approached from the crowd.

"Joshua Wetherwax?"

Stopping short of picking up his dagger, Joshua turned to face the man. "Who's inquiring?"

"I'm Robert Jackson, sir. Served on the Providence for a time."

Joshua recalled the name, if not the face. "Good to see you again, Jackson."

"Likewise. You're a hard man to locate." He reached into his coat pocket and retrieved an envelope with a red wax seal imprint on the back. "I've been holding mail for you, sir."

Joshua's heart leapt, and he tore the letter from the man's grasp, only to hold it in trembling hands. "When—how long ago did you...?"

"Seven months, sir." Jackson struggled with the words. "I—we looked for you, but kept missing you at the fields. Always a camp behind, it seems."

"Fine, fine. Thank you." Joshua broke the seal, and stepped away from the others. He pulled out the letter, glanced over the first few lines, then pulled up a chair, bent over and continued reading.

A shadow fell over him, and a chair squeaked. "What does she say?" Colt's voice asked, calmly from his shoulder. "Not that I'm prying."

Joshua felt the blood drain from his face; his fingertips went numb, and for the second time today a vision of his beloved shattered in his mind. "She came after me."

"What?"

"A year ago. Just after getting my letter. She chartered passage on the steamship California. It left New Orleans on December first. She wrote this letter while approaching Cape Horn, in early January." Joshua held his head in his hands, partially crumpling the letter. "Eight months ago. She should have been here by now!"

He leapt up and raced after Robert Jackson. "Have you seen her?" he shouted. "A woman asking for me?"

Colt, following, put his hand on Joshua's back. "The Cape passage is not an easy one. Hate to be the one to tell you, son, but more ships were lost around those rocks than are probably out in that harbor now."

Jackson waved his hands vigorously. "No sir, the California made it here all right. February twenty-eighth. Quite a big deal, it bein' the first steamer to carry the gold seekers. Jammed pack with 'em too."

Joshua perked up. "Is there a passenger manifest, a list maybe of where they...?"

The young man shook his head. "No, because a couple hundred of 'em crammed on the boat at Panama City, men that crossed from the Caribbean and demanded passage north. Got real ugly. But in any case, you could imagine they weren't takin' good notes on who was where."

Joshua slumped against a wall. "February." He crumpled the letter, then opened and smoothed it out.

Colt approached, slowly. "She may have changed ships—or taken ill and maybe got left behind to recuperate on some nice island. But I'd say give it a good search around here first."

"I'll check," came another voice.

Joshua turned to see Quitch standing behind Colt. He looked disheveled, his clothes askew, and his cheeks smeared with lipstick, but Joshua was actually glad to see him. If anyone could help, it was Quitch. "I'll round up some men, and we'll scour this city for you. If she's here, we'll find her."

"And if she's not?" Joshua muttered. He glanced over at his pile of tokens on the table. Before Quitch could answer, Joshua said: "If not, then I'm going after her. I'll buy a ship, hire a crew, and search the entire coast."

Quitch opened his mouth to protest, but a look from Colt held him back. "Fine," he said at last. "But give us a week."

Joshua left the hotel, and in the bright sunshine, with the gulls cackling and swirling overhead, he almost collapsed. The letter burned in his hand, and the cross felt weightless about his neck. Guilt hammered at his heart: he had defied God, and used his power for greed. Was it any wonder catastrophe had come on the heels of his misdeeds?

He found himself a small, out of the way bar in a back alley. And he drank, and drank. And slept. Sometimes in a dingy room upstairs, sometimes on the floor behind the bar. And finally, days later, he emerged into the painfully bright sunlight, and after clearing his head, he began to run down the dirt-caked streets. Running somewhere, anywhere—away from himself, toward nothing. And ran right into the huge well-dressed man who stood on the docks.

"Glad I caught you!" shouted Samuel Colt. "Sailing out today, but before I leave I have an offer for you."

Joshua glanced over his shoulder, positive Colt spoke to someone else. "I'm sorry, Mr. Colt, what—?"

"Really, Joshua, we've earned the right to use first names. Call me Sam. Listen, I find myself a bit short on cash, having played a bit more after you left. And, after a look at the steamer's common accommodations, I decided I would prefer to sail home in the luxury suite."

"Yes," said Joshua. "Well, I really am a bit low myself..."

Colt waved his hands. "You misunderstand. I am making you an offer for an honest trade. I would like five thousand dollars more than I currently possess." He grinned and reached into his coat and withdrew something.

"And you," he said with a grin, "I believe, would enjoy this very much. You may be the only person who..."

Joshua gasped. "The Dragoons!" He squinted as the box opened and the sun danced over the gold and silver barrels and chambers; he noted the exquisite polish of the ivory handles and how they snugly rested against the velvet. The trigger guards glinted and silver pinpoints danced in his eyes.

"Five thousand," Colt repeated. "Plus a trade for the current Dragoons you wear. Wouldn't want to be defenseless, you understand."

"Of course," said Joshua, still unable to take his eyes off the revolvers. He fumbled with his gun belt, then offered it and his pale steel revolvers to their creator. "I can write you a note to cash at our bank here in town..."

"That's fine. I know yer good for it."

"Are you sure about this?" Joshua asked, finishing the note, and trying to avert his eyes from the open case.

Colt caught Joshua's hand and gave it another vigorous shake. "Not a second thought. I saw the way you looked at these—the way my wife once looked at me before I added a few pounds. You deserve this, and you'll appreciate it like no one else." He stood in the doorway, sunlight framing his bulk. "And I got a feeling you'll be puttin' them to good use."

"Thank you," Joshua whispered, offering a slight bow.

"Good bye," Colt said. "And I hope you find her, or if not—that you discover what you were meant to find."

An hour later, he found Quitch, back at the hotel.

"I want to buy a ship," Joshua said.

But Quitch sadly shook his head and offered Joshua a glass. He poured it full of whiskey. "Joshua. I'm so sorry, old friend. I did some more investigation while you were...busy these past few days. Your Caroline had indeed been on the initial visit of the California. So I checked, as I assume you would have done, had you been sober enough."

Too scared to breathe, much less divert Quitch from his narrative, Joshua let the jab pass. He downed the whiskey.

"So I asked around out at the fields. At Ophir, and Mariposa. Inquired about passengers on that ship."

"And?" Joshua's throat was dry, the glass shook in his hand, and he desperately tried not to look at the faces of the men in a semicircle around him, men who were staring down at their shoes.

Quitch offered Joshua another drink. He slowly shook his head. "There was bad news. From a digger at Angel's Camp. Said a woman had passed during a fever, on the last leg of the trip, after Panama."

Joshua let the glass slip from his fingers, and he barely heard it shatter on the floor. Quitch continued talking, speaking of the quiet on-board service the men had for her, and how they all pitched in to send her body back to Virginia when they arrived in port.

Joshua tuned him out and simply imagined one last embrace, one last chaste kiss in the sun. The rustle of vines along her father's house, and the buzzing of fireflies. He held her fiercely until the tears threatened, then he released the image and took a deep breath.

"I am deeply sorry," Quitch said, and all the others joined in offering their condolences. Joshua lifted his chin and stared at his partner. He would not show any more weakness, although a void had opened at his feet, and his future teetered on uncertainty and hopelessness.

"Come," said Quitch, "perhaps it is fate that I am the one to tell you. As now I can be the one to offer an immediate change of scenery. Get you out of this cesspool, and back out to the mountains and streams you love so well."

Joshua tried to steady himself, taking deep breaths. Quitch was right. He had to move on. "What are you proposing?" he asked. And for the first time he wondered what Quitch's dealings had accomplished; how extensive Quitch's operations might have just become.

Quitch clapped his hands. "Ah, Wetherwax! I propose, simply, that you accompany me on a tour of my new minefields. Come and see what our investments have produced, my friend. Spend a year or so learning the business and seeing the new techniques. I know you'll marvel at what a little ingenuity, a thousand tons of water and some nitroglycerin can accomplish!" His eyes sparkled and a devilish grin pulled at his cheeks.

Joshua nodded. "Fine. What then?"

Quitch shrugged. "Anything you wish. You can work with me—or you can be my scout if that suits you better. Run out into the deeper hills, prospect new sites, and do what you do best. I hear rumors of dust found in the mountains far to the north, and even in Montana and Colorado. The whole region is open to us, my friend."

Joshua pictured it, letting his mind wander. "That sounds perfect." He regarded Quitch quietly, then said, "Thank you, friend."

Quitch slid up close and slipped his arm around Joshua's back. "You can get back everything you have lost. And I'll be here to help you along."

As they made to leave, Joshua retrieved the box from his pack, the gift from Colt. He opened the lid and his fingers lovingly traced the outlines of the chambers, the cool ivory grips, the polished silver barrels. He allowed himself one last fantasy—and imagined for one final moment a caress just as soft against his love's cheek.

And then he let the vision fade, so that only silver and gold—tangible and undying—remained to accept his touch.

Chapter 4: Alaska, 1875

"So that's how you got the guns." Delin said in a dreamy, sleepy voice. The aurora burned fiercely overhead and to the east, a shimmering gauze curtain over the sleepless constellations.

"That, Delin, is how I got the guns." Joshua sipped at stale coffee, lukewarm and bitter, as he huddled in his wool coat and stared into the crackling fire, watching the smoke lazily curl up and obscure the stars. "But don't you go thinkin' gambling is the way to get anything of value. That day damn near ruined me—and cost me my soul. Just as easily I could've lost everything. And if you listened close, you heard that I didn't win those guns; they were given to me, more or less."

"But then you still lost them," Delin said, sitting up in his bedroll. His hair was clumpy and disheveled, his face dirty. Two dogs lay exhausted at his side, snuggling together for warmth. They seemed to prefer Delin to his father.

"I didn't lose them, Delin. You know I gave them away. I told you this story before." Joshua sighed. "Hundreds of times."

"Sorry, Papa." Delin smiled mischievously. "Tell it again. Please?" He yawned and lay back down. "And the part about how you and Mr. Quitch fought, and how you had to run and hide—"

"I didn't run and hide," Joshua snapped. "Apparently I didn't tell the story properly if you believe that."

"—And how you came to Alaska, and how you met Mama and—"

"All right, all right. Promise not to pester me all the way back to the Long House and I'll tell it again."

"Promise!"

"Okay, then. Settle down in your bedroll and prepare yourself for the story—again." Joshua finished his coffee as Delin grinned and hugged one of the dogs, rubbing its ears.

"It starts in Shiloh, Tennessee," Joshua said, his eyes dimming, losing their luster, reflecting the flames and sparks and the swirling embers. "The nation was at war—again. This time, with itself. And Quitch and I, we had to take sides. The Comstock Lode—all our wealth—was in jeopardy. President Lincoln eyed Nevada's silver coffers like a starving wolf circling its unprotected prey. We were being pushed into statehood, and courted strongly by each side."

"But you fought for the South."

Joshua nodded. "General Lee and his men were our friends. Men we served with in the Mexican War. That...and we were promised leadership positions. It wasn't something I was proud of, Delin. Fighting, killing...But it was wartime. And Quitch...he wouldn't take no for an answer. My fortunes and his were one, our destinies ensnared—until that one night."

Chapter 5: Shiloh, Tennessee - April 6, 1862

BROTHER AGAINST BROTHER

After dark, the sky wept. A thunderstorm cracked the heavens and the rains fell and washed seas of blood into the ravines and drenched the wounded where they lay in thousands.

Joshua huddled beneath a splintered tree in a peach orchard his fellow soldiers had grimly taken to calling "the Hornet's Nest." He tore his pale blue eyes off the field of slaughter, praying for less frequent lightning bursts so the dead and wounded would not be lit up in their horrific poses.

Earlier, in a surprise attack, Generals Johnston and Beauregard, with nearly fifty thousand Confederate troops, had swarmed upon the Federal positions, determined to drive them back into the Tennessee River. It was to be the decisive blow at the perfect time, a shattering fist into the Union Army delivered by weathered troops defending their lands. But by the end of the day Johnston was dead, and while Sherman's troops were beaten back past Shiloh's Church, it was not far enough. Natural barriers—swamps, ravines and the high ground at Pittsburg Landing—slowed the Confederate advance and allowed the Federals to fortify their positions. From the hill, great guns bore down on the approaching Confederates, and two gunships in the river mouth rained hellfire upon the valiant troops.

Joshua glanced back during the next flash and saw Benjamin Quitch on the sloped roof of the church, sighting with his telescope and scanning the distant hills for targets; but in the failing light, little could be seen, and the rain effectively doused any fires.

No, there would be no more fighting until dawn—if it ever chose to rise upon this field of horror. The trees were blasted and pierced by hailstorms of lead, and sloping branches hung in misery. The ground was torn and churned by cannon fire, earth and flesh mangled as one. Joshua fought back a surge of nausea, recalling the fires that swept across the hill to the east during the mid-day. The dense carpet of dry leaves had caught fire and roaring flames had consumed the field, incinerating the dead while gorging on the helpless, screeching wounded.

Their cries still echoed in Joshua's skull as he leaned against the tree. His long gray coat, soaked and dripping, appeared black from gunfire and the blood of fellow soldiers.

All day, Joshua and Quitch had tracked the Union commanders, horses, and messengers with fierce success at times. Quitch had enthusiastically whooped after each kill, and cursed every miss, even as he reloaded and sighted another target. When the church had finally been won, the gleam in his eye could not be contained. They spent hours on the rooftop, descending only for additional ammunition.

Sometime near dusk, Joshua had come down, staggering among the dead and wounded, and he collapsed beside a tree. He gave in to a sickness worse than any he'd ever had on the Providence. The stench of burning flesh and blasted bodies mixed with fresh peach blossoms and threatened to overwhelm his sanity.

Word came of Johnston's fall; morale plummeted, and then emotions turned to despair when night descended and Beauregard was unable to rout Sherman's troops. No one voiced the obvious: that tomorrow, barring some miracle, the Confederate regiments would be beaten back by superior numbers. Buell's division of some twenty thousand troops must now be crossing the river up at Pittsburg landing, replenishing the Union lines.

Joshua lifted his face to the sky and willed the pelting rain to wash away his sins, to punish his eyes and remove the visions of such horrors. He opened his collar and let the rainwater blast upon the cross that hung beneath his neck. He dared not speak to God here; he would not impose the slightest unworthy plea for himself while countless souls lay in the greatest agony, and many others had already succumbed.

"Come with me," said an angelic voice that resonated moments later with a roar of thunder.

Startled, Joshua turned to stare into Quitch's bloodshot eyes. And then he followed, wordlessly, as Quitch made his way across the field of the dead. Behind them, men lay huddled in tents or under the meager cover of branches. Some slept. Most stared ahead with hopeless expressions.

Quitch picked his way over bodies, ignoring reaching hands and cries for help. He fixed a bayonet on his rifle as he sloshed through puddles of rainwater and blood, through the battered trees and onto a marshy field beside Owl Creek. Joshua followed at a slower pace. His feet were as numb as his heart, and his rifle dragged along the ground behind him.

He had not once drawn his prized revolvers, the silver and gold Dragoons. Still he dreamed of the promise of that game, the gift of Samuel Colt years ago, ages ago. When his pockets were empty but his heart was still full.

Every so often, Joshua would lovingly trace the wet edges of the ivory handles, feel the trigger points, touch the smooth metal and the inlaid silver and gold designs; but he refused to allow their participation in this unworthy, horrific fight.

He thought back to a night six months ago, back at the Comstock Silver Mine where he had worked at Quitch's side, surveying the mountainside, prospecting new veins. Joshua remembered the fateful decision made in a secret basement room, to aid the South, to do anything they could to prevent Lincoln from seizing their Nevada silver.

Now he gazed up through the descending missiles of water and tried to discern some pattern to their fall; to observe if Fate indeed worked any malefic designs upon his plight.

"Here," said Quitch in the shadows ahead.

Joshua shuffled closer, tripping over a leg and part of a torso as he approached. Finally, he arrived by Quitch's side.

"I saw him in a lightning strike," Quitch whispered, pointing to a blue-suited man on the ground. At first Joshua couldn't understand what they were seeing, wondering if Quitch had finally lost his senses and had gone chasing ghouls.

But then he noticed the stripes on the wounded man's shoulder, the gold tassels on his coat. And he saw Quitch's grin. "Got a live one," he whispered as he raised the bayonet and stepped over the groaning officer.

A jagged, sideways sliver of lightning danced across the hills and in that flash, the wounded officer looked up at Joshua through his one remaining eye. It blinked once, and flickered with thankfulness and the hope of aid. The man's mouth worked, but the ensuing thunder drowned out his words.

Quitch's shadow tensed. He drew the rifle back and sent the bayonet ramming down into the man's thigh, and through—spearing him into the ground. His screams replaced the thunder, but only joined countless others wailing in the night.

Before he realized it, Joshua reached out and yanked Quitch backward. The rifle slipped from his grip as Quitch spun and pushed free of Joshua. The rain slammed down between them as they stood, face to face in the dark, shin-deep in the marsh.

"What are you doing?" Joshua roared, all his anger surging at once, battling through the horror of the day's conflict.

Quitch's hands formed into fists at his side. His shoulders hunched forward and his legs tensed. He pointed back to the officer. "I'm doing what needs to be done!"

"What, torturing a man already in agony?"

"Getting our due! Inflicting deadly anguish upon them so their resolve will crumble."

Joshua shook his head. "That's insane! He won't even make it back to the others. Their reinforcements are here, and they'll renew their attack tomorrow with double our force, and..."

"You know nothing! You never wanted to be here, you don't believe in our cause. You've always been ruled by weakness, fawning over dear, sweet Caroline, as if with our wealth you couldn't have any woman you wanted!"

Joshua staggered as if struck. "Caroline...died trying to join me in California." Horrific images, nightmares that had plagued him for years, sprang into his thoughts, banishing the lightning and the storm. An overpacked boat caught in the storms, braving the Cape passage; his Caroline, feverish, rocking in the ship's hold, wasting away in agony.

"You—" Joshua struggled with restraint, and then finally let it go. "You're a devil!" He spat out the words that had been years in coming, brewing at the back of his throat since a hot California night where Quitch had taken control of their first mining camp by hanging an innocent Chileno man by his neck for all to see.

Quitch tensed; he reached at his belt for something. "And you're a fool, Wetherwax. Ever since the Providence you've been nothing but a sniveling fool, wasting your skills, wasting our friendship. Wasting my time."

Joshua took a step back, and the world seemed to sink deeper into the swamp. Lightning flashed again and painted Quitch with a scalding brightness so intense that Joshua had to look away—but not before seeing that Quitch had pulled his Walker '46 from its holster.

"What are you—?" he stammered, even as Quitch raised the gun and pointed it at Joshua's head.

"I don't need your talents anymore, Joshua," Quitch said, matter-of-factly. "I don't need you."

"No, wait!"

Thunder rocked the hills as the blast went off. Visions of endless wheat fields and mansions of white flew by; majestic mountains swirled in storms of red dust as great ships heaved on Pacific waves and subtle creeks washed over metal pans, leaving fragments of gold dust glittering in his mind.

And a deafening scream silenced the battlefield, drowning out even the most horrific cries. Joshua blinked away the stinging cloud of gunsmoke, amazed he was still standing, and he looked down upon the squirming, crawling form. The scream continued, and when the next lightning burst spread its pointed fingers across the heavens and reflected in the pools and rain-pelted swamp water, he saw his friend writhing upon the ground.

Quitch clutched at his ruined face with one hand as blood sprayed through his fingers; and in his other hand—still raised skyward—lay the ruined heap of the Walker Colt revolver. Shattered and smoldering.

Misfired, Joshua realized at once—even as Quitch rolled to his knees.

Quitch struggled blindly over to his rifle...

And before Joshua could break his paralysis and disbelief at still being alive, Quitch had wrenched the bayonet free from the twitching officer. He lined it up higher, then plunged it down—this time through the man's chest.

Joshua screamed and threw himself upon Quitch. He caught hold of his coat, then hauled him back, turned him around and slammed a fist into his already-bloodied face. A second punch and he felt metal fragments slicing into his knuckles and had a dim realization that the gun had exploded backward—sending fragments into Quitch's face, slicing his cheeks and puncturing his eyes.

He delivered another blow, heedless to Quitch's condition, giving in at last to a wave of rage. Lightning struck again and again; thunder roared, and a crowd of gray-coated men approached, guns drawn.

He set Quitch down, then looked up at the converging soldiers. He saw the fury in their eyes, murder in their thoughts. Here was a traitor, beating one of their own.

Quitch had a crooked, bloody grin as he blindly turned his head this way and that. The rain beat down, pummeling them both, and for a moment frozen in time, Joshua sensed they shared a unified mind and a common thought: that here, on this blood-drenched field, the end had not yet been written.

For either of them. Their paths would cross sometime again, but not soon. Joshua crouched, and as the lightning faded and the men rushed forward, he darted back. He turned and sprinted as fast as his legs would carry him through the deep puddles. Hurtling over bodies and fallen trees, he zigzagged across the marsh, ignoring the blasts of rifles behind him, confident in their inferior marksmanship.

He dashed to the cover of trees and kept running, keeping the Union Army to his right and the Confederates to his left. Desperate to avoid both, he fled straight to the winding creek, then waded across and over to the other side where he dropped to his stomach amid the thick reeds and deeper water.

And he made his way, foot by foot, yard by yard, across a sea of blood and death, under an angry sky blasting the world with its fury.

Sometime—hours, or perhaps only minutes, later—he crawled

atop a soldier not quite dead. In the near-total darkness Joshua couldn't be sure where he was. Cries punctuated the gloom, but voices had ceased and he sensed all the camps and waiting soldiers were far to the south.

As he crawled forward on his knees, a hand reached out from the muddy depths; it clasped his arm and held it in a death-grip. A head appeared in the darkness, but Joshua could not tell if this man lay dying for the North or South.

"Wait," the soldier said in a voice like a hissing teapot. "I beg of you... a favor."

Joshua tried to shake free of the grip, but the faceless man only tightened his hold. "Listen," he whispered. "In my front pocket there's a paper. Take it."

Joshua cleared his throat, glancing around. Impossible to see anything, and the lightning had stopped some time ago. For all he knew, General Sherman stood just ten feet away. "What is it?" he asked, hoping to move on quickly.

He had far to go before dawn, and wanted to get out behind Beauregard's rear flank and on his way around Corinth before much longer. From there he would shed his uniform and hope to have God's blessings for luck and protection as he made his way back west.

"A claim," insisted the dying man, fumbling at his coat. "Take it, please!"

Joshua frowned, trying again to pierce the darkness before the man's face. "A claim to what?"

"...me and four others," he whispered, "registered it with the Mounted Police before I joined up in the Army. Said they'd work it for me. Figured one of us should up and fight in this Great Conflict while the rest stayed behind in the hope of findin' the next big strike."

Joshua perked up, clutching the man's arm. "Where is this claim?"

The man's grip faltered, his fingers relaxed. The swamp bubbled as his body slid backward. "..ska," he managed to say.

"What?" Joshua shook the man once, then reached inside his coat, searching until he found the paper.

The man coughed and his chest heaved in Joshua's arms. But he spoke one last time, getting it right.

"—Alaska!"

Chapter 6: Alaska / Northwest Territories - 1866

AN AUSPICIOUS MEETING

JOSHUA LEFT THE ONE-ROOM CHAPEL with its moss-covered sod roof. He had attended services with seven Tlingit males and two of their wives. Bowing to the splintered wooden cross on the wall, he bade the Russian-trained Eskimo cleric goodbye, and stepped out into the wind. In the pale May sun, his feet crunched across an ice-crusted graveyard as he walked between crosses draped with icicle tears and made his way to the shore.

A man waited for him there. His new partner, Matsei Xien, a Chinaman—a celestial, as they were called back San Francisco. He had been one of the four men working the claim when Joshua had arrived, the dead man's note in his hand.

Xien's face was wrapped in heavy wool scarves that just allowed his eyes and the tip of his red nose to emerge. Together they climbed inside their quayaq and began to paddle across the mist-shrouded inlet. They left Wrangell Island and headed back across the channel, dodging the icy breakup and wagon-sized chunks floating in their path.

They had far to go before nightfall if they hoped to camp at the base of Mount Dewey. Within two weeks they hoped to set out across the treacherous Chilkoot Pass, lugging their supplies and hauling their quayaq. If they made good time they could be at Lake Bennett by month's end, and if the ice had melted by then, it would be clear paddling north along the Yukon River, five hundred miles to the outpost at Fort Reliance.

"Do you feel renewed?" asked Xien, steering at the front of the craft. He and Joshua were dressed alike: heavy parkas underneath thick fox-pelt coats with furry hoods. Their boots were seal-skin interior, thatched with bear fur, rising above their knees over heavy canvas pants.

Joshua did experience a lifting of his spirits, an emotional calm as serene as this implacable landscape. It had been a long trek—a four-week odyssey maneuvering icy ledges across the Chugach range, fording unnamed rivers and traversing endless tundra. Twice they encountered hostile Indians, and twice, Joshua and Xien had to kill to proceed.

For the past four years, Joshua had been impressed with these indigenous people, those they met in peace; advanced and cultured, they were skilled at woodworking, hunting and fishing. He was amazed too, that Russian Orthodox missionaries had schooled so many tribes in languages, religion and arithmetic.

Explorers in this frozen world mainly traveled the coastlines, searching for the Northwest Passage—that mythical link from the Atlantic to the Pacific. They left the interior—its endless tracks of ice, enormous mountain ranges and vast canyons—to that particular breed of adventurer, the prospector. Men who ventured farther and farther north, after exhausting the possibilities of northern California, Montana and Washington.

And like the Russians and the Innuit people scattered about this enormous land, these prospectors soon learned a valuable lesson: that Alaska could not be tamed. To survive you had to let it claim you. To endure its seasons as you could. To suffer through months of darkness and long stretches without food, to endure frigid temperatures that burst even the best thermometers. Every step was a testament to human endurance, and survival depended on prudence—and the whims of the land.

The fog lifted as they pulled up to an icy shorebank, and Joshua reached out to drag the boat onto the ice. He stood and faced the imposing stretch of white leading to the cloud-crowned peaks miles away, and he thought back to a rain-doused night a lifetime ago—a field littered with human suffering and untold death.

Joshua closed his eyes and rubbed his face under his hood, warming his icy cheeks. Today's visit to the chapel had brought out too many disturbing memories. His sins had emerged like cackling ghosts from the crypts in his mind; he had envisioned a line of blue-suited soldiers, bullet holes in their skulls, staring at him from across the mist.

And then Quitch's voice had echoed in his ears. "Giving them their due!" he gleefully shouted, and his face turned, and empty eyesockets glared ahead, and that wicked grin... Joshua had shaken free from those illusions, gripped his cross tight in both hands, and prayed while the minister read from a torn copy of the Gospels. Joshua had called out all his crimes, and he whispered his plea for mercy. He heard no reply but the wind sifting through the cracks in the walls, but that was comfort enough. And now, as he joined Xien, hauling their quayaq up the shore, his friend seemed to sense his thoughts.

"You took an important journey of cleansing," Xien said. "Do not feel guilt that we left the claim unattended."

"It's not that," Joshua said. "Besides, good luck to those working the pits." The ground had been frozen for seven months, and to reach bedrock they had to light daily fires in a hole, then scoop away the softened earth each morning—making progress of only several feet each day. After working several locations, selling their first claim to some Dutch prospectors, they mined with a team of six along the Porcupine River before trying their luck on a rocky patch on one of the lower tributaries. It was work they never tired of, and the rewards—the few ounces a week, the occasional pellet-sized nugget—were secondary to the experience of this dreamlike, often tranquil world.

Joshua grunted as they secured the rope around his shoulders. He started moving, taking the first turn dragging the boat. "I am only concerned about our dwindling supplies, and I hope we can make Forty Mile before our food runs out."

"We will make it," said Xien. "Or we will come across some others who will trade."

"Ever the optimist," said Joshua.

Xien walked ahead, but slowed to let Joshua keep pace. "In this business, there is little point being anything else."

Joshua gazed at the peaks far ahead, and then closer, at the remarkably blue-tinted glacier spilling out into the sea. The sun reflected off the blazing field of ice and pierced at their eyes. They donned their wooden eyeshields—a form of eyewear made by the Tlingits. If left unprotected, their eyes would quickly ache as if drizzled with hard particles of sand, and snow-blindness could occur within hours.

They progressed in silence, suffering the biting cold that still whipped through their layers and began to numb their extremities. Eventually, night descended and the mountains seemed no closer. They made camp, burning the rest of their wood and eating the usual dried pork and beans.

They rose before dawn, and made good time. In six days they had skirted Mt. Dewey and proceeded down a rough, icy ledge into a gorge filled with treacherous ridges and hills, and finally they arrived at the foot of the Chilkoot Pass. Grateful that no Indians were nearby—they had heard the Pass was jealously guarded as a trade route—they crossed without incident and made their way to the icy shore of Lake Bennett. The wide lake, flanked on two sides by steeply rising white cliffs, lured them forward, tempting them to just walk across the thin and cracking ice.

They set the quayaq down and secured a collapsible six-foot pole to its centerpiece, then attached another one across the lower portion of this pole. Xien unraveled the canvas sail from his pack and he and Joshua worked to secure it to the four end posts and the centerpiece. They judged the wind, then adjusted the sail. As the boat lurched forward, they skipped after it, tossed in their packs, then jumped inside even as the ice below their feet cracked slightly and splintered, but held.

"Still a ways till thaw," Joshua said as they sped along at a nice pace, driven by the wind. The quayaq skipped over the smooth lake surface, occasionally hitting a rough patch and requiring some adjustments, but otherwise moving swiftly. They sailed towards the terminus where the Lewes River emptied out and sped northward, ultimately connecting with the Delin.

An hour later they had landed on the far shore, and disassembled the sail. They decided to break for a light snack before continuing on; the next sixty miles or so would have to be partially on foot, down the side of the river, which had begun to crack and flow as rapids tumbled ahead.

Xien suddenly stood up and snapped his head toward the nearby row of spruce trees, heavily sagging with snow. Joshua caught the motion. He tensed, preparing to peel off his gloves in an instant so he could reach into his coat for the revolvers.

The tree limbs rustled and snow crunched—just loud enough to notice, but obviously caused by a stealthy approach. "We've got company," Xien whispered, reaching into the quayaq for the rifle. Joshua's gloves came off, and flashes of silver and gold sparkled off the Dragoons as they drew into the light.

A piercing cry shattered the calm, and three, four, then five forms burst from the trees. At first Joshua thought they were small bears until he realized they were natives dressed in partial bearskins, including the hollowed-out heads used as hoods. Three held spears while the other two ran ahead with rifles aimed.

The two with rifles fired before Joshua could react. A lead slug popped harmlessly into the quayaq, but the other struck home. Xien screamed even as his own shot went wild. Joshua shot both armed men down in seconds, then looked over in horror to see a red geyser spraying from his friend's thigh.

Xien dropped to one knee, and managed to fire even as a howling Tlingit raider leapt on him. The impact threw the Indian backward and left him in a twitching heap. The other two ran past their fallen brothers. One threw a spear that Xien managed to dodge; the other closed in fast on Joshua with an ax.

Concerned with protecting Xien, he fired with the Dragoon in his left hand and let the recoil take him sideways, out of the range of the striking warrior. He spun and saw his shot had struck the target—Xien knelt alone beside three dead attackers.

The final Indian took another swipe at Joshua, and the blade sliced harmlessly through the uppermost layer of his thick pelt coat. Joshua leaned under the Indian's arm, jabbed the gun barrel against the man's throat, locked eyes for an instant of shared animalistic survival, then pulled the trigger.

Through the thick cloud of smoke, he stepped over the native's twitching body, then ran past the blood steaming across the ice. He dropped to his knees beside Xien. Pale and wheezing, the Asian weakly tried to cover the gushing wound with his gloved hands.

Joshua grabbed the nearest Indian and used his dagger to slide open the parka, shredding it into wide strips. He returned to Xien and bound his leg, tightly wrapping the cloth around the wound and stopping the blood flow. He tied a large knot even as his fingers turned crimson.

"Keep... pressure on," Xien muttered, his eyes glazing over, then reasserting focus. "Herbs in my pack. Have to get shelter, and boil leaves. I will instruct you..."

Joshua tried to grin. "What am I, your nurse?"

Xien coughed. "Yes. Most ugly one ever."

Joshua laughed as he slipped under Xien's arm and held him tight, then got to his feet. He started back to the quayaq, dragging Xien along. As they neared the boat, a foul stench wafted over the ridge, blown by a nervous breeze. The sun ducked behind a gray-bottomed cloud and the temperature plummetted all at once.

Xien sniffed, then crunched up his nose. He glanced over to the trees that were oddly quivering, with snow from their tips shaking loose. He trembled in Joshua's arms as he whispered: "Something else is coming."

A strange high-pitched sound whistled through the trees.

And the branches parted, slowly releasing a figure out of a nightmare. It crouched at first, and Joshua's brain refused to process its shape—but then it rose up to full height, easily fifteen feet tall, and nearly six wide. It was covered in thick white fur, like a giant ape, yet pristinely more savage. A blue face with slanted eyes of utter cold, a crunched snout layered with jagged curved teeth.

Xien's grip dug into Joshua's arm. "Run!" he hissed. "I do not believe your guns will stop this thing."

Joshua lowered Xien and released him gently, never taking his eyes off of the monstrous beast as it took one thudding step closer. "What is it?" he whispered as Xien crawled slowly behind the quayaq.

"It goes by many names," Xien whispered back. "And only in legends have I heard of it. Yeti, they call it in the Himalayas. Very deadly." He glanced over to Joshua, and his eyes brimmed with terror. "Our fortunes may have run out, old friend."

The yeti sniffed the air, and a deep growl issued from its insides as plumes of steam gusted into the air. The smell nearly made Joshua retch, but he backed onto the lake, his Dragoons raised, ready with four shells left in each. He would see if guns truly couldn't harm this thing.

One of the Tlingits stirred; not quite dead, he lifted his head and moaned, holding his hand over a chest wound. The sound drew an immediate reaction; in a blur the yeti was upon him, thundering into his ribcage with one enormous taloned foot while reaching down and tearing off a chunk of the Indian's upper body, including the head. It howled to the sky and flung the grisly mass into the trees.

Then it snapped its head around and locked onto Joshua's movement. "Run!" hissed Xien, readying his rifle.

"No," Joshua called back, speaking a little louder. "Don't fire on it until it's chasing me!"

The beast roared and took two crunching steps ahead, bounding off the shore and onto the frozen lake. Joshua narrowed his eyes and took a deep, cold breath to clear his mind. An idea came to him at once like a golden beacon in the night, and he lowered his aim slightly.

Slowly, not to encourage a full chase but enough to lead the beast out a little further, he backed up. Step after step. He felt the miniature cracks open below his boots, and could sense the flow of water several inches down.

The monster took another crunching step and appeared about to give all-out chase and close the thirty feet between them—when it paused and glanced down. A strange grumbling came from its throat and its nostrils flared as it seemed to analyze the pattern of cracks spreading out from its foot.

"Come on!" shouted Joshua, waving his arms. He stepped back with longer strides.

The yeti roared, tensed, and leapt. Joshua almost panicked, seeing how far the creature covered with just one leap, landing nearly ten feet away. The ice splintered, and jagged cracks spread out in five directions. The beast snarled and raised its talons for a strike—

But Joshua started firing, blasting around the beast's feet. He moved his aim after each pull of the trigger, spreading the final shots from each gun into a half circle in the ice several feet in front of the creature.

The wind tossed the black clouds of gunsmoke into the yeti's face, and the great beast coughed and struck at the noxious fumes, and it stomped again, preparing to leap forward and rend Joshua to pieces.

But a great sound like a crack of thunder echoed across the lake, reverberating with smaller cracks, one after the other. And then the howls—sickeningly shrill and desperate—and a great splash. The creature dropped from view, except for its huge arms that raked into the ice, digging up large chunks as they slid backwards, drawn down by its immense weight.

It struggled for one last, desperate pull. Joshua, standing perfectly still just feet away from the start of the hole, admired the attempt and felt a twinge of regret.

It rose on its forearms, sopping wet with stringy tassels of fur covering its eyes and bitter lakewater bursting from its jaws. And then the ice shelf snapped and the beast was gone in one last, great splash.

Joshua slid back, ever so slightly, inching his way with legs spread, trying to evenly distribute his weight. He had the terrifying expectation that a great white fist would burst through the ice and haul him down into the frozen depths, but after two more steps the water in the hole calmed and remained motionless but for a few bubbles.

Joshua let the air out of his lungs and started a quick prayer of thanks—when he noticed movement on the shore. Coming through the trees, a half dozen Indians. Then a few more. His heart sank as he felt the spent Dragoons in his grip.

It would take too long to reload. Xien could kill a few from his vantage point behind the boat, but it would not be enough. Joshua could run, but he would not leave his friend, not this time. Six more Indians emerged, and Joshua sucked in a breath. Something was different, and it took him a moment to see it: these were not warriors, but women. And children. A few carried spears, but no one seemed in a position for battle.

If anything, they appeared to be in awe, like first-time spectators at a circus. Finally, several women broke the paralysis and ran to the fallen men.

Joshua stared out across the splintered lake and locked eyes on one woman—one who seemed caught in his vision, remaining motionless. Finally, she pulled back a hood, and a thick head of blonde hair spilled out, framing a rough yet pleasing face. An older, dark-haired woman ran to her and pointed to the dismembered man, shaking her head. The blonde turned instead to where Xien struggled to stand. She called something to him, and he answered, after a glance to Joshua.

By the time Joshua arrived back on the shore, having inched his way in places, and slid carefully in others, Xien was lying on a canvas stretcher that the tribespeople had brought, anticipating some wounded among their men.

"Put your guns away," Xien said in a weak voice when Joshua returned, warily walking through six of the Tlingit women. They shrank back at his approach, yet seemed overtly curious. The blonde woman knelt beside Xien, and when Joshua neared she glanced up sharply with large eyes of crystal blue.

"We must help your friend," she said in a clear voice, a little forced in its pronunciation, with a touch of the common Russian accent.

Joshua bent down after holstering his pistols, and helped lift the stretcher. "Where are we going?"

"To the Long House," the woman said. "Beyond the trees. We have medicine there and bindings to tend to his wound. I learned English as a young girl, and I can help guide you."

Joshua stopped suddenly, jarring the stretcher, and causing the woman to spin her head back. "Thank you," he said, a hundred questions swirling in his thoughts. "But these men—if they were from your village...?"

"They were," said the woman, her eyes hardening as she looked around at the faces of her fellow women. "But we—I—did not approve of their attacks on outsiders."

Joshua took a deep breath, then said what he had to tell her. "I must admit it was our guns that killed all but one."

She blinked at him. "No. Whether you know it or not, these men were dead the minute the Sesquat smelled them."

Joshua gave Xien a look. "The what?"

The woman glanced out over the lake. "You did what our warriors have been unable to do for generations. Normally the Sesquats do not venture so close to a Long House, preferring to hunt us in small groups—but this one was hungry, and our men were careless." She shook her head. "They should have known that blood would draw the monster. So by their attack on you, they doomed themselves."

Joshua looked back over his shoulder, fearing this Sesquat creature had somehow lumbered out of the ice and stood now at his shoulder, breathing its foul steam upon his neck.

"You killed it," she said, and gave him a look that was part admiration, and part doubt—as if he had just proclaimed himself their savior and demanded worship. "Who would have thought to kill it with water?" She turned from him. "Now, come, we have to get your friend inside quickly."

Joshua followed the surprisingly nimble woman, and they carried Xien together. Xien coughed, and Joshua frowned at him, seeing a playful grin forming under his grimace. "What?"

The smile grew and Xien shook his head. "We will see, but I sense the movings of destiny at work here."

"What?"

The blonde woman turned her head, annoyed at the whispering. She looked at Joshua. "What is your name?"

Taking his eyes off the giggling Xien, he met her gaze and felt his cheeks flush. "Joshua," he said as his mouth went dry. "Joshua Wetherwax, ma'am."

She gave him a curt bow, then continued walking, leading the stretcher into the trees, past the Sesquat's immense footprints and the snapped branches left in its wake.

"Wait!" he said. "That's it for introductions? What's your name, and how do you find yourself among these people?"

"These people?" She stopped, and dropped the front end of the stretcher. Xien groaned while she turned, knelt and lifted the handles again so that she could carry the load, walk backwards and face Joshua at the same time.

Xien smiled again and crossed his arms.

"I meant no offense," Joshua said. "Only...I am shocked to see one so...out of place here. And..."

"Mirna," she snapped. "My name is Mirna Helvoski. And I have been 'out of place,' as you put it, for ten years. Abducted from the aristocratic quarters at Sitka's fortress when I was only twelve."

Joshua swallowed. He had heard about Tlingit raids on Russian settlements. "I'm sorry. Did your people look for you?"

She shrugged. "I am sure they tried, but everyone in my family was killed—my younger brothers butchered before my eyes and my father killed in battle. My mother was taken as a wife by a clan farther north. I heard she died within a year."

They continued walking, slowly and carefully stepping over fallen branches and icy patches. In the distance, down a slight incline and in a clearing, Joshua could see smoke curling from a wooden structure some sixty feet in length, with three levels. Around this house were several smaller homes and sheds.

"I have learned to live with them," Mirna said. "So when missionaries came last year and found me, I told them this is my home. I was married, and had a child..."

Joshua's heart kicked—he wasn't sure why, but a pang of jealousy swept over his thoughts. "Your husband...?" he asked suddenly, afraid of the answer.

She made a motion with her eyes to indicate a place beyond his shoulder. "The one torn in two back there."

Joshua halted, nearly jarring Xien from the stretcher. "Ma'am! You should have said. We must go back and let you grieve for him. I will help to bury the dead and..."

"Tlingits cremate their dead," she corrected, pulling on the handles and walking again, dragging Joshua along. "Besides, I would rather spend my efforts on the living. I will not grieve for that man, and I hold you in no contempt for defending yourself. As I said, he called his doom to him."

Joshua shook his head. "No one deserves that."

Mirna looked at him in wonder. "You are a very odd man."

Xien craned his neck. "You have no idea."

They walked in silence the rest of the way, pausing only once so that Joshua and Xien could stare in awe at the trio of immense totem poles that marked the entrance to the clearing. Dwindling sunlight glinted off a Raven-headed top on the center pole, and its eyes seemed to watch them intently.

The wind blew at Joshua's back, and pushed him closer to Mirna with Xien between them, smiling still. When they reached the Long

House, Mirna spoke in Tlingit to an old man. Several wrinkled gray-haired women approached and took the stretcher from Joshua and Mirna and brought Xien inside. Joshua made to follow but Mirna placed a hand on his chest.

Joshua leaned instinctively towards her, relishing even her slightest touch. He met her eyes, felt a rush of guilt, and looked away. He had shot her husband, and now—being so close to a woman of such placid beauty, deep blue eyes and haunting lips, and that lush mane of bright blonde hair—Caroline's image flashed before him and guilt rose in his heart.

"Your friend is in good hands," Mirna said. "If you still wish to help, find some sticks and help us with the pyre."

A few other men appeared, coming in from the southeast with a caribou carcass and several rabbits. They rushed to the women, spoke in excited tones, then glanced over to Joshua.

"Your fame is spreading," Mirna said. "Be prepared to retell the tale over and over."

Joshua looked up sharply. "We cannot stay. We have to get back to Fort Reliance and..."

She shook her head. "I fear that may be a journey you do not make for some time."

"Is that a threat?" Joshua looked over to the dozen or so young men. A few were rushing to the forest to look after the dead; the others kept watching them and talking.

Mirna laughed. "Who am I to threaten one who has killed a Sesquat? No, I merely tell you that your friend's injury is severe. Looks like his hip is shattered, and he has lost much blood. It may take time for him to heal."

Joshua's heart fell. It was an echo of his own fears. He looked to the door, and made to go inside to speak to Xien.

"Wait," Mirna said, pressing him back with both hands now; she turned her face up to his; they locked eyes again for a moment, and then she stepped back. "Let the shamans work."

Joshua nodded. "Fine, I will wait. And help your people as best I can."

They started to walk back to the forest, and Joshua reloaded one of the Dragoons as they walked. "Just in case," he said. "You tell me there are others like that thing? That...Sesquat, you call it?"

Mirna nodded. "It is what the elder women call it—an easy enough word, something to frighten the children. It means 'Snow Demon.' They have attacked at least a dozen times since I have been with these people. Usually one at a time they come, although once when I went hunting with Mokim's brothers we saw a pair of them chasing a herd of moose."

"This is a strange world," Joshua said. "The beasts and insects here are of such size and ferocity that I fear we will never tame this land." He sighed, and when they cleared the trees he looked out over the frozen lake. "Fortunately, it would take something incredible to lure men here to brave these terrors."

Mirna nodded. "The furs of otter and seal were enough to call my people, and we wisely stayed on the shoreline. Your people, I fear, may come for more dangerous inland treasure."

Joshua gazed over the sun-trickled mountains and stared at the twinkling of ice, dazzling like flecks of gold.

Xien remained unconscious for three days. Then, another four passed before he regained his strength and could stand with the aid of a crutch. In that time Joshua did become a bit of a hero, and he told the story again and again—each time using a few more words in their own language, instead of relying on Mirna as an interpreter.

Joshua met her child that first night, a four-year-old boy named Mikhail. "He is his father's son," Mirna said, shaking her head. "Raucous and rude. Thankfully, his grandmother dotes on him, as I..." She met Joshua's eyes for a moment. "I feel great shame, but I do not love him as I should."

Joshua said nothing, sipping at a strong hot drink made of bark and some distilled plant juice. It tasted worse than moonshine, but somehow left a pleasant aftertaste.

"Mikhail was... forced upon me." She looked away, and incomprehensible sadness loomed in her teardrops and threatened to break free. "I still cried for my family and resisted my new husband's advances. But finally, my heart froze along with this bitter world, and I gave in. I let my will fade."

Joshua opened his mouth, then closed it again. Mirna sat before the fire while the others smoked and told stories. She huddled in a feathered parka and warmed her slender hands in front of flames that danced in her golden hair. Absently, she pulled on a chain around her neck, and out slid a silver crucifix. She touched it with both hands and seemed to draw comfort from it.

Joshua touched his own cross, marveling at this symmetry. He wondered how he had become entangled here and speculated on when they could leave. He glanced over to Xien, who sat braced against a post, sipping a drink and entertaining two young boys with a mining song.

Mirna looked up with a smile. "I am sorry to unburden my sorrows. It has been so long, and I cannot speak to these others. They do not understand what evils they have done, and I truly bear them no malice."

"You are kind," Joshua said, sipping at his drink.

Mirna rolled her eyes. "I do not know if that is true. But come, I think I have made you uncomfortable. Would you sing, smoke and drink with us—or do you wish to remain and talk on things of melancholy?"

"What do you mean?"

Mirna lowered her eyes. "I see great sorrow in your face as well. You have lost much, I think, and have seen horrors that I may never understand."

Joshua let the hot liquid collect in his mouth, staring at her without a thought of what to say. He had been so long without the company of a woman, resisting every attempt on those rare occasions Quitch had dragged him to the city for a visit to the brothel. And as for the recent years, there were no women for thousands of miles where he and Xien worked. And here, now, someone who stunned his very core had just tried to pry open his long-sealed personal crypts.

"Maybe," Mirna said, leaning back and supporting herself on her hands, "you can tell me the story about how you won those guns of yours?"

"What? How do you know...?" He narrowed his eyes at Xien, who glanced up from his singing and winked.

Mirna smiled. "Quite a gambler, I hear."

Joshua shook his head. "Just once, but that's a long story."

"You could tell it to me on the way to Sitka. We will have much time."

"Pardon?"

Mirna beamed. "I have been invited to accompany you back to the port."

Joshua frowned. "Invited by whom, and why are we going there?"

"By Xien, of course. Has he not told you?"

Joshua set down his drink and stood up. Mirna stood with him, and pulled back on his arm. "I am sorry—I think he may have meant to tell you in private."

"Tell me what?" Joshua asked, stepping between the children and standing over Xien.

His friend looked up at him, stopped his singing and lowered his head. "I beg your forgiveness, Joshua. But we will soon be parting company."

"What? No, Xien..."

Xien raised his hands in a prayer-like gesture. "Joshua. I have had more visions while unconscious these past few days."

"Oh, wonderful!"

"Do not scoff—yours have been clearer than you admit."

Joshua started to argue, but thought better of it.

"Besides," said Xien, "you know this has to be. I will never walk again. I cannot pan, dig or operate the rockers. I will never again wade into freezing rapids and scoop out gravel."

Mirna coughed. "Sounds like you are the lucky one."

Xien laughed. "She is good, Joshua. I invited her to join us on the way. Her people will not object, especially since you are so legendary now."

"But why are we going to Sitka?" Joshua asked. "Xien, return with me to Forty Mile. We'll team with other prospectors. You can man the cabin, cook our meals, tend our injuries."

"Joshua," Xien said, shaking his head. "My visions were clear. My ancestors are calling me home. I am to end my days where I began them. I have family to reconcile with before mortality catches me by the tail."

"But..."

"Take me to Sitka. Book me passage aboard one of the Russian whalers. We will find one that can pass the eastern coast of China, and I will go home at last."

Joshua lowered his head, fighting the pull of sadness and the twist of fate. If that shot had been just a little wide, or if he had been quicker in taking out the threat...

"Do not blame yourself," Mirna said, at his side. "He believes this is meant to be, and perhaps it is. God weaves strange patterns."

Choking back his emotions, Joshua could only nod. "Very well. But until that boat leaves, Matsei Xien, you are to pull your weight around here. I want all these people to remember you, and to tell your story for generations."

Xien grinned. "Ah, so we are to be legends together!"

It took nearly three weeks to reach Sitka. In that time Joshua learned from Mirna how to handle a team of dogs like an old master, mushing along behind a sled as Mirna and Xien rested. The temperatures increased steadily, finally lifting above thirty by the end of the month.

During the longer daylight hours and along slower terrain, Xien would read to Mirna and Joshua from one of several old books. He regaled them with complex ancient battles and wondrous stories from an old copy of Herodotus. They marveled at each prophecy that the Delphi Oracle pronounced and how it invariably came true, leveling commoner and king to the same unavoidable fate.

On a sun-warmed afternoon in early June they drove the dogs to the small settlement on the shore, then took passage aboard a dingy to get to the island. The snow was beginning to thaw, and the waters of the Inside Passage were flowing and teeming with newly-hatched fish.

They tied up the malamutes after feeding them the last of their food supplies. Joshua looked around the old settlement, inhabited since 1799, noting the organized layout and the impressive dome of St. Michael's Cathedral.

"The Russians named this place Baranov Island first, then New Archangel," Mirna told them. "But eventually they went back to calling it by a contraction of the Tlingit name, Shee-Atika."

"What does that mean?" Joshua asked, always interested in name derivations.

"The Kiksadi Clan named this island 'Shee', and they lived on the seaward side. So they took to calling their settlement Shee-Atika which means 'people on the outside of Shee.'"

Joshua nodded, smiling as they slowly made their way along a main street, muddy but still mostly hard with frost. Winds carried a bitter chill, but Joshua felt warm nonetheless, supporting Xien on one side as his friend hobbled along using a crutch. Mirna walked ahead with the dogs, intently engrossed in the architecture of the larger buildings, the layout of the main square, and in the people they passed.

"Do you wish to stay here?" Joshua called out. Perhaps that was her true intention—escaping the tribe at last.

"I do not know these people," Mirna said after a pause. "And besides, for the last few minutes I have heard conversation all centered around one thing: they are leaving. Apparently a deal is being made to sell off Alaska to America."

"Truly?" Joshua glanced around, noticing now that some people were indeed packing up, although the Russian flag still waved over the administrative fortress to the west. "No offense, but I hope we do not pay too much."

Mirna shrugged. "Russia has been trying to part with this icy wilderness for decades. Deep in debt, their resources whittled away from wars, they will take any reasonable deal. We did not have your luck in finding gold under our noses."

Joshua thought of telling her about the gold dust they had been panning from creeks and riverbeds throughout this region, but he thought better of it. Besides, these people were single-minded in their focus on furs and pelts, and saw nothing beyond the waterways. If gold did exist here in great quantities, it would once again fortuitously fall into America's hands.

Mirna sighed as she stared ahead. "My earliest memories are of this place." She pointed across the mist-shrouded Inside Passage to the hazy mountains beyond. "That view I remember seeing every morning while my father dealt with fur traders and worked up papers to be sent to St. Petersburg."

"Would you go back with your countrymen?" Joshua asked as they approached the harbor. The smell of salty water and the refuse of the fishing ships wafted onto the shore.

"No," she said, and then Mirna was silent for some time, the wind whipping at her hair as she walked, head raised and hands clasped before her. She seemed like a high priestess walking among her congregation, on the way to the altar.

Joshua stopped. He opened his mouth, but couldn't find any words. Xien noticed his reaction, smiled and turned ahead again, limping along with his crutch and a sack of supplies over his shoulder.

With Mirna translating, they talked to several of the whalers' sea captains. Eventually they struck a nice balance between price and reliability.

The ship left the next morning, but that night Mirna, Joshua and Xien enjoyed the finest meal they could buy with their gold dust, dining at the Regent's administrative hall with a dozen dignitaries and many of the local merchants and traders. They bought new clothes for the event—the finest European styles off the fast frigates in the harbor; they dined on fresh swordfish and enjoyed high quality vodka until late in the evening. A string band played alongside an elegant piano while they traded stories and learned the recent events of the world.

Joshua finally caught up on the outcome of the War; he heard of the Emancipation Proclamation, and nearly wept at the figures of death coming from battles at places like Gettysburg and Antietam. He learned of Lee's admirable surrender, and then he did shed a tear at the brutal assassination of Lincoln. He had another drink, and they all toasted the coming of peace and the end of slavery. And he prayed for the healing of the Union.

Word came that the Comstock Lode still churned out enormous wealth: over one hundred million in gold and silver had been dredged from the depths during the past seven years, and there was no end in sight. How Benjamin must love it, Joshua thought, but then smiled, thinking of Quitch's inability to see it firsthand.

Another trader mentioned a new invention that vastly aided the mining process: a man named Albert Nobel had created a safer, more effective explosive, something called dynamite.

The world turned, and in the course of an evening Joshua felt swept up again in amazing events and sweeping changes. He looked across the table to see Xien and Mirna grinning as they toasted something or other, and ate some kind of delicacy. He felt the twisting of fate and the diverging of paths, and he raised his glass to them both.

In the morning, at the gangplank of the Frieda, Joshua followed through on the decision he had made the night before. He presented Xien first with a heavy bag containing his share and more of all they had panned and mined in the past three years. Nearly thirty pounds worth. Ten thousand dollars—enough to let him live out his life in luxury, and to provide for an extended family back home.

Xien accepted this graciously.

Then Joshua held out the second box, and Xien backed away, hobbling up the mist-shrouded plank. "No, Joshua. Do not..."

"They are gifts to you," he said in a shaking voice. His hands trembled as he held the box, and he noticed Mirna staring in confusion.

"Joshua, they are bound to you. Caught up in your soul, I have seen it. I cannot take those guns. What you do is too noble."

Joshua closed his eyes and shook his head, feeling the cool breeze blowing a calm through his soul. A tender voice seemed to call from the winds of the past, and he echoed Caroline's words from a lifetime ago: "Every gift of noble origin is breathed upon by Hope's perpetual breath. They are pieces of my soul, friend. And that is why you must protect them, as you have guarded my soul many times before."

Xien's hands came out and settled under the box, and for a minute both men held it together. Joshua's hands stopped shaking, and he slid them away. "Take good care of them."

Xien bowed deeply. When he rose, his eyes were full of tears. "I will save them for you, for I feel their part in your story is not quite done."

Joshua smiled. "I would like to believe that, my friend, but Fate would have to work strangely indeed to bring about their return."

"Then think on that, and take those dreams of a reunion with you on your many future quests. But for now..." Xien glanced at Mirna where she waited, wind blowing her hair sideways across her eyes.

"For now, my friend—make up for lost time and elusive dreams. Step out of the past. Walk down this plank and go to your future and the life you deserve."

Joshua backed away, gave a bow in return and watched as the mist circled over Xien, swallowing his body first, leaving only the wooden box held out for a moment, before that too retreated into the shapeless clouds.

Joshua turned, bowed his head, and walked back through the town, realizing only after long minutes of silence that someone held his hand and quietly accompanied him into their future.

Chapter 7: Alaska - June 30, 1868

BIRTH OF A LEGEND

Several leagues upriver from Forty Mile, just north of Beaver Creek, they sat at a perfect site down the hill from their cabin. Bright sunshine danced off Mirna's golden hair, pulled back in long braids—

—and matching the soft, downy hair on the head of their newborn son. The baby giggled on its back on the grass, kicking at the air and swatting at dandelion blossoms. Just beyond their blanket, the great Teslin River churned, continuing its westward bend through the flats, lingering gently in wide inlets before gearing up to charge three hundred miles to the Bering Strait.

Joshua stroked the fine hair on the boy's head, then let the tiny hand clasp his finger. Mirna smiled and leaned in to place a warm, soft kiss on Joshua's lips. Last August, they had been married by a passing Orthodox missionary in a quiet celebration at the Long House. Keeping with the customs of their people, Mirna and Joshua entered the wilderness for their first year together, alone. Mikhail stayed behind, to be cared for by his grandmother. Joshua built a cabin, and they prospected for a time until the bitter snow and ice made it impossible—then they spent the winter indoors, and Joshua had never been happier. By the time the snow thawed, they had read and memorized entire sections of Herodotus, and had acted out every comedy of Shakespeare's. They raised two litters of malamute and husky puppies and taught them to be fierce racing competitors, hardy sled dogs and loving pets.

And by the spring, Mirna was seven months pregnant, and

glowing with happiness. When the time came, a nearby band of Aleuts lent a midwife for the delivery, which was quick and relatively painless, despite Joshua's apprehensions of the great size of the child in her belly.

But the boy emerged, kicking and screaming in his eagerness to join the world. And surely there was some significance to his birthday being the first anniversary of the Alaska purchase.

Both mother and child were healthy and strong. Now, all that remained was to pick a name. All morning, Mirna had been juggling possibilities as she held up the child and posed him in different positions, as if his appearance in varying light would hint at a suitable designation. "I wish I had not already used Mikhail," she said, "but there are other equally strong Christian names. Luke, for instance."

Joshua shook his head, his eyes glazing over as he stared past her. The grip on his finger tightened, and the baby giggled louder as a flock of geese flew overhead.

"Joshua junior?" she suggested.

He said nothing, squinting instead as the kaleidoscopic rays bounced off the river and dazzled his eyes. Fireflies seemed to dance in his vision, and distorted shapes took form.

"Mark? Joseph?"

He closed his eyes. Afterimages like sunspots dazzled behind his lids and the sound of the rushing water overwhelmed his senses. Churning, bubbling, trickling—he picked up every nuance of watery motion, every slap against the rocky shore.

"Simon?"

Again he shook his head. An image formed out of the spots in his vision. And as the mighty Teslin River—the Delin Chu, as the natives called it—coursed through his senses, flooding over his memories with a frothy, thousand-ton mass of water, Joshua opened his eyes.

He gently squeezed the child's fragile hand, and looked into his squinting eyes, then he met Mirna's gaze.

There were tears in his eyes as he told her, and when he did, her smile was wider than he had ever seen. And they looked north together, holding up the child, and they said his name in one voice.

It was, after all, the only name that fit.

CHAPTER 8: CHRISTMAS EVE - 1880

...THE NIGHT BEFORE CHRISTMAS

THE VILLAGE SQUARE BRISTLED WITH activity. A bonfire cackled between the main totem poles, and everywhere elaborately dressed Tlingit men and women danced in the snow while children played with sticks and rope and the elders sang songs to a trio of flutes.

It was mid-afternoon on Christmas Eve, but already near-dark. The bright stars shimmering overhead, flanked by the proudly undulating aurora. Torches burned high atop stakes leading back to the main gate from outside—along the end point of the dogsled course. Mirna and Joshua huddled close together, looks of concern on their faces as they eyed the open gate, awaiting the return of the racers.

"They'll be fine," Joshua assured his wife as she clung to his arm with increasing strength. "Both your boys know what they're doing."

Mirna pressed her face against his cheek, then planted a soft kiss on his lips. "Yes, but they are fiercely competitive. One of them might do something rash to win."

Joshua shrugged and his eyes misted. "Rivals often do."

Mirna looked up at him. "You know he worships you."

"Nonsense," Joshua said, blushing. "He's just growing up fast, and he's voracious to learn everything of the world."

"Takes after his papa." Mirna sighed and held him close, relishing in his warmth, then perked up suddenly at the sound of yelping dogs. Ahead, the flickering torchlight seemed to wave on the racers. The music stopped, and now a low cheering began. The barking grew louder, and suddenly they appeared—a half dozen dogs careening around the bend, kicking up snow and ice and straining against their ropes.

"Who...?"

"Mikhail," Joshua answered, standing on his toes to see over the heads. His heart dipped a little, but recovered when he saw the next sled whip around the bend. There was his little boy pulling on the handles, leaning into the turn as he was taught.

"So close," said Mirna, a little wistfully, but clapping nonetheless as Mikhail's dogs made a right turn and the sled skidded to a stop, spraying snow onto the first row of onlookers. Delin's team roared in from the other side and performed a similar maneuver, but with barely any disturbance in the snow. Joshua frowned and led Mirna closer. One of the dogs was off its harness and sharing the sled with Delin.

As soon as the sled had stopped, their son quickly knelt beside the animal and stroked its head while holding its paw. Delin looked up, tears in his eyes. "We slid on some ice back in the first mile, and Adonis snapped his leg."

On the other side, a crowd of young boys and girls cheered Mikhail's victory and hoisted the boy on their shoulders. Mikhail grinned, raising his hands in triumph.

Delin, however, was focused on the dog. "Got him out of the harness and brought him up here with me. Tried to bind his leg, but then thought we should just get back here fast as possible."

Joshua knelt beside Delin, patting the dog's head. "And you still almost won?"

Delin shrugged, indifferent to the race's outcome. "Can Kreaga heal him?"

Mirna bent down to help Joshua lift the dog. "Sure he can," she promised. "And you did a good thing—that is why the rest of your team ran extra hard for you."

Delin beamed. "Maybe we can race again...?"

"Give it a couple days," Joshua said.

As they walked, Mirna whispered in Delin's ear, "You have won where it counts most." She gave him a tight hug and then playfully yanked his large wool hat over his eyes, then ran to the square. Once he could see again, he took off after her, balling up snow in his mittens as he ran. By the time he reached the square, a full-fledged snowball war had commenced, with projectiles soaring back and forth, everyone choosing a side and taking aim.

Delin sidestepped through the crowd until he bumped up against Mikhail, who suddenly turned and bumped him back so roughly he fell on his side.

"Sorry," Mikhail grunted. "Didn't see you down there—just like I didn't see you anywhere behind me during the race!"

Delin lay there, dusting off his coat, oblivious to the hail of snowy missiles raining down all around him. "Mama told me I did the right thing, helping Adonis with his leg."

Mikhail tossed a snowball at Delin's face—but had it batted away with an angry swipe. He glared down at Delin. "She would say that—your father has turned her into a weakling. She would have been much different if he hadn't come along..."

—and killed my father, Delin expected him to say. But Mikhail got his point across, openly sharing his resentment. He was growing older, starting to partake in the rituals of manhood—and painfully absent at those ceremonies was his father.

Delin got to his knees, muttering under his breath, "Sesquat killed your papa."

Mikhail bent over and gripped Delin by the collar. "You think your precious father is too godly to kill another man? Ask him, then—have him tell you of the wars he's fought. The men he's slaughtered. Then tell me how great he is!"

Delin balled his fists, tensed and started to throw himself into a punch—when a cloud of soft snow blasted into Mikhail's face. A crowd of youngsters cheered from across the square, pointing and laughing.

Mikhail cursed and ran at them, Delin completely forgotten. The music started up again, and Delin stood there alone with his fist raised. Self-conscious and embarrassed suddenly, he lowered his arms, but not before he caught the look from his parents, standing beside the Raven totem.

He stared down at his feet, then turned and trudged back to the Long House. He was tired from the race, and angry at Mikhail's taunts. Sure, he knew Papa did some bad things, but many good ones as well—and at least he had always tried to make the right choices.

Delin stewed as he walked back inside, getting angrier with each step. How dare Mikhail taunt him like that? After everything he and Papa did for this village—so the people could live well and not be hungry like so many other natives he had seen in the wilderness.

He stomped up the roughly-shaped stairs to the third floor where he shared a great room with twelve other boys. He found his cot in the dark, struck a light and ignited a slush lamp. He started to remove his winter clothes when he noticed the three small boxes lying on his blanket.

He heard creaking footsteps behind him and spun around—ready for Mikhail and his friends to ambush him as a joke.

"It's Christmas Eve," said Mirna, reaching the top stair with Joshua. "And I think someone's gifts came a little early."

Delin excitedly tore off his coat, mittens and hat and flung them against a wall while he bent down to open the boxes. He loved this new tradition they shared with him—and maybe because it hadn't caught on among the others, he felt it was their special event. Five years ago he got that pickax, this time...

He flipped off the lid on the first box and stared in confusion at the piece of paper encased in a maplewood frame. It was a sixty-line poem entitled "A Visit From St. Nicholas."

"I thought it fitting," Mirna said. "I wrote it all from memory—my father had made a copy from a magazine some American traders had shown him many years ago. I thought that maybe later we could see if there's some truth to that story—and go out looking for this jolly man and his reindeer."

Delin frowned. "I didn't think there were any reindeer in Alaska."

"There aren't," Joshua admitted. "Except for those on St. Nick's team. And we're lucky there: since we're not too far from the North Pole, we're bound to see him flying overhead."

Delin grinned, reading the words quickly, thrilling to the notion of a sleigh towed by reindeer soaring across the heavens, delivering presents to kids everywhere. His mouth hung open, and his legs felt weak. He looked up after he finished reading, and grinned sheepishly at his parents. "Thank you! And I want to see him! Will the other children get toys, do you think?"

Joshua shrugged. "Maybe... but Saint Nicholas is quite busy helping more desperate children. He may feel these ones have what they need for now."

Delin nodded as if that made perfect sense. Still smiling and holding the framed poem lovingly to his heart, his head snapped around and he looked at the second box, wondering what it could hold.

"That," Joshua said as Delin picked it up, "is something you're old enough to have now. Many times it's given me strength and kept me from falling to evil ways."

Inside the box, something glittered. Delin reached in and clasped his fingers around a thin chain. When he raised it up to the flickering red light, he couldn't believe what he saw.

"Besides," Joshua whispered, kneeling beside him. "Your mother has always been a little jealous of me wearing that."

"I have not," came the reply from the shadows.

"Don't believe her." Joshua took the chain, opened the clasp and secured it around Delin's neck. The cross hung low, almost down to the middle of his chest, but he would grow into it perfectly. "When it was given to me, I was told the same words I'll tell you now: *Every gift of noble origin is breathed upon by Hope's perpetual breath.* Keep it close, and remember your prayers whenever you feel scared."

Delin smiled until his face hurt, still staring down at what, in his mind, was like some powerful magic charm in an old fairy tale; it had seen amazing events and had even played a part in his own destiny. He opened the last box—and found inside six sticks of licorice, each wrapped with a red ribbon. "Yes!" he shouted, immediately breaking one in half and tossing it into his mouth.

"For your sweet tooth," Mirna said.

"I think," Joshua said, "every tooth of his is sweet!"

Delin crunched and grinned happily. Suddenly he felt guilty—receiving all these presents, and he hadn't been prepared to give anything in return. He looked around, as if hoping he may have overlooked something suitable. Oh well, he could make up for it in the future. They were going to have many great Christmases together, and he vowed that next year he would get them something amazing to show how much he loved them.

Later that night, after the younger children were asleep, Delin,

Joshua and Mirna slipped outside. They walked a short distance through the gate, and at a clearing beside the near-frozen lake they gazed up at the sublimely phosphoric aurora and the host of bright stars in the moon-free sky.

They stood, holding hands, with Delin in the middle, watching in wonder. Joshua occasionally named off the constellations to answer Delin's curiosity, blending in their Greek legends and speaking of huge battles and epic love stories—all immortalized in the heavens.

Lost in the vivid tales, Delin only barely recalled why they had come out here in the first place. And as his eyes struggled to stay open, and his yawns grew impossibly strong, he noticed a quiet ringing—as if a bell jingled many miles away, and the sound carried on the winds. It was only later, after groggily climbing onto his papa's back for the return walk to the village, that he wondered if a reindeer-led sleigh flew somewhere out there in the cold, dreaming night.

In the morning, after a huge feast and as more games and races were set to begin, a team of American explorers appeared at the gate. Delin watched from a distance while his father spoke to the men; they shared some food and warm drinks, and then departed. When Joshua returned his expression was unreadable. He met Mirna's questioning look. "They're part of the United States Geological Survey, from something called the Smithsonian Institution. Asking questions about the land and the natural resources."

"Are they looking for gold?" Delin asked, in a voice just above a whisper.

Joshua shrugged. "Looking for many things, mapping out this new American territory. Mostly, though, they want help: guides to take them along the waterways."

Mirna frowned, and looked away. "You aren't going with them, are you?"

"I was thinking about helping them in the spring, since we need to go out anyway for supplies. I told them I would guide them up the Yukon and into the Tanana region where their maps pick up again. Then I might travel back down the Inside Passage. They brought word of a new gold strike there, not far from Sitka."

Delin's eyes lit up. "A gold strike?"

"A man named Henry Juneau and his partners—along with a team of Auk Tlingits—stumbled across something in a gulch there. I hear he's a drunk and a fool, but he got lucky, and now a stampede is on."

"And you want to go there?" Mirna asked sourly.

"We don't need to," Delin said. "I know where there's tons of gold, and..."

"Son! What did I tell you?"

Delin looked away. "I know, but why go looking for more and have to share with all those people when...?"

"It's not just the gold." Joshua sighed. "We'll need supplies, as I said. Also—" He took a deep breath and seemed to be weighing his next words. "—I would like to see if the world has changed any since I've been out here."

"Why do you think people have changed?" Mirna asked. "Or do you just delude yourself because now you are happy?"

"Yes, I'm happy, and yes, I suppose I'm only being optimistic." Joshua looked into Mirna's eyes. "In any case, I want to see how those greenbacks down there are faring."

Mirna shook her head. "Well, if you go, you had better be quick about returning. Delin will miss you."

"What about you?"

"You do not have to ask." Mirna stood up and began pacing.

Delin smiled. He loved when Mama tried to act angry, and he knew Papa adored her for it. "Wait!" He had a sudden idea. "Can I go?"

"Of course not," Mirna snapped.

"Yes," said Joshua.

Delin looked at one then the other.

"I'd like him to come along," Joshua said in a low voice. "It will be a perfect way to continue his studies. He's so far ahead of the other children, and he can learn firsthand from educated men."

Mirna opened her mouth, thinking of an argument, but couldn't find the words. She sat down beside Delin, gave him a deep hug and kissed his forehead. She glared up at Joshua. "In the spring, then. But until you leave, my son and I will be spending a lot of time together to make up for when he's gone."

Joshua agreed. "And do I get the same treatment?"

Mirna smirked and walked off, muttering, "We'll see."

CHAPTER 9: YUKON RIVER - JUNE, 1881

THE GREAT DEBATE

WHEN DELIN WOKE, SQUINTING AT the morning's bright blue sky, he saw that the boat sailed calmly down the immense river. A large sail buckled in the gentle wind and masked the sounds of an argument from the back of the boat.

He stood and stretched, and his long shadow arched over the prow and skittered across the river's blazing surface. A few lazy clouds hung over the distant peaks to the south, but what caught Delin's attention were the great cliffs to the north.

He stumbled to the deck and gripped the rail, staring with his mouth open at the hundred-foot cliffs, and the mud—flowing mud—cascading into the river as the snow melted and ran downhill, tearing away entire chunks from the land.

Delin couldn't believe what he saw—what emerged from the collapsing mudbanks as if disrobing in some morbidly grotesque carnival show. Jutting bones, skulls, heaps of monstrous skeletons, enormous tusks and vertebrate larger than the boat tumbled from their crypts and dove into the churning river.

Motion to his right caught his eye, and he saw his papa there with the man named William Healy Hall. They were gesturing at the cliffs while the other scientist, the man named Garfield, sat and calmly worked at his sketchpad.

Delin walked closer, first ducking under the sail. The voices now took form. His papa's voice, clearly upset: "Nonsense, I tell you, and I insist you recheck your facts!"

Hall pointed to the cliffs. "You are seeing it with your own eyes, sir! There can be no better illustration of the great epochs of history. Huge beasts long since extinct, their remains trapped in successive layers of buildup!"

"Impossible," Joshua shouted. "Maybe they perished in Noah's flood, but to say these... things were roaming the Earth thousands—millions of years before men is blasphemy!"

"Ah, so there it is." Hall threw his arms up in mock disgust. "Your Bible. The word of old scribes trying to pen the unknown and thinking in their own limited terms..."

"Now the Bible is a lie?" Joshua backed up. He swatted at a bug on his neck, then turned to glare at Garfield, who calmly continued to sketch. On the floor beside him were a dozen small wooden cages holding botanical specimens, reptiles and birds.

Delin had taken an active role in helping find such specimens, delighting in the responsibility when they went ashore. They had all interacted quite well until now. Joshua even remarked just last week that he wouldn't be surprised if Delin, with this incredible schooling, became a scientist himself someday. More likely an explorer-scientist, as those were in great demand, Hall said. Especially up in this part of the world—where they had just scratched the surface, mapping but one-fifth of the terrain in a dozen years.

Delin tiptoed closer, eyeing the skeletal debris with a wary eye as he approached the men. His father pointed at Hall, and appeared about to release a vehement tirade, when he noticed Delin standing there, and all his strength seemed to flee at once. "Son—how long have you been awake?"

Delin swallowed hard, and glanced at the faces of each of the men. He shrugged. "Just a few minutes."

Hall straightened his jacket, rolled down his sleeves and fixed his hair under a wide cloth hat. "Sorry to rouse you so early. We were just having a little argument about the age of our planet."

Joshua glared at him. "There is no argument. Turns out science doesn't know everything."

Delin looked at the draining cliffs again. "But... those bones. How did they get there?"

"The Flood drowned those creatures and buried them," Joshua said before Hall could speak, and gave him a warning look.

But Hall turned toward the cliffs. "Yes, of course that's true," he said with a sarcastic tone. "Except, those bones are from creatures that clearly lived in much different times from each other. We have evidence of the Mastodon appearing only in the last fifteen thousand years, while those others were found in geological strata much more ancient."

Delin sucked in his breath, gazing at one particular skull appearing through the drainage—a long-snouted carapace filled with enormous, jagged teeth. "How old is that thing?"

Hall smiled at the boy. "Several million years, I would think. We have paleontologists back at the Smithsonian who are experts in such things, and I can only guess."

"Then," suggested Joshua, "keep your guesses to yourself. Delin, do not listen to this. These men would deny God's role in the past—and probably the present as well."

"Now, sir!"

"Shut it," Joshua hissed, taking Delin by the shoulder. "We are going up front. I suggest you take your drawings and make your notes, but speak to us no more on your theories."

Delin pulled back. "But Papa, what about the Sesquat? Maybe it's one of these older monsters, from before..."

"Sesquat? What's that?" Hall turned around, scratching at his chin where a new mosquito welt had formed.

Delin's eyes lit up. "A huge monster—like a bear, but five times as large. And all white fur, and huge teeth and fast, real fast. They only come out in the snow, and they smell real bad, and..."

"Sounds like a legend we heard," said Garfield, looking up from his sketchpad. "Natives south of Vancouver told us of something they call an Arulataq that matched that description."

"We assumed," said Hall, "they were just speaking mythologically, referencing an ancient snow deity or something."

"Sesquat means 'snow demon'," Delin offered. "And my papa killed one once!"

Hall and Garfield both perked up. "Truly?" Hall asked. "Where was this, and might the remains still be there?"

Joshua sighed and turned his back on them. "Lake Bennett. Good luck dredging the bottom. Now, if you don't mind, we are going up front for our morning meal. And I think—yes, I think our journey together is almost at an end."

"What?" Hall stepped around a chirping bird in the first cage, and tried to follow them—but stopped at Joshua's outstretched hand.

His curls of red hair billowed like the sail at his back. "I have made a mistake, I think, coming with you men, and bringing my son along. Delin and I have a journey to finish and supplies to obtain; and then we must return to our village before winter—which comes early here if you hadn't noticed."

Hall shook his head. "If you leave us now—we cannot pay you the full amount we negotiated. That was for another three weeks, and considerably more navigation."

Joshua patted one of several pouches on his belt. "We don't need your money. In fact," he peered ahead at a rocky ledge. "We will be disembarking there. Delin, ready our supplies."

Delin hung his head, but obeyed. He glanced back at the two scientists, their silhouettes dark against the blue sky. They seemed to be larger than life, and like the indistinct mountains behind them, they appeared infinite and powerful...

And patient.

Chapter 10: Rockwell - October, 1881

RACING WITH THE MOON

THEY ARRIVED LATER THAN PLANNED. It was the first week in October, and the snow had already begun to fall, with several inches frosting their hats by the time they made their way into Silver Bow Basin. Flanked by the coastal mountains on the interior and the Muir glacier to the north, this location was perfect for a gold rush. The new town was currently called Rockwell, after the commander of the Navy steamer in the Gastineau Channel, but there was talk that if Henry Juneau continued complaining, the miners were going to give in and name the town after him.

The Navy had come with the first prospectors to provide some basic law and order, but like most boomtowns, excesses and vices were unavoidable. Already saloons dotted the valley, their rickety structures looking more inviting than the host of miners' shacks thrown up haphazardly beside the streams. Red lamps hung outside homes upon a hill, and seeing them, Joshua muttered as they dragged their supplies across a makeshift wooden bridge.

"Don't make eye contact with anyone," Joshua instructed as they approached the start of the camp. Men busily cleaned their diggings and started fires for their evening meals. "Just follow me. We'll eat, and then get our supplies."

"And buy some dogs and a sled!" Delin said, wearily but with an edge of enthusiasm. It had been a long and stressful three-month hike across difficult terrain. After they had left the scientists, Delin picked his words carefully, seeing that his papa was unusually frustrated and quick to anger. The bedtime stories were no more;

Papa silently turned in under their tent, with his back to Delin. They woke before first light, wordlessly packed up and moved out.

They traveled in that fashion for the last month, his father only speaking kindly to him once when he was violently ill for several days. After weeks had passed, Delin actually hoped to get sick again, so that maybe Papa's heart would soften once more. But instead, the silence grew, and the days progressed in unendurable gloom. Papa's attention seemed to be in another world altogether. They trudged ahead through days of unending rain, mud and freezing slush, which had blessedly turned to snow just days earlier.

Now, Delin set foot in town with the slim hope that the presence of other prospectors would lift his papa's spirits. Delin did his best to keep up, as Papa wove a trail around discarded cradles, shovels and picks. Some men ate sitting around a campfire, the fish sizzling in pans, while others spooned a clam-stew into their mouths.

With Delin in tow, Joshua led the way past the diggers' encampments into what seemed to be a main square: a dozen hastily-constructed storefronts, a supply office, an assayer, and—set back a ways, in the darker shadows behind a laundry hut—a larger structure made of loose-fitting boards. Men were lining up to enter this place, jostling to get inside.

Delin noticed his father staring in that direction and was about to ask what was in there, when Joshua reached back and pulled him in the opposite direction. They entered a cabin that turned out to be larger inside than Delin expected. Joshua made a path through the standing crowd and arrived at a bar where he ordered two bowls of clam stew and a chunk of bread.

He paid with a small pinch of gold dust, and Delin couldn't believe that their meal just cost an ounce of gold. Joshua watched the room as he ate, and as the brown stew clung to his beard, his eyes darted back and forth. As soon as he finished, and before Delin could even take his third spoonful, he stood up and muscled back to the bar.

He returned in less than a minute with a full bottle clasped in his hand. He dragged a chair with him, taken from another miner who had just finished. He set the bottle down on an overturned barrel, staring at it like he was preparing to duel an old adversary. Delin set his dish down, cold and unfinished. He scratched his neck and was about to say something; to finally break the silence and ask if he had done something horribly wrong.

But Joshua reached inside his coat, under his shirt's collar—and it took Delin too long to realize what his father sought. The chain—the cross! "Papa," he said, his voice barely audible in the din of the crowd. Delin fumbled under his shirt and started to pull out the cross, the gift from his father last Christmas.

But Joshua was already leaning forward; he gripped the bottle like a sword-hilt, and in one swift motion, turned it upside down and let it pour into his mouth. Delin took a step back, bumping into someone who cursed and pushed him back. He stumbled and jarred his knee against the barrel, and the bottle slammed back down on it, just in front of Delin's face. He saw with alarm that it was half-empty. The ripe stink of heavy whiskey wafted from above, and his father stood up sharply.

He looked down, as if noticing Delin for the first time. Some mixture of recognition and guilt flashed in his eyes, but clouded over quickly. He set a small pouch onto the barrel, after weighing it in his palm. "Should be enough there. Buy us food and supplies for the trip back. And buy some dogs too."

"Wh—where will I find dogs?" Delin managed to ask, standing up straight. He had the sudden idea that if he acted responsibly now, maybe Papa would be okay.

Joshua waved over his shoulder in a broad gesture. "Proprietor told me they have several dozen in a clearing at the gulch. Use 'em for racing and fighting."

Delin frowned. "Fighting?"

"Never mind that. Just buy us a team and train them if they need it. And then, keep out of trouble."

"Yes, Papa," Delin said, but he was suddenly concerned. This would all take time, and just how long was he going to be on his own? "But where...?"

"I'll find you when I'm ready."

Delin saw an immense sadness in Papa's eyes, and it looked like he was about to say something—to apologize maybe—but then his jaw tightened, his lips curled back, and his fists clenched. He patted the four other sacks of gold dust secured to his belt, then he strode through the crowd, pushing people out of his way.

Delin grabbed the pouch, stuffed it deep in his front pocket, and ran after his father. He darted around barrels, sidestepped muddy boots and lunged through the door just before it closed. Out in the square, snowflakes whipped in an angry wind as men rushed about, holding their hats.

Looking in both directions, scanning the heads of everyone nearby, he failed to see the telltale red hair. He started walking, and was jostled along in the general direction of the crowd—toward that singular structure in the darker section. The one with the ramshackle boards and the slanted roof.

He heard his papa's voice ahead in the crowd. Arguing, and insistent. Something about "having the gold to play," and that someone "better let me in."

Delin pushed past a foul-smelling miner and saw a man in an enormous coat holding a rifle and guarding the main door. Stacks of weapons were heaped by his feet. Two more men he let by only after they opened their coats to his inspection.

Heart pounding, Delin slipped around the side, keeping out of sight of the man at the door. He crept close to the boarded wall and positioned himself so he could peek through a vertical gap in the poorly-positioned boards. He tried different angles, and from what he could see it was a crowded room, where smoke drifted heavily and red lamps cast faces in devilish hues. Men played at cards and dice, and Delin noticed a strange wheel in the far corner.

A few women milled about in exotic tight dresses and curled-up hair, with their faces painted and lips bright. They refilled the cups of thirsty gamblers who took every chance they could to grope the girls. There: in the center of the floor, his father pushed his way toward a table where six men sat playing a card game. For one shining moment Delin actually expected his father to flip over the table, grab some of the men by their collars and send them on their way; but instead, he pulled over a free chair and slid into a narrow space between two men who eyed him warily.

—until he pulled out one pouch of gold, opened it and allowed everyone to peek inside. He set this down, along with his nearly empty bottle, rolled up his sleeves and pointed at the space in front of him.

Somebody walked into Delin's sightline, and he backed away,

looking for another gap. He had to see—and despite Papa's instructions, he knew he needed to stay. Part of him hoped he could witness another epic card game like the one with Colt long ago, but somehow he knew this was different.

It was just as Papa had warned him so many times: evil and greed. Both were strong in this place, and now Papa had fallen into their clutches. Delin could smell it everywhere, and he knew that this town would destroy them if they stayed.

His mind made up, feeling a surge of strength, he ran around the corner and confidently approached the man at the door. The last man in line had entered, and now the entrance was dark, just the tip of the guard's pipe flickering red.

"You lost, kid?"

Delin squared his shoulders and lifted his head. He knew he just had to get by this man and he'd be able to say the right words to Papa. He would tell him to remember those lessons—to recall the words of his friend Matsei Xien, and to remember Mama's love waiting back home.

And yes, to remember God. Delin wasn't sure why Papa let those scientists crush his faith; he didn't see what was so devastating about their theories. Surely, in all his years prospecting, Papa must have realized that gold's very existence in such predictable locations proved the great age of the earth.

That didn't bother Delin. It was clear that God's hand was at work in all of that. It was obvious that the Creator, with infinite patience, set all this in motion so that, eons later, men could be drawn here. To explore, to search, and yes—Delin saw it clearly now—to come face to face with their own devils.

It was all a big snare—one that could be avoided, if men had the skill to take only enough not to spring that trap.

Excited that he was going to save his papa, Delin lifted his pouch of gold. "I'm going in," he said sternly.

The man tipped his hat back and removed his pipe. He gave Delin a look of amused curiosity. "Whatcha got there?"

Delin opened the pouch slightly and tilted it forward. "Gold dust," he said. "You're gonna let me in, and..."

"And someone'll just take it from you." The man shook his head, eyed the pouch for a second, then took a puff on his pipe.

"Get outta here, kid. And hide that pouch. Yer lucky I'm the one to see it. Most others would kick you down and run off with it, seein' as you probably stole it in the first place."

"Did not!" Delin fumed. "Panned this myself!" And lots more, he wanted to shout, but Papa's warnings still rung in his ears.

"Ya don't say?" The man sighed. "Listen, there's still some laws around here, and yer too young, so beat it."

"But, I have to..."

"And stay away from Velma's Ridge too—not that you'd know what to do with the ladies up there, but they'd just as soon take all your gold and show you some tricks for when yer older."

"But, my father's in there!" Delin blurted out at last.

The man raised his hat and narrowed his eyes. "Ah, so that's it! Well, in that case, yer definitely not getting' in."

"But..."

"Man goes in here, it's for a reason. And he'll come out when he's done—or when he's lost everything."

Delin's shoulders sagged and he looked down at his muddy boots as snowflakes stung at back of his neck like angry flies. "That's what I'm afraid of."

"Go, kid. He'll find you when he's ready."

Delin nodded. "Any chance you can give a message to him?"

He shook his head. "I don't run errands for kids, and don't even think of payin' me. I'm tellin' you for the last time—hide that pouch and get on about your business."

Delin turned to go. "Wait," he called back. "I'm supposed to buy some dogs for our trip home. Where are they?"

The man motioned to his left, down the hill from the red-light area Delin had been warned about. "Down in the clearing there. There's a race set for ten tonight, so after that, I'm guessin' you'd be able to buy some—the losers at any rate."

"What's this race?"

"Don't worry about it. Just go. Yer gettin' on my nerves."

With a heavy sigh, Delin trudged away. He shuffled down the rough path to the clearing. Halfway there, he stopped to put on his mittens and hat, and as he set off again he hugged his shoulders and looked up. The snow whipped down from the black void and danced across his vision. He closed his eyes and imagined a far-off sled towed by reindeer, racing through the skies at the jolly commands of its rider.

Even that thought failed to bring a smile on this darkest of nights. Last Christmas seemed so long ago it must have happened to another child, in another age.

When he arrived at the base of the hill, he saw a row of large tents, and heard whining and barking from within. At tables set up all around, it looked like men were arguing as they drank from flasks and had their meals.

Delin walked through the flattened snow and made his way to the largest tent. Everyone seemed to ignore him, although at one table an older teenager gorged himself on what looked like a roasted rabbit and watched Delin pass. The boy wore a heavy black coat with thick yellowish fur for a collar, and a necklace of seal tusks circled his throat, giving the appearance of a set of growling teeth.

Turning away from the strangely-dressed boy, Delin entered through a flap in the tent. The barking stopped all at once, as several dozen dogs looked his way. They were all sizes, although most were full-grown malamutes or huskies, with thick yellow-gray hair, long snouts and bushy tails. The tent held three partitions, each section separated by a row of crates, confining a team of dogs within.

Delin had walked in on the first team, all huddled together; they had been growling and nipping at each other, but now padded over to him and sniffed at his feet and hands.

Delin smiled; he knelt down and whispered Innuit greetings in their ears. Several of them whined and crouched in a playful stance, prepared for a tussle.

"Hey!" a voice shouted, and for the first time Delin noticed that someone sat on a stool in the corner. "Leave 'em alone! Stop tormenting the poor things."

An old, thin man in a long coat struggled to rise, then sat back down with a wheezing sound. When Delin stepped around the dogs and came closer, he realized the man wasn't really that old—perhaps his papa's age—but extremely pale and haggard. He stunk of that whiskey smell, and Delin noticed the two empty bottles at his feet. "Sir?"

"Yeah, whaddya want? Why you here?"

Delin pat one of the huskies behind the ears as it jumped on him and pawed at his chest. "I need to buy some dogs."

The man squinted and shook a finger at him. "These ain't fightin' dogs, so tell that fool Branling to get his own!"

"Don't need them to fight, sir. Need a team to take me and my papa back to the interior."

The man perked up. "Your pa's got money?"

Delin reached into his pocket—then left his hand there. "Yes," he said. "He does. My name's Delin Wetherwax, and my papa's Joshua. He's up... playing games now, but he sent me down to check on some dogs."

"Delin, eh? That's an appropriate name. Well, I got the dogs, and I'm looking to sell." He noticed Delin's wandering eye. "No, don't go looking at them other teams. First off, the ones right next door here aren't racers. They're the ones bred for fightin'."

Delin scratched his head as he shook his leg free of one of the dogs that had taken an unconventional interest. "What do they fight?" he asked, envisioning vicious guardian dogs, attacking dangerous Indians or violent grizzlies.

"Each other, of course," said the man with a laugh. "Big money in it, too. Men around here so starved for action, they bet on anything."

Delin looked over at the ten dogs at the other side of the crates, and saw that indeed, some of them had nasty red smears on their coats. One's ears were chewed through and another limped on a clearly broken leg.

He thought back to last Christmas, and his father's words came back to him: *I want to see if the world has changed any*. If this was a change, Delin thought, then he didn't want to imagine how vile it had been in Papa's day.

"Now," said the man, staggering to his feet. "My name's Elrod Jarsey, and I'll sell you my dogs—for the right price."

Delin nodded. He would pay anything just to get these dogs out of this awful town. He only wished he could take them all.

"But," Elrod said, "they got one more race to run. Against them dogs in the last section there."

"What race?" Delin asked, then began to understand; if the miners were so desperate enough to bet on dog fights, then surely they were eager to stage even grander events.

"We've had five dogsled races since first snowfall. And that damn half-breed's won 'em all. That's why I'm gettin' drunk." He leaned in close, glanced around and whispered. "Planning to put my last five ounces on that kid, then I'll throw this race and at least make enough to get outta here."

Delin's attention stayed back on the part about a dogsled race. A thought occurred to him, but he shook it away as quick as it came, focusing on fulfilling his instructions. "So how much do you want for them?"

Elrod scratched his chin. "'Bout three pounds should do it. Got that kind of dust?"

Delin pulled out the leather pouch and hefted it in his hands. "Feels like only two."

"Hmm. How 'bout your old man? He got more?"

"Maybe—I hope." Delin turned, hanging his head. "I guess I can come back when I find him."

"Yeah, I guess so." Elrod sat down again and lifted one of the empty bottles.

Delin stared at him, thinking. Finally, he said, "You gonna race drunk?"

Elrod shrugged. "Like I said, I'm plannin' to bet on the other kid. Don't matter what I do now—although the odds are pretty bad, and I ain't gonna make much money."

A plan was brimming in Delin's thoughts, and his pulse quickened. "What are the odds of your team winning?"

Elrod laughed. "Thirty to one. Some suckers will take it, though. Hell, them odds are better than finding gold out there anymore!"

Delin petted the dog that was licking his hand—the lead dog, Delin guessed, the friskiest and strongest. "Listen, mister. I got an idea: how about you bet on this team?"

"What, are you daft, kid? Didn't you hear—?"

"And I win it for you."

Elrod choked, continuing his laugh in a distorted sound. "'Scuse me? You?"

"Yes sir. I've been racing in my village for years, and I was trained by my papa, plus some Indian mushers, and..."

"Indians, eh?" Elrod leaned forward. "If that's true, maybe you do got a shot. Seems to work for that other kid."

"So let me do it!" Delin begged. "You can bet on me—your five ounces at thirty-to-one, that's... um, a hundred-fifty ounces for you if I win! And all I want are the dogs."

Elrod looked at him with his mouth open. "Damn, son, I don't know if you really got talent, or if you're just plain stupid, but..." He rubbed at his patchy skull and seemed lost in thought.

Delin folded his hands together, rubbing them to keep warm, even as the dogs continued to jump on him playfully.

"Hell, the dogs take to you more than me." He staggered to his feet. "A'right, let's go out and sign you up."

Delin clapped, and the dogs barked. Out into the cold, the young teen that had given Delin the glaring look before was now standing on a chair and shouting to a group of fans. His necklace of tusks clanked together as he spun around. He slid the furry hood over his head and he even let out a growl, to the delight of the drunken men, who rushed to place more bets.

"Who's he?" Delin asked.

"Not sure if it's his half-breed name or just something he picked for these events, but he calls himself Moon Chaser."

The team consisted of four Siberian Huskies, two Malamutes and the lead dog: a Canadian Eskimo husky, an extraordinary white and brown mix. Delin named this one Blitzen; he then proceeded on a sudden whim to name the rest after the other reindeer in that poem he loved so much.

He called out their names, kneeling in the snow and fixing their harnesses. After attaching the gangline firmly to the sled's handlebars, he went to work tearing small strips out of a canvas tarp he had acquired from Elrod's supplies. These he tied with a bit of twine around each dog's paws, starting from the back. Back at the Long House, to protect the dogs' feet, Delin and Mikhail used a set of specially made buckskin moccasins every time they raced.

Here, Delin had to make do. He was surprised to see Moon Chaser's team didn't wear any. His opponent paced up and down, yelling something at each dog. Then he bent down and pushed one, then the next, roughly taunting them until they snapped back.

Antagonizing them, Delin realized. Making them so angry that they'd tear out at the start and ride hard for the whole track. Delin tied the last coverings around Blitzen's hind feet, and then put his arms around the dog's neck. Its opaque blue eyes blinked at him, and its tongue lapped at his neck as he whispered in its ear. "We're going to win," he said, and reached over to stroke Dunder, a foot behind the lead.

They had been fed an hour ago, out of Elrod's last barrel of pork and rice mush. His final words to Delin had been to warn him of Moon Chaser's tactics on the course. "That son of a bitch will try to trip you up. Nudge you into a tree or down the hillside if he can."

Elrod was now up at the betting table, struggling against the crowd of fevered gamblers. A few who had already bet on Elrod demanded refunds once they learned of the change—to no avail—and the odds had climbed to 35-to-1.

Delin tried to focus only on his team, getting them used to his voice, looking each dog in the eyes. Finally, he made his way to the sled. The snow had stopped falling and the clouds were peeling away like a stage curtain, revealing the eager, starry-eyed spectators beyond.

A large bearded man yelled for them to come and take their starting positions; but first, Delin's opponent sauntered over. Blitzen and Comet snarled and snapped as Moon Chaser approached. His seal tusks clanked as he walked, and his bear-fur boots kicked up clouds of snow with each stomping tread. He was nearly a foot taller than Delin, and his face was ghoulishly taut, as if he'd starved himself for weeks.

"*Chung-ti—ala reg ley!*" he grunted, and spat directly on Delin's sled, just in front of the footboards. Delin looked up, disgusted, and the crescent moon glittered just over the boy's head, framing his imitation lion's mane like a halo.

Delin removed his right mitten, then struck his hand forward. "Good luck," he said, trying to smile.

"*Chung-ti—ala reg ley!*" Moon Chaser hissed again, louder, then raised his fingers to his teeth and made chomping sounds.

Delin lowered his hand. He knew enough Tlingit to understand what was said, even if this dialect was a little strange. Moon Chaser had just promised that after he won, his dogs would be turned loose on Delin to devour his flesh.

Delin looked down. "*Al, chan-ila Ugnari,*" he said, and then added the translation: "May you lose more gracefully than you boast."

Moon Chaser's eyes went wide—whether from the shock that Delin knew Tlingit or because of the words themselves, Delin wasn't sure, but he didn't stick around to find out. With a quick snap of the towline, he pursed his lips and made a kissing sound; Blitzen barked and strained and pulled forward, joined by the other six dogs aligned side by side in the standard tandem pattern.

Moments later, at the starting post, Moon Chaser's dogs appeared to the left, snarling and snapping at each other. Delin allowed himself one quick glance to the right to see hundreds of men huddled together in the field, standing beside well-positioned bonfires for warmth.

It must have dropped below negative ten degrees by now, but Delin barely noticed. Beyond the steam billowing from his mouth, the air actually tasted sweet, dancing with flavors from the fried foods cooking up around the town and the burning birch branches, and the incredibly pure glacier air from the north.

He tensed, digging with his boot points into the snow behind the footboards, while tightly gripping the handlebars. He stared ahead, focusing his breathing, sensing the feel of the sled and the strength of the snow. He tried to see along the length of the first mile before the bend. He was already disadvantaged in never having raced this course, and he felt a sudden doubt creep inside his skin.

But then, a smile came to his chafing lips. Suddenly he pulled off a mitten and reached inside his shirt. The gold cross came out, and he let it hang over the top of his coat.

A man ran up to the starting post. The flaming torch danced wildly at his approach; he nodded to both contestants, then raised the gun, closed his eyes... and pulled the trigger.

And then Delin was running as fast as he'd ever run, pushing with all his weight behind the dogs as they yelped and burst forward. Ice kicked back into his face, but he kept running, seeing for one satisfactory moment that Moon Chaser's sled lagged behind by several feet.

The crowd bellowed like some subterranean dragon snorting fire and rumbling about in a cavern. The wind whipped at his hat and tried to slip inside his clothes, and his cross flew about his neck in the icy wind. He took four more large steps, then jumped onto the runner boards and shouted "*Amma!*" to speed up. Ahead, the newly-dusted snow field lay in pristine tranquillity, shimmering in the moonlight and beckoning him on.

He relished in the feeling of control, holding power over these magnificent creatures, unleashing their natural instincts. His heart surged as he sensed the astonishment of the crowd, then he filtered their presence away and became one with the sled team. His lips curled back and he crouched and shifted his weight as needed; when they hit bumps and icy patches he controlled the sled's traction and direction.

In several minutes that seemed to pass in quick heartbeats, they were coming up on the first turn, a slight incline gradually bending to the left. One mile lay behind them, and while the shadows were deeper out here, the moonlight seemed fiercer, and the snow basked in an eerie luminescence. For a brief moment Delin's sled went airborne after a bump, and he seemed frozen in time, gazing at the channel and the perfection of the glittering whitecaps. Then he landed, yelled "*IU, IU!*" and steered the dogs to the left—

—just as Moon Chaser's team came in hard, closing the gap, then turning sharply at the last moment. Their sleds banged together and Delin barely held on. The force of the collision pushed him out of the way of a backhanded swipe as Moon Chaser took a swing at his head.

Delin imagined for an instant he was back at the village, racing against Mikhail, who used these same tactics. Delin drove ahead, pulling right to get some distance between them, then angled back in when he had a slight lead.

Moon Chaser's dogs snarled and snapped at Delin's, but they gave way, overmatched by the inertia of the crossing team. He noticed with concern that Moon Chaser used his whip to actually snap at the dogs themselves—cracking against their hindquarters to spur them on—instead of skillfully snapping at the air to indicate which direction to move. Delin uncoiled his own whip, shouted "*ILI, ILI!*" and cracked it to the right side. Blitzen responded perfectly, drawing the team back to the center and gaining ground on Moon Chaser, who had to arc around a bumpy area and connect back to the path.

They plowed through a series of drifts, blown in during the day; Delin's sled bumped and slowed as the dogs had to trudge through the deeper snow.

Moon Chaser caught up swiftly, driving his team through the path made by Delin's sled. The dogs barked and nipped at his legs, then banked around when they came to a flatter section. With the newfound momentum, Moon Chaser cracked his whip again and again, and his team swerved around and raced past Delin's, their sleds momentarily side by side.

For a brief instant Delin and Moon Chaser stared into each other's eyes from four feet away. Moon Chaser's hair whipped along behind him as his necklace slammed down against his chest with every bump in the terrain. He grinned suddenly; Delin flinched as his opponent swung his arm and the whip came cracking around toward his head.

Delin ducked; he felt a thump on his skull and his hat flew off, yanked free by the leather whip. Moon Chaser cursed and raised his arm again, but Delin leaned over and snapped out with his own whip. It struck like an attacking cobra and circled around Moon Chaser's wrist.

Before Delin could react, Moon Chaser caught the whip cord with his free hand and yanked it hard across his body. Delin let out a scream as he lost his footing and hurtled off the sled. He spun in the air and slammed hard onto the ice. The whip, still caught on Moon Chaser's wrist, dragged Delin along behind the sled. Through the jarring impacts and painful bumps, he looked past the spraying snow and saw his team slowing, veering off to the right.

He spun and managed to get to his feet, then ran to keep up. He grabbed hold of the whip, and for an instant thought about yanking it back and pulling Moon Chaser off his sled as well, which would force them both into a foot race back to their sleds. But just then the sled hit a large crest and launched in the air; Moon Chaser, holding on dearly to the handles with his free hand, pulled Delin ahead with the momentum.

Delin staggered and remained on his feet—barely. Noticing how close he was, he leapt with all his might, and connected with the shocked rider, slamming Moon Chaser forward and down onto the wooden flatbed.

He turned and yelled, "*Amma!*" as he glanced back to his sled. He saw the dogs perk up at his voice; they looked in his direction, then pulled toward him.

A fist slammed into his chin and bright lights exploded in his vision.

"Good-bye, yellow-hair!" Moon Chaser sneered, his breath foul even in the pure air. Dazed, Delin teetered back. The heel of his boots scraped on the snow, and then something whistled toward his face. He moved at the last moment, but not far enough. The blow glanced off his temple, knocked him sideways and sent him rolling off the sled. He tumbled over and over, scraping his face against the ice until finally coming to a rest on his back, staring up at the haughty moon as it rose triumphantly higher.

Moon Chaser's laughter faded and all hope fled in one painful groan. He imagined the future of his life sprawling forward: that he and Papa would be stuck in this town forever. Their gold gone, and with no way to get home now before the worst of winter; they would miss Christmas with Mama, would miss the feasts and the songs—and they might not even survive in this dreadful place.

Delin lifted his head, and through his starry vision he focused on the dogs bounding toward him. Blitzen ran up first, then Dunder and Dasher, on either side of his body with their ropes just clearing his face; then the others ran by: Comet and Prancer, Vixen, and Dancer, who snorted and took a lick at his face in mid-stride.

With a grunt, Delin rolled and reached for the incoming sled. At first he didn't think there was any way he would catch the left sideframe, let alone hang onto it. But it came up swiftly and jarred his wrist as the flatbed caught under his ribs. He rolled and circled his other arm around. Holding tight, he was dragged for a while, his legs trailing along behind the sled.

He tasted blood but he was thankful for the bitter cold that numbed the bruises and scrapes on his face. Sensing the team slowing down, he struggled and pulled his knees up onto the wood slats. Rising slowly, he righted himself, then peered ahead at the dogs. Their gait subdued, they looked nervous and confused.

He made a kissing sound to let them know he was back. Wobbling, he scanned the path ahead and quickly located the dark shape of Moon Chaser's team, leading by at least ten lengths and nearing the second bend.

Delin shifted his weight to the left, then reached over and pulled on the gangline and eased the team back on a straight path. Then he leaned in and shouted, in force: "*AMMA!*"

The dogs reacted, pulling and scraping, yelping with excitement and hot in pursuit. Still a chance, Delin thought. They had two more turns before the finish, and Delin could only hope to shorten the gap before Moon Chaser knew he was back on the trail.

Without a whip, Delin had to be extra diligent and skillful with his verbal commands. He shouted through the spreading numbness, shrugging off what seemed like rapidly decreasing temperatures and a bitter wind sweeping in from the west.

For the next ten minutes, the race's outcome was out of his hands. He had done what he could—the dogs were at the highest level of excitement he had ever seen in these breeds, and following Moon Chaser's tactic, they were set in the leader's wake, traveling easily over the snow flattened by his sled.

Delin let out a deep breath and tried to relax before the final urgent push—if there was to be one. In the time before they reached the last turn, he allowed his mind to wander. Thoughts came to him and slid away with such speed he imagined them to be snowflakes hurtling by. He reflected on the things he'd learned in the past year: the miracles of nature, the incredible diversity of this vast land. He thought of the treasure lying in wait in the riverbeds and creek shores, and deep under the ground.

Then he thought of his papa, and his heart cracked again. A prayer, fleeting but intense, left his frozen lips. Be strong, Delin cried. Resist if you can, and whether I win or lose, I will come get you, and we'll leave this place.

The wind tore at his scalp; without his hat for protection his whole head felt so bitterly cold, but again he tried to think of other things. Above, the aurora had appeared, magnificently swaying like gossamer emerald filaments. A faint crackling accompanied the dancing lights and reminded Delin of the native legend from his village. The shamans said that only those who had died violent deaths could make it across the great abyss at the northern edge of the world, where the dome of heaven met the land and the spirits of the sky waited with torches to guide the newcomers. On the other side, they played at football with a walrus skull and had great feasts, and spoke to the living in those crackling whispers.

Delin thought, too, on other legends that echoed these themes. He recalled reading in an old Russian fable book how the Norse believed the Lights were reflections off the shields of the warrior maidens: the Valkyries.

Painfully, he took his eyes off the cosmic wonder, looked ahead and saw that his dogs had closed the gap to only four lengths—and were still gaining as they went into the final turn.

But there, as Moon Chaser whipped his team around the bend, he shot a glance behind. And Delin could see the whites of his eyes, and the lips that curled into an angry sneer. The Tlingit boy shouted orders at his team and cracked down the whip again and again across their backs.

Delin felt his anger boiling, and he braced himself; he shouted the command for "left" and leaned into the turn. He kicked out with his right foot for added speed, pushing the sled along. He hadn't realized it from the cursory inspection of the track, but this last leg was up a gradual incline, and the dogs whined as they dug into the rising terrain. They still gained on Moon Chaser, but more slowly. Within one length, Delin could tell his opponent had lost his confidence, raging with the whip while glancing back at Delin's approach.

When the gap closed to within the reach of Moon Chaser's whip, Delin decided they had to pull out of the trail and swerve to the side to begin a pass. "*ILI!*" he roared, and tugged the gangline to the right. As they started to pull alongside, Moon Chaser attacked with a crack of his whip.

Delin was ready. He had shed his mittens, letting them drop on the flatbed. And as the whip uncoiled and shot across, he ducked at once and reached up to grab it as it passed overhead. He caught it just as it straightened out—and he stood and pulled.

Moon Chaser lurched sideways, but wisely dropped the whip at once. Delin was so startled by the lack of resistance that the whip flew out of his cold fingers as well, sailing off into the darkness.

Delin's sled was only about five feet behind Moon Chaser's, and a moment of hope rose in his chest. The torch smoke was visible up ahead, on top of a steeper rise to the finish line. Large crowds lined either side of the posts, straining to see who was in the lead.

Then something whistled through the air, and Delin reflexively threw himself to one side and gasped as the knife-point of a large ceremonial blade slammed into the upright plank above his fingers. Moon Chaser yelled something—a curse Delin recalled Mikhail often uttering—and then he turned and bent forward, screaming at the dogs. The knife hilt, made of caribou antler and decorated with a crescent moon design, shuddered with the sled's vibrations. Delin only glared at the blade, and let it fuel his determination.

He fought for purchase with his boot on every backward kick, but he noticed their ascent slowing. The dogs were tiring, still heroically pushing ahead, but it wasn't enough. They weren't gaining any more, and the last one hundred feet very well could have been the distance to the moon. Delin saw all this and understood: they were not going to make it. Moon Chaser's team just had to keep this pace—which was Delin's best—and they would win.

A quick thought occurred to him, and he rationalized that it was his only chance. Moon Chaser was heavier than he, and his opponent's sled was a little longer and had a few more boards to slow it down. Also, his dogs seemed a bit chunkier; at least some of them, perhaps feeding too well on their winnings lately.

Delin had a weight advantage. Not enough, as it was, to win, but he knew of one way to increase his chances. He leaned forward and yelled so all his dogs could hear the strength in his voice, the determination and urgency in his command. Then after locking eyes with Moon Chaser for an instant, Delin leapt into the air—and let go of the handlebars.

The sled shot on ahead and he tumbled backward, landing hard on the snow and rolling awkwardly. He gained his feet and took off up the incline, watching the speeding sleds. He ran after them, bounded up the hill to where it leveled off, then stopped to watch both teams clearing the gateposts.

Delin dropped to his knees, peering ahead anxiously, unable to discern which had crossed first. But then he looked at his opponent, and he knew...

Moon Chaser dropped the rope brake, leapt off his sled and started punching the ground. Then he raced to one of the nearby administrators and grabbed him by the collar, fiercely shaking him and pointing to the other sled until a small crowd rushed to the man's defense and dragged the boy away.

Delin got up and staggered forward, and in a daze he crossed the finish line, aware of the stares of hundreds on slack-jawed men around him. It was clear they were in shock—many of them didn't know what to make of it. But several bookies were running about, assuring everyone that what happened was legal: the rules stated that the winner would be the team that had the first dog to cross the finish line, regardless of whether the rider was on the sled or not.

Delin looked around for Elrod, and then saw him off to the side. On his knees, tearing up vouchers. He met Delin's stare, and then sadly shook his head and turned away, and Delin understood: at the last moment, he had gone for the safe win.

Barking dogs drew his attention, and before he could get out of the way, Blitzen and Dunder, leading the team back around, leapt on him. He fell back, grinning and hugging them as they playfully licked his face. Soon, he was enveloped by all seven dogs, getting tangled up in their ropes.

"Well done, boy." Delin looked up to see a red-faced bookie, his wide-brimmed hat on sideways, hands on his hips, looking down at him. The man leaned forward and placed a shiny, gold-covered lamp into his freezing hands; it felt light, yet magical, as if the trophy might just spit out a Djinni offering his fondest wishes.

A man in a long coat staggered up behind the bookie, set up a tripod and attached a large wooden box to it. Then he struggled to hold up something that looked like a rake without teeth. "Hold still," he called as he opened a slot in the box, "and try to keep them dogs from jumping." Then a hissing sound, a burst of smoke and a pop of light, a flare growing brighter and brighter. Delin blinked and tried to keep his eyes open—and the dogs still—for what seemed way too long. The cameraman kept repeating, "Almost there, almost finished." And then it was done and the man was packing up his gear in a hurry and then heading back to his studio.

The bookie grinned and helped Delin to his feet. "You can get yourself a tintype of that down at the newspaper office tonight. By the way, what do you go by?"

"Delin, sir. Delin Wetherwax."

The man nodded. "Nice competitive feel to that. How about

staying on for a couple weeks? Maybe the whole season?"

Delin glanced over to see the crowd still subduing Moon Chaser. "Well, sir..."

"He regrets to decline that offer," said a familiar voice at his back.

And Delin leapt up, pushing through the barking dogs to face his father, standing there in the moonlight. A moment of fear swallowed Delin's thoughts. The guard from the gambling shack stood behind his papa.

"This is my boy," Joshua said to the bookie. "And I must respectfully inform you that we are due back at our village in short order." He offered a thin smile to Delin. "Where I have a lot of making up to do to a couple loved ones."

The bookie's frown softened, and he let out a sigh. "Very well, then. Godspeed to you."

Joshua looked up at the comment. "I hope so. Oh, and sir, how do I go about cashing in on my bet?"

Delin gasped, looking from the voucher in his papa's hands to the bookie's suddenly dropping expression. "Ah, well." The bookie took the paper, studied it, then reached into a medium-sized sack secured to his belt. "I remember you—last one to get a bet in. Lucky fella," he said, weighing out a sizable and heavy portion of gold dust.

Joshua took the pouch and hefted it. "I trust this will not be significantly less than the ten pounds I have earned."

"You will find I have been fair, sir. Good day."

Joshua turned to the man at his side and measured out a couple ounces. "For your kindness to my son."

"Don't mention it. Heard about the young'un in the race, and I figured, well... his dad could wager better on his son than on cards." He tipped his hat. "Nice race, kid." Then he turned and followed the crowd back to the saloons.

Joshua lifted his face, squinted up at the brilliant moon, then took a deep breath. When he opened his eyes, he knelt in front of Delin, and had to fend off the affectionate dogs looking to sniff him and nip on his sleeves.

He reached out and touched the cross hanging visibly but crookedly over Delin's coat. "I'm sorry," he said. "Sorry for how I've been, and what you had to do to bring me back. But thank you, son, for doing it."

Delin smiled, and his eyes threatened to overflow with tears of happiness. He wanted to hug his father, but stood there, too self-conscious with the crowd watching them.

"Now," said Joshua, rubbing his head, then fixing Delin's coat. "Let's see about sobering me up with some coffee and getting you a hot drink and some rest."

"And some food for my dogs! I named them after Saint Nick's reindeer."

"Really? All of them?"

Delin looked sheepish. "I only had seven dogs, so I left Cupid out. Didn't need him getting all lovey during the race."

Joshua put his arm around his son and they led the dogs up the side of the hill. He slid his rifle over his other shoulder and glared at a few men who were angrily looking at Delin and muttering under their breath.

"Let's get home," he said.

Chapter 11: Alaska - December, 1881

LOSS

DELIN AWOKE WITH A MUFFLED scream, and in the dark it took almost a full minute to recognize the surroundings. He finally smelled the smoldering fire from the great room, and he felt the warmth of the heavy goose-down covers. He felt Mama stir, then mumble something and turn to her side.

He had been ripped from another nightmare. When Papa had gone away, the dreams had begun, and he had begged to sleep with the adults. The reunion with Mama had been sweet, and the next day they had gone out to the hot springs, the three of them in the sulfur baths in the caves. That had worked wonders for Delin, easing all his aches and chills, and renewing his rosy cheeks. But Papa seemed no better. He stared only at the chain around Delin's neck, and it seemed some great battle warred behind his eyes.

Mama knew it too, and afterward Delin saw them spending hours together alone. Going for long walks, or sitting out by the totems. She, too, was helpless to lift his mood, and at last, six days ago, he announced that he would be going into the wilderness for some time. To be alone and reconnect with his soul and his faith, if possible.

Delin told himself he would be patient, but he was so excited to start the new prospecting season with Papa. And as he watched his father disappear through the gates, dragging his pack and lumbering out with only a rifle and his thoughts, Delin inched closer to Mama and held her hand as the winds kicked in and blew a wall of snow between them and the departing figure.

The nightmares began that night. *A red-eyed snow creature tracks his father in the whirling winds. It toys with him, leaving signs of its presence, but never attacking. At the end it's always the same—Papa stumbles into a clearing and finds his wife and son, frozen in ice with their mouths open in silent screams. And a crowd of giant Sesquats shake free of the snow drifts and descend upon him.*

Still trembling, Delin slid out from the covers and quietly got to his feet. He stopped and listened. There were about twenty women and older men inside on this level, and ten children asleep above. The other men and teenagers had all gone out last week for the monthly hunt, and would not return until tomorrow.

He tiptoed down the stairs. After first retrieving his clothes—the heavy wool pants, thick black sweater and his boots—he made his way in the dark, zeroing in on the glowing of the fire's embers. He dressed by the hearth, then retrieved his coat and hat from a side room.

Finally suited up, he found the main door and slipped outside into the somber, blue-tinged night. He took a few steps in the crunchy snow, breathed in the crisp air, and then turned his face to the heavens, following the tail of the Bear to Arcturus, the main star in the Bootes the hunter. Some comfort came in that association, as if by locating that star so quickly, maybe it meant Papa would swiftly find what he sought in the wild, and he would return soon.

Delin shuffled quietly to the supply shed on the east side of the village, intending to look in on the dogs. When he opened the heavy door he said, "It's me, boys." In the darkness he heard the answering whines and padding of feet. Blitzen came bounding over and stood on hind legs, licking at Delin's face. The smell of kerosene was strong in here. Six barrels rested in one corner, and they were frequently opened for refilling the lamps of the Long House. Four rifles lay against the wall, beside piles of freshly chopped wood. It seemed like only yesterday that Delin was climbing up the nearby ladder to the second floor, helping to pack away their supplies.

He made his way through the rambunctious dogs and lit the glass-enclosed kerosene lamp on the far wall. In the flickering light, he wrestled several dogs at a time, enjoying this morning romp. But moments later, he noticed Prancer was standing away from the others. With its ears back and fur bristling, the malamute focused at the partially-open door. A couple seconds later, Delin heard a low growling.

Then the others picked up on it too, and playtime ceased at once. They crept to the door, baring their teeth. Delin tiptoed between them and, heart pounding, he peeked outside.

At first he saw nothing. Just the silvery phosphorescence trickling from the tree boughs onto the village square. The Raven-headed totem stood there impassively, but by a trick of shadow it seemed to have one eye looking at the Long House. Delin focused there, and at first saw nothing whatsoever.

But then, on the snow-covered roof, a barely visible patch of white broke free from the background. Delin squinted, trying to make it out. Prancer uttered a menacing growl, just as something creaked overhead. Delin continued staring, though, and then he saw it—and his heart lurched. The shape moved faster this time, shambling sideways, and when it stood up its great white bulk blotted out the stars.

Sesquat—the thought shook Delin with fear. His legs trembled and his mouth went dry. And then, he caught motion near the gate. Another form, taller but more agile, slipped over the wooden wall and dropped soundlessly. It made its way to the Long House entrance, just as the one from the roof crept to the side of the main door.

And again, something creaked above. On the shed's roof, Delin realized with a fright, just as Dunder and Vixen backed up, turned their snouts to the ceiling and let loose a furious round of barks and snarls. Delin rushed to the wall with the rifles even as dust fell from the ceiling and heavy thuds pounded their way to the edge.

He grabbed the nearest—a heavy Winchester .44. He turned and cocked the chamber, just as Papa had showed him on many outings. Trying to check his fear, he choked down a terrible sense of doom. The timing of these foul creatures was perfect: to strike just as all the men and older boys were away.

They were nearly defenseless. Maybe the medicine man and several of the women inside had rifles nearby, but against a force like this? These thoughts rushed by in a blur while the dogs massed before the door, snarling. At the top of the doorframe, four enormous talons bound with white fur gripped the edge of the wood and pulled it back slowly.

Three dogs leapt ahead just as Delin pulled the trigger, aiming at a spot just under the doorframe. He jumped through the cloud of gunsmoke as the rest of the dogs raced from the room. They leapt on the Sesquat as it staggered backward. This was a small one, at least from what Delin could tell; maybe ten feet tall, thinner and probably much younger than the one on the Long House roof. But it was quicker, too, dodging out of the way of the snapping jaws and moving in to take a swipe at Prancer. Delin took another shot, and saw a satisfying blotch of red appear on the thing's shoulder.

He heard a commotion to his left; more snarls, the splintering of wood, and then bloodcurdling screams. "Long House!" Delin shouted at the dogs. "Attack!"

It took a second for them to react, to tear themselves away from the current quarry; but most of them obeyed, racing to the broken front door and jumping over the splintered pieces. Only Dunder and Blitzen remained, circling the closest foe. The Sesquat poised, crouching low and snapping its great jaws. Delin aimed at its face and fired. Somehow the snow monster dashed to the side, and the bullet sailed into the far gate.

He cocked the rifle again as the creature rushed, and the dogs leapt on its legs and bit into its calves. Delin jumped out of the way of a huge hand that slammed into the spot he had just been, then turned and fired, this time into its skull. Something echoed like a hammer slamming into metal, and when the smoke cleared, the beast had made it back to its feet, kicked away the attacking dogs, and held its bloodied head in its huge talons.

Delin's hopes soared for a moment. The dogs continuously jumped forward and back, and Dunder took a vicious bite at the Sesquat's thigh, then darted away before the swiping fist could connect.

Delin reloaded and advanced—and then heard his mother's scream amidst new gunfire. He paused, fleetingly tempted to actually kill one of the monstrous things, to finish it off right now while it was wounded, but he turned and ran to the Long House, calling Dunder and Blitzen to follow.

Before he got halfway across the square, three figures appeared in the doorway: his mother and Kreaga the Medicine Man, and they held the elder Mother Frelda between them. Her head was twisted sideways, a great red spot covering one side of her face, and her nightdress was a sheet of blood. They staggered out, and relief washed across Mirna's face when she saw Delin, the dogs and his rifle.

He started to run to her, even as he heard the painful yelping of dogs and the piercing screams of children in the darkness, but then her eyes widened and she pointed over his shoulder and screamed out a warning.

Delin ducked flat and rolled, just as a flash of white roared over his body. Someone grunted, and a horrible sound of shattering bones echoed in the clearing. Delin got up, and as his dogs raced by, he saw the wounded Sesquat rising up with Kreaga in its grasp, viciously shaking the man and crushing his ribcage. Frelda lay in a heap several feet away.

Mirna staggered away in shock, and the overwhelming stench of the Sesquat wafted over the clearing. Delin got to his knees and fired another time, and a patch of red erupted from the monster's back just as Dunder and Blitzen pounced on its thigh.

"To the shed!" Delin shouted as he ran to his mother's side. Surprising himself with his strength, he hauled Mirna to her feet, put her arm around his shoulder and backpedaled.

Delin watched desperately as his two favorite dogs put up a valiant fight, snarling and lunging despite glancing blows and sideswipes from the Sesquat's talons. Suddenly the creature tossed the medicine man's corpse to one side, then pounced and lunged swiftly, and caught Blitzen's hind legs; it lifted the dog and threw it like a rag toy into the nearby wall.

Delin started forward. "No!" Mirna shouted. "Leave them! Into the shed, it's our only chance."

"But the children!" Delin gasped. And the dogs!

"Now!" Mama shouted, and yanked on his shoulder; he turned and obeyed, running inside. As soon as they both were in, he glanced back to see his mother pulling the door shut, and in the closing gap, he saw a great bloodied face tear itself out of Dunder's twitching body.

It looked up at him, snarling, and then it jumped—but the door slammed shut, and Mirna threw the wooden bolt across the frame. She quickly ran to the wall with the rifles and snatched one up even as the door quaked with an immense collision.

"Mama…?" Delin held the gun in his shaking hands as tears formed on his cheeks. What could they do? Where could they go?

"Shush, honey," she said, loading two more shells into her rifle, and handing a fistful to him. "Take these, reload and head up the ladder to top level."

"But..."

"Wait there for me. I have an idea."

The door groaned and a sideways crack appeared in its middle. The lamp tossed wild shadows across the supplies as Delin backed away and made for the ladder.

"Wait," Mirna commanded, as she set the rifle against one of the barrels of kerosene. She gripped a barrel, twisted off the cover, then pulled it forward and stepped out of the way as the contents spilled out, gushing over the wood floor and spreading toward the door.

"Take that lamp with you." she instructed as she started opening another barrel. The door frame buckled again, and something landed on the roof. A horrible whistling sound chilled Delin's blood and suddenly there were three sounds out there: one on the roof, and the other two out in front.

That meant their business in Long House was over, Delin thought gravely, as he detached the lamp and climbed the ladder. Almost there, he paused, took out his cross and said a silent prayer for the villagers' souls. The roof shook, and scratching and clawing sounded from just over his head.

At the top, he almost dropped the lamp when he heard the sound of wood rending and splitting from below. He bent down, turned and reloaded the rifle. In the flickering light he lay flat and scanned the shadows.

There was his mother, kneeling in a growing pool of kerosene, tugging on another barrel. Three of the six were empty and tilted over, and the overpowering smell almost made him retch; but at last, he understood what Mama was doing. He only hoped she wouldn't run out of time.

"Mama!" he called, just above a whisper, as he readied the lamp to throw. "Come up here. That's enough."

She glanced up, and in her eyes he saw desperate resignation, and a touch of longing. In a soft voice, she said: "Take care of your papa."

Confused, Delin was about to beg her to hurry when he realized something was wrong. It was the silence. The roof was utterly quiet, and the hammer-blows against the door had ceased.

Mirna lowered her eyes, then slowly turned her head to look over her shoulder, and Delin followed her line of sight. The floor up here had concealed the view of the door below, but now Delin gasped as a lumbering white form hunkered into view, ducking to fit under the low ceiling. It proceeded slowly, sniffing and snarling.

For a moment, Delin didn't understand why Mama wasn't moving—either running to the ladder or reaching for the rifle. Then he understood. The shadows were deep down there, and she was partially concealed. And also, she was soaked in kerosene, her smell effectively masked.

Delin dared to hope, and to breathe. He set down the lamp, lifted the rifle and aimed for the creature's head. This was the first Sesquat he had seen on the Long House roof, larger than the one he had scuffled with. He steadied his aim, but then a new shape moved into the line of fire.

Another Sesquat, slightly smaller, but crouched over and snorting. Its feet splashed on the kerosene, and it got on all fours, sniffing the air and whipping its head about.

Delin changed his aim to the newcomer, even as he saw from the corner of his eye that the third monster had crawled into view. Now his heart fell, and for an aching moment he listened, hoping any second to hear his father's Dragoons, somehow miraculously returned, arriving in time to blast these foul beasts with their holy vengeance.

But only the wind whistled back at him, and somewhere in the distance came the pained cry of a wounded dog. Delin held his breath, said a prayer, and aimed at the nearest head.

Before he could fire, a voice whispered, "The lamp!"

Delin blinked, and looked away from his target. He saw the whites of his mama's eyes, pleading up at him. She still knelt in the midst of the three creatures; the beasts that now heard her voice and snarled, tensing.

"Throw it, Delin!" she yelled as a white blur fell upon her and great talons whipped back and forth.

With a cry, Delin fired wildly then let the rifle drop with the recoil. He spun and scooped up the lamp; he stood up high, holding it above him like a blazing beacon. He shouted down to the creatures, and up to the heavens, and to the entire vast wilderness. He screamed until his lungs burned, and even the Sesquats stopped in their slaughter to look up at him.

Three monstrous faces ringed with blood-spattered fur and ravenous fangs turned upwards, and crimson eyes of intense animal cruelty locked onto him, yet flickered with a kind of hesitation, seeing one so bold and angered.

The smaller one backed away, recognizing Delin's scent, and holding its wounded head. Delin glared down at them, and saw the mangled body in the largest one's grip; the twitching form of his mother, whose head turned, and a blood-soaked face sought him out. "Please..." came the desperate whisper.

It was an action he never recalled making in any conscious way. For the rest of his life, he only remembered crying out, "Goodbye, Mama," as his arm descended; then watching with detached interest as the globe-shaped lamp spun around and around and fell between the two larger Sesquats. The sound of shattering glass reached his ears a second before a whoosh and a blast of heat.

Then, the light—a white-hot burst of seething fire, and then a scarlet cloud erupted as the flames ignited the remaining full barrels. Something slammed against his back, he tasted blood, and then he had the amusing sight of the starlit sky streaking across his vision.

And he floated, sailing in a great downward arc. There was the roof of the supply shed—in flames—and a small hole in the top where he had been blasted out. He continued falling, and he watched as the entire building erupted in another fiery explosion, and flames and columns of smoke roared from all sides and shot up through the collapsing roof.

Next, the wind rushed out of his body as he slammed into a deep snow drift, then rolled forward, the momentum carrying him to the icy ground, where he tumbled onto his back. Still without sensation, physical or emotional, he could only stare back at the burning shed; at the nexus of his dreams and nightmares, where both were devoured by fire.

The first sense to return was his hearing, and it took several moments for him to place the hideous howling that carried over the freezing wind currents. Then he saw the three burning figures stumbling about the wreckage, flailing wildly. Two of them—the larger two—were engulfed in fire; it roared through their fur and flesh and seared away muscle and incinerated bones. They collapsed at the same time into the deeper flames that greedily finished consuming them.

Guess they don't like fire or water, Delin thought without amusement.

The third shape—the smallest, youngest of the three—howled and rolled, diving in and out of the snow, stamping at its left side and finally putting out the flames. It rocked back on its feet and screamed out a fearsome cry. Smoking, it staggered into the clearing, then it stopped, turned toward Delin's position, and sniffed, cocking its head.

Delin managed to blink, then struggled to sit up, but groaned with the flaring pain from his back. The beast lumbered toward him. Dragging its blackened leg and shaking its seared right arm, it came. And Delin got a good look at the massive burns: scorched fur and singed flesh all the way up its side, even onto its raw and blistered face.

As it stomped closer and closer, its normally hideous stink merged with the unbearable odor of charred flesh. It snarled and lowered its head, sniffing. And when it came within ten feet, it slowed, flexing its claws.

Delin forced his lips to make a grin. He was about to die. Despite such sacrifice, and such luck, his story would be snuffed out. The worst part was, no one would know how hard they had fought. He groaned, but then met the fierce stare of the monster as it pawed at the ground, and sniffed again in Delin's direction. Motionless, Delin laughed and managed to speak. "You're the one that stinks, Sesquat."

It growled, tensed, and raised a taloned fist.

"Go ahead," Delin said, grateful for the numbness. Maybe he wouldn't feel the pain, and it would be like a gentle tugging that eased his soul from this frozen place. He closed his eyes, and pictured Mama waiting for him...

—maybe in the Northern Lights, holding a dazzling shield and riding on horseback with a legion of Valkyries.

The creature roared, and something warm sprayed down on Delin. And then he heard the loud echo, followed by another. Then another.

The Sesquat howled. Delin opened his eyes—only to see the monster fleeing, bounding away as ice exploded around its feet, coinciding with loud reports in the distance.

Delin raised his head and watched the beast scrambling about the clearing, then finally leaping onto the back wall. It turned and spun its head around, locking its eyes on Delin's. A gunshot exploded against the wood at its feet, but still it hung there, staring into Delin's very soul, and he stared back. Time seemed to slow, the flames curled in lazy circular patterns, and the smoke blew across his vision with minute patience. The two adversaries shared an eternal connection, and every emotion seemed to transfer back and forth.

And Delin started laughing—because that was the only sound he could make, the only noise that could dispel the madness of this morning, the only thing he could do...

...Even as the men came running, some of them still firing, racing through the gate in the dawn's slow rise. The shadows fled before their feet, and even the flames flickered and subsided. Cries of anguish filled the air, and men and boys rushed about, scrambling and looking for survivors.

Delin glanced up, high up, into the face of the Raven atop the largest totem. He doesn't seem to be grieving, Delin thought. Odd—it's almost as if he intended this, as if no life should be without its grief, without its pain.

Without its loss.

Delin blinked up at Raven, and his laughter died. He wanted to scream, wanted to leap to his feet, take a rifle and fire up at the haughty bird-god. Wanted it to feel this same pain, to understand what it was like.

But he just lay there, and the shadows of the men fell upon him as the sun rose above their shoulders. And then the Indians were pushed aside by one who came, out of breath and desperately anxious. Papa knelt at his side and strong hands slid under his body. Delin sighed and turned his head away so the falling tears wouldn't catch on his father's beard.

"Delin..." came the voice, hollow and distant, spoken out of some far abyss. He choked as he rose, carried between a crowd of horror-struck hunters. And there in the distance—was that Mikhail kneeling in the smoldering ruins and shaking his fist?

Delin tried to reach out to his half-brother, tried to call to him but his throat was full of ice, and he couldn't breathe. It was only later that he realized his papa held him so tightly that he nearly crushed his lungs.

"I'm sorry, so sorry..." came the voice at his ear.

And the winds blew and the sun rose.

And the world of his childhood closed with a whimper over the frozen clearing.

Chapter 12: Fort Reliance - 1882

RECOVERY AND A LETTER FROM THE PAST

AFTER THE QUIET SERVICE BEFORE the Spirit House, the missionary blessed Delin and his father while Mikhail and the other Tlingit men sent glares their way. They were all gathered for the dedication ceremony, over the west bank of Lake Bennett, within rifle distance of where, ages ago, a great beast had been felled and a love had arisen.

Mirna's body was buried in the ground according to Joshua's wishes, but only after a fierce argument with Mikhail. In the Tlingit tradition, the deceased were cremated, and Mikhail insisted on the same for his mother, but Joshua's Christian intentions and forceful demands won out. The others were cremated, and this traditional Spirit House had been constructed over their potted remains and built atop Mirna's grave. It was a small log hut with intricately carved animal designs and nature scenes, and like all Spirit Houses, it was intended to be venerated and protected by the living for generations.

It took four months before the ceremonies could begin, before the village was rebuilt, the ground thawed and the Spirit House erected. Delin had spent the first month in the care of the shamans, with Joshua always at his side. He recovered quickly, and as soon as his body was fit, Joshua took him to Fort Reliance, to be away from the memories and the recriminating stares of Mikhail and the others. To be away from the place they no longer belonged.

Now it was finished. "Let's go home," Joshua said quietly, after thanking the gray-bearded missionary and giving him a pouch of gold dust for his mission.

With the fierce stares of Mikhail and the others at their backs, Delin and Joshua returned to the lake and to the waiting quayaq. Delin noticed Papa seemed increasingly tense the farther they ventured from the village; he kept casting furtive glances to the spruces, scanning their branches for any movement, eyeing the shadows.

He felt his father's eagerness to return to the safety of the supply station, with its fortified structures and high walls—and armed men. Delin didn't mind spending the months with those other traders and prospectors, and many of them had come to know the not-so-little boy with the blond curls—the kid with the Midas Touch, they took to calling him. These men had been out at the streams with him and his papa, and had laughed at the boy just poking around with the pickax, tasting the blade.

But whether they were in the Porcupine River tributaries, on the banks of the Peel, or just off the Yukon itself, he would always find something that would bring the others running.

It was mid-September when Delin and Joshua finally returned to their small cabin on the hillside overlooking the fort. They had missed a good two months of prime panning and prospecting, but Delin noticed Papa seemed more at ease than he had in the past nine months, as if the dedication ceremony had finally offered solace and closure.

In hindsight, it was only his papa's extreme emotional sadness that kept Delin's spirits afloat. He had bounced back from the horror of that night almost miraculously, drawn out from under the shell of desolation only to honor Mama's last request: Take care of your papa.

Take care of him... It was the ever-repeating echo in his mind, and Delin no longer held back. Fifteen now, having celebrated his birthday quietly while paddling downriver, his words spilled out even as they were thought, and his heart seemed to pull all the strings. Like the time last night when they had left the campfire and hiked back up to the cabin, pausing halfway to look up at the ribbony trails of the aurora just as it appeared briefly to the north.

"Do you think we can see Mama's soul in there?" Delin asked directly, pointing and tugging on his father's sleeve. Joshua stopped. His body seemed to deflate, his eyes widened and his pupils reflected the multicolored radiance. Delin could tell he wrestled with the beliefs that usually rallied his soul.

"Maybe," he whispered simply, and gripped Delin's hand for just a moment. "Maybe she does ride among their brilliant members. But for now, I know one little boy—I'm sorry, young man—who needs to go to sleep."

"Can I read a little first?" Delin asked. They had a small stash of books in the cabin, collected over the past year from travelers.

"Which book?" Joshua asked. "Aren't you reading three or four at once?"

"Nah, only two: The Odyssey and the Inferno."

Joshua laughed. "Nice light bedtime reading."

Delin tried not to smile. He loved their themes of great journeys, vast searches across fantastic realms, and quests for cherished loves. It all seemed fitting, and yet... he read with a fevered pace, as if he needed to get through these works as background information for something—like studying up on maps of a land he was about to visit.

"Fine, read by candlelight while your father sleeps."

"Thank you!"

"Come on," Joshua said, giving one last glance to the already fading lights in the sky. "She's saying good night."

Delin followed, and at the door to the cabin, he pushed away the heavy curls from his eyes. Soft wisps of fuzz were beginning to form on his upper lip and his chin, manhood peeking through the youthful skin. When Joshua's footsteps echoed from inside, he whispered: "Good night, Mama."

On the day of the first snowfall, during the third week of October, a small brig came up the Yukon River and dispatched two men with a sack of mail. They made their way across the willow brush and through forests of birch and spruce, and came to Fort Reliance. Their imminent presence sparked something of a celebration. News-starved men waited hours for their arrival, flags waved, and guns were fired into the air.

On a log table beside the west wall, Delin ate a hunk of sourdough and sipped at a steaming cup of bacon stew while he watched the commotion. Still mourning the loss of his valiant dogs and hoping to buy more someday soon, Delin drank down a hot tea mixture and watched as the arriving postmen were greeted like national war heroes. He shook his head, feeling blessed to have been born into the one place he belonged, into a world that seemed constructed just for him.

A flash of red hair in the crowd caught his eye. Papa, returning from the general store with an armful of cans and some jars of oil, stopped short. A man was calling Joshua's name, and holding something up.

Delin stood, and his long legs trembled. A letter? Finding them here? No one knew about them except the villagers back on Lake Bennett, and they would have just sent a scout if it was something urgent. Maybe it was the Chinaman—Xien—his father's friend? That hope faded when he saw the shock on Papa's face, and he thought only one thing, that somehow his papa's old enemy had tracked him down. Benjamin Quitch.

But then Papa's expression changed; his mouth dropped and his eyes went wide. He staggered and gripped the other man for support, then shot a glance to Delin. He tore open the seal and removed the three pages within. Delin dropped his spoon and made to run to him, when Joshua held up a hand. His eyes scanned back and forth over the first few lines.

And emotion erupted in a flood that Delin hadn't seen since Mama's death—and even then. This, this was different. Joshua made it to a nearby table, sat on a bench and read frantically, from one page to the next. Delin shuffled closer, quietly.

After what seemed like the passage of great ages—like those long, dusty epochs advocated by the scientists—Joshua lowered the letter, but still gripped the pages tightly as if fearing the wind would cruelly snatch them away. He looked up, and as his face fell out of the shadows, he said, "It's from Caroline."

It was the first time Joshua had ever let him taste alcohol. "Just a sip," he told Delin back in their cabin, when he had opened a dirt-caked bottle. "I have a feeling we might both need it at this point—and I would rather be with you for your first drink."

He eyed Delin intently across the table and over the flickering candles. "You haven't had a nip before, have you, boy? Not back in Rockwell when I was away?"

Delin shook his head as he held the metal cup in both trembling hands. He wasn't sure what he feared more—tasting this noxious liquid, or reading what was in that letter.

"Good," said Joshua. "Beware the drink, and only do it in moderation. Otherwise, if you must—say, if it's terribly cold outside, or if it's just your soul that's freezing—then only indulge around those you trust."

"Got it," said Delin, eager to get this drink over with so he could learn about the mysterious letter. He brought the cup to his lips.

"Whoa!" Joshua said, and reached out to stay his son's hand. He raised his own glass, and his sad eyes held Delin's. "We must toast. As a wise Celestial once said: 'To life's surprises, which often are as cruel as its inevitabilities.'"

Delin clinked his glass against his father's, then brought the splash of whiskey to his mouth and downed the cup. The taste of fire roared across his tongue and down his throat, and he held back a scream. He had to show his strength...

But instead of a laugh or a mocking sound, his father only pulled out the three sheets of hand-scrawled paper, sighed, and handed them over to Delin. "I can't read this aloud—and I would spare you seeing your father choked up on his emotions."

Delin took the pages. "It's okay, Papa. I'll read it."

"Good, and when you're done I want you to be my voice of reason and tell me if my intentions now are unwise. For I cannot make the decision that is before me."

Swallowing hard, fighting back the bitter swelling in his throat, Delin drew a candle closer, and by its flickering radiance, read the words from his father's one-time fiancée.

My dearest Joshua. How cruel has Fate been.

To have had us almost cross paths those many years ago. But if there is any hope, any breath left in this husk of the thing once called love, I must pray that this letter finds you, and finds you willing.

Willing to listen. Willing to forgive.

I will be brief, and can only tell you as plainly as I can, for other explanations are lacking. I must rely upon your Christian sensibilities to at least hear me out. Know this first: that as soon as I learned the truth—when I heard the rumors of how he was blinded, and whose name he curses in his sleep—then I spared no effort in trying to find you.

He is the most black-hearted of beasts. I realized the obvious truth when he returned from the War: that he stole me away from you, as callously as the Devil pries goodness from the soul. He did it—convinced me of your murder in the gold fields by vengeful Mexicans, then persuaded me of his desire to care for me as you would have.

Joshua, I am so sorry. When I arrived in San Francisco I was lost, desperate and out of my element, surrounded by sudden power and luxury, thrust into a role of businesswoman and confidant. I did things I am so ashamed of. Things that were accomplished only under the sway of opium and heavy drink. Ever since setting foot off of the California, that vessel which almost became my tomb, I evolved into something other than the fine mannered lady you loved.

I will not speak of my employ in various disreputable places in the Bay city, or of how one fateful night I thought I saw you down the stairs from my landing, involved in a card game and looking up at me through a haze of smoke. I will not speak of the shame I felt in that moment or the certainty that I could not let you see me in that condition.

But that was the night that changed my life. For it was then that I met the man who came up those stairs—the man who would, like the sinewy serpent in the garden, offer me power and knowledge to send me far from the gates of Paradise.

I am sorry, my dear Joshua. How utterly has my soul wept at the cruel acts in this life's drama. He whittled away at the foundations of my heart, chiseling free the stones you and I had so carefully molded. I later learned the horrible truth. He paid the courier to hold back my letter—the first letter I had written as our boat sailed around the Cape. He held it back, and delivered it in a callous, deliberate method, knowing it would crush your soul, your optimism, and keep you from leaving his employ. And also, giving himself ample time to conquer in your stead.

Like those suitors who moved in on Penelope while Odysseus sailed lost in the Aegean, Benjamin Quitch is your malicious Neptune, your deadly nemesis. He sent you hence, and then—God forgive me—I yielded instead of standing rock solid and true.

I am no heroine in a Greek fable, Joshua, no true maiden deserving of your slightest glance. And I ask nothing for myself of you. Only I write to warn you of his surging hatred. He thinks of little else, even while his mines here continue to churn out millions every year, and his pockets grow fatter beyond imagination. Everyone he touches is ruined.

Myself included—and my son as well.

Yes—and here is the greatest sadness, my deepest regret. That I stayed with this monster for one purpose: I saw in this child's unexpected appearance a chance at redemption. It is false pride, I know, but I expected some last, desperate hope for my own salvation: that despite the evil I invited across my threshold, there was some good I was meant to do.

And when little Jericho was born, perfectly innocent, I knew what it was. Here was a clean slate, and I wielded the quill. I would make of this child everything his father was not. I would mold him to be the man I once intended to grow old with. Carve into his soul all the kindness and love that his mother once had, until his father came along and swept it away.

I thought it would be easy. Benjamin was never around, as you know. I saw him only on a handful of occasions each year. But something changed when I became pregnant. He called in his favors—to men like William Ralston—and I was released from my role at the resorts.

Quitch called me back to him, and here in Nevada I have stayed ever since. Sixteen years, locked away like some medieval princess in the high tower at his factory at the Comstock. And, since Jericho's birth, Benjamin has been at my side at all times. He delegated most of the mining work and financing to his superintendents, and to that dreadful Doctor Dreggel. And for the first five years, Benjamin was a doting father, winning over the boy's affections and always treating him with such kindness that for a time—a short time—I actually dared to hope that fatherhood had caused a reversal in his nature.

But it was not to be. When the boy was old enough, Benjamin took him to the mines, and ever since he left my chambers without so much as a glance goodbye, he has walked in his father's shadow.

I see it now—the subtle designs of Fate, or a cruel God. That I chose the name Jericho is fitting. I had sought only for a Biblical name, something sounding much like your own in syllables and feel. But it was actually much more appropriate. I remember fondly your love for word derivations and deeper meanings beyond the surface.

Jericho—the place where the walls fell.

I sought to mold in my child the resistant stonework that should have been mine. The strength of character I should have had. I tried, Joshua, God how I tried.

But once again, Benjamin Quitch struck me down, and my labors on Jericho's behalf were just as feeble. All his goodness is crumbled to dust.

Just last week, at sixteen and only a foot shorter than his father, the boy stood watch over the elevator cart on the northeast expanse and let two men fall to their deaths rather than risk the loss of one cart of ore. And worse, upon bringing up their shattered bodies and eviscerated limbs, I watched from a distance as he gleefully described the condition of the corpses to his blind father.

Jericho serves him now in all things, and has become his eyes; it is as if Benjamin has created a younger, healthier extension of himself to do all the vile things he can no longer enjoy to the fullest.

I cannot bear it. I have lost all, Joshua. And I can only beg you, if this letter should find you in the wilderness where I have heard word of your deeds and your remarkable existence—that if you should read this, guard yourself. Guard against his spies, and keep alert. Even great Alaska and the Canadian expanse are not large enough to hide you from this blind demon and his malevolent son, should they turn their full resources to your capture.

There is nothing left for me. I spend the weeks and months holed up in my chambers, seeing no one. Dreaming only, I stare out my window and see not the crisscrossed hills, or the cars that spit forth from the hellish depths with their foul cargo. No, I peer farther back. To a time long ago, and those fateful steps off a gangplank onto a new land in search of my old love.

I had such good intentions, Joshua. Remember that always, if ever we are to meet again.

I hear, as I said, many rumors. One is that you have a son of your own. I am sure he is made in your likeness, his heart is pure and his soul clean.

I wish he could have been ours, as I wish many things. May life be kind to you, and may God bless you always.

Yours, Caroline.

When Delin finished, his own tears barely held at bay, distraught as much for his concern over this woman he never met as he was for his father, he set down the papers and reached for the bottle and a cup. "May I have another sip, Papa?"

Joshua, sitting in the corner, his chin propped up in his crossed hands, grunted, and when he turned from the stove's heat, his eyes came away wet. "Just a swallow, boy—don't let the taste of it go to your head."

Delin poured a splash, then brought it to his lips. He saw his father watching him, then paused and set it down, untouched. His head had cleared on its own, and seeing his papa hunched over, his expression pained, wrestling with those inner torments, Delin knew what he should say.

"We're going to her, aren't we, Papa?"

Joshua closed his eyes and held his face in his hands. "I don't know. How can I go back there? She..."

"Needs us, Papa."

A weak smile tugged at his lip. "You're a good son, you know that? I am proud of you. But this—it's too dangerous. We'll be risking our lives for someone that... That..."

He turned and punched the wall. "Damn it!" He bit his knuckle, leaned forward and started rocking. "I'm sorry, so sorry. I don't know if I can forgive. The years I struggled with her loss, blaming myself, suffering with the guilt."

"But, Papa. She's alive." Delin walked quietly to stand behind his sobbing father. "Alive when you thought her dead. And during those years, her sadness has been just as great."

"She's not your mother, and she's no longer my responsibility."

"No, she's not, but..." Delin looked to the top level of the bookshelf—to the stereograph of his father and Benjamin Quitch standing outside the Comstock. He often wondered why Papa kept that reminder out in plain view, and now he thought he might have the answer. He took a deep breath, knowing he was about to change their lives with his next words.

"*But Quitch is.*"

His father stiffened, and he slowly sat up. Then he stood and his hands dropped to his hips, as if seeking the familiar handles of his departed Dragoons. "You're right," he whispered.

"And you read what Caroline said—he's looking for you anyway. Why not go to him? Surprise him!"

"And his son?"

Delin trembled as an unseen wind rushed through his body. Something came to him, a memory from one of the Services several months ago. "Jericho!" he said suddenly. "In the Bible!"

"What?"

Maybe there was something of Fate or the Divine at work here. Caroline's selection of that name—did its full meaning escape her? Delin met his father's inquisitive look. "Who was it that brought down Jericho's walls?"

Joshua's eyes went wide, and his teeth peeked out from a widening grin. "Of course! But in *that* battle, Joshua had seven priests with him blowing on ram's horns, and he made his entire army shout at the same time. He had all that help."

Delin shrugged and gave a sheepish grin. "And you've got me. What're we waiting for?"

Joshua embraced his son, and for the rest of the night, until both were too weary to keep their eyes open, he told Delin stories of his youth. Of Caroline and their early courting, of the hills of Virginia and the world so far away, yet somehow back within reach.

And in the morning, they began to pack.

Chapter 13: Nevada - December 12, 1882

RETURN TO COMSTOCK

THEY ARRIVED IN SAN FRANCISCO just as the sun came up over the Sierras. When they disembarked from the steamer, it was in a heady rush to get through the city and arrange a trip upriver to Sacramento.

Delin knew his papa wanted to spend as little time as possible in this city—in any city—but he was astounded by the sheer mass of population, unable to believe so many people could live in so small a place. He must have stood on the dock for almost a minute until Joshua dragged him away. The crowds rushed by, people with fancy clothes and top hats mingling with dirty, foul-smelling vagrants.

Joshua pulled him along and they scurried up a great hill, then continued on to the port around the northeast section of the city, where they bought passage on a mid-sized brig.

When they reached Sacramento, it was Joshua's turn to be astonished. The western terminus of the Transcontinental Railroad was waiting for them. A dusty locomotive stood ahead of some twenty passenger and cargo cars, and a small crowd jostled to get on board, waving their tickets in the sun.

"Too bad they didn't finish this sooner," Delin said in awe, after the porter had taken their tickets and ushered them into the dining car. "Back in 'sixty-two you could have used it to get to the War faster. It could have taken you all the way to Shiloh in just days instead of months!"

Joshua nodded as he adjusted his wide-brimmed leather hat and stared out at the rising Sierras. His face darkened as they traveled under a cloud, and his eyes took on a welling of pain, as if unwillingly reviewing past sights.

Delin noticed the changed expression and thought to divert the subject. "Are we going to go through a tunnel?"

Joshua sighed. "Sure—a large one. Blasted through the mountain by the Celestials."

"They were good with gunpowder?"

"Quite," Joshua said with a smile and when his eyes closed, Delin wondered what his father saw in the dark.

The train rolled on, and murmurs of conversation made their way through the crowded cart. Combined with the banging of silverware, spoons chinking inside of teacups and forks stabbing at plates, it all formed an original symphony in Delin's ears.

And while Papa was lost in thought, Delin listened in on a half-dozen conversations, hearing all sorts of things about the country and the world. He keyed in on one discussion concerning Alaska: a table of gentlemen in black suits and spectacles discussed the Navy's governing of the land, and how the pressure from settlers—most of them in the panhandle region—was leading to the introduction of some sort of civil and judicial law. One of them seemed to ridicule the notion that the land would ever become anything of value to the United States, and he hoped that Congress wouldn't waste more than a handful of judges and officials on its administration.

At another table, two ladies and two elderly men spoke in hushed, jealous tones about the amount of wealth streaming out of Comstock from Virginia City and making its way back to San Francisco. Delin learned that Virginia City boasted over eighteen thousand people now, and hundreds of mines. Nevada had become a state in 1864, and progress came quickly with the railroad. But some muffled voices contended that the greatest wealth had already been discovered, processed and carted away, and Delin heard staggering numbers—figures in the range of twenty or thirty million dollars being extracted every year.

The the incredible scenery rolled by in a blur as the sun began its descent below the dark peaks behind them. Ahead, the land shimmered in various hues of purple, white and rust. Sickly shrubs dotted the ground as far as Delin could see, along with huge patches of severed tree trunks, remnants of a once-mighty forest.

Shortly after they rode through the last tunnel in the Sierras, Delin had his first bite of steak—a medium-rare slab of juicy meat that he imagined tasted just a little sweeter than heaven. A pile of potatoes and a side of carrots rounded out his first meal on a train, and after he finished a deliciously sweet dessert, he looked up to see Papa grinning at him.

"Wipe your mouth, son," Joshua said with a glance about the car. "We don't want to attract any attention from this point on. So that means you act the part of a well-bred California boy. You keep your eyes down and you don't make any outbursts..."

"Or chew with my mouth open?"

"Exactly."

Delin folded his napkin and sat back with his hands in his lap. "Do you think they'll be looking for us?"

Joshua adjusted his hat, pushing a few red strands out of sight. "Knowing Quitch, I would expect so."

Nearly an hour before they were to reach their destination, Delin saw his father nodding off at their table. He had just finished a cup of coffee, and it was odd that he should be so tired all of a sudden, but Delin decided Papa needed the rest. After getting up quietly, he headed for the door at the rear, intending to get some air outside.

Between the cars, he stood on the metal walkway and watched the stars through the gap in the train sections. The air was crisp and would have felt much cooler if not for the smoke puffing from the locomotive three sections ahead, and the heat from the long day still radiating off the metal cars. Delin sighed, and wondered at fate—or whatever God had in store for him. Why was he here now—and was Mama's death necessary to push him out of that reclusive existence?

Maybe it was like Kreaga the Shaman had told him those many years ago: the Creator expected him to use his talent for the good of others. At the time, Delin supposed that meant for the good of the village. Now, though, with their departure from Alaska, he wondered if a wider population could benefit from his gifts.

He smiled and was about to let his mind wander, when the next car's door jolted open and banged against the wall, just inches from his face. Delin ducked out of the way and almost slipped off the train itself, spinning around at the last moment and catching himself on an exterior ladder. He climbed around and hung to the outside of the train, peeking his head around.

Two men in long brown coats walked out. They wore white hats that were either just purchased or recently cleaned, contrasting with the dirt and dust on the rest of their clothes. The first man spit an unsightly gob of tobacco at his feet, then put his hands on his hips. When the coat pulled away from his body, Delin noticed the shine of a black revolver at the man's belt, beside a silver star.

"We arrive in an hour," he grunted to his friend. And when he talked, Delin saw that his mouth glittered—it took a moment to realize that several teeth must be made of silver.

The other man, shorter and a little heavier, spat as well, and shook some dirt off his boot. "Let's get him now, then."

The man with the silver teeth nodded. "Can't believe he took the bait."

"In a such a hurry to rescue her. Never suspected we let the letter get on through."

Delin nearly choked on his tongue. He shifted to the side, and pulled himself out of sight, fighting the whipping wind and the smoke blowing past. He shuddered. Did they know Papa traveled with his son?

He had to find a hat, or another disguise—and they had to get off this train!

"All right then," Silver Teeth said and stomped on ahead. "Let's move."

After they passed into the dining car, Delin swung himself around, landed and slipped through the closing door. Seeing no alternative, he skipped around the men and raced forward, only to see a man sitting with Papa.

Delin froze, and the two men behind him came to a stop on either side of him, their hands on their revolvers.

And the thin, ghoulish-looking man at the table smiled as he reached for the coffee cup in front of Joshua. He inspected it, then nodded. "Good. Gentlemen, he is ours."

"Thanks, Dr. Dreggel," said Silver Teeth, clamping a huge hand on Delin's neck. "Too bad this one doesn't drink coffee."

The bald man lifted his bony shoulders in a shrug. "Not to worry.

Let him sit and watch his father dozing peacefully until we reach Comstock, and then take him up to the mine."

The hand shoved him forward, and the two men slid into the booth beside him, trapping him against the window. Delin's hopes disintegrated as he watched Papa, who looked pale and helpless, jostling with the motion of the train.

Delin simmered and tried to push back against the weight of these lawmen. *I won't let it happen again*, he thought. *I'll save him like I should have saved Mama. There won't be any fearsome monsters up ahead at that mine. Only men.*

Only men, Delin repeated to himself, hoping to find some comfort in the words. *Just one man in particular. And his son.* Delin shivered, and something told him that, even so, maybe there were worse monsters loose in the world than the Sesquats.

REUNION

"Welcome to the Comstock Lode, little Wetherwax. My son tells me the resemblance to your father is uncanny, so I will take his word for it."

After a perilous mine car ascent, Delin had been led inside the mountain, through a series of winding passages and timber beam-supported corridors; he now stood in a large, hollowed-out chamber with black-sooted walls and a huge, steam-driven hoist against the far wall. An enormous spool with cranks, pipes and gears surrounded the coiled rope attached to a waiting cage. Oil lamps burned in the unevenly-hacked walls, and the whole cavern danced in crudely twisted shadows and reeked of smoke and burning metal.

After a minute spent adjusting to the light and allowing his pounding heart to calm, Delin took note of the people inside. Apart from the hideously thin Dr. Dreggel, with his labored breathing and incessant wheezing, there was a sweaty-faced man operating the controls on the hoist. The two lawmen from the train stood in front of one of the elevator cages, with their backs to Delin.

Then there was the man who spoke—a tall figure in a black suit and a vest dotted with glittering silver buttons, large as twenty-dollar gold eagles. He was hatless, and wore small, dark spectacles, as if the lenses had been painted over and reflected nothing beyond or within. A razor-thin mustache framed his lips, and his thinning hair was greased back in ropy threads across his glistening skull.

The man said, "Your father's stink is about you boy, and believe me, in the past few minutes, I've had more than enough time to reacquaint myself with the Wetherwax stench."

"Save it, Quitch," a defiant voice said from the back of the room. The two men in leather coats stepped away and revealed their prisoner.

"Papa!" Delin shouted, seeing him for the first time since they left the train; his hands were bound behind his back, his face bruised and his lip cut, but otherwise he was grinning and full of energy.

"Delin. Are you hurt?"

"Not yet," said a new voice, with a powerful and youthful inflection. A young man emerged from the shadows. Slightly shorter than his father, Jericho Quitch was dressed in a plaid vest, with rolled-up sleeves, pressed black slacks and shiny boots. His long face narrowed to a point on his hairless chin under a bowler hat, where dark curls waved from its cap. Dancing flames reflected in his pupils like tiny eruptions on the surface of two dark, lifeless planets.

He glanced back at Joshua, then returned his attention to Delin. "'A tree is recognized by its fruit,' eh, Father?"

"Indeed," said the elder Quitch as he cocked his head. "Hmm, Matthew is it not? Chapter twelve..."

"Verse twenty-three," Jericho finished. He bowed slightly to Delin. "An education spent in the endless study of Scripture. A little hobby of mine, the sole valuable gift my mother ever sent my way. Perhaps..."

He glanced back to Joshua. "Perhaps she meant to mold me after someone else she once loved?"

Joshua's face darkened. "Sadly, those Biblical lessons do not appear to have taken root."

"Oh, I think they have. I'm quite excellent at finding the perfect quote for any occasion. Take for instance, the circumstances by which you left my father."

Quitch grunted, and lifted his spectacled face to the high ceiling. His son continued: "'Forsake not an old friend. For the new is not comparable to him.' —Ecclesiastes nine, verse ten." Jericho spun around in a full circle, tilting on one heel with his hands outstretched, as if expecting applause.

Delin frowned, dismayed but distracted by the rough hands of the other two guards, holding his shoulders.

"Or how about this one?" Jericho asked, sauntering over to Joshua, boldly leaning forward, until their faces were just inches apart. "'The wicked flee when no man pursueth, but the righteous are bold as a lion.' Proverbs, twenty-seven..."

"—Twenty-*eight*, verse one." Joshua corrected. "Pick and choose all the passages you like, boy. I fled from your father's evil before he could corrupt me, and my only regret is that the misfire of his gun did not penetrate further beyond his eyes."

Quitch gasped, but Joshua kept going. "Release your mother, boy, and release us. There's still hope for you."

Jericho merely grunted, then tried to think of a retort.

Joshua looked over Jericho's shoulder and called out, "Come, Benjamin, does your boy speak and see for you? Have you no senses left of your own?"

Quitch turned toward the sound of Joshua's voice. Then he pointed toward the entrance, beyond Delin. "Fortunately, old friend, after you robbed me of my sight, I did develop the other senses. Namely, touch."

A cool breeze and the scent of cinnamon wafted by, and Delin caught a glimpse of blonde hair, and a long gray dress, and then the woman the guards led into the room was snatched by the wrist and dragged forward. She cried out as Quitch spun her sharply and wrapped one hand around her breast and the other about her throat, facing her toward the elevator cages.

"Caroline!" Joshua seemed to deflate at her sight, and only Silver Teeth's grip prevented him from collapsing. Delin saw such pain in his father's eyes that he knew Quitch had won. Forget the Biblical parallels, forget the interweaving of destiny or the faint breath of angel wings. The Devil held sway here, and up on this mountainside, near the foul-smelling pits dug deep into the fiery bowels of the earth, it would end for them.

"I'm sorry," Delin heard the woman whisper, and in those two words, more emotion spoke than in her entire letter. Joshua screamed and lunged—one last ditch effort, but the men were too strong and held him fast.

Jericho chuckled; he had glided over to his father's side, and he whispered in his ear.

"Ah, quite true, my son." Quitch eased his hold on Caroline, then pushed her to one side where she stumbled and fell to her knees. Not more than five feet from Delin, he reached out to her, but his own guards pulled him back.

Quitch waved a multi-ringed hand in the air. "My son reminds me of the rumors I'd heard, old friend. Something about your wife—what was it? Oh yes, she was slaughtered by some hairy arctic monster. How tragic!"

Joshua moaned and hung his head.

Quitch snickered. "Never were too lucky in love, were you? I hear too that you deserted her when she needed you, just as you deserted our unit back in Shiloh..."

"Beast!" Caroline hissed, on her hands and knees, her blonde hair, graying at the sides, mopping on the greasy floor.

"Please, mother," Jericho said, spreading out his arms again. "Look at all we've done for this town, for our investors, and for the city of San Francisco. The majestic palaces there upon Nob Hill, the great opera house here, all built upon our silver. Thousands of families enjoying comfortable lives thanks to us. Haven't we earned the right to a little revenge?"

"A petty thing, really," Quitch added, slapping his son on the shoulder. "A bit of closure. It's been a long time since Shiloh, dear Joshua."

Joshua regained his feet, and his composure. He held his chin up, and did his best not to look toward Caroline. "Very well, Benjamin. Then take your revenge as you see fit. But let my son go, and release Caroline."

Quitch shook his head, smiling. He gingerly walked up to Joshua, led along by his son. When he was close enough he reached out and grabbed hold of Joshua's smooth chin. "Ah, shaved, for once. Can't imagine how you look now, but I can only think back to our youthful days on the docks in Richmond, before you could even grow a mustache.

"Remember our fateful last day on the Providence?" Quitch moved his face closer until his dark glasses misted with Joshua's breath. "I spoke to you of a grand destiny, and you weakly went along with it, even though I knew you doubted my vision. I succeeded despite you, Joshua Wetherwax.

"Now I've drawn you back in. Actually it's more like I reached the other side of a chessboard, and already having my queen, I requested you—a mere knight—to return to the game. But it's only to teach you a lesson."

"What lesson is that?" Joshua whispered. "You've already taught me everything about evil there is to know, and I've spent a lifetime trying to cleanse it from my soul."

Jericho muttered something that Delin couldn't quite hear. He only saw his father and his old enemy face to face. Movement caught his eye; Caroline had turned her head to him, and she was staring, open-mouthed.

It took Delin a moment to realize what it was she focused on, and then he understood. The gold cross around his neck—it had come out from under his collar, and now swung below his chin, glinting in the lamplight and sparkling like a firefly in Caroline's eyes. Tears fell down her cheeks, and amidst her soft sobs, Delin saw a tiny smile break free.

Quitch's voice boomed across the walls and echoed down into the mineshaft. "No, Joshua. Don't worry about your son or Caroline now. They are beyond your control, and you should only prepare yourself for what lies ahead." Quitch backed away, walking slowly to the great machinery of the hoist.

"I have thought many long years on the nature of my revenge, and how best to exact it. Of course I could just pluck out your eyes, but no; that would be far too easy."

Jericho snickered in agreement. And Dr. Dreggel wheezed uncomfortably.

"No, I have something much more fitting." Quitch pointed to the man at the controls, then waved his other hand toward Joshua, and the lawmen at his side immediately moved him toward the open cage. "You will be taken down to the deepest shaft, the one we have labeled Mahomet."

Delin gasped. That name! He had just read about that. A devil in the Inferno; the corrupter of Christianity.

"It's only two thousand feet deep," Quitch continued. "Not the furthest we've gone, but—unfortunately for several hapless miners—quite deadly. Steam down there reaches a hundred forty degrees, and I'm not sure, but there could be some breaches where the scalding water has plunged into the shafts. We only dug about five hundred feet; found nothing of consequence, and were forced to leave it or else bring in some heavy pumps.

"Who knows?" Quitch said with a grunt. "Maybe, given time, your prospecting skills could save Mahomet and turn a profit down there, but I doubt you'll have such time. Also, in case I hadn't mentioned it yet—you won't have any light." Quitch buttoned his coat and held out his arm for Jericho to take and lead him.

Quitch paused at the chamber entrance, just feet from where Delin battled with his rage. "You may last a half hour down there in the dark—maybe only ten minutes. My only misgiving is that I cannot actually see your face as you as you die."

Jericho cleared his throat. "But don't worry, father, I'll remind you often of how he looks right now. That face of fear and oh-so-tragic disbelief."

"Your son, by the way," Quitch added, "will be put to work down in the lower levels of my factory. Helping at the vats with Dr. Dreggel. Maybe shoveling out the processed silver. Do him good, I suspect, to perform some honest work."

"Quitch!" Joshua yelled as he was dragged back into the cage and held there by the two men—both of whom were accompanying him down to the lowest levels to ensure he got off at the right stop.

"Yes, old friend? What, do you need, some last words?"

Joshua took a deep breath, and closed his eyes. "Your son loves to quote the Bible. Here's one for you, and may you hear it for the rest of your blessedly short life. 'Go now, ye rich men, weep and howl for your miseries that shall come upon you. Your gold and silver is cankered, and the rust of them shall be a witness against you, and shall eat your flesh as it were fire. Ye have heaped treasure together for the last days!'"

Jericho snorted. "James. Five, one to three." Something passed across his expression—something unreadable to Delin, but he actually thought it might have been grudging respect.

Then the elder Quitch yelled to the hoist man, "Drop him!"

The levers groaned and squealed, and the great spool began to turn. Delin pulled at the rough hands, but couldn't move. Caroline stood and stumbled forward, hands out to Joshua—but the cage was shaking, moving.

Joshua called out, "Delin!" And as Silver Teeth and his partner held him inside the cage, Joshua curiously lifted one leg—just a couple inches—but enough that Delin could notice.

His eyes went wide and his mouth opened. There was a glint of silver peeking out from his papa's boot. Caroline stopped short as well—she had seen it too.

The dagger. Her dagger, the silver blade she had given him a lifetime ago, the very jeweled weapon that almost found its way into Samuel Colt's possession in that poker game. The dagger. Delin held to that thought, and the expression of secret victory on Papa's face, as the cage descended with a horrifying rattle. The huge spool spun around with dizzying speed, and steam hissed out from the pipes and pulleys.

Almost a full minute passed in silence, as Quitch and Jericho stood, waiting for the spool to slow and then come to a complete stop.

When it did so, the ensuing quiet was something Delin sensed was a good sign. Quitch seemed nervous. He cocked his head, straining for the subterranean sounds that maybe only he could hear.

Finally, the bell above the hoist rang, triggered by the tug rope far below. The signal to raise the cage received, even if it was later than expected, settled Quitch's agitation. He smoothed out his coat and rubbed his perspiring forehead.

Jericho took off his hat and did the same, running his fingers through the wet black curls. "We'll pay the Reno lawmen back at the casino, I expect. They've earned their reward."

"Quite so," said Quitch.

The rope hissed and re-coiled even faster than it had spun down. Caroline continued to shuffle forward, toward the awaiting cage's cradle. She held her hands clasped against her chest and mumbled something in quiet to herself.

"Mother, get away from there." Jericho strode forward and reached for her—only to have her yank her arm away, and then point with a trembling hand.

The cage reappeared, rocking to a hard stop and clanging against the metal frame. It shook loosely and creaked on its hinges. "No..." Jericho mouthed. "It can't be."

"What?" asked Quitch. "What, WHAT?"

Caroline turned, straightened her shoulders, and smiled, holding her chin up high. "Tell him, son. Tell your father. Give him bad news for once."

"What!" Quitch roared and stumbled forward. He waved his arms until he caught Jericho, then gripped him about the lapels.

"Dead," Jericho said at last. "They're dead."

"Who?"

"Morty and Harrison. The men from Reno."

Quitch's shoulders sagged. "How?"

"Dagger, by the looks of it," Jericho said. The color had gone from his cheeks, and he wobbled uncertainly on his feet.

Delin strained and tilted his head until he could see around Caroline. The two bodies were in a heap on top of each other. A lot of blood was spattered about their clothes. And the silver hilt stood embedded in the chest of the man he had been calling Silver Teeth.

Smiling, even in the face of such violence, Delin gave in to a burst of laughter. Quitch pointed in his direction. "Take that boy away and shut him up."

"Go ahead," Delin taunted. "My father's coming for me."

Quitch spun around and slapped Jericho blindly in the chest. "Get the maps out, now! Find out what other shafts he could have gotten into before they reached Mahomet."

"There's only a couple, father, and we have men down there, and..."

"Send more, then! I want those shafts searched and when they find him, don't hesitate—I want a pick in his skull, or a drill bored through his foul heart."

"Yes, father!"

"NOW!"

Caroline chuckled and clapped her hands together.

And the last thing Delin saw before Dr. Dreggel and his cronies dragged him away was Quitch shuffling around, blindly flailing his arms, trying to grab hold of his laughing wife, who kept dancing and spinning out of his reach.

Delin was put to work immediately upon reaching the factory. After the two-minute descent on the rail car down the side of Mt.

Davidson, they finally banked around a series of rounded turns and rolled along a straight path into what looked like an enormous barn door. It turned out to be just the top level of eight immense floors in Quitch's processing mill.

Dreggel and two lanky men with sidearms led Delin down a sturdy wooden staircase around and around into the guts of the mill. Delin gaped in astonishment at each level's tremendous machines, starting with the black-iron crushers at the top—the great pounding pillars that repetitively beat down upon the ore dropping from the cars above. The remaining fist-sized chunks were then pitched down to the next level—to the stamps, where Delin paused briefly to watch these pieces mix with tons of water, then get strained and smashed again.

Pushed ahead and nearly tripping down the stairs, Delin peeked out at the next level, which held the vanners: huge belts that further winnowed out worthless minerals. Finally, the resulting mixture poured into one of twenty immense amalgamating vats on the next level.

"This is where you're to work, boy!" Dreggel hissed with glee in his voice. His breath wheezed and he spread out his arms as if embracing the entire floor and its cyclopean denizens, the great vats: tanks of mercury, sulfur, chlorides and trace amounts of other volatile chemicals. Dozens of haggard, grease-soaked men looked up from their tasks, and to Delin they seemed like the souls of the lost, gazing up from their personal hells to glimpse their returning master.

The floor shook with steam-driven power, and the vats trembled while other great pans gurgled out a sloppy, scalding mixture that seeped down pipes to the final level below. There, the settling tanks took the liquid sludge and separated mercury from the gold and silver, and then flushed the tailings out onto the mountainside.

"Set him up on number twelve!" Dreggel ordered, shouting over the tremendous grinding and hissing. The two men dragged Delin down the final steps and marched him through pockets of hot steam and foul odors. The sun lit up two rows of windows with the false light of hope, but everyone's eyes were hooded and their faces grim as they poured out chemicals and shoveled steaming sludge. Others operated great wheels on top of the vats, controlling the flows in and out of the tanks.

Dreggel climbed a steeply turning staircase to a solid metal platform outside his office. This was his perch, where he controlled the entire process at the mill—from ordering supplies and devising chemical combinations to creating and delivering the final output. Delin watched him ascend until clouds of steam got in the way, and the next thing he knew he was herded into the midst of a dozen men with shovels working alongside a fifty-foot long belt. A bubbling mixture swirled by, and the men pushed at it, shoveling it along, directing the flow into certain runoffs at the direction of superintendents.

The two gunmen caught a superintendent's eye and nudged Delin. "New kid," one of them said. "He doesn't leave here. Lock him in the supply room at the end of the shift."

The superintendent—a short man with bushy brown sideburns and wearing filthy overalls—nodded and said, "To work, kid. Cousin Jack there to your left will show you what to do. Lunch is at noon, then you'll work straight through till six."

Delin wheezed. The air was brutal, almost unbearably hot, and the foul reek of chemicals burned at his eyes.

"What're they payin' ee, my son?" The man to his left, the one called Cousin Jack, asked, shoveling with a grunt and grinning at him. He was missing three front teeth.

"Nothin'," Delin replied, taking the shovel he offered. He wasn't sure how much this man knew or whether everyone was in league with Quitch, so he didn't want to elaborate.

"I hear that, my 'andsome lad. Never pays us enough." He slammed down the shovel then fired it forward and scooped it up. "See that there? More silver in that there scoopfull than my whole clan ever mined back in Cornwall."

Delin hefted the shovel. "You're from England?"

"Right'ee are, lad. Come to California just after the gold was all gone from them forty-niners. Then missed the boat at Leadville. Never got to see the damn Elephant."

"Not many did," Delin answered, and closed his eyes for a moment. Going to see the Elephant. That was a phrase his papa had explained to him years ago—the story went that some hopeful forty-niner, newly arrived in California, heard about a visiting circus and spared no effort to catch up to it, to reach his burning goal of seeing an elephant. That story took on such a mythic character it got wrapped up in the notion of men expending their dreams and sometimes their very lives, all to experience a gold strike firsthand.

Jack nodded as if Delin's answer held an immeasurable wealth of wisdom. "I even missed out on Black Hills in 'sixty-four. So now I'm up here, makin' just about the same—six dollars a day. Minin's in my family's blood, and I don't get to do none of it. Not like in the beginnin' when the mine owners 'preciated the value of a good Cornishman."

"Know what you mean," Delin said and sent his shovel into the steaming mass in imitation of what the others were doing. "Except I'm a prospector."

"No kiddin?" Jack laughed. "Yer probably too young to be frequentin' the taverns 'round here, but did you ever hear the old prospecting joke us Cornishmen like to tell?"

"What's that?" Delin asked, holding his breath.

"If anyone asks us where they can find some gold, we answer, 'Well, sorr, where gold is, it is, and where it ain't, there I be!'"

Delin thought for a moment, then grinned. He decided at the very least, he could trust a man who knew how to joke about his predicament. So he took a deep breath, and the next time the superintendent looked away, Delin told the Cornishman who he was and why he needed to escape.

The day passed, and Delin and Jack didn't get much chance to talk. After lunch—a quart of water and a cold ham and sourdough roll—they were separated, and Delin was sent to the end of the line where the superintendent could watch him closely, directly under the office window of Dr. Dreggel. Every so often he'd look up, and most times that pale bald skull would be peering down at him.

At lunch, Jack had brought him over to meet his mates—men with names like Martie and Jenkins. He explained Delin's plight to them, and they uttered foul curses when Delin got to the part about his papa being sent below.

"Quitches—the two of them," Jack hissed. "Both the same side of a bad shilling. Tell ee what, we'll keep our ears open, and Martie here'll send word to his brother. Ee's a blasting foreman down in the shaft called Seventh Circle. They'll be on the lookout fer yer pa, and protect him as best they can."

Delin grinned and almost cried his thanks. He hoped it wasn't too late for such aid. He went back to work, and somehow the hours passed; his muscles almost gave out, straining as they'd never worked before. Finally, at six, the shift ended. The cars stopped coming from the mines, and the men went home.

The superintendent led Delin to a dark supply cabinet. Inside was a single cot amidst crates, boxes, shovels and other tools. The door locked behind him and the lamp went out. Delin was sure he could find something in here to help him escape, but right now, after that day of grueling work, he could only stumble to the hard cot and fall face-down.

He was fast asleep in minutes.

When he awoke in the dark, a cloaked figure knelt beside him holding a candle and pressing a finger to his lips.

"I don't have much time," came the voice, and Delin barely registered it. Familiar, somehow—and then came the scent of cinnamon. The finger traced his cheeks, then descended to his chin—and lowered to his neck where long nails pricked lightly at his skin and touched the gold chain.

"This was mine once," came the whisper. "When I gave it to him, he looked much like you do now. Every bit as beautiful."

"Caroline..." Delin said, and glanced around in the dark room, suspicious of the shadows huddled in the corners.

"Hush, just listen." Soft blue eyes held onto his, and blonde strands poked from under the hood. "I'm taking a great chance, but it's long overdue. My husband and my son are still up at the mine entrance, poring over the maps, sending down search parties and scouts—murderers."

Delin choked back a cry.

"Don't worry," she said. "They're going to the wrong place. I know where he is."

"What?"

"Your new friends here. One of them sent word to me through a series of couriers and coded signals." She smiled. "You must have made quite an impact on them."

Delin shrugged. "They don't like their boss much either."

"Modest too, like your father." Caroline regarded him silently in the faint candlelight. "Tell me quickly, if you will: what was your mother like?"

Delin opened his mouth, struggling for the words to describe her. Instead, he just said what came to mind. "She was... everything that you meant to him. And giving up this cross was the hardest thing he's ever done. But he wanted me to have it, and he told me something—*that every gift of noble origin*—"

"—Is breathed upon by Hope's perpetual breath!" A soft sob escaped from the hood. "Oh God, Wordsworth. He remembered. Things should have been so different. I made such errors."

"So did Papa," Delin said. "At least, that's what he believes."

She held up a hand. "No more. 'Waste not fresh tears over past griefs.'" She tried to smile. "That's my own favorite quote, but I forget where I heard it."

Delin was about to tell her it was from Euripides, a Greek philosopher in 400 BC, but felt he should hold back.

"Tell your father that, if you two should make it out of here."

Delin reached and touched her hand. "We came for you, and we're leaving with you."

She shook her head. "I don't deserve to be rescued."

"But you will be," Delin said with a determined smile. "Where's Papa?"

Caroline took a breath. "He's found friends. An unlikely discovery—but just what Benjamin and Jericho were afraid of. Last week they had sealed off part of Seventh Circle where the miners had made a big strike."

"Sealed it off?"

"And locked the men inside. Oh, they've been sending down food and water, and the superintendents have orders to keep digging, but nothing gets brought out until Benjamin can manipulate the stock."

"What?" This place was every bit as convoluted and bizarre as he had imagined, and worse.

"He's buying up shares in that mine now when the prices are low, and then he'll leak out the word of the strikes, boost its value and sell them after demand soars."

"So what is Papa doing?"

Caroline smiled. "He found a way in to their sealed-off section through an old sump tunnel. The way the Cornishmen tell it—if I understood properly—he's freed the men down there, and now they are working their way up through the tunnels, pipes and lattices."

Delin imagined it all—his papa and a crowd of men behind him, with their miners' helmets and lamps blazing the way up narrow spaces and deserted passages.

"Here," said Caroline and presented Delin with a silvery object. "I took it off the dead man without Jericho's notice. Take it, and when the time comes, use it if you have to."

He held the cold hilt and stared at the reflective silver edge on the dagger that had recently killed two men. Delin met her warm stare, and his lips dried and his throat locked in a held breath. He couldn't think of what to say.

But she could, and with a desolate look of loss settling in her eyes, she spoke. "I don't know if your valiant rescue will succeed, dear boy. And I fear—no, I see—for myself, nothing beyond tomorrow. But you will go on, I know. Don't ever let the world take away your spirit."

She touched his face with both hands, then placed a soft kiss on his forehead, and lingered there as if savoring a long-misplaced treasure. Then she broke away, spun around and blew out the candle. In the darkness, her footsteps were muffled, and the door creaking, closing and locking, ended all sign of her presence.

Delin lay back, gripping the dagger tightly to his breast. He thought about calling after her and convincing her to flee into town, but logic held him back. No, he had earned friends here, friends he would need tomorrow. When Papa came out, he wouldn't be alone. And this time they would have the advantage.

He closed his eyes, and when he quickly lapsed into a dream, he stepped into a world of ice and snow, where a great lumbering beast with red eyes and charred flesh patiently waited in the blizzard for his return.

Chapter 15: Nevada - December 13, 1882

SHOWDOWN

IT WAS FIVE THIRTY WHEN the superintendent woke him up. "Move it, kid." He dragged Delin outside and pointed to the enormous belts churning into motion between two huge vats. "Silver never sleeps, and gold's impatient."

The rest of the floor was in motion; men crawled around ledges and stairways, and operated wheels and levers. Steam hissed from everywhere and intense heat blew across his face. Delin looked past the foreman and saw Jack and Martie at their posts, stretching and rubbing their hands together. Jack caught his eye, winked, and gripped the shovel handle like an ax. Something's up, he understood. Whatever happened, he'd be ready. The dagger was strapped with a shoelace down inside his boot, with his pant leg over it—just as Papa had done.

He thought of his poor dogs, how they had fought by his side last year. Was it only last year? Now he had new allies, and an enemy just as dangerous. And now...

"Hey, kid! You're wanted up there." He stopped short as the foreman pointed to the top of the winding metal staircase, to the ledge where Dr. Dreggel stood and waved a bony hand.

Delin pulled back, and glanced over to the Cornishman, who saw Dreggel, then looked away. "Don't make a scene," the superintendent hissed in his ear. "Follow me."

Grudgingly, Delin went with him. They ascended slowly, their heavy boots clanging on the stairs like death knells. The railing was hot to the touch, and Delin wished he had brought his gloves.

Finally, at the top, he paused and stared out at the entire area, the twenty steaming vats, the scores of men shoveling and grinding the processed ore.

Directly below, almost thirty feet down, an open tank churned with a frothy, gray bubbling mass, and steam rose right up to his feet.

"My contribution to the Comstock fortune," Dr. Dreggel said, sliding over to the waist-high rail beside Delin. He wore a perfectly-clean white silk shirt, a dark vest that seemed too big for his bony torso, and a checkered bow-tie. Spidery fingers tapped against each other as he peered through his thick glasses and surveyed the floor. "The result of years of trial and error—the perfect blend of chemicals."

His nose made an odd clicking noise. "The alchemists of old could only dream of this, but I have achieved it."

"Why am I here?" Delin asked, eager to get away.

Dreggel lowered his head. "I have been given permission to try out a new drug of mine. An elixir, if you will. One that will be used on the miners on the deepest levels."

Delin coughed, and glanced down again. Some of the men around his workstation were missing. He had to keep the doctor talking. "What does this drug of yours do?"

"It holds down body temperature. Men can only work in fifteen minute shifts down in the mines, and must carry loads of ice just to survive." Dreggel shook his head. "That must change. This mine, and Quitch's corporation, must pull ahead of the others. The riches are hiding deeper and deeper, resisting our innovations. Silver is drying up at the Comstock, boy, and unless we go after it, deeper, we'll be finished here before too long."

"Isn't that the way of all gold and silver strikes?" Delin asked. "Nothing lasts forever, or did you expect it to?"

Dreggel shot him a look. "Considerable investments have been made here. Just look around. Machinery, construction, trade. A thriving economic system has sprung up, from the Coast and back, all supported by what we do."

He turned and stalked back into the office, waving for Delin to follow. "We are not giving up until every ounce has been plucked, pulverized, amalgamated and purified."

"I'm not taking any drug of yours," Delin said, following slowly.

The foreman came along and stood in the doorway. Delin glanced around the cramped, one-window room. The single desk was a polished cherry wood, with nothing but a neat stack of papers and a set of clear glass beakers in the middle. The far wall supported a large bookshelf packed with medical and scientific texts.

But what drew his attention, tugging at it gently as if to point out what was so out of place, was the cloaked figure sitting at a chair in the far-left corner.

"Ah, yes," Dr. Dreggel said, pointing. "My first trial. Last night I caught her leaving your room. A simple cloth soaked with a chemical treatment—one that young Jericho employs quite frequently and with great success on the girls in the French Quarter—and she was out."

"Caroline, no!"

"Stay right where you are, kid."

Delin glanced back and saw a revolver pointed at him.

"Now," Dr. Dreggel said. "Where was I? Oh yes. Her husband offered her use as a test case. You're actually quite lucky, boy—the first trial was meant for you."

"Is she—?"

A moan escaped from the hood, and her chin emerged into the light, then her face. But her eyes were still closed.

Dreggel shrugged. "She is not dead. However, her body temperature is dangerously low. She may not recover if it drops any further."

Delin seethed. "Then get her warmer—bring her blankets!"

"Yes, I may have to do that. Since I do not believe Quitch will be happy if she dies. At least, not in such a peaceful way."

Delin stared at him, this diminutive bald man who seemed so void of any warmth himself. "Monster," he whispered.

"Now, now. You should be grateful. I took my time. Learned from my errors. Reduced the weighting of certain ingredients." He held up a flask filled with a blue-green liquid. "This may be it. Now, drink it down without a fuss."

"No."

Dreggel smiled. "Come, I'm offering a day away from the grueling labor down there. Just a quick drink, and then you can stay up here for some tests and observations."

At his back, the foreman grunted, and in the corner of Delin's eye, Caroline stirred. Stalling, Delin asked, "It doesn't taste as bad as whiskey, does it?"

"I would guess not." Dreggel placed the flask in Delin's reluctantly-offered hand. "Bottoms up, as we say in Berlin."

"*Aullaqtuq*," Delin replied, holding up the glass. "As we say in Alaska." *I'm leaving.* It was now or never. He couldn't count on whatever the Cornishmen were doing down on the work floor, so he opened his mouth as if to take a sip, then spun on his heels. He had just one moment to register the shock on the foreman's face and see that he had lowered the revolver. And then Delin launched the flask with all his strength.

It sailed true, struck with a heavy thud against the man's forehead—and then shattered. He screamed, rocked back, but didn't go down. Instead, he tried to aim the gun—but the liquid stung at his eyes.

Delin lunged, slammed his shoulder into the man's gut and grabbed hold of the gun with both hands. They struggled, and Delin switched his grip on the gun and swung upwards with it—connecting solidly with the foreman's chin. He rocked back and went down. Out cold.

Delin got to his feet and spun around—sure that it would be too late, that Dr. Dreggel was right behind him, ready to stab him with a needle or worse.

When he turned, he saw that it was worse. The little man stood beside the overturned chair. Caroline was on her feet, but only weakly—held up by his arm around her neck. In his other hand, Dreggel held a scalpel to her throat. Her eyes fluttered open and she tried to focus. "Joshua?"

"Hush!" Dreggel commanded. "Now, boy. Drop the gun!"

Delin wavered, still holding it trained on the doctor's bald head. This would be his first-ever shot with a revolver, and with Caroline so close, her hair in tangles and caught in her captor's face, it would have to be a miracle shot.

He raised his hands. "All right." He bent down and let it drop to the floor.

Dr. Dreggel pushed Caroline forward. "Move outside," he ordered.

"Is that you, Joshua?" Caroline's head sagged and one eye opened, straining to make out Delin's face. "I've missed you."

Delin backed away, stepping over the foreman. He took one step on the metal ledge, then another. “Yes,” he said, not knowing how else to respond.

“Joshua?” Caroline called, more desperate this time. “I can’t see. It’s been so dark, and so cold.”

“I’m here,” Delin said. “I’m with you.”

“Touching,” Dreggel said with a sneer. “Now move back.”

Delin took another step, and then saw motion to his left. Someone coming up the stairs. When he caught the bushy blond hair, the dirt-stained faces, and the cautionary finger on Jack’s lips, he turned back to Dreggel, stone-faced.

And the doctor came forward, pushing Caroline out first. She shivered in her white nightdress and sandals, and her face was deathly pale. In the corner of his eye, Delin saw Jack and Martie arrive on the ledge, then press themselves against the office wall.

They raised their shovels. And Delin took another step back, until he felt the railing at his waist and the heat from the boiling vat below.

“Now,” said Dr. Dreggel, taking another step out. “Stand there while I summon my—”

“Already here, laddie!” Jack shouted as he brought down the shovel. It clanged against the doctor’s shoulder and knocked him away from Caroline where he spun and hit the doorframe, then fell inside.

Martie caught Caroline as she fell. Delin ripped the dagger free from his boot, and made to pounce on the doctor.

But Jack stood between them and held out a restraining hand. “Whoa there, lad! Jes calm eeself down with that sticker. No sense you losin’ yer soul for murderin’ som’un.”

Delin lowered the blade, suddenly recalling similar words, and another hand that had once stayed Papa’s vengeance.

“’Sides,” Jack said, “we got the situation under wraps.” He pointed down to the floor, and Delin risked a glance. The workers were standing in a crowd around five foremen who looked to be on their knees. Several mates were waving up to them.

Martie waved back. “See, boy, ‘s’all good. I hear your pa’s coming out of the mine up at the top any minute, so we’ll rush there to greet ‘im.”

Jack grinned. “See, lad, that’s the way we do it in Cornwall. Us miners know how to treat a friend in need. We—"

A spot of red burst through his chest, and the loud pop didn't register in Delin's ears until Jack had toppled over sideways. And as the cloud of black smoke wafted out from the office, Dr. Dreggel emerged, favoring his wounded shoulder and pointing the revolver at Delin. In his other hand he still gripped the scalpel like a miniature sword.

He lined up a second shot when Martie screamed and lunged. The shot rang out and a man grunted just as Caroline, unsupported, collapsed on the top stair. Blood flew from Martie's side as he crumpled beside his friend, and then Delin yelled out. He swung with the dagger and slashed Dreggel's wrist just above the hand. The gun dropped, but the scalpel arced around toward his head.

Delin had an image of a huge talon slicing toward him, and for an instant he was back in the Tlingit courtyard, snow slapping at his face and the Sesquat advancing in a blur. He ducked instinctively and dropped to his knees. When the swing went wide and he sensed the body above him, Delin stood and tilted backward, flipping the weight off his shoulders.

Dr. Dreggel screamed as he rolled, lifted off his feet and flung into the air over Delin's back. His knee banged the railing, and his hand reached out for it—and caught the metal just as his body went over. He howled, but held on, his feet dangling thirty feet over the boiling vat.

His glasses immediately fogged up, and he spat while kicking and thrashing. Delin stood and bent over the rail. And for just an instant, he thought about prying the fingers loose, but it was a swiftly-passing guilty thought. The next moment he was reaching down to grab the doctor's wrist.

When suddenly Martie, back on his feet, ran to the rail and swung down with the backside of his shovel, slamming Dreggel's fingers and shattering them all against the hot metal. Delin gasped and looked over, only to catch the distant expression on Dreggel's face an instant before he fell into the boiling liquid of his own proud concoction. A molten splash surged up several feet, then spread out in concentric ripples. And no further sign appeared of the doctor.

"Martie," Delin shouted, seeing the blood.

"'Tis a scratch, lad," he said, holding his side. "Not like poor

Jack, who's gone on, ee has."

Delin looked to the body, but then caught another movement. Caroline struggled to rise, and her eyes were misted over. "Joshua, where are you? Father's home, you have to leave now."

"Here," Delin said when he reached her. He slipped her arm over his shoulders. "Let's help her down." He and Martie took her to the stairs and led her to the floor, where the others waited. By then, she had regained some color, and could stand on her own, but she still seemed out of it, lost in a hazy dream.

"Can she climb?" Martie asked.

"Doubt it," Delin said. "Can we leave her here?"

"'Kay. Brown and Willis'll look after the lass. Let's you and I get up there to that mine."

They ran up the main stairwell, together with seven other men, leaving the rest on the main floor to watch the loyal foremen. At the top only two empty cars waited, and men were already piling in. Delin and Martie got in the first car just as it kicked into motion, and Delin looked down, glad to see Martie had retrieved the revolver from the ledge.

"A car's coming this way," Delin said, pointing ahead. They had gone not more than thirty yards when the oncoming car came racing toward them.

"On the parallel tracks," Martie said. There were two sets, one for climbing and one for descending cars. "Cain't tell who 'tis."

Delin leaned forward in the rocking car, trying not to glance down. The drop here was about a hundred feet, and at the bottom, he could only see rust-colored rocks, boulders and earth fouled by the mill deposits. He peered ahead, and could make out six figures in the car. Martie operated the brake, slowing the car. He kept his revolver out of sight, but ready.

Then the sun peeked through a fat bulge of gray clouds, and the man in the head of the oncoming car seemed to glow. Despite the grime, dirt and ash in his hair, enough red poked through to catch in the sunlight and dazzle like a beacon.

"Papa!" Delin shouted and leapt from the car onto the tracks ahead. He ran towards the slowing car, then stopped as Joshua hopped out and embraced his son. The wind picked up and cooled their faces and dried what looked like tears from Joshua's soot-streaked cheeks.

"God be thanked," he said, gripping Delin tightly. He gave a wary glance to Martie, but then Delin pointed back to the mill. "Dr. Dreggel's dead, and the men are revolting, and Caroline is safe, and..."

"Easy, easy. Did you say Caroline is there?"

"Yes, and..."

"Let's go then. I don't know where Quitch and his son are. It's possible they might try to retake the mill."

Joshua led Delin into the crowded car with him, and they made room for Martie, who then released the brake. When they reached the insides of the mill, the others had gathered near the entrance, and someone was leading Caroline up the stairs.

"What's goin' on?" Martie asked, jumping out.

"Police are inside," the newcomer said. Whole platoon, seems like. Freein' the supers and arrestin' our mates."

"No..."

"Yep," the man said. "I seen 'em comin', and had the others hold 'em back while I take the lady up here. Figger we can get her up the tracks, then she and the lad and his pa can hoof it down the other side."

"Good idea," Martie said, as Joshua rushed by him. The crowd parted as he raced to Caroline. He searched her eyes, and for a moment Delin thought—hoped—he would just scoop her up in a great bear hug, but he stopped. Touched her face gently.

"My God," he whispered. "She's so cold."

"Joshua?" Caroline blinked and her eyes tried to focus. "My, you're filthy. Quit that job at the docks, I told you. Bad people out there. No good having friends like them."

He shot Delin a glance as he gently took her hand. Delin joined them and helped her along. "That doctor gave her something. It lowered her temperature, but messed up her mind."

Joshua helped her into the returning car, and once the three of them were inside, Martie offered the revolver to Joshua. "Might be's you need it."

"What about you?" Delin asked from inside. Already he could hear shouts from the stairwell, and pounding feet.

Martie shrugged. "Me and the boys'll come out okay. Blame the whole thing on that mad doctor. Go on, we'll hold 'em off 'slong as we can."

"Good luck," Joshua said. A quick handshake and they were gone—just as a group of men appeared from below. The car could still be stopped from down there, but hopefully they'd get far enough to continue on foot.

Delin stood in the back as Caroline sank to her knees, shivering. "Papa?"

He turned, squinting in the bright sun. "Yes?"

Delin held up the cross from around his neck. "I prayed that you'd escape."

"I know you did." He ran his hand over Delin's curly head. "We're going to make it. The miners I let out will spread the word, and Quitch will be in great trouble, I suspect."

Delin nodded. The wind tugged at his shirt and hair, and the car seemed to be pushing harder to get up the steepest ascent. "Will we come back for him?"

Joshua shook his head. "No, son. I'm done with revenge." He looked down at Caroline who was shivering and muttering to herself. "We have what we came for, and should count our blessings. We need to get her some medical help, and then—if it's all right with you, if you've had your fill of civilization—I'd like to go home."

Delin grinned and clapped his hands. "Perfect!"

Joshua smiled, but then the car stopped, braking abruptly. "Damn," he spat, looking back. Way down the hill, along the straight run of tracks, small specks ran about in the mill entrance. "Okay, let's get out and run for the mineshaft."

"Is it safe up there?" Delin asked as they lifted Caroline.

"I hope so," he answered, but his eyes looked worried. They lifted Caroline out, and Joshua scooped her up in his arms. "I'll carry her for the steeper part, then maybe she can walk."

Following behind them, Delin glanced back down, expecting to see another car on its way up, but nothing emerged from that dark interior. As he climbed, the dagger in his boot started to prick his skin, so he removed it and carried it. The sunlight glinted off its blade and sent sparkles ahead.

Joshua saw the blade and smiled. "You look like a young Greek hero—was it Theseus? The guy who fought Medusa."

"Perseus," Delin corrected. "Theseus killed the Minotaur."

"Oh, yes, how could I forget?"

Delin grinned, and clasped the handle tighter.

"At least that blade's stayed in the Wetherwax family," his papa added. "Almost had that thing won from me way back when."

I know, and I'll never lose it, Delin thought. They climbed until Papa's breathing became shallow, about the same time the tracks leveled off, then rose up at a much lower angle.

Only another twenty yards to the top: a timber-framed dark entrance set into the cliff face above a precipitous drop. Delin looked down and saw the steep, rocky descent and wondered how these tracks were ever constructed. It had to be over two hundred feet straight down until the mountain jutted out and angled back toward the mill.

Joshua set Caroline down, and she reluctantly stood, still keeping her arms about his neck. Delin took another look back, but now couldn't even see the factory. If anyone pursued them, they were going slowly.

"Come on," Joshua said. "Almost there." The revolver was tucked into his belt and he used both hands to steady Caroline as she shuffled up the tracks.

"Where are we going?" she asked. "Is it time for tea?"

Joshua helped her along. "No, darling. Not yet."

"I'm so cold. We should get inside by the fire. Father will welcome you now, you know. You're a great man."

Joshua paused. He looked into Caroline's face, and Delin imagined for a minute what they must have been like, all those years ago. A pang of guilt rushed through him that he could be happy with someone other than his mother, but...

But then a chill rushed by suddenly, like a warning. They were close the top. Another car sat facing them just ten feet away. It seemed empty, but Delin strained to see inside, sure he had seen something moving in there a second ago.

Joshua had started again, holding Caroline about the waist. He was smiling, and so was she. Her eyes sparkled slightly, and a little color had returned to her cheeks. They were nearing the car on their right. Delin's palms were sweating, and the knife handle loosened. He moved to catch up, and then saw it—

—not from the car, but from higher up. In the shadows. Someone emerged, followed by another person. Let it be Papa's friends, Delin prayed. Please...

Then Caroline dropped back and the arm about her withdrew. "Delin, be ready!" Joshua shouted, and the revolver came out.

The second man, dressed all in black with a wide hat, aimed a rifle at them. But that was as far as he got before a blast from the revolver caught him in the throat and knocked him down.

Joshua steadily moved the gun a couple inches to the left, and trained it on the blind man standing on the precipice. "Quitch!"

Delin caught Caroline and held her as she swayed, dangerously close to falling off the edge; he pulled her to the safety of the middle, held her tight with his left hand and readied his dagger. It was still about a thirty-foot throw, but if anyone else appeared, he would try it.

"Joshua, my friend!" exclaimed Quitch, alone with his hands folded. "Good to hear your voice again. We had a devil of a time down there searching for you. Tricky, beating us out."

"The tricks end now," Joshua said. "Just one shot, and I'll finish the job you started back in Shiloh."

Quitch spread out his arms. "I'm unarmed. And blind, or have you forgotten? You going to shoot me in cold blood?"

"Maybe I've finally learned something from you."

"What will your boy think?"

Joshua hesitated, then glanced over his shoulder at Delin, his eyes searching.

Don't worry about me, Delin meant to say. End this, he wanted to shout. It's a trap—it has to be.

All those things, any of those things, he should have said. But the words failed, his mouth hung open, and his papa hesitated. And in that moment, the car beside them shifted, and something emerged in a blur. Delin shouted and let go of Caroline, turning to throw the blade.

But Jericho Quitch rose out from the car, pointed a large, double-barreled rifle, aimed and fired. The roar bellowed across the valley and it seemed the sky went black. Warm liquid splashed onto Delin, and the smell of death rocked him backward.

The dagger flew, but sailed wide of its mark, clanging off the cliff face and dropping out of sight. And Jericho smiled, cocked the rifle and stepped out of the car.

A muffled, throaty cry reached Delin's ears after the gunshot's echoes had faded. And through the thin smoke blown his way, his papa looked up at him from a kneeling position. A great red hole had appeared in his back, just under his neck. Bloody pieces of his shirt had spread out from the impact like a daisy's petals.

"Who's been shot?" asked Quitch from above, inching his way down, feeling out with his feet for the wooden planks.

Jericho cleared his throat. "Just a nuisance. An obstacle surmounted at last."

Delin reached for his papa, heedless of Jericho, of Caroline, of Quitch approaching unsteadily. Numb, he made to grab Papa's quivering hand. Inches apart, the distance closed, and their fingertips touched for an instant.

"My son," Joshua whispered. "Mind your lessons..."

"Please," Delin cried, before his papa tipped, wobbling. Delin scrambled to his feet and lunged to grab him when a rifle butt jabbed his stomach and pushed him back.

Jericho snickered, and then pressed his boot against Joshua's chest. "For dust you are, and to dust you will return." Jericho savored the moment, then kicked out. And Delin's last glimpse of his father was of a man with his hands clasped as if deep in prayer, his eyes closed and his face at peace.

He tipped over, and dropped out of sight.

A scream tore the breath from the day, and it took an endless stretch of time measured not in moments, minutes or hours, for Delin to realize it was not his own, nor his father's. Caroline, shrieking, had pushed past him. She knocked Jericho aside and ran up to Benjamin Quitch.

She pounded at his chest, slapped his face, then finally threw her arms around him and beat at his neck and back. Jericho aimed the rifle, but lowered it immediately, as the pair spun around and around.

"Woman!" Benjamin Quitch shouted. "What are you doing? Unhand me—or guide to my son!"

Caroline calmed down, then let up on her hold, but still clung tightly to him. They were just past the cliff face, and Caroline's feet were only inches from the edge. “My husband,” she said, and buried her face in his chest.

His hands up in the air, his dark glasses pointing skyward, Quitch laughed. And Jericho lowered the weapon, aiming it instead at Delin, who still remained on his knees, staring in disbelief at the space where Joshua had just been.

Quitch softly pat Caroline’s head and smoothed her ruffled hair. “My dear. It’s over at last. We can now truly be together. Now you can be my eyes.” His face turned toward his son and his lips curled into a twisted smile.

“Yes,” Caroline said, and she turned in the same direction—only a little lower. Her eyes sought out Delin’s, and when he despondently lifted his head and saw her, he noticed the brilliance of her focus, the intent of her stare. She was out of her malaise, or enough so to act.

“Yes, dear Benjamin,” she said, still staring right at Delin. “I will be your eyes. Follow where I lead.”

Delin swallowed hard, and tensed. He didn’t know what to expect, but whatever was about to happen, he had to get up, to flee—or kill Jericho, better yet.

“Trust me,” Caroline said, and the next instant was only a blur in Delin’s eyes. He saw that she had bent her knees and tightened her grip around Quitch’s neck. But then—she was sailing backwards, throwing herself over the side. Benjamin Quitch hurtled over with her, arms flailing, legs kicking out like a spastic vaudeville puppet with its strings tangled up.

And then they were both gone and only one long, dwindling scream remained in their place.

“Father!” Jericho shouted as he moved, far too late. And then Delin was on his back, pounding him down, and then kicking and rolling. Certain he had sent his father’s murderer over the edge, he got up and ran toward the top.

A blast tore by his shoulder, and the heat stung at his skin. He stopped, turned and saw the boy reloading. Jericho hung with one leg on the tracks, the other dangling over and his stomach flat on the boards.

Delin swore, and then changed directions—and took three big steps, then jumped into the waiting mine car. Another shell sailed overhead and cracked into the mountainside.

He located the handbrake, just as he saw Jericho rising, cocking the rifle and raising it for another shot. Delin pressed the release as he remembered Martie had done, then threw his weight behind a push that set it free.

He looked sideways and the ferocity of his glare stayed Jericho's hand. And in the next moment, both boys, both suddenly orphans, stared at each other with a surging malevolence, an emotion so strong Delin sensed it could not have come from him.

An arctic wind cut through his soul, and the image of a raven floated in his mind; the foul stench of the Sesquat wafted in his senses and he heard its bellowing cry deep in his soul, the echo of the enemy before him now.

And then he ducked, and the car rocked with an impact. The car gained velocity and roared back down the tracks, down the mountainside, and away from the gun that kept firing and firing, blasting harmlessly into the air, drowning out the tortured screams of its user.

Delin sat and held back his tears. Not yet, not until this was over. When he thought it was safe, he peered over the edge and saw the approaching factory, its entrance still dark and empty. But he wasn't going to risk it.

No, he'd brake the car soon. Just up ahead, around the curve. He could see the drop from there to the ground was manageable. A simple climb down the timbers.

Then he'd be on the ground, and could chart his way around those gullies and make it overland to the Chinese encampment he had seen earlier. He was getting out of this place. Honoring his father's wishes. Minding those lessons.

Living to fight another day.

And, he imagined—starting to grieve. For his papa, and at last, for Mama, and for Caroline as well. He'd grieve for them all, and one day, when he made it back to Alaska and the land that was his home, he would sit out every night. Waiting and hoping.

Longing for the green shimmers of the Northern Lights, the undulating bands of luminosity, and the glittering shields of the spirits.

And on those nights, he would see them again.

BOOK TWO

"Moralizing, I observed, then, that 'all that glitters is not gold....' (but) I could go further than that, and lay it up among my treasures of knowledge, that nothing that glitters is gold."
—Mark Twain, Roughing It

Chapter 16: Northern California - December 5, 1889

CLIMBING MOUNT SHASTA

At three o'clock in the morning, the brilliance of the stars extended like eight-point lances. The planets dazzled like miniature suns, the soft folds of the Milky Way waxed in transparent glory and the heavens seemed only an arm-length away. The split precipices of the cratered summit waited above, between the steam vents and hissing lava beds.

These two explorers were not the first to ascend this most beautiful—if debatably second-highest—mountain in California, but to do so in the midst of winter, with heavy storm clouds threatening, made it dangerously exciting. For the adventurers Thomas Jacobson and Stephan Moore, that was the thrill: to climb this majestic juggernaut at a time no one else would dare.

Even the noted naturalist John Muir, who had reached the summit several times in the last decade, hadn't braved it this late in the season. And there would be no help from the townspeople down in Strawberry Valley. The hotels had closed for the year; the leagues of resort-seekers had returned to their cities on the coast weeks ago, having soaked in the medicinal hot springs and relished in the beauty of the meadows under the perpetually snow-capped Mt. Shasta.

Below them lay almost twelve thousand feet of the most beautiful landscape either had ever seen. Dense carpets of cascading snow drifts unrolled in steep angles down to the timber line. But it was here, beside the venting fumaroles and the sulfuric gasses hissing from the mountain, that Jacobson and Moore almost lost their nerve.

The ascent seemed unmanageable. Normally, climbers made camp at the edge of the timber line, then pushed to the summit and back down on the following day—when conditions were amenable, such as in late July or August. Now, however, the adventurers second-guessed themselves, and as the storm clouds massed, unveiling dark cumulous banners, they debated heading back down.

Then, sudden fortune arrived in the form of a guide. A lone wanderer emerged from the frosty darkness, as if summoned from the heart of the ancient volcano. His beard ice-coated, his eyebrows bushy and his blue eyes aglow, he came to them just as the sun descended and the winds roared, when it seemed the mountain itself tried to shake them off its hide.

He neither offered a name, nor asked theirs; and he did not question their decision to brave Shasta so late. He helped them dig out a trench beside the fissures and light a fire from old fir logs. Then he shared some dried venison and settled down to wait out the storm.

As they shivered on one side and roasted on the other, depending on whether back or front faced the hissing vents, they tried to keep their spirits up, and asked their guide for some local history, peppering him with questions to pass the time.

"We hear gold was discovered in the valley, back in the fifties," Moore said, sipping his coffee.

The guide pulled at his nose, keeping it warm, then brushed off the snow from his mustache. His face and body outwardly suggested a young man, perhaps in his early twenties, but his eyes told a different story—as if they belonged to one who had borne witness to several full lifetimes.

"Aye," he said. "You heard true. The 'Niners ventured north, following the Sierras, hoping for similar discoveries like those dying out in the Sacramento Valley. Prospectors looked, found a little, and Strawberry Valley got its start, but the stampede didn't last long."

"Mined out quickly?" Moore asked.

"Nah," said the guide, and he tapped his boot against the lava rock beside the fire. "Shasta was too fiery in her youth, too reckless. Volcanic soil and glacial activity are not the best midwives for the delivery of gold. No, for that birth you need some fiercely running streams and active erosion."

Moore scratched at his back, and steam slipped around his cheeks. "Do you know why this mountain is called 'Shasta'?"

Their guide laughed to himself. "Many people have their own thoughts on that. But the truth is, the Russians named it first. Settling at Bodega on the coast, they could see this mountain, rising starkly white. They called it 'Tehastal', which means white, or pure mountain. American settlers spelled it phonetically as Chasta, then dropped the hard ch for an S."

The guide then pulled out a small brownish stick that even in the blowing winds produced a strong fragrance of licorice. As he started nibbling, he said, "But that was before my time."

"And how long have you been here, sir?" asked Moore.

The guide chewed on the licorice stick some more, but selfishly didn't offer them any. "Seven years, give or take. Too long. Too long away from my home and my... remaining family. The mineral springs have been calming and rejuvenating, but I must soon move on. Return to my responsibilities. Return to use my gifts to benefit those who need them most."

Moore shivered and stamped his feet. His face, beaten by the wind, felt like it had been doused with ice water. "Seven years... Doing what in that time, may I ask?"

The guide shrugged. "Odd jobs. Chopping at the timber mills, some railroad work. Prospecting."

"Oh, a prospector!" snapped Jacobson. "Maybe you've heard the rumors down in the valley?"

The man cocked a frosty eyebrow and crunched down on another bite of licorice. "Rumors?"

"Yes, about a wild man, some kind of legendary prospector. Living on this mountain—or maybe even inside it, if you believe all the drunken tales. Apparently he only ventures into town for occasional supplies."

"And always pays in gold dust or nuggets," said Moore. "And buys kerosene, and... gunpowder, and—what was it?"

Jacobson looked up sharply, with eyes wide. "Candy, I thought, of some kind…?"

The guide glared at them. "Rubbish," he said with a grunt. "What else do they say about this man?"

Moore glanced at his friend, then moved closer, inching away from this mysterious guide. The constellations sparkled icily overhead, with the Great Bear twisting sideways over a world of cloud-ringed peaks and frosty ridges.

"Well," Moore said in a low voice, scratching at his frozen pants. "His first name is something unique—the name of a lake or river or something..."

"Like Mississippi Mike, or Yellowstone McGrain."

"Yeah, and we hear his mother was an Indian woman who was eaten by polar bear..."

"And his father was a miner killed by one of the Silver Barons in Virginia City."

The guide suddenly perked up. "Interesting. And what is the news out of Virginia City—what of this Baron?"

Jacobson shrugged. "Only a bit of legend—can't believe too much of what you hear, especially in the taverns down there. But the way it sounds, this rich gentleman, who had lost his sight in the War, had a tragic accident."

"Oh yes!" Moore chimed in. "Fell right down the side of Mt. Davidson he did, and accidentally brought down his lovely wife with him."

"Yep, sad as that was, worse thing is—the couple's son saw it all. Went a little mad, the boy did. Of course, he inherited the mine and the great big factory, but sold out as soon as possible."

"Good thing, too," said Moore, choking on fumes and a collection of scattered ice crystals wafting in the air. "Production at Comstock has slowed down and the fortunes are all dried out. So he up and got out just in time."

A dark shadow crossed the guide's expression. "And where, did you hear, is this son now?"

"I think he moved on to some other venture up north—along the coast of Alaska. Bought out a share from the Russian-American Company. Shipping, I think."

"Whaling," Jacobson corrected, and nearly bit his frozen lip when he saw the guide's sudden reaction. The bearded man threw down his cup and stood up sharply.

"Enough rest," he announced. "The storm's below us, and the way is clear above. Let's make for the summit."

"But sir!" Moore objected, trying to rise and shake off the icicles that had formed over his clothes.

"No more talk," the guide muttered, striking out with a long walking stick, and kicking through a patch of deep snow.

They followed on aching, near-frozen legs, hurrying to catch up but never seeming to match the man's hearty energy or renewed purpose. In time, as they climbed, ascending a labyrinth of treacherous inclines and frosted ledges, floundering in deep drifts up to their waist, they reached the mile and a half-wide ruined crater of the summit. Two enormous snow and ice fields greeted them, bounded by crumbling ridges and peaks, and to the south—a narrowly rising spire that marked the extreme summit.

"There!" yelled the guide, shouting into the intense, swirling wind and pointing to a metallic structure rising twelve feet high. It reflected the starlight, and seemed to scintillate with a host of kaleidoscopic energy. "The geodesic marker erected in 1875 by the geologists from the Smithsonian."

Moore nodded—he and Jacobson had seen it from Sacramento, taking detailed readings with their telescope and wondering if they would ever have the good fortune to see it up close.

Suddenly, they noticed they were alone. Moore reached for Jacobson's arm, and then he saw motion to their left. Their guide had run off to a nearby patch of rocks and was crouching in a fissure.

"What's he doing?" shouted Moore, struggling to make his voice heard.

"No idea!" Jacobson yelled back, even as the man turned, collected something, and then ran over to them.

He had a bulging pack over one arm, and what looked like a rickety wooden sled in the other. The strange man slid to a stop. The frosty gale pushed at them and all three men braced themselves, rocking back and forth in a cyclone of crystalline snow that fluttered about them like a swarm of butterflies.

"And now," the guide yelled, "I must bid you goodbye."

"What?" Moore yelled.

"Congratulations on your ascent! I would suggest you enjoy the view while you can. The Pleiades are rising just to your south, and Mars is in alignment with Antares to the east."

They looked at him blankly.

"Then," he continued, "you should venture back down to the steam fissures and wait until sunrise to start your descent."

"What about you?" Jacobson cried.

The man lifted his sled, then pointed to the west, and his bushy beard and mustache flapped in excitement. "I have another way down!"

With one last grin and a wave, he turned and raced for the western edge of the summit. They raced after him, navigating the cratered pits, frozen outcroppings and gusting side winds. Gingerly, they approached the drop-off and held on to a spiky protrusion of lava rock. Together, Moore and Jacobson peered over the edge, expecting the worst.

Instead, they gazed down at the starlit field of snow, the thick, luxurious drifts flowing in steep drops. The mountainside seemed to glow with subtle blues and purples, and pockets of shadow transitioned into glittering, sparkling hills of crystalline beauty. A single sled trail marred the pristine imagery, etching a bold track across the drifts and kicking up snow like flaky dust in a gentle breeze. The ascending particles twinkled like fireflies, lingered, then scattered in the wind.

And a single, joyous yell, a sound of riotous glee and natural wonderment, careened up the steep cliffside, until, miles below, the boundless congregation of hungry storm clouds finally swallowed it up.

Chapter 17: Alaska - 1890-1892

THE SEARCH FOR MIKHAIL

The Raven-headed totem pole peered down at the new arrival through the crisp spring air. Icicles perched on its rotting wooden beak and crusty moss discolored its once-vibrant eyes.

Delin met the Raven's woody stare, and the two remained locked in mutual consideration as the mid-day shadows, already long, shrank away from the clearing. Delin pulled his fur-lined hood back, and his thick curls of golden hair danced in the polar breezes. Behind him, the Long House stood in wretched decay. The winds whistled through the broken west wall, and the sagging roof creaked under the oppressive weight of successively brutal winters.

The crunching footsteps he had been hearing for several minutes now grew louder, like drumbeats in his ears. Finally, he tore his gaze away from the unapologetic Raven and faced the newcomer.

"*Agaripoq*," said the gray-haired old man leaning on a worn, knobbed stick. "It is good to see you, young Wetherwax. You have stolen your father's stature and your mother's eyes." He bowed his head. "I must assume then, that your father has joined Mirna in the Great Dark?"

"Sadly, he has," Delin said, bowing as well.

"If you come to pay respects, you are late." The old man pointed his stick toward the crop of advancing trees and the overgrown path to the lake. "The few who came, visited the Spirit House last month, for the final time."

"Final? What's happened? Where's everyone gone?"

"West," said the elder, as he stared into the ruins of the Long House. His eyes flickered as if witnessing a much different and lively scene. "White men—your people—came through for the past five, six years, requesting guides, navigators and hunters. Mainly hunters."

Delin frowned—to have come this far inland, their need must have been great. "What do they hunt?"

"Walrus, seal and otter. Mostly, they hunt the bowback."

"Whales," Delin whispered. And a cloud of red passed before his eyes. He had tried desperately to push away thoughts of revenge, to quell the flames of anger that had been rekindled on Mt. Shasta. That was three months ago, and it marked the end of his solitary retreat. Since then, during the slow travel north, competing drives vied for his destination. Revenge and closure on one side, obligation on the other.

"Yes," said the elder. "Two great fleets. One from the Northeast States, the other from Seattle." His dark eyes clouded and he shook his head sadly. "Soon, great Bowback will be gone, along with seal and otter. Dark times have come."

Darker still, Delin thought, if any of those boats are owned by Jericho Quitch. "And many Tlingits have joined?"

"Many, for payment in your coin. Terrible work. Entire years away from their families, away from the land." He waved his arm toward the decomposing structures. "From the village."

"What about my half-brother? What of Mikhail Leadfoot?"

"Joined a ship, last summer."

Delin sighed, expecting as much, as if the trail he had tried to avoid—the one marked with blood—had looped back around and merged with his chosen path. So, my conflicting desires have become one, and all roads lead back to Him. He put his gloved hands on the elder's shoulders. "Where will you go?"

The elder glanced over his shoulder, toward the lake and the trees. Delin noticed a group of Tlingits huddled there. Men and women, a few children. "I go with them. We travel to Skagway, Place of the Winds—where some of the younger men will join their older brothers with the whalers. The rest of us, I suspect, will scatter among those winds."

"No," Delin implored. "Surely there are other tribes along the great rivers? The Chilkoots or the Aleuts..."

"Have their own problems. Food hunted away, men leaving for the cities. Villages crushed by new diseases." He shook his head. "And the great demon, alcohol, snares many."

Delin swallowed, then patted the elder's shoulders and bowed. He glanced to the others, and noticed several frisky Innuit sled dogs among them. He smiled and his heart skipped as he watched them nip and paw at each other. Finally, he made a decision. "Elder, might I humbly request passage with your people?"

"You are always welcome among us," the elder said. "That terrible day, the Sesquats took more than your mother's life. You did what you could, and destroyed two of them—a greater triumph than even your father had managed—yet the others resented you for it."

Delin lowered his eyes. "For not saving anyone else."

The elder shrugged. "Raven called them away. It was their time to fly with him."

Delin risked a last glance up to the totem, then caught up to the departing elder and asked if he could make just one last stop. "I would like to see her again," Delin said, even as two of the gray and white dogs raced up to him, sniffing and nipping at his gloves like he was their returning favorite friend.

"Of course," said the elder as he crunched along the hard snow and joined his people. "We will wait for you."

Delin thanked him and went with one dog following, staying at his heels with its nose to the ground, whining softly. When he reached the clearing, the dog stopped and sat at a distance, seemingly out of respect—or perhaps sensing something around the moss-covered hut set in the encroaching woods.

Delin glanced around the clearing carefully, noting any movements. Across Northern California and up into Washington and Canada, he had been wary. With every mile further north, his fear had steadily grown, and many nights by campfire he had imagined rustling in the dark woods, and thought he could almost smell the foul stench of the creature, its scorched flesh still reeking. Alternating images of red-eyed snow monsters and a black-haired, Bible-quoting fiend had plagued his dreams.

Now, with the weight of urgency guiding his feet, Delin approached the Spirit House and said what he needed to say. Apologized for his absence. For failing to honor her last request and look after Papa. For neglecting his responsibilities, hiding in the mountains when he should have been avenging his father and helping his people.

He promised Mama he'd do better. He would find Mikhail and save him. And he would find enough gold to help these people.

The dog wagged its tail and spun around when he rejoined the others; and with a last glance toward the ruins of his childhood home, Delin embarked for the coast.

As promised, Captain Tobias came to see Delin after they'd safely maneuvered out of Skagway's port. He left his first mate in command of the wheel, trusting him to navigate the Aegis through the smaller islands of the Inside Passage and out into the Pacific. Tobias found his one paying passenger on the stern, gripping the ice-crusted ropes and holding on for dear life as the brig rocked with the sea's gyrations.

"First time at sea?" Tobias asked, approaching his unsteady guest.

"Second," Delin said. "Although the first was on a steamer many years ago. Sitka to San Francisco."

"Ah," Tobias said with a grunt. "Steamer. Then it's as I said—your first time at sea. Until you've experienced one of these..." he pointed to the billowing sails, the creaking ropes and twisting beams. "You haven't truly been at sea."

Delin, turning pale, had to stop and bend over, hoping the nausea would pass. "Not sure I like it."

"I noticed. Maybe a drink would help you along? Come downstairs with the officers."

"Are you sure? I am imposing upon you enough as it is. I have licorice—and it works wonders with nausea."

"Licorice instead of liquor? Are you mad?"

Delin sent him a dull look and choked back on bile. The smell venting up from the holds was ferociously vile—the remains of two adult bowback were down there. Twenty-five hundred pounds of baleen—the prized mouth-bone, and fifty gallons of whale oil. That was another reason he remained above.

Earlier, he had asked some subtle questions about the fleet's ownership, and had determined that this ship and twelve others were owned by the Northeast Company, rivals of Quitch's fleet. They each had their prowling zones, and rarely did the two intersect; and Quitch's ships never docked in Skagway, preferring the more civilized cities of Vancouver or Seattle.

"Come," Tobias said. "I bring good news—I have checked the logs and I have found your brother's ship."

Delin's face brightened, even as a wave of icy water splashed over the side and drenched him again.

With his soaked white beard and weather-cracked face, the Captain looked like a Biblical Noah, standing on the Ark's prow as the wrath of God erupted upon the world. "Yes. Mikhail Leadfoot is on the Nordic Hunter, captained by my old friend Harris Green from Boston."

"And?" Delin urged, hoping he had further news.

"And, my friend, we're catching up to her right now."

With that, the Captain stutter-stepped past Delin, made his way to the stairwell and descended to the officers' quarters. Slowly, carefully, Delin followed.

He found Mikhail the next morning in the cargo hold of the Nordic Hunter, after rowing over with Captain Tobias to board it. Below deck, the men were crowding around some tables, gambling before setting out on the hunt.

Mikhail, his long hair braided behind his sloping forehead, was dressed in western style pants, boots, and a vest over a shirtless chest. He intently focused on the three hollowed out conch shells before him on an overturned barrel. A large man behind the trunk shifted the shells with a fluid motion.

Mikhail looked at the pile of coins by his right hand, then started to point to the center one—when Delin stepped in, took his wrist and moved it one shell over to the left. "Try this one, brother."

In a flash, Mikhail had Delin by the collar, and his other hand had formed into a fist. The other Tlingits moved in, two of them drawing their knives.

"Is that any way to greet your brother?"

Recognition flashed in Mikhail's eyes, along with alarm and

surprise—and then a shadow crossed his expression. He released his grip, after first pushing Delin backwards. "What is this? How did you find me here?"

"I've been looking for you," Delin said. "Went to the village, and was told by the elders that..."

"I don't care what the elders told you." Mikhail glared at him. Then he turned and with a defiant look toward Delin, lifted the middle shell—and cursed.

The man behind the table smirked, then lifted the leftmost shell to reveal the black marble. Mikhail shook his head and stared at Delin. "Right again. As always, you are blessed by the gods."

Delin frowned, not understanding the intensity of his sarcasm. "It's nothing so mysterious. My papa taught me how this game cheats men, and how you can cheat it back."

"Your precious father." Mikhail turned his head and spat on the boards. "Like his son, a man who can do no wrong—except when it comes to protecting his woman. Maybe he's here as well? Is this to be a family reunion?"

Delin backed away. "He's dead. Murdered."

A smile crossed Mikhail's lips. "Then we are even."

Anticipating that remark, Delin moved on. "I visited our mother's Spirit House three months ago."

"Late again for the anniversary."

"Nevertheless, I know she wants us to reconcile."

Mikhail stared for a minute as the boat creaked and swayed. Then he threw his head back and laughed. "What—have you come to rescue me?"

"Come home. Your people need you. They are scattering, unbound by the strong ties they once had."

"Before your people came and uprooted us."

"Alaska is a big place, brother. 'My people,' as you call them, will not go everywhere." As long as the gold eludes them, he thought hopefully. "There are many other areas, rivers, lakes—sacred mountains. Don't leave them all unattended after being their stewards for so long."

Mikhail snorted and joked about something with his friends.

Delin sighed. "Mikhail. I have sought you out because I know that's what Mama wanted. If you tell me to go, I will. But I promise you, I will stay by your side if you ask."

Mikhail thought for a moment. "If that's the case, brother, then I hope you like whaling, because I intend to stay with this crew. I am a great hunter—the lead harpooner, and I'm paid above all these others. Don't try to deny me this. You have your skills at prospecting—and, from what I hear, you've even improved at dog sledding."

"Heard from who?"

Shrugging, Mikhail said, "Oh, other tribes. They spoke of a great competition in Juneau, and a young boy who beat the great Moon Chaser on his first outing."

Delin risked a smile. "I had some luck."

"Or maybe you learned well from your half-brother?"

"Maybe," Delin admitted, and followed Mikhail up to the top deck. Out in the morning breeze and spreading blue sky, Mikhail went on to tell him of Moon Chaser's comeback, how he had never lost another race since then. At Juneau, at Skagway, at Sitka. He raced wherever there were men and gambling, and had apparently grown a following of henchmen–a band of other Tlingits and half-breeds that called themselves The Outcasts.

"So what's it to be?" Mikhail asked, eventually tired of talking about the past. "Are you going to join me here, or do we part ways again—this time, hopefully for good?"

Delin stood and faced Mikhail. "Where's your captain?"

The next two years were only a blur of salty, wet and violent images, a series of tintype-like stills in his memory. But he would always look back on this time as an existence as pure and direct as mountain snow. A bonding with Mikhail, slow to start, soon warmed as the months at sea dragged on, as countless whale-hunts merged into one blend of fierce, bloody quests, tempered by weeks of calm. There were images of Mikhail shirtless in the sun, poised on the prow with his great iron harpoon, tensing and throwing at just the perfect moment. There were nights in the holds below, drinking tankards of ale and telling grand stories with the men.

Slowly he and Mikhail became friends, as the teamwork of the hunt, the kill and the cleanup drew them close. Delin bit back his revulsion and gradually learned the ways of the sea—how to chase after whales in the small boats the Tlingits called umiaks; how to attach the ropes and row to ice sheets and carve up the great beasts. Noble creatures, all, Delin begged God for forgiveness after every slaughter—explaining that what he did, he did for a higher purpose.

A year passed, and then, near the end of July, Delin found himself on the prow of the Nordic Hunter, beside his brother. Something felt different—the depth of the clouds, the heaviness in the air, the scattering of fog above the peaks of Mt. Osborn, fifty miles north of Nome. He shivered and rubbed his hands together as he approached his half-brother.

"Do you feel it?" Delin asked as the boat's masts creaked and whispered tiny groans in a strangely-subdued wind. The Bering Sea was a calm gray expanse to the west, muddled with heavy ice floes and drifting bergs.

Without acknowledging Delin's presence, Mikhail grunted. "Bitter cold coming fast. Wind moving in the wrong direction."

"It's early," Delin said with alarm, gazing out over the waters, seeing the distant blurs of the other whalers. The Aegis was out there, as were ten others in their fleet. Plus, they had word that the Seattle fleet was just a little further north, pursuing a school of humpback. Quitch's boats were near, Delin thought. Perhaps Jericho himself captained one.

"Too early," Mikhail agreed. "This time of year, winds always blow out, pushing the ice floes away, not towards us."

"Always," Delin said warily, "to us doesn't mean the same to the sea."

Mikhail nodded. "The other Tlingits feel it as well. I've heard them whispering. They're scared."

Typically, another two months were left before the ice closed in and ended the hunts until spring. The whalers would finish their grim work and head south to unload their catches—and then sail to various ports to restock, or try their luck off the shores off of Vancouver and Washington.

"We have to warn the sea captains," Delin said suddenly, wringing his hands on the cold wooden rail. Mikhail's unsmiling face met his look and he nodded grimly.

In the end, they had less time than they thought. In two days, the ice encroached upon the fleet like an advancing, insatiable mudslide. They awoke to hear great cracking explosions and thought they must be near a coastal glacier, as the compressing and breaking sounds were common there—but soon they heard other noises. The cries and screaming of men pitched into the freezing waters as the brutal ice bit through the defenseless hulls of the ships.

The Nordic Hunter had dropped back in the night, after Delin had finally persuaded the First Officer to at least pursue some leads down along the southerly currents, outside of the major collection of ice floes. When they broke off, the Aegis was obliged to follow, so only two ships were far enough out of the way by the time the sun vainly peaked through overcast skies upon a scene of impending carnage.

Delin and Mikhail watched from the railing of the stern. Watched while the Nordic Hunter and the Aegis fled south with all possible speed, but ultimately to no avail. The winds died and they floundered, at the mercy of the oncoming ice. Twenty-two ships were caught, snared in a rapid freeze as temperatures plunged to twenty below in the small hours of the night and the winds blew the ice back upon the fleets, sealing them in. Wood splintered, bows cracked and great seams were rent through the vessels. After a series of meetings, the sea captains voted unanimously to do the right thing—the only course by which history would judge them favorably. To save twelve hundred lives, they had to flee; but by doing so, they would lose a fortune in whale catches, plus the fleet itself.

The whaleboats were lowered, and men pushed, dragged and paddled where possible, struggling to make it to the safety of nearby islands. Delin and Mikhail pressed on in their small umiak to the small beach town called Nome and settled to wait there, along with two hundred other boats and the remaining crew and captains of the other fleets. They watched helplessly as their vessels were moored, and some were mercilessly crushed.

In the gaining light, as the ice sparkled in the brutal cold, Delin saw what looked like movement far out to sea. He walked unsteadily past the somber crew, and came up behind Captain Tobias, who stood with Captain Green a distance away from the others. "May I borrow your telescope?" he asked.

Tobias, his eyes hooded, and his expression unreadable, pulled the device from inside his coat. Breath tumbled in a clouded rush from his nostrils, mimicking the expelling air from the whales they had hunted. Tears had frozen on his cheeks as he watched the ice consume his vessel.

Delin extended the scope, aimed at the distant speck and brought his eye to the glass. One lone ship had cleared the ice. It raced ahead of the lagging floes and heedlessly stopped for no rescue of its brethren. Delin scanned the deck, trying to control his shivering hands and steady the image. Finally the view settled on the promenade and he found the main wheel. A man stood there, barking orders. He was dressed in red and gray layers, with a wide Napoleonic hat and an enormous cloak that billowed behind him like shadowy dragon wings, flapping majestically and propelling the vessel to safety.

"Jericho," Delin said, expelling the word with contempt.

They stayed at Nome for three days before the house-sized ice chunks blew away from the shores, the storms subsided, and the scout ship returned with the good news of rescue. In that time, living in huts and cabins among several intrepid trappers, Delin spent his mornings out on the beach, examining the soil and making occasional digs when he knew he was unobserved. Traveling over steep dunes, out of sight of the others, he struck at the sand and sifted it with a small pan.

Gold, he found, after rinsing out the black sand and plucking the heavy flakes from the bottom. A lot of it. He surveyed the expanse of the dunes, noted the landscape and the weathering of the rocks; he studied the deposits placed here in ancient times by receding glaciers, as if offering in patience a gift to the future. He panned more and more, and finally, on the day before the rescue ships arrived, he had collected two full, small sacks. Easily twenty-five pounds, he thought, of what tasted like very pure gold.

On that last night, Mikhail noticed him coming back from the beaches. Drunk, he eyed the sacks, and when he and Delin were alone in the back of one of the small cabins, he demanded to be shown what Delin was doing.

His eyes lit up when Delin reluctantly opened the bag, but his smile dropped right away. "So you thought to keep this from me too, eh brother? Now that our ship is sunk and my career destroyed, you revert to your old ways."

"Mikhail, no!" Delin shook his head, holding the heavy bag out before him apologetically. "I only wanted to keep this find from the others—or else these men, these white men you so despise—will come here in droves, and this stretch of land will draw others out here, looking for similar finds, and..."

"Spare me," Mikhail blasted back, and turned away. He extinguished the lamps, and went quickly to sleep. Delin joined him a little later, tossed and turned for hours, then finally drifted into a troubled sleep.

When he awoke, the scout ship had returned, and the men were excitedly packing up.

But Mikhail was not among them. He had disappeared in the night. And he took with him the two sacks of gold.

Chapter 18: March, 1895

CAUGHT BY THE SHORE

TWO YEARS HAD PASSED. TWO years since Mikhail had left him, taking his gold and running for parts unknown. Two years since the tragedy in the ice, the disaster that set back the Pacific whaling industry. He had shut both Mikhail and Quitch out of his thoughts as best he could. Pursuing them was simply not an option. He had had enough of the sea, enough of taking orders.

The wilderness called him back, and he gladly answered, rejoining the great vastness of the arctic world. He returned to the glaciers, the tundra, the great peaks and winding rivers and streams. A land—for all intents and purposes—empty of men, unmarred by human greed.

So he selected a place that tugged most on his heart, a view that inspired his soul. This promontory was high above the Yukon River, just ten miles away from the Canadian border and within a day's sledding to Fort Reliance. Deciding it could easily serve as his sanctuary, he carved out a home from the mighty alpines, and in the summer months he fused it with layers of sod, mud, sealskin and thatch. He placed inside all the memories of his father and the priceless items of his childhood.

He bought another team of dogs—eight of them this time, and named them after St. Nick's reindeer. He prospected occasionally in the spring, and returned to the haunts of his youth; he made two pilgrimages to the Spirit House to visit with Mirna and to stroll among the ruins of the Long House. The Raven totem was gone on his return—only a stump remained. Perhaps, Delin thought with a smile, Raven left on his own, called from this world to join the ancestors and await a hopeful resurgence of his people.

Finally, after two years, his cabin had become stifling. The loneliness started to creep in. His current pack of dogs were only so good for breaking the long lapses in companionship, and the forests and hills beyond often took on the long shadows of menace. More than once the dogs would growl and point their snouts to some dark patch in the trees, or they would focus their attention on a nearby hill, bristling. Delin would wait by the cabin door, poised with his last purchase—a Winchester Repeating Carbine rifle—gripped tightly in his hands while he tried to discern any sign of the Sesquat.

But if it was out there, it acted with infinite patience and restraint. Hoping perhaps, for a time when Delin would let his guard down or when his dogs were no longer a threat.

Delin's diggings had grown. The pile of nuggets and dust had become too heavy, and he wasn't re-supplying as often as he used to. Finally, he decided to convert all the gold he had found so far. However, remembering his father's lessons, he realized that showing up with this much gold—or any sizable amount, for that matter—in Fort Reliance, Dawson, Skagway or even Juneau, would be too dangerous.

Given time and the insatiable curiosity of men, the secret would get out. They'd trace his comings and goings, find his haunts. Narrow it down to the Thron-diuck basin, and the tributaries there. Delin was surprised the strike hadn't already been found. Other prospectors were roaming those hills. Not many, but a handful—and even as green as they were, they could get lucky. In any case, Delin decided to cash in what he had—but to do that he needed a larger city, somewhere he could trade in portions to various bankers or mints without raising too much interest. He would go to Seattle.

He packed up the gold and some supplies, and he harnessed the dogs. They left the next morning—the first of April—and made for Skagway.

If all went well, he'd be back home within a month, with money enough for five years of supplies. Maybe while in Seattle he would even purchase some new books, or update his collection of the classics. He expected to have a good deal of free time.

Expectations, however, had a way of not following the rules. On the last day before reaching Skagway, mushing south along the shores at the foothills of the Chugach, he came upon a man running from the shore. The man was dressed in a heavy jacket, but Delin nonetheless recognized the uniform of the Canadian Mounted Police. The Mountie staggered up the hill from the ice-coated inlet. His face was bloody and he held his side.

"Help," he choked, seeing Delin and his dogs. The Mountie pointed over the hill to the shore, where Delin could now make out a party of six men. They all seemed to be carrying clubs, and they were swinging indiscriminately at what looked like kneeling forms on the ground.

"Sea otters," the Mountie said in a gasp. "Those men—hunting illegally."

Delin pulled back on the ropes and drew the dogs to a stop, whistling at them to be quiet. "Illegal?" Delin frowned; he couldn't keep track of what laws existed—if any did. Alaska still did not have territorial status, and operated loosely under Oregon's adopted laws; by order of the U.S. Organic Act, twelve administrating judges visited various areas once a year to hear trials and pass sentences.

"Joint treaty," the Mountie said, wheezing and holding his bloodied forehead. "Signed two years ago to protect the extermination of seal, walrus and otter along these coasts. U.S. resources are limited for this sort of thing, so we were asked to lend some assistance."

"I see," said Delin, glancing back to the shore. Now he heard the baleful cries of the otter, the almost-human screams as the men moved haphazardly through the waddling creatures, bashing their skulls in with swift efficiency.

The Mountie pointed to the rifle in Delin's sled. "Sir, if you could assist me. I need to arrest those men. They have two boats anchored just past the ice, and if I don't get them now, they'll escape and continue this criminal activity."

Still staring at the carnage on the shore, Delin felt the emptiness in his heart; it was as if all his emotions had been leeched away through great loss, and now he had no sympathy left to offer. He sighed and shook his head. This is not my fight, he thought, and tried to think of a nice way to let the Mountie down. At the least he could offer to take the man to Skagway for medical attention.

"Please, sir!" the Mountie pleaded. "We cannot let this stand! Especially when they flaunt our laws—and even have the gall to quote scripture in their defense!"

Delin froze; his head spun around—to the Mountie, then back to the shore. "Scripture, you say?" He strained and tried to see closer, tried to make out some features on the men.

"Yes, the taller one—I think their leader. When I confronted him, he just laughed and spouted out some verses—I can't remember what. Something about 'a time to reap and sow, and a time to kill...'"

Delin's mouth opened, and he reached for his rifle. "Ecclesiastes," came his answer, and then he was off, bounding from the sled. Rifle in hand, he yelled back, "Watch my dogs!"

He was down the hill and upon them before they had a chance to notice. The screeching of the dying otter blocked out the sound of his approaching footsteps. Delin burst into their midst, bashing the closest man in the side of the face just as he was in the act of clubbing another otter. Scanning the other men quickly, he located his quarry. Indeed the tallest one, Jericho Quitch stood with a long, curved ivory club in each hand, the tips spattered in gore and brains; he wheeled around and around, chasing the fleeing animals and smashing with abandon.

With a roar, Delin sped toward him, stopping once to land a blow on the forehead of a hunter that suddenly turned in his direction, alarmed that an intruder was in their midst. Knocking the man to the ground, Delin wheeled, brought the rifle to his shoulder and aimed.

A sudden calm descended upon the shore—animal and man alike ceased their struggles and turned to the newcomer. Delin stood on a blood-drenched field of ice, with the shore only twenty feet distant. Thin ice masses had formed in irregular pockets and already mingled along the subsiding waves.

And Jericho Quitch pulled back his hood and straightened to his full height. He turned and lowered the clubs while he regarded the interloper. Blood and bits of bone dripped form the clubs onto the white snow.

Delin lined up the shot, aiming between Jericho's eyes. His

heart was pounding and the wind hissed through his ears, bristling his thick beard and stinging his eyes. But he focused and tensed his trigger finger. One shot, and all the pain of the past could be eradicated. One shot, and this monster before him would be sent back to hell. One shot, and he would do what he should have done back at the Comstock—if he had been quicker with the knife, or if he had listened to his intuition and examined the car where this treacherous fiend had hidden.

But he paused, and remembered another time a Wetherwax had shown restraint—and then he remembered that a moment of just such weakness (or goodness) had cost papa his life. Renewed in his thirst for vengeance, Delin gritted his teeth, steadied the rifle and took a deep breath.

From his right a crunching sound reached his ears a moment too late. He saw Jericho smile—and then a blurry club whistled down and cracked against his rifle barrel. The gun went off—blasting into the ice several feet ahead. Then Delin jumped back—out of the reach of another club swung by a raging dark-skinned man.

Delin dodged, then slipped under the man's arm and rammed his fist into the soft flesh under his ribs. He went down in a groan; but then three others—all but Jericho and the first man Delin had knocked out—were approaching. And to his horror, he saw that two of them had revolvers.

Delin shot a glare to Jericho, and for a moment something like recognition flashed in the other man's eyes; above that cruelly-drawn face, the strangely handsome angelic countenance.

"Wait!" ordered Jericho to his men, who immediately paused. "Who are you?"

Trembling, chest heaving with short, thin gasps of air, Delin felt as if Jericho drew the very breath from his lungs through some arcane incantation. He offered up a short prayer, hoping that time had changed his appearance. Surely the thick blond beard, the bushy, unkempt hair, the gaining of at least another hundred pounds—he was a far cry from the thin, wiry youth Jericho last saw back on those mine tracks.

"No one," Delin answered, gathering his courage, and redirecting his stare. "Just a trapper who came upon a beaten Mountie."

"Ah," Jericho said, nodding slowly. "So, you are merely a do-gooder. Well, that is commendable, for as it says in the Good Book: 'Though I have knowledge and faith so I can remove mountains, if I have not charity I am nothing'."

Delin fumed, but still wouldn't meet those eyes. He only glanced back up the hill, to the tiny vision of his dogsled team. Now he cursed his rashness; he should have untethered them—at least Dunder and Blitzen—and brought them with him for backup. Instead, he had to hope the Mountie would see his predicament and flee, taking the dogs to safety. Now, with the calm acceptance that he was about to die, Delin only cared about protecting the interior from Jericho's greed. The sack of gold at his belt was a giveaway—if they found it, they would torture him until he revealed its origin.

There was no way he would lead Jericho Quitch to the interior, to allow him to repeat his father's corruption and devastation here. Jericho had clearly moved on from mining, but with recent failures in whaling—and with the possibility of soon experiencing the same from otter hunting restrictions—he might be looking for a return to his first love.

"Men," Jericho said. "Get him. Morris and Yaeger—take this fool back to San Francisco with you. Bring him before Judge Harris Marks—the man owes me his position. Just tell him I want this criminal locked away for a long time." Jericho smiled. "The rest of you, I think this shows us it's high time to leave this hellish place. Time to enter politics, I think—where there's still money to be made and power to wield. Let's go back to Reno."

Thinking fast, Delin turned and fled. Not to the hills, as they would have expected, but toward the shore. Unhooking the heavy bags of gold at his belt as he stumbled, tripped and staggered outward, he crunched through the brittle ice. Shouts of the pursuers rang in his ears—and then a patch of ice ahead exploded with a gunshot. Stopping just six feet from the icy waters, Delin braced his feet, grabbed the bags in both hands, spun around like a Greek discus thrower, then launched them. Sailing in high arcs, the bags dropped like boulders, crashing through thin ice and disappearing into the frozen waters.

Delin dropped to his knees, smiling as frost collected in his curly mustache.

"What was that?" Jericho shouted.

"Just some family heirlooms," Delin said, lowering his head as if awaiting the executioner's ax. Jericho muttered something else—but whatever he said, it was swallowed up by the crackling snow, and the whistling of an ivory club. A stinging sensation wracked the back of his head—like a thousand bumblebees attacking at once. Delin's vision exploded into a galaxy of red-blue stars, and then he saw no more.

Chapter 19: San Francisco - April 15, 1895

THE BARGAIN IN SAN FRANCISCO

Delin wondered if Raven, reunited with his mother in the spirit world, might not be calling some of the shots after all. Down here in this grimy, overcrowded prison up the side of Telegraph Hill, not far from where Papa had played cards with Sam Colt decades ago, Delin stood against metal bars, looking across the narrow corridor to another other set of cages and into the eyes of his half-brother.

Mikhail, no less surprised, stared back in amazement. Once, was coincidence enough, but now, in jail himself—it was too much to accept. "So, you've found me again."

Delin nodded, massaging the back of his head where the bruise still stung. "Although not on purpose this time."

"Let me guess," Mikhail said with a dour look. "You were arrested for being a nuisance?"

Delin ignored the jab. "What did you do with my gold?"

"Spent it, of course," Mikhail said.

"On what? And how? All at once, or prudently, a little at a time?" Delin prayed Mikhail had not made a big mistake worse by drawing attention to the find. Gold could ultimately be traced back to a particular region, based on the level and type of impurities it bonded with. As the glaciers had pushed south during the great ice ages, the mixture of elements dragged along with them became more complex, so that the gold found in South America might only be 40% pure, while most found in California was around 90%. But Delin had already quietly assayed some of his findings from Canada and the eastern edge of Alaska, and found they were nearly 98% pure. That kind of enviable composition would draw immediate notice, and cause a major stampede.

"Oh, stop fretting!" Mikhail turned around and paced to the back wall where he promptly sat on a rickety wooden bench. He was alone in the cell—for now—while Delin shared his cell with three other men, all newcomers awaiting trial.

"No one cares for your little gold finds," Mikhail said. "People here wager that much on a single hand of Faro—or spend as much for a night at the Nob Hill resorts."

Delin grunted. "All the same, I hope you kept quiet. Where are your friends—the others who left the fleet?"

Mikhail shrugged. "Took off last month when I was caught."

"What did you do?"

Again, Mikhail shrugged. He picked at his tooth with a fingernail. "Bunch of things."

A heavyset bald man leaning against the wall jabbed Delin's arm. "Yer friend there had his way with a young lady who didn't much care for him. That's what I hear."

"Shut up!" Mikhail hissed. "You're only jealous an Indian can get a pretty white girl."

The bald man winked at Delin. "Lady was only fifteen. And had a rich daddy. Yer pal's in for life—which might not last too long down here."

Delin sighed, gripping the cold bars for comfort. He stared at his half-brother and could only shake his head. "I'm sorry, Mikhail. There's not much I can do—I'm in for what looks like a long stretch as well."

He sat down, and proceeded to talk, to tell Mikhail—whether he was listening or not—about Alaska, about their home. He continued on into the night, his cellmates occasionally chiming in with a question or two, glad to have something else to focus on. He spoke of the fur trade and the whaling industry's depopulation of the seas; he waxed about the ruin of the old village and the breakup of the tribe.

Finally, around dawn—from what he could tell by the meager

light streaming from distant windows—an iron door opened and footsteps approached. Prisoners shuffled to their feet, hoping for a visitor or a lawyer.

Delin stood. A good foot taller than the others in his cell, he could see the two men passing by the cells. Both wore uniforms—one the dark blue of the U.S. Army, the other the red and brown of the Canadian Mounted Police. Recognition dawned on Delin, just as the Mountie caught sight of his blond hair poking above the others' shoulders. "There he is!"

Delin pushed through and stepped up to the bars. The Mountie, bandages on his head and bruises marking his cheeks like ashen makeup, thrust out his hand. "Good sir! My apologies for your predicament. I did all I could after Skagway to return to your rescue. Failing that, I scoured the ports of Seattle and Vancouver, telegraphing dockmasters until I found a ship and a prisoner from Alaska."

Delin shook the man's hand, then glanced at the Army soldier who promptly cleared his throat. "I am Lieutenant James Bradley, and I am accompanying Mr. Benneforth here on your behalf. I am entrusted to obtain your freedom."

Delin sighed in relief. "But what about the fur traders? And—what of my dogs?"

"Easy there," said the Mountie. "I've left your dogs in the dockmaster's care back in Skagway."

Lt. Bradley shifted his feet. "And—ah, as for those traders. Well, we haven't been able to identify any of them, and their vessels are long gone."

"The pelts and tusks?" asked Delin.

"Sold, most likely. Up in Vancouver or Portland."

Delin rapped on the bars. "What about that Judge—Marks? He knew the traders, their leader especially. And..."

"Now, sir," said Lt. Bradley. "Keep to matters at present and trust the U.S. Army to handle other crimes. Mind such advice next time you try to single-handedly enforce laws against a gang of men more than your equal."

Delin took that to mean that Marks might at least be under investigation. "Very well," he said as they started to unlock his cell. "But..." He looked across the corridor.

Mikhail leaned against the wall of his cell, his arms crossed. He shook his head. "Well, that does it, then."

"Mikhail..."

"No. It's clear to me now that my doomed life has come to an insulting conclusion." He shook a fist to the ceiling, to the wooden cross-hatched beams eight feet above. "The ancestors, our spirits—all are nothing compared to your God, who it seems has lowered down your salvation once more."

Delin stepped out of the cell, standing between the two uniformed men. "Brother, I promise I will do all I can to get you out of here. Or at least to lessen your time."

"Spare me your words. Go, live your charmed life and leave me to rot." He turned his back on Delin. "Finish what your father started when he arrived, bringing death with him."

"Mikhail!"

"Come on," said the lieutenant, and pulled Delin away.

Outside, when the jail's iron door clanged shut and the three of them stood in a brightly-lit office, the officer regarded Delin with an odd look. "You know," he said. "There might be a way we can make a deal regarding your friend down there."

"How?" Delin asked, yanked out of a sullen depression. He would do anything to break Mikhail's long-standing anger; his bitterness.

Benneforth cleared his throat. "Yes, well. Given your obvious concern over the well-being of the Alaskan resources and the indigenous people there..."

"Go on," Delin said, scratching at his mustache. He smelled cooked eggs and ham somewhere close—perhaps in the next room, and his stomach flipped ravenously.

Benneworth continued. "The U.S. Government has recently funded a project for just such purposes. Concerned with the declining populations of seal and other inland game, they have given in to one proponent's idea to import new game."

"What kind of game?" Delin asked. "And from where?"

"From Russia," Lt. Bradley said.

"Reindeer," Benneworth added. "Maybe two thousand at first, from what I hear."

Delin coughed. "And this project will do what? Ship these

reindeer across the Bering Strait and introduce them to the Alaskan wilds?"

"Precisely," said Benneworth. "With the hopes that they will take root in similar environments and multiply—and can then be used by the Innuit peoples for food, milk, and as pack animals."

Delin scratched his head. "Probably won't work. Different terrain, different people. Noble idea, though."

"Well," said Lt. Bradley, "if anyone can make it work, it's Sheldon Jackson—the missionary who's been pushing this idea to Congress for years."

Delin nodded. He'd heard of Jackson. An explorer and visitor to many Innuit villages up and down the coast, he had been setting up Presbyterian missions in many remote areas, and had, through the Organic Act, been made chief educator of the region, which led him to send many teachers out to the rural locations. "What would you need me to do?"

"Jackson needs help," Benneworth said. "A man such as yourself—one who knows the waters and the land and the people. You'd be valuable to the success of this project."

"What's the time period?" Delin asked.

Lt. Bradley shrugged. "Two, three years, maybe."

Delin considered it. "And what of Mikhail Leadfoot's sentence? What can you do to help him?"

"Well," said Lt. Bradley. "I'd have to review his case, but if he's done anything short of murder, I could promise to commute his sentence to, say... five years?"

Delin grinned. Without a second thought, he held out his hand. "You have a deal, if you can honor that pledge."

Benneworth and Bradley smiled. They all shook hands.

After, Delin asked to be allowed to tell Mikhail the good news. They agreed, and he raced back inside the jail. Down the concrete stairs and along the shadowy corridor.

The men in his old cell were shouting, even as he came closer. But not to him. They were pointing and yelling across the way, to Mikhail's cell. Delin slowed, and when the others saw him, they quieted down immediately and backed away.

"What?" he shouted, and suddenly his heart seized up.

At Mikhail's cell, he could only stare in horror at the shirtless man swinging a foot off the ground beside the kicked-over bench. The shreds of his shirt were tied together, wrapped around his neck and secured over a beam on the ceiling.

Delin lowered his head to the dirt-caked floor. Somewhere, he thought he heard a woman sobbing, her muffled cries carried over the winds from the north.

And, with a desolate sigh, he wept with her.

As he walked up the corridor, through the rushing guards, he made the decision to keep his promise. Regardless of the bargain's futility, Delin saw in this action a way to honor Mikhail. In the end, the mission had other rewards.

When he emerged into the light, with the tears dried on his cheeks, he asked when he could meet this Sheldon Jackson.

Chapter 20: February, 1898

REINDEER HERDING AND THE KLONDIKE EXPOSED

THE DOGS CHASED AFTER THE herd, nipping at their hooves, yelping and barking. Delin watched with pride from an icy promontory that led down from the mountains and to the flatlands, heading towards Nulato. Some two hundred reindeer had survived the odyssey from Siberia across the Strait and then over difficult ice passes and ravines—nearly a hundred mile trek from the sea. The harsh wind blew over the blue-gray glaciers to the north and carried an even deeper chill, one that somehow left these animals unfazed.

The dogs were in heaven, Delin thought, watching Comet and Vixen teaming up to lead a straying pair of reindeer back to the herd. Toward the south, the frozen Yukon River still lay dreaming of spring, while the reindeer fed on willow brush and other hearty shrubs.

Crunching footsteps behind him grew louder, until a pair of black boots trimmed with fox hair stopped at eye level on a ledge above. "God be praised."

Delin looked up, squinting as the mid-day sun, in its feeble northern pass, backlit Sheldon Jackson. Even in silhouette and viewed from below, the man was diminutive—barely five-foot-one. He nonetheless dressed as an imposing explorer. In this, the start of their third year together, Delin never knew Jackson to be sick, fatigued or even depressed despite the arduous travel, the brutal months at sea, and the crossing back and forth from Russia. With his neatly trimmed black beard and mustache, heavy sideburns and bushy eyebrows, military-style coat with colorful patches on his shoulders, Jackson looked and acted the part of a commander. Three other men, all recently imported Laplanders, made this journey with him, helping to hunt, chop wood for fires, tend the reindeer, and spread the Good Word.

"Yes," Delin said, glancing back to the valley as the sun danced on the tips of two hundred antlers. They galloped in a wide path, spreading out like an advancing army upon the wilderness. "God be praised indeed."

"Think they'll survive?" Jackson asked, digging into a pouch for some tobacco, and packing his pipe.

Delin shrugged. "They should. Anyway, if you believe Clement Clarke Moore, Saint Nick's been living up here for hundreds of years with eight of these creatures."

"Sacrilegious nonsense!" Jackson blurted, and followed it up with a cough of vanilla-scented pipe smoke. "If you ask me, that damned story's taken the Devil's hold among the simpletons back east. Mark my words—one day people will forget that the birth of Christ happened on Christmas, and they'll substitute such divinity for this red-suited fat man's holiday. You realize that Santa is an anagram for Satan, don't you?"

Delin smiled to himself. "Actually, I think you'll find it means 'Saint'—from the Dutch Sinter Klaus, or Saint Nicholas, who lived around the time official Christianity got its start and was revered by many countries across Europe."

Jackson frowned at him, then coughed again. "We'll respectfully disagree, then. As we have on many points these past few years. I wonder, if your father was as devout a Presbyterian as you claim, how you come to question so much of what the Lord shows us to be true."

Delin shook his head. He didn't want to get into this again, but Jackson kept harping on him. "Honestly," Delin said, giving him a sideways glance, "of late, the actions of certain so-claimed 'men of God' have given me reason to question, and to look elsewhere for truth. Or at least not shut other doors."

"Again," Jackson muttered, "with your rubbish. These natives are begging for salvation. That you are blind to this fact still, after all we have seen, amazes me."

Then send me away, Delin mused. I've had enough of this mission. Enough of seeing all the money slated to help Alaska and its native people instead go towards funding missionary schools and churches where the only ones to benefit are the re-located American settlers you've brought up here. Plus, you disappear most of the winter, socializing back in Washington with politicians and clergymen.

As if reading his thoughts, Jackson brought up a proposal, after first checking his leather-bound journal with its maps and notes. "Mr. Wetherwax. A thought occurred to me. We are low on supplies. Ahead of us lies the frozen Yukon River. Perhaps you could follow it to St. Michael, then cross the Norton Sound to Nome. There you can pick up our schooner from its wharf. You've had enough experience piloting that craft, and should be able to do so on your own now."

"Where do you want me to go?"

"To Skagway, or better yet, Seattle."

Delin regarded him quietly, wishing they were at least on equal footing. The silhouettes of the other three men had arranged themselves like guardian statues behind Jackson. "What do you need?" Delin asked gloomily, feeling like an errand boy.

"Salt, cured meat, flour. I will give you government notes for your expenses." Jackson straightened his coat and glanced out over the valley. "Yes, after Nulato I think we'll make our way to the mission at Desolation Point. Return to us there—but be quick about it, and leave Nome as soon as the ice permits. We'll have only a short period when the seas are ice-free, and I'll be damned if I let another winter keep me up here. I want to get back to Washington as soon as possible, before the damn Democrats ruin all my work up here."

"It will take some time to arrange," Delin said as he looked out over the herd. "And I am not leaving my dogs."

"Understood," Jackson said. "It looks like they have done their part, anyway. Obedient creatures." He glared down at Delin. "Your three years are almost up, you know."

"Three months, eight days left," Delin said.

Jackson coughed again and took another puff. “Quite. Well, what I’m hinting at, my boy, is that if you were to find yourself too indisposed to make the return trip, kindly contract a captain to do so for you.”

“I will return,” Delin insisted. “I don’t break my promises.” Unlike some.

Sheldon Jackson regarded Delin with one eye in the sun and the other bound in shade. Delin tucked his coat tighter around himself, trembling slightly with a renewed chill. Without another word, he set off down the rocky path and tread through a thin layer of snow, following in the multitude of hoofprints.

And then he half-walked, half-ran to the river, with the dogs chasing him, full of anticipation for a new adventure.

He reached Nome on the twenty-fourth of February, nine days after he set out. They had made frequent stops: to fish, to sleep, and sometimes just to relieve the dogs’ boredom. In a promising location outside of the Anvil Creek, he had dug up the earth under the previous night’s fire and cleared nearly six ounces worth of shining gold flakes.

At Nome, he found Jackson’s schooner, one of four boats at the lone dock. The harbor was mostly ice-free, and the waterways looked manageable—surprisingly so, this early in the year. Deciding to chance it, Delin readied the ship, stopping first at the general store where he glanced at the latest San Francisco newspaper.

“War,” he noted, glancing at the headlines. “Again. Spain this time?”

The clerk, a thin, spectacled man nodded. “Lousy Spaniards sunk one of our ships in Havana. The Maine. Sneaky surprise attack, too, although they actually denied doin’ the deed.”

“So why are we fighting?”

“Well, if you listen to that Hearst fella who runs the paper...”

“George Hearst?” Delin recalled the stories Papa told him, about how Hearst was an expert prospector himself, and had done well at Comstock before going on to strike it even richer at Black Hills, South Dakota.

“No, not him. His son, Randolph. Owns the paper and, some say, most of the city. According to him, it’s our God-directed mission to kick the Spanish outta the whole hemisphere."

Delin nodded absently. He glanced over the counter and pointed to a shelf and several jars. "Those licorice sticks?"

"Yep," the clerk said cheerily, as if happy to discuss something other than the War. "Two for a penny."

Not wishing to convert Jackson's bonds just yet, Delin grinned and reached for his leather pouch. "How many for a pinch of gold?"

His supplies adequate for the trip south, he set off alone, working the sail and rudder on the small schooner. He could have brought on a crew, but the men around the docks were quietly reserved, avoiding contact and going about their business. Sensing something was amiss, Delin nonetheless put it out of his mind, assuming it had to do with apprehension from the onset of this Spanish-American War.

He sailed south, and the wind at his back was already turning colder. He steered through the waters where only five years ago, and much later in the spring, a score of great whaling vessels had met their match on the icy teeth of an early freeze. Foregoing Skagway—which, as he neared, lay enshrouded in heavy fog—he pressed on to Seattle. It would do for him to clear his head and go someplace new, he thought. And since Jackson's paying for it anyway...

He thought about his obligations and his promise many times during the long twelve-day sail. Many nights, with the ship anchored while he rested with the dogs in the dark quarters below, he thought about the needs of the natives and the missionary dream of Jackson's. And he felt as adrift as if he had lifted the anchor and sent the schooner into the rough seas.

In the midst of these raging internal doubts he rounded the final cliffs outside of Seattle and entered Schwabacher's Wharf. After so long at sea, witnessing no other signs of civilization, the sight of so many ships packed into the bay was astounding. There were brigs, men-of-war, steamers and frigates. Dingies, tugboats and ferries. Some were docked, others barreling out with such speed that Delin's craft heaved upon their wakes.

He steered for one pier that had recently emptied. As he approached, he scanned the decks of the departing boats, and his concern mounted. Something was at work here, perhaps the War again—but these didn't look like slack-eyed conscripts or even gung-ho warriors. There was a different kind of excitement in their expressions.

The passengers were an odd assortment; men from every walk of life prowled the decks, dressed as differently as could be—from three piece suits and top hats to grimy coats, ragged jackets and dusty hats. And livestock—horses, mules, goats and chickens. Delin took off his hat and scratched his head as he prepared to dock. The temperature was surprisingly moderate, but for some reason a chill crept slowly up his spine.

When at last he found a free space and had tethered the boat, the dogs began whining to be let off. Delin saw a small group of men coming up the pier toward him. He counted three of them, with a fourth lagging behind, but they were moving quite slowly, lugging immense packs. Frowning, Delin stepped onto the wooden pier, motioning first for his dogs to stay on the boat.

The men came to him, gasping from the exertion. He was so bemused by their appearance and attire that he almost failed to notice the incredible scene behind them, in the city's harbor square. When he finally focused on it, he opened his mouth in shock, and the nagging chill spread to his extremities.

What looked like an army swarmed in that cramped space between the buildings, dockhouses and fences. They packed the roads and stormed the wharf, clamoring for passage away, moving like a colony of determined ants.

"What is this?" Delin whispered as the four men stopped before him.

The closest, a well-dressed dark-haired man, glanced over his shoulder, then looked back, confused. The next man back, an Oriental—small and thin, clothed in gray trousers, a silken black vest and a wide cattle-herder's hat—stepped forward. "Do you not know?"

"Are you from the North Pole or something?" asked the third man—a Chilean, by his accent. Tall and heavy-set, with tattoos of dolphins on the sides of his neck.

Delin took notice of the men's belongings. Besides the heavy luggage, they carried a small cast-iron stove, a netted bag full of pots and pans, a violin case, an assortment of picks, shovels, pry bars and axes, and a curious-looking metal rod, forked at the top.

The Oriental man noticed Delin's attention and picked up the staff. "Divining rod!" he exclaimed.

"Yes," said the younger man. "Chang-Sai here claims to have the gift of dowsing. Using this doo-hickey here, he can scour the land and help our team find the gold."

Delin's heart stuttered. The dogs cried and lay down. Only Dunder stayed tense, growling. "Gold?" Delin asked, and leaned against a wooden post, fearing the answer.

"Of course," the young man answered, pronouncing the words very slowly. "You haven't heard?"

"All over the news, since August," said the Chilean. "Two steamers docked almost at the same time—in Seattle and also down there in San Francisco. Couple men aboard had sacks full of gold—nuggets, flakes and dust. Incredibly pure, ninety-eight percent, some say."

"They were just tossing small rocks out into the crowd—that's how much they found up there," said the younger man.

Delin closed his eyes and forced his lips to move, asking "Up where?" even as he envisioned a peaceful, sunny day in the past, and pictured a young boy with a small pick bounding through the streams in an uncluttered natural landscape.

"The Klondike!" three of them said at once.

The Chilean adjusted the heavy pack on his shoulder. "Some Indian name, I think, for an area up in that Delin Territory."

"Thron-diuck," Delin heard himself say, correcting the men, although he assumed the name had been altered in its pronunciation.

"Ah, so you know it," said the well-dressed man. "Well, an injun named Skookum Jim and some of his prospector friends, one called Carmack I think..."

"George Washington Carmack," Delin said, remembering he met the man ten years ago while prospecting.

"Yep, he found the first site, staked off some land, and before they knew it everyone from Fort Reliance down to Dyea were headin' there."

"Only hope there's some left for us," said the Chilean, looking over the armada in the bay, and the leagues of men on the shore. "Comin' from all over, they are. Men just leavin' their jobs and up and running north where the gold's just lyin' there for the taking."

"But it's near impossible to get a boat now," the Chinaman said. "And prices are soaring out of control. Started out at two hundred for a ticket, now it's a thousand. That's why we were hoping..."

Delin groaned and rubbed his temples. The internal debate about his next course of action had suddenly been evaporated in the blistering heat of this new revelation. But in the end, after only seconds of consideration that felt like long months, he made the only decision he could.

Like his father long years ago, faced with a similar choice, he gave in. Deserted his stint with the army. Broke a promise, and fled his duty. Whether it was simply to walk in Papa's footsteps—or whether he just needed to see if he could prevent the ruin of his homeland, he wasn't sure.

In either case, the gold had finally called him back.

After introductions, Delin discovered the well-dressed man, Floyd Miller, was from Boston. The Chinaman, Chang-Sai, had been working the mines in Leadville, Colorado until recently—until a strange dream urged him to head to the northwest and await his destiny. The Chilean was Martino Christos, and had been employed as a strong man in a traveling circus outside of Spokane when he heard the news.

There was a fourth, a brown-haired young man, covered in a heavy wool coat and a brightly-dyed yellow cotton hat, who stayed back from the group and said little.

Delin cleared his throat. "My conditions are, first—you pay for passage on this vessel and also for its return to Barrow. And second, I expect payment for my services as guide."

Floyd glanced at Martino. "Do we need a guide?"

Delin shrugged. "How are you planning to get to the gold fields?"

Floyd took a breath and spoke as if he'd done his research. "We're aiming to sail up the Inside Passage past Skagway and on to Dyea, where we'll disembark and head for the Chilkoot Pass, and over that onto Dawson where..."

"Hold on. The Chilkoot Pass? Is that where most of these crowds are going?"

"I believe so—it's the quickest way. Could go all the way up past the Aleutians to St. Michael by steamer and make our way to the Delin and then sail over to Dawson—but that's a thousand mile trip."

"Thirteen hundred fifty-five from the Alaskan Coast, to be exact," Delin said. "Go on."

"There's the White Pass—but we've already heard too many horror stories about that one. We could sail to Valdez and go over the glaciers to the flats and across to Dawson, but—"

"But the glacier is immense, and access is straight up. You'll never make it with heavy supplies."

"Right, so that leaves the Chilkoot. It's only twenty-seven miles overland that way until Lake Bennett, and then a quick jaunt, well—five hundred miles, but it's all on the water—up the Delin to Dawson. We'd get there weeks ahead of those taking the all-water route."

"The Chilkoot Pass." Delin stared at his feet. The Chilkoot tribes had only recently given up travel rights to that trail to the Canadians. They had only allowed one explorer to pass through in the last sixty years—besides his father and Matsei Xien long ago, who had slipped through unnoticed. The Pass was on the Alaskan-Canadian border, and was a difficult trail in any season. Sheer cliffs, jagged rockslides, and a very narrow and steep trail over the mountains. And just getting to the Pass involved crossing dangerous terrain—bogs, cliffs and canyons. Delin stared at each of them in turn. "It's suicide—especially in winter."

"Well," Floyd said, "gold makes men find a way."

"All the same," Delin responded, "you need a guide—and a dogsled team." He motioned to the growling dogs inside the boat, and the men peered in and clapped each other on the back.

Martino laughed. "You may be our godsend, sir."

"Truly the spirits are with us," Chang-Sai announced. "It is as my dream foretold. And besides, with the name Delin, you must be good luck."

Delin pressed on, resisting his curiosity about the man's prophetic dream. "My third condition is that certain things stay on this pier.

Namely—that."

Chang-Sai's expression fell as Delin pointed to his divining rod. "No..."

"Yes," Delin insisted. "And any other nonsense items you've been sold by unscrupulous know-nothings. There are no quick and easy devices that will do this work for you. You either have it in your blood to prospect, or you get lucky. Nothing else. Stick with me, however, and I'll give you pointers, such as how to read the land, how to prospect by the bending of streams, and how to trace the ancient river beds. Gold—I'll teach you to crawl inside its head, understand its characteristics and its motivations, and in a sense, become it. You'll know where gold goes and why it stays there. You'll understand its hundred million year love affair with the Earth's evolution, and then and only then, can you find it."

The men nodded, awed—even Chang-Sai, who reluctantly dropped his metal staff. And for the first time, Delin focused on the fourth man, hanging back. "What's his deal?" Delin whispered to Floyd.

Floyd shook his head. "We don't know. Can't seem to get rid of him though—he latched on to us in the crowd back there. Apparently his original group kicked him out."

"That true?" Delin asked. "What's your name, kid?"

"Oscar," the young man said, looking down and pushing a blond lock of hair from his face. "Oscar Leopold McCloud." He coughed, lifted his eyes and offered a weak smile. "The third. But please, just call me McCloud."

Floyd appeared bemused. "The third? You mean there were two others like you?"

"Yes," said McCloud, quietly, then perked up. "And they were all miners, back in Austria."

"Good," said Delin. "Although, I'm quite familiar with the look of those who have the hunger for mining, and I have to say in you it seems to be lacking. You sure you're set on this?"

"No he's not," said Chang-Sai. "A man is born to only one purpose. Mr. McCloud's is not to prospect, as he told us."

Delin raised an eyebrow. "Then...?"

Floyd and Martino glanced at each other, then chuckled.

McCloud straightened his shoulders. "I'm just going along

because of family duty. It's what they wanted of me."

"But...?" Delin prodded.

"But," McCloud continued, "I never cared for it. All that dirt. Filth under the fingernails and mud on your shoes." He shrugged. "If I don't happen to get lucky and succeed at it with the first pan, I plan to go back to my main wish."

"Tell them," Chang-Sai urged. "Don't listen to these other two when they laugh at you. Tell Mr. Wetherwax."

McCloud sighed. "I want to be a dentist!"

Martino and Floyd cackled, biting their knuckles and trying to look away from the blushing youth.

Delin nodded thoughtfully, then took the young man's pack and hefted it over his shoulder. "I'm not laughing. In the camps, where all those men have gold to spend and no one to fix their rotting teeth, you may be the only one to strike it rich."

He tossed the pack onto the boat and started loading the rest of their luggage. "Welcome aboard, gentlemen, let's step to it. Croesus never dallied on the shores of Persia while treasure awaited. Who knows, maybe you'll amass the riches of Solomon—but more likely you'll end up paupers or salmon fishers."

He glanced at McCloud. "Or dentists. Either way, you're about to have the adventure of your lives!"

CHAPTER 21: APRIL, 1898

ACROSS THE CHILKOOT PASS

IT TURNED OUT THEY COULDN'T get close to the docks at Dyea. Abandoned boats were moored for hundreds of feet out. Like the skeletal remnants of an ancient navy, the vessels labored to stay afloat in the frigid waters, their hulls scraping against each other, huddling for warmth.

Delin maneuvered their schooner as close as possible, finally using the oars to thread a path to a rocky abutment. They unloaded the supplies carefully along a wooden plank and set off on jagged and wet footing. The dogs led the way, Prancer and Vixen ahead of the pack, yelping with excitement at the scent of home. On the shore, crowds stormed the port like an invading force. With them came horses, mules and sheep, and cages of chickens, huge chests—armoires, even—a piano and a cello, cases full of food, and weapons: rifles, pistols, knives, dynamite and blasting powder. Moving among the men were natives, mostly Chilkat Indians, although Delin recognized a few Tlingits. They carried sleds and harnesses, and a few had dogs in tow, and were offering their services as guides—at very high rates.

Delin found a flat patch of land and set about hooking up the dogs. "Stove, tools and some of the food supplies can go on the sled," he told them, readying the straps. "And if you don't have the required amount of supplies..."

"We're set," said Martino, slinging an extra sack over his shoulder, then pulling out a crumpled piece of paper from his coat pocket. "Leaflets were given out in Seattle. The Canadian government insists on at least twelve hundred pounds of supplies before customs will let you cross the border."

God bless those Canadians, Delin thought as he scanned the small typescript and read the list of suggested items. The list was probably saving countless lives. Since the Klondike was in Canadian territory, and they were likely monitoring the Chilkoot Pass, the White Pass and the river entrance, they were wisely insisting that only serious miners make this attempt. Once at Dawson City, where food could only be brought in by boat during the summer, gold-seekers would need enough to last the winter.

"Damn near broke us," Floyd said. "A little forewarning before setting out from St. Louis would have been nice."

"But we managed," said Chang-Sai, with a tip of his hat. His high cheekbones and tanned skin stretched with his smile. Delin imagined those eyes had seen a great many hardships, and had endured some fierce discrimination—although it seemed on this rush so much more diversity existed, and tolerance. As if, preparing for the devastating cold when all men would be indistinguishable in their layers of wool, the single drive toward gold would unite them in ways the earlier rushes had not.

However, it was still early in the strike, and excitement and hopes were high. Delin fully expected that when the truth set in, when the harsh conditions took their toll and when mocking failure reared its head, the darker side of humanity would show its ugly face once more.

"My guess," Delin said, "is that there will also be a customs charge by the Mounties to cross the Chilkoot Pass."

Floyd nodded. "A percentage of weight, at the checkpoint. Heard all about it, and we're set." He glanced back at McCloud, who was trying to get a leather case over his shoulder. "Although I'm not sure about him."

McCloud looked up and spoke through a tightly-bundled orange scarf. "I have money left."

"Probably from his daddy," Floyd whispered.

"Enough," said Chang-Sai. "Everyone has his place."

"His," said Floyd, "should be somewhere else."

Delin glanced back at the youth, but if McCloud took offense to the latest jab, he didn't show it. Instead, he ran off and began bartering with a group of Tlingits. When he returned, he had exchanged his dull frock coat for a multi-colored parka that matched his scarf and red mittens.

Someone up ahead began a song, and after a few minutes everyone down the line picked up the words. As Delin cracked the whip to the right of Dunder's ears, they lurched forward, with the men trotting along behind the sled.

"Oh, to the Klondike! We've paid our fare,
Our golden slippers soon we'll wear
We'll live on pig and polar bear
And gather the nuggets we know are there!"

When the song reached their group, only McCloud began to sing, his voice tumbling in clear, lofty tones, overshadowing everyone else's attempts. Delin started humming in time. The dogs whined. Approaching the rugged foothills, the wind met them with a chilled, bitter foreshadowing of things to come.

Four days later, after leaving the place called Canyon City, with its boulders and rock-strewn trails, they traveled all day, occasionally pulling ahead of slower moving travelers. At times, as they ascended muddy, frosty trails, they saw the littered remnants of those who had already passed by. There were broken cabinets and chests too heavy to carry—splintered and hewn for their wood; at one bend, at the base of a rocky incline, they saw the discarded piano, its keys shattered and its legs sawed off for firewood. As the hours passed in a muscle-numbing pace, as the snow began to fall in drifting whirls, the items discarded became grimmer. Here was a horse, its legs broken under the strain, shot in the head. There, a pair of mules and an ox, likewise shot, their brains painting the snow-sculpted hills.

Delin heard rumors that on the White Pass trail, over two thousand animals had perished already—and the rush was not even a year old. Over thirty-five thousand men had made the journey to Alaska last autumn, and if rumors were to be believed, Delin and his little partnership were among another hundred thousand on their way. The economic collapse of 1893 had led the country into its worst financial crisis since the Revolution, and for men on both coasts, the American Dream had crumbled around them. The country had needed this gold rush more than ever—and it seemed to come just at the right time.

By nightfall on March twenty-eighth, Delin's team reached the base of the Chilkoot Pass, the place they called Sheep's Camp—a valley surrounded by high cliffs and peaks, where in the past, only mountain goats could be seen. In the fading sunlight they could still make out the mass of humanity stepping into line to join the hundreds on their way up—a long, unbroken chain of hopeful miners ascending the last, brutal approach. And there, at what seemed to be a region near the top, stood the Scales—a ledge a half-mile beneath the Chilkoot Pass, aptly named as the place where each prospective miner had his gear re-weighed, and where they were cleared to move on up the pass, or were rejected.

Delin took a deep breath and surveyed that last ascent of the pass itself—an incomprehensible climb up a thirty-five degree angle. After resting at the Scales, most climbers got in line and used a tow cable attached at the top; they pulled themselves up—along with however much of their supplies they could carry. As bad as it was—and as challenging as it appeared at first sight—the worse news, the understanding that nearly turned back everyone that heard it, was that the trip had to be made many, many times. To carry up over a thousand pounds of supplies and equipment took, on average, thirty-five trips. So the apparently shorter route of a mere twenty-seven miles on a map turned out to be over a thousand miles of actual walking—a trip that could take up to three months. You made it to the top, dropped off your gear in a big dump along with everyone else's, staked it and covered it with a tarp, then began the slow descent back down for the rest. For some of the braver souls, the descent was a little easier—just slide down a carved-out trail like a human toboggan.

Delin urged them all to get some sleep here at Sheep's Camp among the tents and shanties. If they got up at first light, they could make it up the three and a half mile ascent to the Scales and be there by late afternoon—perhaps in time to make one trip to the top and back. Then, if they could average three trips a day, they could be over the pass by late April. The weather, although freezing and bitter, hadn't left much snow on base where they had begun—although a two week blizzard had dumped tremendous levels on the Pass itself, and drifts were very heavy near the top.

They settled under a makeshift shelter. The dogs collapsed together in a contented heap outside, utterly exhausted. They had eaten well—better than the men, Floyd complained, but hushed up after a look from Delin. Everyone but McCloud took a swig from a passing bottle of vile moonshine that Martino had brewed back home; then everyone bedded down for the night.

Less than three hours later, in the still of the night when even the wind had retired, Delin found himself jarred awake. Attuned as he was to any sound out of the ordinary, he perked up and heard stealthy footfalls around the dying fire. A dark shadow crouched there, scattering something beside the flickering logs. Reaching for his knife—Moon Chaser's old antler-handled blade he had kept as a keepsake—Delin rolled silently out from the bearskin blanket. He tiptoed past McCloud as he snored under a velvet blanket that looked like it should be hanging on a castle wall, and he crept to the figure. He moved closer—and saw a glint of steel.

"Do not be alarmed." The man hadn't turned or even flinched at Delin's approach. And it took a moment for Delin to place the voice.

"Chang-Sai?" he whispered.

"Yes." The Chinaman set down his blade, got on his knees and peered in front of him. Delin took a step to the side, and gasped when he saw blood and what looked like entrails.

"Chicken," Chang-Sai explained, pointing at the spread of internal organs, and there, to the side, the disemboweled, headless creature. "Bought it off the Idaho company. We'll eat it tomorrow, but I needed to study something."

"What?" Delin asked, then understood. He thought of Herodotus's Oracles, the seers who used various scrying techniques to tell the future. "You're reading the entrails?"

Chang-Sai nodded and held up a hand. "Bad dream last night. Could not understand it. Ancestors' power weak this far north. I decided to consult for myself."

Delin put away the knife and sat cross-legged beside the Oriental. "What was your dream?"

Chang-Sai shook his head. "Fleeting images. Whirling blizzards. A high peak, and great drifts of snow."

Delin nodded. "Go on."

"Something up there, waiting for us. Something… not right. Not human, not animal. An evil spirit clothed in white."

Delin's skin crawled under his thick clothes, and his senses quickened. He scanned the darkness ahead and behind, over the leagues of men and beasts huddled in their tents or out in the open beside smoldering fires.

Chang-Sai focused again on the still-steaming entrails. "The dream cut off quickly, but I had the sense that this creature—or several of them—were waiting. But not for us all, as I had thought at first."

Chang-Sai sighed. "This spread, this placement, confirms it. I asked if it sought us out specifically."

Delin's throat went dry; he wanted to dismiss all of this, to proudly proclaim he didn't believe in a word, but he managed to ask anyway: "What does it say?"

Chang-Sai looked up, and his face modestly clothed itself in darkness. "It says no. But then, I asked if these devils were after you."

Delin sat perfectly still.

Chang-Sai's words slithered from the darkness. "I no longer believe," he said, turning his head, "that teaming with you has, in fact, been a good thing."

After a minute of stillness, Delin reached out and laid a hand on the man's shoulder. "I can't say I blame you." He looked ahead, up the last trail that led to the Scales. "You have my permission to journey this next part without me. I will repay you the difference, and..."

"No," Chang-Sai said with defiance. "I cannot fight what brought me here. My ancestors spoke of a destiny, of my fate to be reached on this trail in the days to come. I do not know what it is, but I do know that not all destinies are happy ones." He stood up, brushed off his pants, and faced the dark cliffs ahead. "A man can only be one thing, and I go tomorrow to be that."

On the second day and the sixth trip up the Pass, Floyd actually felt confident enough to take the lead from Delin. The dogs were tethered far below, at the western edge of the Scales with the rest of their supplies. Delin led the men for the first four hours after sunrise; taking a path a short distance away from the main line of climbers—a side route traveled by a few of the Chilkat Indian guides. They ascended rugged steps carved out of the ice and rock—an alternate path from the "Golden Stairs" followed by most of the others. Even after the snows intensified, turning to heavy squalls by afternoon, the heavily trod steps remained visible. Soon, in the blinding, swirling blizzard, they traveled as if by instinct, their numb limbs conditioned to the route.

Falling in line behind Floyd and Martino, Delin climbed shoulder to shoulder with Chang-Sai while McCloud trudged along behind, looking more and more miserable with each trip.

Delin turned into the swirling, stinging wind. He had fixed on his snowshoes, which helped to steadily distribute the extra weight he carried on his back—a full forty pounds more than the others. "Hey, McCloud! How're you doin' back there?"

Covered in sticky snow, with icicles dangling from his nose and poking from under his hat, McCloud tried to smile underneath his frosty scarf. "Never better!" he shouted back. "Just using this time to think about teeth—and how mine are chattering so hard I fear they'll break!"

Delin laughed. "At least you can fix 'em if they do, right?"

"Sure," said McCloud, leaning closer and peering into Delin's face, past the snow-crusted beard and mustache. "I must say, I'm a bit surprised at how clean and straight your teeth are. I'd assumed a man such as yourself..."

"Would've lost 'em by now?"

"Something like that. Don't get me wrong, I'm sure you're good at what you do, but well, let's face it. Living out here, with no clear hygiene, eating food that's likely too raw, or diseased and soft, and drinking and smoking too much..."

Delin shrugged. "Don't do much of the latter two, especially smoking. And my papa taught me to beware the dangers of drinking—nothing more than the occasional warm up beverage or two with fellow prospectors. No, my only vice is the love of licorice sticks." He shot McCloud a look. "You're not going to tell me they'll rot my teeth now, are you?"

"Oh no," McCloud said, looking away. "You should be fine unless you're eating a ton of them or something."

"Well…"

"It's a known fact that entire regiments of Napoleon's troops had their teeth turn black after chewing too many during extended tours of battle."

Delin's smile vanished.

"But your choppers seem fine. And besides, licorice has many long-term benefits. In addition to aiding in the quenching of thirst, it helps your immune system, aids digestion, fights coughs and otherwise keeps you healthy."

"That it does," Delin said, nodding in satisfaction. He turned and trudged ahead, assisting Chang-Sai.

"Delin?" the Oriental said after gasping for air as they passed the midpoint. The storm had passed, and the snows stopped their assault on the climbers. Over Chang-Sai's right shoulder, not more than fifty feet away, an endless line of dark figures broke the featureless white landscape, hauling their supplies up the fierce incline.

"Yes?"

"I was thinking about my vision the other night. My dream." He gazed up the cliffside, past the jagged boulder-sized outcrops and frosted ledges to the barely-discernible summit four hundred feet ahead. "And I fear... whatever it is, it will happen soon."

Clasping his arm again, Delin shook his head. "Don't be afraid. You're surrounded by an army of men, with the Northwest Mounted Police up on the crest. We're all in this together and nothing's going to attack us out here." He made himself say the words, but at the same time he was scanning the ridge. Something up there looked odd. Hard to tell from here, but something about those deeper packets of white drew his attention; the three indistinct house-sized shapes that he swore weren't there on the last ascent. In his imagination, they shifted and slowly moved in unison above the heavy drifts.

More than once he thought he caught a glimpse of blinking red pinpoints. He sniffed the air, and strained to hear any telltale bellows or whistling sounds. But there was nothing, although his ears, covered with earmuffs and a thick wool hood, couldn't pick out much beyond the howling wind.

Chang-Sai moved along, clinging to Delin as he carefully placed each boot ahead of the last. "All the same, sir. I would ask—no, beg—a favor of you."

"Name it!" Delin shouted, and rubbed at his face with his frosty gloves, trying to warm up the skin on his exposed nose and cheeks. Their mercury had stopped responding several hours ago—frozen, itself; which indicated it had to be lower than thirty-eight below zero. There were other tests they could use for lower temperatures—whiskey had a freezing point of negative fifty-five, for instance; but no one wanted to check that sobering fact just yet.

"If anything should happen to me," Chang-Sai said, "I would beg you to honor a sacred tradition in my family. My bones..."

"What?" Delin asked, not hearing the rest.

"My remains!" Chang-Sai shouted. "Send them to my family in China to be buried with my ancestors. To Tianjin, on the west bend of the Beiho River. Hsian-xi is my family name."

Delin stopped and pulled back his hood and looked into the face of the Chinaman. He stuck out his hand. "You have my word. In such an unfortunate—and hopefully distant event—I will send them there by fastest steamer."

Chang-Sai bowed, then gripped Delin's hand. "Thank you, guide." With slow determination, he turned his head up toward the ridge—from where a strange, undulating sound descended, as if carried by the advance of tiny, nugget-sized snowballs. A high-pitched wail, buffeted by the winds and muzzled by the chill, began with a whimper then rose until all the men ahead and behind stopped in their tracks and lifted their heads.

Far below came the frantic warning of dogs barking.

"It is time," Chang-Sai voiced, the words sounding like a vibrating drum in Delin's ears.

And Delin stared, mouth open in disbelief. Three gray-shaded forms lurched and ducked away from the ledge above them—between Delin's trail and the main line of ascending gold-rushers. And then it seemed the sky erupted—just as the ground trembled and the Pass shook with a low and menacing roar, like a big cat that had cornered its prey.

Men everywhere dropped their supplies and stared in abject horror and disbelief. After enduring so much just to get here—now this.

A wall of tumbling ice and snow hundreds of feet wide advanced upon them—shook loose from the heavy buildup of weeks upon weeks of great snowfalls, then jarred free by something only Delin had seen: a trio of fiendish beasts above, perhaps acting out of fury, perhaps in some last ditch effort to prevent the gross invasion of their realm.

Delin yelled "RUN!" and grabbed for Chang-Sai, but the man had already disappeared as the first wave of the avalanche struck. His hand fumbled across Delin's for a second, then he was gone, just before a roaring, tumbling force knocked Delin sideways. He scrambled to keep his feet, then he leapt and spun in the direction he hoped was away from danger.

The next few minutes were nothing but a jumbled series of chaotic images and brutal, unrelenting volumes of snow. Snow, tons of it, piling and piling down around him and over him, and then—miraculously, under him. It actually lifted and knocked him free as the great wave roared down the Pass. As he tumbled, alone now, grunting with each impact and trying to see something beyond the chunks of ice bursting into the air, he managed to get his pick free of his belt. On the next roll he struck out and dug its point deep, striking into the underlying drift.

With a grunt, his body straightened. He tucked his head down and pulled up his knees and let the less forceful dregs of the avalanche pass overhead and around him. Then, with all his strength, he pushed with his feet and cleared a path free with his back, erupting into the clear air and standing waist-deep in a drift, three-quarters of the way back down the mountain.

He stared up at what looked like a different landscape. A pristine covering of new, deep snow, punctuated by a few errant ice chunks and larger snowballs, led the way back to the summit. A weak sun simmered through an overcast sky drizzled with floating debris.

And then men were rushing past him, staggering up the hill. And others were stumbling down to help—climbers who had been unloading at the top when disaster struck. And then came the Mounties, racing with their picks and ropes. And then he could hear again—shouts and cries for help. The baneful howling of the dogs, barking to be free of their tethers. Somebody please let them loose, Delin thought grimly. We're going to need their noses very soon.

He pulled himself out, ripping the pick free as well, then stood unsteadily and forced his legs to move, to ascend. He scanned the ground and started to see things: hands sticking up—some of them waving frantically, others limp and lifeless. Delin continued climbing, scraping at the loose snow as he moved, listening for any sounds of trapped men. Something crunched behind him and he turned. There was Martino, the big Chilean looking no worse, except for the expression of shock on his face. He pointed up ahead, and they both quickened their pace to reach the red mittened hand waving to them.

They dropped to their knees and had the arm free in seconds. Half a minute later they were dragging McCloud out. He shook his head and brushed off his body, while Delin and Martino cautiously watched him. "No broken bones?" Delin asked.

McCloud coughed out chunks of snow. "Apparently not."

"Miracle," Martino said, then pushed past the grinning man and scanned up the hill.

"Floyd?" Delin asked.

"Down there," Martino said, motioning to the Scales.

Delin breathed in relief. "Good, then..."

"No," Martino said, shaking his head. "He was crushed and dragged all the way down. Died in my arms."

"Oh no," McCloud whispered. "What about Chang-Sai?"

A dozen men trudged past them, carrying picks and shovels. The wind slowed; then, out of respect, it stopped. The Pass turned silent but for a few muffled cries of the dying.

Delin closed his eyes and lifted his face to the impassive sky as if to ask an answer of its infinity—to kindly deliver some kind of explanation of this whole comedy of life and death.

"We have to find his body," he said at last. "I have a promise to keep."

When April third came to a close, the men huddled in makeshift tents at the Scales, sitting soberly by a score of fires, and they took measure of the disaster. Sixty men, including Chang-Sai and Floyd, had lost their lives. *Sixty*. Delin stirred a pot of steaming beans over the fire and looked into its red depths, lost in thought. Another seventy-five men were injured—half of them too badly to continue.

They would be heading back to Dyea at first light, returning as casualties of a war never fought, from a battlefield never reached.

"And you?" McCloud asked finally, while Martino came and scooped himself out a portion of dinner. "Will you stay with us to Dawson, or..."

"I will continue on," Delin said. "I have two promises to honor—first to get you to the Klondike. The other, to Chang-Sai, can be fulfilled later." He looked past the smoking fires to a dark section of land on the southern edge of the cliff's base. Rows of markers stood there, indicating the fresh graves dug all afternoon with great difficulty in the frozen ground. The team members of the fallen men made the decision whether to bury the dead here, or to send them back and pay for the transport. Most elected to keep the bodies here—some claimed they would return and re-inter the remains at a later time, when they headed back this way with their riches.

McCloud read his expression. "You'll have to dig him up?"

"The cold will preserve him."

"Not worried about cold," Martino grunted and pointed up the Pass. "More concerned about the thaw. And mudslides. Hate to be headin' up this pass for the first time in summer and seein' them bodies suddenly wash up at my feet!"

Delin shuddered. Maybe I'll come for him earlier, then. Standing, he looked up at the dark silhouette of the Chilkoot Pass. He followed the moon-dappled edges and crooks to the barely-visible outline of the summit, where a few bold stars dared to show themselves. They sparkled, urging the mortals below to ignore this setback; to shake it off and continue upwards, and never forget the glittering prize waiting over the ridge.

But Delin scanned the top for other figures. For anything that moved. For loping sentinels that patrolled above like the three-headed Cerberus guarding the gates of Hell.

Anger smoldered in his soul. He thought of Mama, of her sacrifice and those haunting nightmares that had plagued his dreams ever since; he smelled the raw stench of scarred fur again and his hand found the rifle at his side and clenched its cold barrel.

I will find you. Soon. And this will end.

Chapter 22: Yukon Territory - May 1898—June, 1899

IN THE KLONDIKE

On May twenty-ninth, the first cracks appeared in the ice on Lake Bennett. Seven thousand boats patiently waited on the shore. They waited another two days until the ice had melted enough to take sail, and then they groaned under the collective weight of over twenty thousand men and several hundred women. The fleet had been constructed using any and every available material, and countless axes had broken in the chopping of nearby trees.

At last, on June first, with sails made from canvas, from blankets, coats, bloomers and sheets, the fleet set off. Delin, McCloud and Martino, however, were not among those that left on the first of June. They had gotten a jump on the others, borrowing a technique Delin recalled from his father's stories—attaching sails to their triangular-shaped craft and setting out over the ice. Only, he modified the approach a little and harnessed the dogs, letting them try their art at hauling and running with the wind to help carry the load.

It worked well—to the chagrin of those they left on the shores. A shout rose in the early dawn, as a crowd formed and waved them on. McCloud stood up on the prow in his unbuttoned tunic and a green beret—which he took off and waved euphorically in the air.

Now, nearly a week later, they traveled with the dogs inside as the fast moving, nearly ice-free river carried them along. And in those long days of sail, while the glacial salts in the Yukon River hissed with their boat's passing, and as they steered around floating driftwood, Delin thought back to the start of spring on the shores of Lake Bennett. When the briar roses opened and the bluebells blossomed, and they had set about to build their boat.

They had first traveled up to his old Tlingit village, with his dogs yelping and skipping ahead, noses to the ground, thrilled at recognizing the old scents. But when they approached the clearing, they stopped all at once, laid down and let Delin pass through them.

Dragging his feet, he made his way to the center of the old courtyard; and he turned in a slow circle, surveying the field of hacked trees and mangled stumps, looking out over the piles of earth and rubble. There was nothing left. Not even one stick. All the wood from the Long House, the sheds and outlying shacks—all gone, carved up by the others for their boats.

Dejected and numb, Delin staggered away and walked, then trotted, then ran. And he found himself at the spot where his mother's Spirit House had been. With a cry, he dropped to his knees and placed his forehead against the damp earth, beside a small trio of stone markers—the only signs left indicating the foundation of some other structure.

"I'm sorry, Mama," he cried, breathing the words into the porous mud as his fingers dug into the earth. The cross around his neck slipped free and brushed against the ground.

Someone cleared his throat and a hand appeared, which Delin took. McCloud helped him up. They wordlessly returned to the lakeside, and walked among the crowds, among the thousands of men sawing and sanding, hammering and polishing.

And Delin turned his tear-speckled face back towards the path to the clearing—realizing it would surely be unrecognizable now to Joshua. To Mirna. To Mikhail. Probably, Delin thought, even to the Sesquat.

And for an instant, as chills ran across his arms, he imagined he saw a little boy standing beside a creek off in the distance, holding up a rock and gazing back in wonder at him and the sadness in his eyes.

They made it through the rapids—with a little help and advice from several pilots who had gone this far and had decided to offer their services to the hordes on their way. One of them was an aspiring young author. London, Delin recalled. Jack London—and he had to admit, the man had a way with words, and an obvious appreciation for the natural beauty of this land. Despite the swarms of mosquitoes rising from the muskeg moss on the river banks, plaguing them for much of the way, London was a cheery fellow who took an instant liking to Delin's dogs, spending hours on the shore running and chasing them around.

Finally, they moved on, with London promising to meet them later and try his luck at prospecting—after first earning some more money piloting people through the rapids. And so the trio sailed on, weeks ahead of the others, and passed into the days of the northern sun, where its light greeted them for over twenty hours at a time. Finally, at the end of their long journey, they followed a pair of bald eagles as they glided, flying over Dawson City, leading the way to the prize.

After mooring their boat, they walked about the burgeoning boomtown and were amazed at the extent of construction: houses, stores, town halls, churches, an endless array of saloons and dance halls; several banks and two sawmills which constantly operated, churning out lumber for more construction. Once in the hills, away from all the commotion and crowds, Delin carefully selected from among several hundred available claims, foregoing most and striking out for some of the more inaccessible areas, surmising they would have been the least inspected—and perhaps, the most promising.

They settled for a hundred square foot section on the fourth bend of Monte Cristo creek, registered their claim, then got to work. Even McCloud did his fair share, and did it without complaining, despite the rising heat, the hundred-degree summer days, and the host of painful flies and mosquitoes. They dug and picked and sifted and pried loose the earth and rocks—and for a long time, that was their life. Toiling for six hours after breakfast, then a quick lunch of ham sandwiches on sourdough bread, then another seven hours until the usual pork and beans dinner. Then, back to clean out their diggings, apply the quicksilver to free the gold. Inspect the day's take, and prepare for tomorrow's efforts.

The sacks of extracted gold grew heavier and heavier. Not exceptionally so, like some of the earlier prospectors—those like the Lucky Swede or Big Alex Macdonald, who had bought up over a hundred other claims and hired men out to work them. Delin occasionally walked around in the late hours of the evening, when it was still light after midnight and men were drinking and singing, telling stories of their successes and failures. He toured the other sites, and looked upon some with jealousy, recalling his time here as a young boy, and remembering how Papa had told him to only take a little. Was this what I left it for? he wondered. For these men to get rich, and then spend it like water down in the saloons?

One day in mid June, as thousands of new arrivals were coming in—more and more every day—Delin and McCloud were visiting Dawson to replace a pick and buy a new shovel when they got caught in a huge crowd in the public square. A man stood on a porch and shouted out the headlines from a paper brought by steamer.

"What's he sayin'?" McCloud asked, standing on his toes.

"War's over," Delin replied. "A final battle in Manila Bay, then the Spanish surrendered to Admiral Dewey."

"Well, that's done then." McCloud said with a smile."I bet that's the last war we'll see for a while. No one will want to tangle with us. The next century will be all about peace!"

"Yes, that and dental hygiene." Delin slapped the young man on the back. He guided them through the cheering crowd as men tossed their hats and shouted their excitement.

They continued on to the general store, haggled a little, but were ultimately dismayed at the price of basic materials. It was truly a seller's market, with demand causing everything to become almost as valuable as the gold they were digging up. Dawson City parted a man from his diggings as fast as possible. And for most of the forty thousand that would make it here, it took from them everything but their memories. Only a few lucky thousand made any significant finds, but it was the glaring success of a couple hundred ostentatious miners that lent hope to all the others.

Men like Alexander Pantages, who soon opened a theater and went on to fund many more. And others like Charlie Kimball who would lose over three hundred thousand dollars in a three month drinking and gambling spree.

The months passed. And the work continued. By the time the ground finally froze in October and the easy digging came to an end, Delin's team had switched claims three times, buying out or trading for ones that impatient miners were quick to hand over.

By the end of the season, the three of them had collected over two hundred pounds worth of gold. Almost thirty-two thousand dollars worth, or ten thousand apiece.

"Not bad," Martino said over a celebratory glass of whiskey in early October as they sat around a campfire outside their tents. The sun had descended, again returning to an appropriate schedule for a few months, enjoying this basic complacency before it prepared to disappear for most of the day.

"Not at all," Delin agreed, raising his glass and draining it. He sucked in a breath and shook his head, then licked the drops from his ragged mustache. "What do you say, Mr. McCloud? Did you do your old family proud?"

McCloud looked up from his glass, and smiled. He had recently washed his face, and had taken his nightly cold bath, so he looked prim and clean. "Uh, yeah. Sure. But I was thinking—ten thousand. That's a lot. Enough, really to..."

"To what?" Martino said with a belch. "Get yourself some gold teeth?"

"No," McCloud said. "To buy an office. A dentist's office. Here in town."

Neither Delin nor Martino laughed. Instead, they looked at each other and smiled. "You've earned it," Delin said at last, and poured another round for all of them. "And you're probably smart to do it now—before the winter sets in. Otherwise, if we stay out here, it's all about fire setting—digging out the top layers of frosted earth, lighting a fire to melt the topsoil, then digging some more. All winter long."

"No thanks!" McCloud said, shaking his head and admiring his fingernails, proud that he had just saved them from devastation. "I believe then, this is where our partnership ends."

"Just as well," said Martino. "I got an offer from some Cheechakos from southern California. Wanting me to help strike up along Porcupine Creek at the bottom of the Dome."

"You're welcome to it," Delin said. "You have no more to learn from me, my friend."

"Thank you," Martino said, extending his hand and taking Delin's in a firm shake. "Best of luck to you—although I suspect you don't need it."

"We all do," Delin said. "Just some more than others. And I have other goals that will be needing a little help."

"Okay then," McCloud said. "I'll be off to town in the morning, and I expect to see both of you at my office in the next couple months." He waved a scolding finger at Delin. "And go easy on those licorice sticks."

Delin never did stop in for an appointment, although he did meet up with Dr. McCloud on several occasions in the winter and early spring. In those long months he had spent a great deal of time in Dawson, experiencing what a big city was like. Nearly forty thousand people lived there now—easily a rival of Seattle or Portland, and the largest city in Canada. He experienced culture, at last, in its many forms: reveling in renditions of Shakespeare at a local theater, then almost weeping in a grand opera hall to the scores of Puccini, Haydn and Handel.

He read voraciously, and spent months at a lower-cost hotel off of Front Street—one that let him keep his dogs in a side room out back. His money went far, as he spent it judiciously, staying away from the gambling halls and saloons. He drank occasionally with the miners, and he found himself welcome in most bars, but was a little embarrassed to learn he had become famous—probably from McCloud as he tended to his patients.

Some asked if it was true that he could prospect any land, and if he had once thrown away a fortune in gold rather than let thieves find it. Others whispered behind his back that his father and mother were killed by Indians; still others contradicted those rumors and said that bears had killed his folks. A couple from Juneau related that he won the biggest stakes in a dogsled race as a kid, upsetting the champion—who even now continued to race, unbeaten ever since.

And if they gave him enough drinks, Delin might spill a story or two of his own, not always telling the truth, but often enough. There was gossip that he'd found a five pound nugget—which would make it the largest one ever discovered—larger even than Big Alex MacDonald's three and a half pounder he was so proud of. This rumor *was* true, but Delin would never admit it, and he kept that little find hidden away.

And life went on, much the same, until the end of spring.

Until a steamer came to town and docked—the same day Delin contemplated heading back to his claim to start prospecting for another season.

It was on that morning that McCloud ran to Delin's hotel, pounded on the door and told him the news. Delin emerged, blinking in the fierce sunlight—light that hadn't been so intense in many, many months. He quickly looked past McCloud to see the unusually large number of people on the street, all heading toward the docks. Many of them were loaded up with luggage and packs of supplies.

"Uh oh," he groaned. "Where are they going now?" He knew word had gotten out that the Klondike was running its course—all the good placer finds were snapped up and worked already, and there was nothing for the majority of people to do other than lose their remaining money—or head home.

"Another find!" McCloud shouted, pointing. "All the way on the coast. At..."

"Let me guess," Delin said, leaning against the doorframe. He closed his eyes and tasted the familiar twinge of saltwater, and he felt a cool chill race down his spine. "Nome."

McCloud coughed, choking on his surprise. "How did you...?"

Delin shrugged. "I was there first. So, what are you going to do?"

"I don't know. That's why I came to you, to ask your advice. Is there enough at Nome?"

"No, of course not. Not for an army like this. Those beaches will be staked out and dredged and upturned in weeks. And despite what I managed to find, it won't be easy for the common folk after the first layers are gone. They'll need the bigger machines, drills and sifters."

"Yeah," McCloud said, as if seeing it all in his head. "But still—they'll need a dentist, right?"

"Of course." Delin sighed. "I guess you should go, then."

McCloud gave him a sour look. "But... you're not coming? To a gold rush? Gold... I did say that, didn't I? Or maybe you didn't hear...?"

"I heard. And you heard me. I'm sitting this one out." Delin took McCloud's hand and shook it. "Good luck, kid. Maybe we'll meet again after all this madness is over, and you can pull my teeth or something."

"But—what will you do?"

Delin had thought about that a lot lately, and had come to a decision. "Close out the claim," he said at last. "Sell it for what I can—maybe to old Bill Macdonald. By my reputation, and his indebtedness, I'm sure I can wiggle a little extra out of him. Then, I think it's off to honor my second promise."

"Chang-Sai?"

"Right. His image plagues my dreams, and I can't rest. I think of him, rotting in the earth back there at the Chilkoot Pass. I worry about mudslides. And animals." He hung his head. "No, I want to leave tomorrow. I'll head back upriver with the dogs and anyone who wants to join me."

McCloud sighed. "Very good, then. You're an honorable man. Tell that old Chang-Sai I miss him dearly, and have him pray to his ancestors, or his gods or whatever, for me."

Delin smiled. "I'll do that. Goodbye, McCloud."

Chapter 23: 1900

THE BOXER REBELLION AND A GIFT'S RETURN

By the time he reached Skagway the snows had melted and spring had reclaimed the world with the tenderness of a returning lover. Despite the beauty of the new season, Delin wished he had come during the winter. He had dug up Chang-Sai's bones and wrapped them in salts and a heavy tarp, but still, the winter months underground had kept the remains a little too fresh for Delin to bear. Cremation would have been good, he thought, but he didn't know the customs of the Chinese. If he sent back just a jar of ashes instead of actual bones, would that sacrilege doom poor Chang-Sai to an afterlife of never-ending torment?

No, he decided to bring the bones, securing them on the sled while he walked behind the dogs and made for Skagway.

Carefully treading Skagway's muddy streets, he made his way to the start of the plank sidewalks where he tethered his dogs against on a railing. Although this town had a reputation for being the most lawless place in Alaska a few years back, when Jefferson "Soapy" Smith and his gang of thugs were in charge, it had since improved, taken back by its outraged citizens after Soapy was killed in a gunfight.

In one tavern, a place called Clancy's Saloon, he found the dockmaster. "I understand what you're lookin' for," said the stocky man with a Georgian accent. "But all the ships out in the dock now—none of them are captained by anyone I'd call trustworthy. 'Specially with the stuff goin' on up at Nome."

Delin bought the man a drink. "So what do you suggest?"

"There's a Navy gunboat picking up supplies and dropping off some administrators or such. Word is, their next port is exactly where you want to go."

"What?"

"Yep," the dockmaster said. "Some kind of trouble in China. That Secretary of State John Hay stirred up a real hornet's nest over there with his whole 'Open Door' trade policy. You know them slanty-eyes, though—never trusting foreigners. Five thousand years without one inside the borders, and then we expect 'em to change in just a few years? So now a bunch of 'em—a secret society called the Boxers on account of their fancy martial arts skills—are stormin' the places where the foreign diplomats are stayin'. Rioting, killing and lootin' and stuff."

"No kidding?"

"Nope. Christian missions especially been targeted I hear. Chinese converts gettin' killed by the thousands. Main foreign compound near Peking's all barricaded off and just a couple hundred U.S. and Europeans are keeping out ten thousand of those maniacs. I hear that eight other countries are each sendin' in a couple thousand troops. Some kind of 'relief force'."

Delin scratched his beard and stared at the bottom of his glass. "Not too sure the Navy will have time for such an errand as I'm looking for."

"Nope," said the dockmaster. "Doesn't sound like it. But you can try 'em."

Thanking the man, Delin left a coin for the barkeep and set out for the docks.

"Well, well." The broad shouldered man stood with his hands on his hips at the dock, in front of the *Valencia*'s gangplank. "I thought you'd be off to Nome by now, or did you strike it so rich in the Klondike that it doesn't matter?"

Delin groaned. *Of all the people. The world really was too small a place.* "Lieutenant James Bradley. Nice to see you again. Not out searching for me all this time, I hope?"

"Don't flatter yourself, man," Bradley said. "Besides, I was shocked you put up with Sheldon Jackson as long as you did—especially when there was nothing in it for you anymore."

Delin looked down at his boots. "Well, to answer your question, no I didn't strike it all that rich in the Klondike, but I did make some good friends. One of them..." he pointed over his shoulder to the dogsled. "One didn't make it."

Bradley raised his eyebrows and looked over his shoulder. "Sorry about that, but don't they have a morgue in this town?"

"He's not from here," Delin replied. "In fact, his dying wish was to have his body returned to his family."

"Always nice to be with family," Bradley said, taking out a cigar and looking in his pockets for a light. "So, let me guess—you're trying to honor that promise? You've got a nasty habit of doing that, you know? So, you want to send him off, but the only problem is there are no boats."

"Correct." Delin watched him light the end of the cigar and take a deep puff. "I come to you not because you're the only trustworthy ship captain here, but because you and my late friend may be heading to the same destination."

Bradley coughed up a cloud of thick smoke. "Sorry? Wait—your pal's a Chinaman?"

"Yes."

"First Indians, now Celestials? Wetherwax, you don't seem to have much luck in keeping your foreign friends alive."

Delin thought about correcting his assumption that Native Indians were foreigners, but passed it up. "I need to send him back to Tianjin—I believe it's a village on the way to Peking."

"It is, but it might be damn hard to find anyone there." He took another drag on the cigar. "I can't play postal worker, not while we have people in there getting killed. Sorry, but..."

"Then let me go with you." Delin said it so fast he almost didn't think about the words until they were out of his mouth.

"Excuse me? You asking to join up again?"

"No," Delin said. "But well... yes. If it's a relief mission, then I do volunteer."

Bradley looked back over the gangplank. "We've got a lot of men already, many of them sailors just signing on for the duty, backing up a minimal contingent. But... I suppose one more wouldn't hurt."

Delin smiled weakly. Somehow he had just been sucked into a battle, drawn into events beyond his control. All due to a promise made over a year ago in the snow. "All right, then. Just let me find a kennel for my dogs—you can take me back here when it's over, right?"

Lieutenant Bradley smiled and blew a smoke ring towards the nearby mountain peaks. "We'll find a way to get you home, don't worry. But now, hurry up—the Forbidden City awaits!"

They landed at Taku on July sixth, in sweltering humidity with a thick haze in the air. Two other American warships plus a fleet of allied forces were already in the harbor, flags waving and the colors hanging limp in a sluggish breeze. The port city was a scarred, blistering hell, with flames racing through entire streets and columns of smoke spiraling skyward. Along the smaller canals and tributaries feeding the sea came an assortment of bloated corpses from somewhere inland, and the stench overpowered the gunsmoke and fumes.

Crowds of Chinese had gathered, their faces grim and impassive; many were injured and sought medical aid aboard the sidewheeler, *Monocacy*, and the relief contingents remaining on board did what they could, but made room first for the injured among the returning Allied troops.

Delin reluctantly ambled off the ship after everyone else had marched out in file; he had watched them disembark, eager for battle after weeks at sea. In dark blue shirts and khaki pants, with an assortment of rifles, pistols and bayonets, they started on their way to Tianjin—to the missions and delegations desperately waiting for aid. Their goal was to take that city first, with its two main arsenals and its command of the waterways, and then move on to Peking—although they feared it was already too late for those diplomats and their families.

With canons roaring in the distance and gunfire whistling by from unseen snipers, Delin descended alone down the plank, with Chang-Sai's bones carefully wrapped in linens and tucked away in his backpack. He ran quickly past the demolished shopfronts and tried to imagine the beauty that this ancient architecture once presented.

He had his rifle and enough rounds to get out of any minor skirmish, but suddenly thrust into this unfamiliar world, he felt like an invader; and it seemed the entire land stood ready to defend itself with a limitless supply of warriors.

Someone came running up to him—another American sailor from the *McAvoy*. "To the train!" he yelled. "Tracks are over there. We got word it's finally been repaired after all that sabotage and we can get the cars through to Tianjin."

Delin followed the man, and soon their regiment merged with a squadron of British troops. Delin got into the third car just in time, sweating and breathing heavily—and then they were off. Soon, the land of rugged mountains, endless rice fields and meandering rivers revealed itself. Strange birds and large insects darted around the train and flew away. A drought had recently ravaged the country, and everywhere people were huddled, watching soberly as the train laden with foreign soldiers sped by.

Buildings were in ruins, homes demolished and looted. Churches and missions—those Delin could identify as such—were charred-out ruins. Bodies littered the ground and floated like driftwood in the creeks. Dogs fought over the corpses.

Delin turned away, and instead focused on the faces of the men packed inside with him. One, the young man who had called to him outside, was staring at him. Delin nodded and tried to smile. "Only my second time on a train," he said.

The sailor shrugged. "I've seen better."

"Me too!" Delin exclaimed, and proceeded to tell him about the dining car on the train from Sacramento to Reno, including details about the sumptuous steak dinner. Afterward, he heard more about the current conflict. The Imperial troops were mobilized now, Delin learned—siding with the Boxers in the attempt to expel the foreigners. Some even said the Dowager Empress had played at a game to incite the Brotherhood into action, hoping the delegations would leave on their own before it came to outright war.

There had been no word from Peking—after nearly thirty-five days of siege. Delin held out little hope for the men and their families; he could see the resolution on many Chinese faces out there. More than once, small bands of white and red garbed Boxers had approached the train and opened fire. They had quickly been shot down or scared off, but everyone felt they would be coming back, or waiting ahead in greater numbers. Finally, all conversation ceased as the sun descended, and the men decided to catch some rest while they had the chance.

They finally arrived at Tianjin in the small hours of the night. Delin was awakened by the young sailor and brought outside. A contingent of German and French troops had set up a makeshift barricade around the train station, having secured it quietly upon arriving. A Major Waller, from the *U.S.S. Solance*, trotted over on horseback, leading a squadron of maybe three dozen men. “You there!” he called, noticing Delin was the only one not heading off with specific duties. “Can you shoot?”

“Sorry?” Delin looked up groggily. He tried to stand at attention or salute, but didn’t know what to do with the backpack of bones sliding off his shoulder.

“Shoot! Can you fight, or are you here for the scenery?”

Delin stammered. “My papa was a sharpshooter in the Mexican War and the Civil War, and...”

“Didn’t ask about your daddy. Unless he taught you every morning, and your eyes are good, or unless you been trained out in the wilds of Alaska, then you’re no use.”

“Actually. Everything you just said is true.”

Waller regarded him as if he just spoke in tongues. “Well then, take up position on that parapet there and watch for snipers. And defend this station as best you can with these others.”

Staring at the backside of the Major’s horse, Delin swallowed hard and lifted his rifle with shaking hands. Someone came by and gave him a box of ammunition, and as dawn spread silken rays through the smoke and lit up the congested villages, mud walls, brick buildings and the flags of the foreign consulates, he climbed the steps to his position.

Cramping himself into a little nook behind some crumbled masonry on the second level, he looked out over the ruined structures, past the flames and smoke. A mile in the distance the native city of Tianjin lay huddled behind two great walls, thirty feet high, with four gates each, heavily fortified. Mounted cannons commenced firing from those walls, and the shelling of the Allied-occupied districts—and the liberated compounds of the foreign legations—began again.

Delin cringed, never having imagined the intensity of the sound of a shell exploding into a wall, or a house. He watched, open-mouthed, as multi-colored uniforms ran through the streets, ducking for cover, running for positions ordered by the Major and the respective commanders. He watched as great twelve-pound guns were wheeled up out of the railroad cars and dragged into positions—the very guns from some of the battleships back in the harbor at Taku.

For the next six hours, Delin sat perched in that position, watching the battle unfold, amazed at the give and take, the explosions on both sides. He wondered about the damage done to the interior of Tianjin City—it was impossible to see the result after the shells flew over the wall and only huge, twisting coils of smoke arose from beyond.

Shortly before noon on the second day, the Boxer assault began. With advance warning of gunfire and with men running back to the barricades, the regiments prepared themselves. With pistols and rifles, most of the contingents knelt behind the barriers or crouched beside fallen masonry. A pair of Germans manned the huge Colt Automatic, which had been set up between a high stack of sandbags.

Everyone seemed to take a deep breath, having been at this before. And then the hordes appeared, clearing the wall of the French compound ahead, and racing for the railway station. Swords and clubs drawn, those in the front line screamed and raced headlong into the first volley of gunfire, and the Colt's loud greeting sent dozens down in the next seconds.

Delin sighted from his position on the wall and chose a target several rows back—a man readying a rifle as he ran. He closed his eyes for a second, then opened them and took his finger off the trigger—to reach into his shirt and clasp the golden cross there. Forgive me, he thought, and felt a flash of vision—a memory, almost—of a rain-swept Tennessee field, and two men atop a church firing into a crowd of blue.

Then the image cleared and the current danger loomed, as the force of Boxers stormed right up to the barricades. The Allies stood from behind their barricades, pistols firing, bayonets thrusting.

Delin found his target, and fired.

The first kill, someone had once told him, was the hardest.

Three hours later, after the Boxers had been driven back and then repulsed two more times, Delin could swear that wasn't true. Every time he pulled the trigger he had felt the same horrible finality, the snuffing out of a life from above. As if he were God, indiscriminately pointing and choosing who to remove from this world.

Finally, the first day's battles ended. Night fell, and the railway station held, despite heavy Allied losses. A full thirty percent of their strength had been lost, as well as half their ammunition. Delin was starting to know how the delegates and the small band of defenders in Peking must be feeling.

And this was just the first day.

Three more days passed in similar fashion. Occasionally, the Allied defenders got reinforcements from the field—men returning from other missions, from securing other parts of the villages outside Tianjin. But Delin stayed on while others took a welcome change from this deadly detail. He eventually moved to a more secure position on a rooftop overlooking the station—and outside of the range of Tianjin's guns. He took time to rest, and he slept somehow through the shelling, the stray, whistling bullets and the wailing of the injured—Chinese and Europeans alike.

On the fourth day, July thirteenth, a train arrived again, to the shouts and bugle calls of the defenders. Major Waller and his officers were present to greet the new arrivals—Brigadier General Dorward of Britain, ranking officer for all the armies, and Colonel Robert Meade, U.S. ranking commander and veteran of the Civil War. They had arrived four days after Delin's ship, and brought with them over two thousand multinational troops, supplies and more guns—which they quickly moved into position to strike at Tianjin.

The commanders drew up a plan and commenced their fire the next morning, shelling the walls and focusing on the South Gate while the infantry began to advance.

Relieved to be free from railway station guard, Delin managed to slip away from Major Waller's notice in the midst of all the preparations and fighting. He made his way around the ruined French compound and started exploring the villages, hoping to find someone who could speak English and Chinese, and could help him find Chang-Sai's people. He hoped his good intentions weren't in vain, and prayed Chang's family hadn't been killed or uprooted. Few homes were intact, and the ones that were had been looted, although the inhabitants seemed more relieved than anything that they at least still had their lives, perhaps expecting much worse from a conquering army.

After difficult traveling, keeping to the walls where possible and ducking every time he heard a whistling shell overhead, he eventually found himself in front of a burning frame of a church. A large cross smoldered on a pile of charred timbers and crumbled masonry. Bodies lay strewn in the wreckage, and a trio of pigtailed heads—severed—stood on stakes in the church field. A single yellow flower bloomed against a shattered wall, humbly bowing its petals.

Delin looked, peering over the rubble, and after a sudden lull in cannon blasts, the sound of crying finally reached his ears. Sitting in the corner was a young Chinese girl, her white dress in tatters, her arms and legs singed and bruised.

She held a tiny blackened wooden cross in her callused hands, and when she saw him she shrunk back and turned her head, expecting a gunshot or bayonet to end her cries. Delin instead set down his rifle and knelt in front of her, hands open. "Hey," he whispered. "You have to get out of here."

She looked at him blankly, not understanding. Then, her tears came again and the cross fell from her fingers. She looked at her blackened hands, glanced over to the headless, burned bodies in the rubble, and sobbed.

Delin reached out and gently took her chin in his fingers, and pulled her gaze away. Happily, she didn't resist. Perhaps too numb, he thought. And then he did the only thing he could think of—he pulled out the cross from around his neck. He unclasped the chain. And slowly, very slowly, he moved to secure it around the girl's neck. Pushing aside her matted hair, he snapped the clasp gently, and only when he stood back and looked down did he realize she had stopped crying.

Instead, she gazed with wide eyes at the shining cross held in her palm. She blinked repeatedly, as if clearing out the dust along with the evil she had seen. Then she looked up and smiled.

"That was very nice," said a voice at his back.

Delin spun, reaching for the rifle—but then froze. A white woman stood there. Standing straight and proper amidst the smoke and sputtering flames, she wore a light gray suit, ruffled blouse and some kind of tall, flowery hat. She spoke something in Mandarin to the girl, who answered, pointing to Delin, then back at the ruin of the church.

The woman nodded, then regarded Delin with a smile. "Hashi thanks you, foreign devil. And I thank you."

"Who are you?" Delin asked, swallowing hard. This seemed surreal. A man suddenly appeared. Likewise dressed in a proper suit and business hat, he stepped gingerly through the wreckage until he came to the woman's side and put his arm around her protectively.

"Name's Hoover," said the man. Herbert and Lou."

The woman blushed and bowed. "Aren't you a little lost? Your regiments are attacking the city now, and I daresay they need all of you chaps."

"Honey," said Herbert, "maybe the man has other responsibilities. We're not all warriors."

"No," Delin said. "We're not. At least not willingly. And what about you—are you with the British Legation?"

"We are," Hoover said. "Although we're Americans—from Newberg, Oregon actually. Been employed with a British mining firm for some years though."

Lou patted her husband's chest. "On his first assignment, in 1897, Bert was sent to Australia and managed to find his company a gold vein worth millions."

"This," Hoover said, waving his hand at all the wreckage and violence, "was my reward. Where are you from, my good man?"

"Alaska," he replied. "Delin Weatherwax. A bit into mining and prospecting myself. Listen, I don't mean to take up your time with this, but I notice, ma'am, that you speak the language."

"I do. Bert only picked up a little here and there, but I seem to have a knack for it. Came in useful this past month, I can tell you. We've actually been out every day, trying to help the people where we can, especially those at the missions."

Delin nodded, impressed but impatient. “I am looking for someone—a family, actually. I have the remains of a man named Chang-Sai, and I have promised to return him to his family—the Hsian-xi clan of the west bend of the Beiho River.” Delin hoped he said that right, desperately trying to remember the last words of his friend. “Do you know them?”

Lou glanced at her husband, then shook her head. “I do not, but I can take you to someone who will.”

“Who?”

She pointed to the west, toward a collection of mud walls; and beyond them—an intact structure looming against a backdrop of smoke and ruin. “One of the elders—a wealthy man who has helped the people of this village for two decades. He has his family home behind the Apostolic Mission. Both buildings have thankfully escaped major damage.”

“We’ll take you to see the elder,” Herbert said. “And along the way you can tell me about Alaska—how are the people doing up there? Is the lawlessness as bad as they say? Do the people really want self-government?”

“Bert!” Lou scolded. “Not everyone wants to talk politics.”

“Ah,” Delin said. “Don’t get me started. If only I had Roosevelt’s ear. The abuses going on up there, the way outside companies are reaping Alaska’s resources without having to pay taxes, the callous uprooting of the native people and the misallocation of funds...”

Herbert Hoover nodded vigorously, as if taking mental notes to recall at a later time. “Tell me more...”

Outside of the Mission, passing through a crowd of Chinese, their expressions forlorn and miserable, Delin noticed that they were being followed. The little girl, still holding the gold cross out before her like a Communion wafer, skipped along, keeping pace.

Around the back of the western wall was a slight trail that led to a home nestled within a grove of bullet-ridden cypress trees and surrounded closely by six smaller houses, three of them destroyed. Chinese men walked about, sifting through the rubble, collecting what personal items they could and bringing them to the temporary shelter of the elder’s home.

Up a short flight of stairs, Delin followed the Hoovers to a landing under a sloping gabled roof. Twin Celestial jade lions guarded each side of the main door. Lou bowed and spoke to a servant who looked back at Delin, then ushered them inside.

"This is where we'll take our leave," Lou told Delin. "You're in good hands now, and we have much more work to do."

Herbert shook his hand firmly. "Pleasure to meet you, chap. Once this is over, if I ever get to Alaska, I'll look you up, and we can have a drink and share prospecting stories."

Delin grinned. "I'd like that very much, sir."

As they left, Delin turned and watched an old, wizened man being wheeled into the plainly-decorated room. A young man with a long, braided ponytail maneuvered him carefully around the items set here and there from displaced family and friends.

"My apologies," the elder said, looking about the room. "Normally the parlor is a place of great serenity. To make one's visitors at ease."

Delin bowed as he had seen the Hoovers do. "No apology necessary. In fact, I feel I must apologize—for my countrymen and for what they and their allies have done to your villages."

The old man waved away the sentiment. "We brought it upon ourselves with thousands of years of perceived superiority. And what we have done to our own people is worse than anything you foreigners could possibly conceive."

Delin shifted uncomfortably when the chair rolled to within several feet. He noticed that the old man's left leg seemed withered and useless while the rest of him appeared in good condition; his eyes sparkled with a youthful vigor he hadn't expected, and while bald, the gray hairs on his chin and mustache remained bold and pronounced. An old scar ran across his cheek.

"You speak very good English," Delin said.

The man nodded. "In my youth, much time I spent among your kind. Been all over the world. California, Australia..."

"Father," whispered the boy at his back. "Be done with this quickly; there are still Boxers about, and to see the American here..."

The old man waved his son back, then leaned ahead in his chair, scrutinizing Delin closely. "My eyes are not so good," he said. "Step closer."

Delin swallowed and took a step—but then withdrew as the little girl suddenly darted around his legs and ran up to the old man and threw her arms around his neck.

"One of my many grand-daughters," he said, grinning and pulling away to look at her. He said something in Mandarin while he stroked her hair. Nodding, he glanced up at Delin, then back to the girl, and spoke some more.

Then, suddenly, an incredible change came over him. His body went rigid, his eyes bulged and his mouth worked as if struggling for the words. Sunlight streaming in from the east window glinted off the gold cross on the girl's neck, and dazzling pinpoints danced across the old man's face, lighting up his newly-forming smile.

He sat up in a flash, lips quivering, hands trembling. He wheeled himself closer to Delin. "Take off your hat, please."

Fearing that he had greatly disrespected this man and his house, and had probably made a big mistake giving the cross away, putting the child in danger, Delin lifted his hat. He brought it to his chest as he bowed his head.

He heard a gasp, then a soft, murmuring laughter like the gentle rolling of a stream over ice-coated rocks. When he looked, the old man was urgently whispering something to his son and pointing to the other room. The boy bowed, glanced at Delin, then darted off.

The old man turned his face up to Delin's. His eyes roamed over him, studying his hair, his eyes, his beard. And he nodded over and over, clapping to himself, as if proud to be the only one to catch the joke.

"I'm sorry," Delin said at last, while hearing what sounded like drawers opening and closing in the other room. A shell exploded in the distance, and sporadic gunfire rattled the windows. "I'm really just looking for a certain family. I have the bones of a man with me—he died in the Klondike, digging for gold, and I promised..."

"Ah!" said the old man when his son returned with a small cherry wood box and placed it reverently in his father's hands. The old man carefully stroked the box cover as if soothing a precious pet. Still grinning, he tapped the edges. "Just like him, you are. Always trying to honor your promises."

Delin shook his head slowly. "Like who?" What was going on here? It seemed everyone was in on the joke, and he was left in the dark. "Listen. I have this man's remains, plus some gold he managed to find."

Already having decided to part with the five-pound nugget, the scene of devastation and loss all around this village only strengthened that resolve. He planned to tell Chang-Sai's family that their relative had honored them by finding the largest nugget in the Klondike. He reached into his bag and offered the leather pouch and the heavy nugget to the old man.

His son took the pouch, looked inside, and whistled. "Generous, too, like him," the old man said. "What was it he once told me? 'Every gift of noble origin...'"

Delin's heart stopped. And the words slipped out of his mouth: "*—is breathed upon by hope's perpetual breath!*"

The old man nodded. And he lifted the cover of the polished wooden box.

Delin's eyes went wide, his knees buckled, and he dropped to a crouch—at eye-level with the glittering revolvers resting on the velvet interior, dazzling in their polished sheen and trembling with an imperceptible excitement.

"I believe," said Matsei Xien, "these are yours."

Seven cups of tea, two bowls of boiled rice and eight hours later, when night covered the silent battlefield, Delin stood and shook Xien's hand. He bowed again, and finally, there were no more words to be spoken.

They had each shared stories and eagerly related events beyond the other's experience, filling in the years. They spoke of silver and gold, of mines and creeks. Of Quitch and Caroline, Mirna and Joshua—and they shared tears. They spoke in hushed whispers about the Yeti, the Sesquat—the nemesis Xien told him he would one day meet again; their destinies were entwined, Xien insisted, every bit as much as these gold and silver Dragoons were bound up with his family.

Destiny had called him back here, Xien claimed. Chang-Sai, and the avalanche and the war—all had their part, intricate pieces in a tapestry of fate. Delin didn't know what to believe, and he wondered to himself at the unerring spell of coincidence. It was hard to believe in destiny, or even in God, when such suffering, evil and horror existed—the worst examples going on just outside this home.

But he couldn't doubt where he wound up. Full circle, brought to the man his father had trusted above anyone else, to the one who safeguarded the treasure Joshua would have loved to pass on to his son.

And now, walking amidst the flickering shadows of twisted, shattered walls and crumbling homes, his hands held the loaded Dragoons at his sides. He strode with long, purposeful steps, his boots crunching over loose stone, glass and wood. Walking, he didn't know where, just feeling the weight of the four-pound guns in his hands and following where they seemed to pull him—toward the northeast, toward the walled city. Toward where the Allies were retreating even now, back to the safety of the trenches after a brutal day of little gain against the fortified Tianjin Boxers.

Delin walked past the troops as they ran in the other direction; he pushed through Germans, Austrians, British and Russians. He headed across the watery rice field, which the Boxers had flooded by strategically diverting the canals. He stepped over bodies and trudged through pools of red. Overhead, the constellations tried unsuccessfully to burn through the smoky haze of battle; and darkness, thick and palpable, held onto the battlefield and clung to the distant walls.

But still Delin walked, his fingers caressing the polished metal chambers, the ivory handles. He walked, splashing without concern through the death field, the almost mile-long march to the wall, where just a few lone figures patrolled at this late hour.

In time, he heard splashing footfalls at his back, and glanced over his shoulder to see a large force following, some of them hurrying to catch up. Men of every color uniform marched behind him, perhaps believing he had a plan and needed backup. To his left, a group of Japanese soldiers, emboldened by his apparent bravery, whispered among themselves, then took off at a faster pace—heading to the South Gate and readying what looked like large, taped collections of dynamite.

Gunfire spat from the wall as they approached, and Delin calmly aimed to the thirty-foot height and fired the first shot back. A dark form twisted, then plummeted from the top. Then, rifles blasted, men shouted, and the advance was on.

Minutes later, the Japanese came running back from the gate—all but one, who stayed behind to light the wet fuses at closer range. His silhouette was obliterated in the ensuing blast—a great fireball that rocked the wall, blew apart the huge gate and sent clouds of smoke into the sky.

A thousand men took up the charge, racing around Delin and pouring through the demolished gate. Four thousand more launched out of their trenches back in the villages and came rushing out to join in the capture of Tianjin.

Delin stepped into the smoke and walked blindly through, into the great walled city. Troops rushed by, shouting and firing at the routed Boxers, engaging the entrenched enemy where they stood, and pursuing them when the fled.

He had been told that the Boxers believed they were endowed with sorcerous powers, making them invulnerable to the foreigners. But here, as their city was violated and destroyed, Delin felt somehow infused with his own brand of immortality—perhaps granted by the mighty Dragoons in his hands. He felt surrounded by an aura of protection as if his own ancestors cradled him a sheath of invincibility.

A Boxer ran up to him with a sword drawn. Delin shot him in the face, then turned and fired with his left hand, knocking another one down in the midst of striking a Russian fighter. He fired seven more times, slowly, unerringly, as he wandered through the narrow passages between homes and buildings. He ignored the huddled villagers, the women and children and the old men kneeling by their smoking homes.

The shelling over the wall had been intense, and damage inside was severe. Nearly every building was in ruin, every home a smoking huddle of scorched and fused debris. Bodies and limbs were strewn about. Men crawled with broken legs and crushed arms, massive wounds and burns.

Delin walked past them all, directed somehow to one particular building—a halfway-destroyed administrative-looking structure. He walked inside, guns ready. Two Chinese knelt inside in the shadows. They held rifles. Both fired.

Both missed.

Delin shot twice and silenced them, then put the hot guns, their chambers empty, into his backpack. He walked to a pile of rubble and glanced around the burned-out interior. The sun was peeking up over the far wall now, and the sky brightened with a crimson hue. Through the shattered windows and broken masonry, troops could be seen racing by, still firing, but less than before. The rout was on, the Boxers streaming from the city or surrendering by the hundreds.

Tianjin had fallen after its long siege, and now the Allies could mount their advance to Peking. Unified and in control of the waterways and the railroad, they would go on to rescue the legations after fifty-five days of holding out, and they would force great concessions from the Dowager Empress.

But Delin didn't think about any of that. Instead, his attention focused on the rubble around his feet and strewn about the office building. He got to one knee and examined a curiously shiny chunk of masonry, noting the fused material heated onto the brick and concrete. He got up and walked around, removing a short steel knife from his pack and poking at various sections of the debris.

Eventually, a big grin appeared under his bushy mustache, and thirty minutes later, when the Corporal he had requested arrived, looking annoyed, Delin was still smiling. "I hear the Allies are carving up the city into districts for themselves."

"That's true," said the Corporal. "Everyone's trying to get their share of whatever's around for the taking—spices, silk, other goods. Why are you asking?"

Delin smiled. "I would do everything possible to make sure you get this building in the U.S. zone."

The corporal glanced around in obvious distaste. "Why?"

Tapping his foot on a chuck of rubble, Delin said, "I'm guessing this was the salt supply office."

"Okay. So?"

"So, the Chinese traded in salt for the exchange of precious metals from the other provinces. Everything funneled through Tianjin, through here." Xien had told him as much last night. "The Salt Administrator held a storehouse of all that wealth."

"And?"

"And—for external purposes, China is under the Silver Standard, requiring all foreign trade elements to pay for their goods only in silver bullion."

The Corporal's eyes brightened. "Then..."

"Yes," Delin said. "You're looking at what I'd estimate to be around fifteen thousand pounds of silver bullion."

"Fifteen thousand..." The Corporal looked dizzy. He did the calculations, at $35 per pound... "That's over a half million dollars!"

"Yes. Most of it's fused with the wreckage here—but can be easily separated. Ask Mr. Hoover out at the British Legation about that. In the meantime, I'd suggest posting some guards, and getting an assayer down here."

The Corporal nodded. "I believe the U.S. Legation has a member of J.P. Morgan's New York Financial Company present—he can value the silver, and then probably we'll need to ship it to Shanghai and our agents there to hold for removal back home..."

Delin nodded rapidly as he made to leave. "Yes, yes. Do what you need to do."

"Hey!" the Corporal called. "What's your name, soldier?"

Looking back, Delin smiled. "I'm no soldier. I'm a prospector. And I'm going home."

The peaks of the Chugach Mountain range never looked so good. That was, until he was looking at them from the other side, with Dunder and Blitzen racing ahead, happily pulling the light sled with Delin on it, mushing down the trail toward his cabin.

It had been a long trip home, involving three stop-overs—in the Philippines, then to Guam, and finally over to Seattle where he boarded a steamer for Skagway. Almost four weeks had passed since Tianjin fell. But it seemed like years, even decades, had spun by. That was, until he returned to the wild interior, to the vast reaches and infinite mountain ranges. There, time always seemed irrelevant. The land was beyond all measurement, outside of the count of hours, days and years.

And it was in such a dreamlike state that he resumed his quiet life in the cabin on the edge of the Alaskan border overlooking the grand Yukon River.

The years passed. And in such a place, he barely noticed.

Seasons all merged into one long experience of timeless beauty with perfect cycles of light and dark, hot and cold, hunger and plenty.

The world moved on, unchanging until one brisk morning before the sun struggled to rise in the near-perpetual gloom. When the aurora burned in fierce ribbons and majestic spirals.

Until a growl from the dogs broke Delin's silent contemplation on the edge of the cliff.

Until the great white beast burst from the forest, tracked by the hunters.

Until he met Eloise, and time once again clicked into place.

And then the weeks were chronicled by the stories he wove to her in the blizzard; in the solace of his cabin, while the dogs whined outside, patiently waiting for him to finish.

BOOK THREE

"Thinking to get all the gold the goose could give he killed it and opened it, only to find—nothing."
—Aesop, The Goose With the Golden Eggs

Chapter 24: Alaska/Yukon Territory – 1906-1908

PROSPECTING WITH ELOISE

By the light of a candle, nearly melted down to a stub on the table beside a frosted jar full of licorice sticks, Eloise carefully made her way inside the cabin.

Delin's powerful snores drowned out her limping footfalls, and she took a moment to glance at him, lying there curled up like a dog on a bed of furs upon the floor, having spent most of the night there beside her bed while she dozed.

Eloise smiled and watched him sleep, seeing the bushy mustache fluttering with his shallow breaths, watching his eyelids tremble and his legs twitch. She put a hand to her mouth to stop from giggling. Perhaps he really had lived too long among the dogs, she thought, but at the same time she wondered what visions crossed behind those dark lids, what memories were sculpted and wrought in his dreamscape.

And how much of what he had told her was the truth? She had listened rapturously over the past two weeks as he nursed her back to health, and as the blizzard raged and ultimately passed on, satisfied its part had been played.

She sighed and continued her shuffling to the door, treating her ankle gingerly. She meant to bundle up and relieve herself outside—which would be a welcome change to that embarrassing chamber pot Delin had graciously endured all this time. Almost to the door, she stopped, peeked back at the sleeping man, then turned to the small wooden box on a shelf to her right. She was mesmerized by how the candlelight lovingly traced the silver features and settled into the golden etchings of the twin Dragoons. She slowly reached out and was surprised to see her fingers trembling, as if sneaking a touch of some sacred Vatican relic. When her skin met the cold metal, a shudder ran up her arm and she drew her hand away.

Her vision spotted now with sparkling star-points, she let her attention wander, looking at the other relics in this museum of a man's life, and as she noted each one in turn, her earlier idea resurfaced. Why not? she thought. The appeal of such an exhibit might be just what the Smithsonian needed, a nice contrast to all its animal specimens and excavated bones.

Eloise trembled with mounting excitement as she carefully worked her way around the cabin's walls. Stopping at each item, she bent down to inspect them—a tintype here of a young boy accepting a trophy, looking bewildered and surrounded by a half-dozen sled-dogs. Next, a knife with a caribou-antler hilt and an etching of a half moon on it. Relics from Juneau, she thought, nodding as if verifying one part of the tale.

And here—was that an actual bar of silver? Stamped with some kind of Chinese symbol? That little devil, Eloise mused. Took one for himself—good for him.

And there—a stererograph—two photographs side by side in a device with a viewer. When she peered through the lenses, the figures leapt out in three dimensions: a handsome-looking young prospector and a dark, narrow faced man standing before a rain-swept mountainside. Comstock, the title read, 1862.

She was about to continue when she noticed the snoring had stopped. Blinking, Eloise lifted her face from the viewer and turned slowly. In the flickering stove light, Delin rubbed his head, yawned, stretched and sat up, crossing his legs.

"Good looking guy, my papa—wasn't he?"

Eloise winced. "I'm sorry, I didn't—"

Delin held up a hand. "Snoop all you want. I'm just glad to see you up and walking again."

"Thanks to you," Eloise said. She pointed to the stereograph. "So, that's Benjamin Quitch, right?"

Delin's smile vanished. He looked down and straightened the rugs and blankets.

"Sorry," Eloise whispered. "But whatever happened to his son—

to Jericho?" She hated to admit it, but she wanted more of the story, and had to know how that villain met his end. Surely, he wasn't still out and about, thriving all this time...

"He's out there somewhere," Delin said, as if reading her thoughts. "Though I don't feel anything toward him anymore. Maybe it's the beauty up here, the infinite peace of it all." He shrugged. "It has a way of making you forget your hurts."

"But he murdered your father! If you found him now—things are so different. Laws and decent society—you could have him jailed, maybe even executed."

Delin got up slowly. "Things are not that different, I'd wager. He mentioned something about politics when I last ran into him outside of Skagway. And he had judicial connections. I don't think there's any way justice will reach him unless it comes from the end of pistol."

Eloise let a smile loose and her eyes flickered to the Dragoons. "Maybe that's as it should be... Don't you want to—?"

"No!" Delin snapped. "Do you think I don't lie awake imagining just such a thing? How I wish I could look up at the Northern Lights and speak to Papa and tell him I've avenged him? But when I sit there in the cold and ask just those questions of the night sky, I hear nothing back. No stirring in the heavens, no trembling in the mountains."

He shook his head. "Vengeance is irrelevant, and time will take care of Jericho Quitch. As Chang-Sai told me, everyone is born to one thing, one purpose. Mine isn't revenge."

Eloise limped over to a chair and sat down. She leaned forward, looking into his eyes. "Then what do you think it is?"

Yawning, Delin got to his feet. He smiled at her, then grabbed a coffee pot. "Right now, my one purpose is to get some coffee. Then, it's to go take a run with the dogs, to see what the storm has left us and determine when we can make for Dawson. Have to get you back to civilization soon before they mount a rescue party and throw me in jail for kidnapping. You know how I detest confinement!"

Eloise made a pouting face, and looked over to her notebook, filled almost three-quarters of the way with hastily-scrawled notes. She tapped her fingers on the cold table and watched her breath form icy steam in front of her face.

"What?" Delin asked, readying the coffee pot. "Don't tell me you're not ready to go?"

Eloise blinked, crossed her arms and rubbed her shoulders. She would enjoy a hot bath and a real dinner, but... "Well, I suppose I am. But I feel like I'll be returning empty-handed."

"Ah," Delin said. "You came out here with a mission, and you'll be returning with nothing. No giant carcass, no piece of the monster you sought."

"Right," she admitted. "The others in my team will go on to collect more grants, gain professorships and ultimately publish their articles and inspire the world, while I'll return with only a harrowing story about a man who saved my life."

Delin grinned. "You got 'em beat there, right?"

"I suppose so," she said with a shrug.

Delin offered her a cup and let her choose the sweet licorice tea or the bitter coffee. "So, is that what you want? Is that your purpose—fame and success?"

Eloise sighed. "Not when you put it that way. I always thought I'd be pushing the boundaries of knowledge, finding some great truths about the world. Or even just about people. What makes us who we are?" She picked up the gold-plated trophy Delin had won so long ago, and held it up. "Maybe I just want my own recognition somehow."

Delin set down the hot water. "You've got time—you're young. And the world is still new. Approach it with the same tenacity you hunted that Sesquat, and I have no doubt we'll all be reading about you soon."

Her eyes down, Eloise looked away—and Delin couldn't tell for sure, but he thought he saw a trickling of cold tears forming on her cheeks.

"Maybe I'm impatient," she said quietly, reverently setting down the trophy. "Or maybe I just don't have that much time."

Delin opened his mouth, thinking of a witty comeback, when she spun around suddenly.

"Let's not go back to Dawson," she said, a rosy flush to her face, the tears—if there were any—dried already. "Why don't we work out a deal? I'll stay on for the prospecting season with you. You teach me everything you taught your group back in the Klondike—and then, when I return to Washington, hopefully with some gold of my own, I'll be able to personally describe the life of a prospector. And along with the stories you've told me, that might almost make up for knocking my Sesquat off the cliff."

"Whoa!" Delin backed up, holding out his hands. His heart pounded and as he looked into the young woman's passionate blue eyes. With her wispy hair in tangles over her forehead and tickling her cheeks, he found himself at a loss for words.

"Why not?" Eloise asked. "Do you have other plans? Got a ladyfriend on her way from Seattle?"

"No," Delin said, blushing and grateful for the thick beard to hide it. "But... you don't know the first thing about gold. And I'm too tired to teach it all again. I just want solitude and quiet. I've got my books, my dogs, and the whole world out here to occupy myself."

"Ah yes," Eloise said. "Your solace. More like your hideaway. If that story you told me wasn't exaggerated for my benefit, then if you ask me, it seems like there were a lot of promises you set out to keep, and the big ones—the most important—slipped through your grasp."

Delin's mouth went dry; he looked down at her feet, and he shivered in a sudden chill.

She moved closer to him, and, to her surprise, she found herself reaching out and touching his arm, and she looked up into his eyes. "Help me. And come back to the world. Step into it with me. Teach me. We're not too different, you and I. I retreated into the dusty libraries and dark cellars of a museum for half my life when my parents died. My uncle couldn't understand it, but he let me go. Sometimes I wish he had been more forceful, and maybe I wouldn't have found myself out in the middle of nowhere, aiming a gun at some frozen monster."

Delin smiled weakly, squirming in her touch. Outside, he heard one of the dogs whining.

"But then again," she said, "if he had restrained me, I wouldn't be here, talking to you, and hearing about your life. And who knows—maybe it's as your papa's friend said, and destiny is working its way through all of us. Come on—if you waste away out here alone, no one will know your story, no one will ever care, and they'll just find you out here someday, frozen, and no one will have a clue who you were."

"Well," Delin said, shifting his feet. "They know me down in the city."

"Yes, but they'll forget, in time. Your name and your legend will fade. Do you want that?"

Delin shrugged. "Why not? Everything fades in time."

"Not gold," Eloise said, standing back. She lifted her face, and waited for her words to settle in.

After several long seconds passed, Delin actually found himself smiling. "You have me there, Miss Griffith. Gold does not fade. It keeps its luster, its brilliance, over the millennia. Great civilizations fall into ruin or get swallowed up by the sea. Yet dig up their treasures—and the gold remains as it was."

"See!" Eloise exclaimed. "I do know something about gold. I know more than that, too."

"Oh, do tell?" Delin poured his coffee, stirred in some sugar, then pulled up a chair.

"Well, I know it's one of the heaviest metals. A cubic foot of pure gold weighs over one-point-five thousand pounds."

"Okay, you're two for two," Delin voiced, raising his cup.

"Thanks," Eloise said with a sneer. "And I know that it's extremely malleable—one ounce can be pounded into an incredibly thin sheet—I think someone once quoted a figure like one hundred square feet..."

"Sounds about right," Delin said. "Amazing thing, gold. And hard to believe that up until the last century, it was over the broken bodies of thousands of slaves that kings and pharaohs dug up the great caches of old. Today," he kicked at one of the full sacks at his feet. "Anybody with a spoon and a pan can do it."

Eloise smiled. "I'd like to borrow a pan, then. And I think I have a spoon in my pack."

Delin looked at her seriously.

"Please," Eloise said. "Teach me. Let me learn something other than what I've found in books. Until now, gold was only a symbol on the table of elements. 'Au', from the Latin, shining dawn. Like in…"

She looked up suddenly. "Like in... Aurora."

The coffee cup fell from Delin's fingers and hot coffee spilled over his leg. He shot to his feet, his eyes aglow.

Eloise shrank bank, fearful suddenly, and a little unnerved that he seemed to be eyeing her in a new, appreciative light.

"Dear me," Delin whispered. "You actually told me something I should have known, but didn't." After a minute in deep thought, he finally reached out his hand.

Slowly, she took it and felt his gentle squeeze as he pulled her toward him and she withered under his gaze.

"Eloise of the Sun. My dear Miss Griffith." He backed up and bowed to her, then kissed her hand like a nobleman. "You have your wish."

The one season rolled into another, and the days, weeks and months slipped by as they can only do in a place of such timelessness. But to Eloise, this time was among her most cherished. After an exhilarating sled ride through the frozen lands and over the ice-coated Yukon River, they had reached Dawson by late March. After purchasing supplies and more food, and after only a quick overnight in separate rooms at Belinda Mulrooney's Imperial Hotel with its magnificent fireplace and hot baths, they left town again. Eloise sat on the sled with the supplies as Delin raced along behind it, occasionally leaping onto the running boards when the terrain permitted.

Soon they were heading south, following the Yukon River, moving swiftly through Canadian territory. They camped twice a day, then once for the night, and the weather let them be, although the crisp nights and cloudless skies drove the temperatures far below zero. Several weeks later, Cupid gave birth to two puppies, and Delin and Eloise camped for a time, raising the animals. Taking the small litter as a sign, he named them Dunder and Blitzen to replace the two he had lost to the Sesquat.

The snows receded as they moved further south, the days grew longer and the ice on the river began to break up, separating reluctantly in a week-long ritual. Delin guided them just past his namesake, the Teslin River where several fast-moving streams wove down the hill.

"You have to remember," he told her as he squinted against the glare from the white-capped mountains, "this one thing, above all else when prospecting: gold is a lonely orphan. It wants nothing more than to return to its birthplace."

"Orphan," Eloise repeated with a sigh, carefully setting her boots down into the muddy earth. "Right. And where is this birthplace? Oh, I get it—where it was created. Deep in the earth, with all that heat, pressure and excitement."

"You have it!" Delin said, clapping and then pulling out his pick and striding ahead of her. "After that, just rely on logic and common sense. Thrust violently from its home, sent thousands of feet above the sea in an upswelling of earth and rock. And then, over eons and eons, rain and erosion carved out trails for it. Which paths would it take to get back down?"

Eloise thought for a moment as she trudged ahead, trying to keep up. The dogs were circling Delin, leading him ahead. "Uh... well, the easiest path, I suppose."

"Exactly!" Delin looked back at her, grinning under all that bushy hair. "The shortest routes, hugging the inside of creek bends. Also, with such heavy weight, gold looks to rest occasionally—and will pick the softer ground as its bed."

As he droned on about the likeliest locations to find their treasure, she tried to picture him clean-shaven—or at least groomed, and it sparked her imagination—and other vivid fantasies which she quickly pushed aside. Not much chance of that, she thought. Past time for a husband. Past time for a lot of things... She thought back to her last trip to the physician in Washington, and remembered the way her uncle had held her hand and the doctor shook his head. She kept seeing that nurse in the doorway, peeking in curiously, as if trying to see what futility looked like.

But it wouldn't happen soon, she told herself. Still several years before it got really bad, the physician had told her. She could still function—although he hadn't expected her to travel, and definitely not like this. She had taken a chance, hoping that it was just this kind of immersion in nature, surrounded by this wondrous scenery, that just might lift her soul and cure her body. If not, if things deteriorated, she would throw herself into her work and create something permanent in the midst of all this limited mortality. Some way for her name to live on.

Standing shin-deep in the cold flowing creek, balancing on some flat rocks, Eloise smiled as she listened to Delin rattle on. Three of the dogs surrounded him, snapping at the water, trying to catch the spawning fish. He motioned to the mountains and waved his pick at a sandy outcropping ahead, then pointed to a twisting riverbend behind them. His words cascaded like the distant waterfalls, and his enthusiasm surrounded him and drew her in.

"You'd make a great father," she said suddenly, interrupting a digression on the comparative weight of gold.

"What?" Delin stepped past the dogs and reached the drier side of the creek. "Me? You have to be kidding."

Eloise splashed along, carefully dodging the struggling salmon; she almost reached the bank, then slipped—

—and fast as a cat, Delin caught her. He lifted her by the arms, effortlessly plucking her from the water. On the shore, Eloise met his vibrant eyes and smiled. She pulled away slowly, then looked to the glowing sun. "You're a wonderful teacher, and I can tell you were so perfectly influenced by your father."

Delin forced a laugh. "Yes, but... children? Nah..."

Eloise shook her head, still smiling. "Any son or daughter would be so enthralled by you. If you had a child, what would you name it?"

Scratching his beard, Delin looked down to his boots. "Good question. I think that would be a difficult, agonizing decision. My parents thought for ages before settling on mine. And I'd want to choose something equally powerful—obviously with my understanding of the Classics, plus various etymology influences, I'd want to select something meaningful, something..."

"I get it," Eloise said, cutting him off. She started unpacking her bag, setting up camp. She shot him a grin, then said, "I'm sure your child would be quite beautiful."

Delin shrugged. "Well, probably won't happen." He stuck his pick in the sandy earth, then tasted the tip. "Aww, shucks—nothing! How about we continue to prospect around this area for a few weeks, then make for Juneau? Plenty of salmon to eat around here."

Eloise nodded. It would be nice to visit a city again. She had heard that Alaska's capital had officially been moved to Juneau from Sitka. "We could see the Treadwell Mines on Douglas Island," she offered. "I'd like to write about that—the hundreds employed in the mines and at the stamp mills. Sounds like a Comstock of the North."

"You can do that. I'll stay in Juneau and read the papers."

"Okay then." Eloise crossed her arms and looked back to the sled that they'd have to drag over the creek. "Do we have enough gold for a long stay there? I don't mean to impose, but the Smithsonian funds I came with are nearly depleted, and..."

"Consider your expenses covered," Delin said, "by an interested benefactor. Think of me as your sponsor—except that I insist on your presence with me at dinner, and if I need a date for the opera..."

Eloise blushed, and pushed away some errant hairs from her eyes. "Will you rent me a separate room in the hotel?"

"A suite!" Delin beamed. "That way, we can still read to each other at night, before turning in."

"You've grown used to this," Eloise said coyly. "To me."

Delin looked away. "I have, and I must confess there's been no one like you to talk to. No one to share the poems and books. No one to listen to my ramblings on the world, no one..."

"But the dogs," Eloise giggled. "And they don't appreciate Shakespeare. Fine, I'll stay in your suite, and be your date for the shows you want to see. But I do have to do some work here and there."

"You will, you will." Delin beamed. "And you'll start tomorrow. I'm having you dig out a promising spot on the west bank. We'll be sifting and panning all day. I'll build a rocker, and we'll see what secrets this creek has that make the salmon love it so."

"I thought we had enough gold?"

"It's not just the gold, dear Eloise." Delin grinned at her and rubbed his hands for warmth. "It's the adventure. It's the seeking that's the attraction, the way prospecting fills your soul with hope in a way nothing else in life can. Faced with disappointment in one pan, you're always telling yourself—maybe the next one. Or the next. Then there's the sand bar up ahead, or that crevice there!"

Eloise swallowed hard. Trembling, she listened. And her body tingled. She felt her pains shifting, loosening, and washing away, along with her doubts and fears.

"You'll see," Delin continued, "that what we do will energize your body and soul; it will be like the grand quests of old—those fortune-seekers who endured every horror the world threw at them, steadfastly hunting for the prize—even if such a thing only existed in legend."

Eloise turned away, a tear in her eye. She knelt, and with shaking hands, unwrapped her tools.

They approached Juneau from the north, passing the Wrangell Mountains and St. Elias. The first snowflakes of the season were falling, and Eloise caught some on her tongue, and giggled. The past two months had been miraculous, as Delin had promised. They had found only a little gold, maybe two pounds worth altogether after searching hundreds of sites. But his promises came true—it was the quest that had made the difference. Her steps were lighter, her mood positively shining, and her health better than it had been in years. It was enough, almost, to let her dare question if the consumption had been beaten back completely.

But at some point, she found it didn't really matter. A new hope had settled in, and if some days she didn't feel good, then there were always others. And others ahead of that. Smiling, she followed along after the dogs, petting each one as she stepped among them.

They walked in silence beside the great Mendenhall glacier, awed by its illusionary proximity and its dazzling blue sheen; they felt its radiating cold and its slumbering power.

And finally, in mid-October, they came to Juneau.

Eloise watched Delin's reaction, and she realized this was the first time back here since the race, twenty-five years ago. He stood at the start of a hill, looking down on the sprawling city, the homes and buildings stretching in precise gridlines across the valley. He took in the great hotels, the opera houses and theaters, the baseball field and park, the cannery by the Channel, and the ferries that left frequently, carrying miners over to Douglas Island to work the Treadwell. Great columns of smoke reached into the hazy sky from the island, as three shifts toiled each day, and two hundred stamp mills constantly ground the ore dragged up from the depths.

As Delin shuddered, looking at the mills and thinking of another such site, years ago, Eloise walked by and tugged lightly on his jacket sleeve to pull him along. Together, with the dogs pulling the sled over melting snows, they entered Juneau.

The next month was spent in a rush of culture, a frenzied experience of sight and sound. It was as much a novelty for Eloise, who hadn't socialized much back in Washington, as it was for Delin. They rented a suite of rooms on the third floor of the Morgana Hotel on Front Street—after Delin had first left the dogs in the care of a farmer on the eastern hills. Then they visited the bank, where Delin exchanged two of the four sacks of gold. Armed now with fifteen thousand dollars, amazed that the bankers didn't even bat an eye, he and Eloise went on a small shopping spree. They visited the clothiers, Kaufman and Co., and left with crisp new fashions—elegant ball gowns and casual evening dresses for Eloise, and several crisp suits for Delin. New shoes, and polished leather boots. Then on to the barber—at Eloise's insistence, and when Delin emerged from inside, standing in the cool air with his brown suit and silk tie, with his smooth face and chiseled jawline seen for the first time, his hair short and cropped, but still curly, Eloise whistled appreciatively.

"Worth the wait," she said, then stepped up to him, slid her arm into his, adjusted the strap of her blue-gray bonnet, and proceeded to walk with him to the theater. They caught a presentation of *Twelfth Night* that evening, and dined by candlelight on king crab with Takou hash and stuffed porcupine. They drank wines from France and Germany, imported just that day from the last steamer of the season.

The next night was an opera, and the next—a silent movie played to a packed house of rowdy men and women, thrilling to the piano accompaniment. They went dancing in grand ballrooms, and attended boxing matches and card parties. The days grew colder, and the snows came, but the town kept going without losing stride. Delin discovered the library the next week, and that led to days and nights of reading—in the hotel lounge, in their suite, or out in the park. New classics were available—*Dr. Jekyll and Mr. Hyde*, *A Tale of Two Cities* and Eloise's instant favorite, *A Christmas Carol*. And then came *The Call of the Wild*, and *Huckleberry Finn*—and Delin proudly told Eloise that his father had met Mr. Twain once in Virginia City, and reminded her that he himself had sailed with Mr. London.

They continued in this adventure of a different sort—and Delin's money went far; they became something of celebrities, and gossip spread about the famed prospector and the 'museum lady'. But they didn't care; Delin bought rounds for townspeople at Epestyn's Smokery and Billiard Hall, and crowds gathered to thrill at his stories of the early mining days. Men from the Treadwell peppered him with questions about Comstock, and Eloise took it all in, jotting notes occasionally, and sometimes interviewing other miners and foremen.

They bought a box camera—the new invention by that Eastman fellow, something that everyone seemed to have. And just as quickly, the world in all its beauty and ugliness was free to capture and save for later review. Eloise often left on long walks through the carefully-shoveled streets, snapping pictures of the distant glacier, the mist-shrouded peaks of Mt. Ogden, and the halibut boats out braving the icy floes of the Gastineau Channel. She shot images of the returning miners, and even captured an injured driller carted off the ferry in obvious agony.

The days passed. Christmas came, and with it, the town erupted in an unexpectedly jovial celebration. The Treadwell closed—for one of only three days in the year—and the streets of Juneau were lined with parades. Electric lights had found their way to a few homes and main avenues, and on Christmas Eve, thousands sang and thrilled to the glowing colors while a muted aurora sparkled overhead.

After the ceremony, Eloise and Delin visited the dogs and presented each one with a meaty steak bone; then they attended a midnight ceremony at the Cathedral. When they finally returned to their suite, it was nearly three a.m. They lounged in their church clothes beside the fireplace, reciting stanzas from *A Visit From St. Nicholas* and sipping warm cinnamon rum until, just as dawn was peeking through the embroidered silk curtains, they decided St. Nick wouldn't be coming tonight after all, and they exchanged presents of their own.

Eloise bought Delin a leather-bound edition of *Gulliver's Travels*. Delin grinned and held the book close to his heart, having already heard parts of the stories from the other readers in Juneau. Eloise opened her gift and let out a soft sob as she slid the framed portrait out from the cardboard wrappings.

"When did you have this done?" she asked, eyes wide and filling with tears.

Delin laughed and crawled beside her so they could look together—at the two of them standing in a field against the backdrop of the lofty mountains, and surrounded by the dogs, sitting around them as if posing. "Mr. Harris attended to my request—rather surreptitiously, as I instructed. Then, I took it to Johnson's darkroom and had it enlarged and framed, and..."

"It's perfect!" she announced, tracing the glass-covered images with a trembling finger. Her eyes were distant, as if viewing something placed impossibly far in the future, like a child enviously watching a sibling's graduation.

Suddenly, she turned to Delin and threw her arms around his neck. "Merry Christmas, my love!"

Delin froze, and Eloise tensed at once, still clinging tightly to him. She pulled away slowly, and locked her eyes on his. Before she knew it she was standing, and pulling him with her. She set the photograph on a chair, stood on her toes and leaned forward. "I'm sorry for saying that if it embarrassed you," she whispered, when her lips were just inches from his. "But I can't help it."

A tear slid down her cheek, and Delin bent to kiss it away. She trembled, and he could feel her heart hammering in her breast. His heart pounded in time, inevitably, and as he met her eyes again, he felt overwhelmed with the emotions staring back at him.

And he said the only thing he knew to be the truth. "Ever since you pulled back that hood and yelled at me for killing your quarry, ever since you sat on my sled and fired that rifle over my shoulder—I've loved you."

Eloise made a slight gasp, and would have dropped out of his arms if he hadn't held her tight. She pressed tight against him as the sunlight danced inside the room and birds started their morning songs outside the window.

Delin whispered, "In all my years of prospecting and searching for the most valued substance in the planet..."

"Shhh," Eloise whispered, shaking her head as their lips touched. "I think we have one more gift to share."

Slowly, calmly, they walked hand in hand to Eloise's bedroom.

She closed the heavy drapes, lit several candles and pulled him into bed, where they celebrated Christmas with joy, with tears and laughter, love and passion; and finally, complete happiness.

On New Year's Eve they met the territorial governor of Alaska, Wilford Hoggatt, at dinner in the hotel restaurant. He made his way to them where they sat among a table of tourists, teachers and miners.

"So, you two are the big fuss around here," Hoggatt said, raising his glass of champagne. He looked radiant in a white suit coat and black pants and bowtie. He bowed to them and pulled up a chair, sitting between Delin and Eloise.

After introductions, Hoggatt spent the better part of an hour talking about the challenges Alaska faced, the ongoing struggle for representation and legitimacy. "Oh, the States are fine with taking our gold, our salmon and our seal, ravaging our seas and our lands, but never a tax dollar comes back to us."

"But surely you get the tourism and the wealth all those workers bring?" Eloise spoke softly, after a mouthful of caviar. She reached under the table and gave Delin's hand a squeeze, and he smiled, fondly recalling their last few days together and the bliss of their lovemaking.

"True," Hoggatt said, "but that pales before what should be ours. No, men like Solomon Guggenheim and J.P. Morgan just skate in, set up their operations, and funnel every cent back out to their New York coffers. The Alaska Syndicate, they're calling themselves, and with a couple dozen other politicians and bigshots, they're running this land, count on it."

He snorted. "I have a title, and they're building me a nice governor's house on the hill—which I'll have to pass on to the next guy in a couple years—but other than that and the fact that I need to give an annual report to Congress this year, I don't have much to do."

Delin tightened his grip on Eloise's hand. "Sounds like you better make a compelling report, then, on your visit to Congress."

Hoggatt sighed. "That's just it, I fear I cannot. I am needed here—I can't be away for the nearly four weeks it would take, sailing to Seattle, then going by rail to Washington and back. No, I will just do as my predecessors did, and send a written report—for all the good it will do."

Delin nodded, staring at his half-finished dinner of caribou steak and russet potatoes. He felt something was coming, and was sure the governor's appearance at this moment was far from coincidence.

"You know," Hoggatt said, "There's a way you can help."

Delin looked around. "Who?"

Hoggatt smiled and pointed with his champagne glass at the two of them. "I've been talking this week with the colleagues of this lovely lady."

Eloise blinked. "The others from the Smithsonian? Here?"

"Yes," Hoggatt said. "Came in by dogsled on Saturday. When I told them about you—and our famed guest here—residents now for some two months, they were overjoyed. Seems they thought some mishap occurred. Something about a great monster you came up here to hunt, and when they found the body of your guide..."

"Oh, no," Eloise said, holding her fingers to her lips. "I sent a letter from Dawson to the Smithsonian, letting them know I was fine, but apparently the others never got word."

"Not to worry," Hoggatt said. "I set them straight. And after their relief, came some jests about your mission, but that is neither here nor there. I am speaking to you of a way you two can help me to help Alaska."

"How?" Eloise asked, looking from Hoggatt to Delin.

"Well," he said. "I hear that after next month, and as soon as the ice permits, your colleagues are heading back to Washington. Obviously, they wish you to return with them."

Eloise turned pale. "But, I don't know if..."

Hoggatt held up his hand. He leaned forward on his elbows and stared at Delin until he felt uncomfortable. "Hear me out. I think what would make the best impression on those short-sighted Congressmen would be the delivery of my report, followed up by a first-hand accounting from one of Alaska's finest."

Delin's lips went dry, and he felt Eloise squeeze his hand tighter, and then she turned and gave him a calculated look. "You mean...?"

Hoggatt nodded. "Come, Mr. Wetherwax, who better to represent this land, in all its rugged glory? From what I've heard, there is no one so well-suited to speak on its behalf. Yours could be a powerful voice, a representative of the success of this place—you've been here since boyhood and seen its transformation. And I know you are deeply committed to maintaining Alaska's natural resources and its culture."

Eloise was enthusiastic. "You could come back with me! See my home, experience my world for a change..."

"Say yes," Hoggatt urged. "Please—don't miss this opportunity. I can't do it, and any plea from someone who has only lived here a few years would fall on indifferent ears."

"Please," Eloise whispered, leaning toward him and holding his hand again. "Come with me."

Delin trembled, and it seemed the walls and the people were just illusions, sifting away in his vision—and there stood the mountains and the fog-crowned peaks, the vast lands of tundra, the glaciers and canyons, rivers and hills. He saw everything at once, and it all seemed to patiently quiver under his gaze.

"Okay," he whispered. "Yes." He looked into Eloise's eyes, and gave a cautious smile at her joyous reaction. She hugged him fiercely. Hoggatt shook his hand. They all shared a toast, and then began to plan.

Chapter 25: Washington, D.C. - April, 1908

A TRIP TO THE CAPITOL

At the Smithsonian, standing on the marble floor of the first level, Delin nearly blacked out when he came face to face with the enormous bronzed dinosaur skull. Jagged dragon's teeth grinned down at him while empty eyesockets as large as his head peered through his soul—and sent his memories sprawling back to a warm April day, sailing on the Tanana River as great muddy flows dredged out the bones of ages past.

He held Eloise's hand in a fierce grip. She pressed herself against him. "I'm here," she whispered and pulled him away, just as he sensed the shadow of his father approaching, his footsteps creaking over the buzzing of mosquitoes.

He blinked away the past and took a deep breath as she led him away from the main exhibit. Eloise pinched him. "I think I fared better against your live monsters up there than you're doing against these dead ones."

Delin blushed. His face was still clean-shaven, and he wore his best navy blue suit; he itched under the starched shirt and vest, and the gold cufflinks scraped at his skin. Still, he was happy to look the part outside, even while he was full of dread on the inside, horrified of standing before all those powerful delegates in a few hours.

"Yes, well, you don't have to go and plead before Congress. So I'm still ahead of you there."

"I'll give you that," Eloise said. She led him to the next exhibit, then on to other wings, proudly showing off her workplace, spinning tales of each relic and every specimen. Where they were found, who was involved, and what they represented. They walked through crowds of tourists, all shuffling in amazement at the wonders of their natural world.

Just after noon, Delin kissed Eloise goodbye at the steps of the Capitol building. She hugged him tight and assured him he would do splendidly. They were ready for him, having received Hoggatt's report last week, and now a uniformed escort was set to take him inside. Eloise promised to wait for him at her apartment on Twentieth Street—where they had stayed last night—and they would celebrate his return with an elegant dinner followed by an opera at the Grand Theater.

He left her, their hands touching and parting slowly, and Eloise had the sudden, horrible sense that Delin foresaw something dire, some horrible event to tear them apart. She saw it in his eyes—a flashing doubt for just a moment; then it was gone. He was smiling and confident, and he went up the stairs and into the building just as a cool wind tossed a few scattered cherry blossoms across the steps.

She sighed, then grimaced and bent over. *Not now*, she thought. *Please*. The feeling passed, but the nausea remained, and she only barely managed to flag down a coach and request to be taken to the hospital.

"Gentlemen," said the Speaker, a gray-haired heavy-set man with spectacles, "we have a special guest today. All the way from Alaska. On the behalf of Governor Wilford Hoggatt, this man—who requested to talk under anonymous conditions so that we might judge only his words—is here today to speak for Alaska. To tell us of its people, land and culture."

Delin stood, looking up at the smoke-filled rows, past polished wooden desktops to the shadowy faces staring back at him. Half-filled glasses lay beside notes, and everywhere Congressmen yawned and stretched—some of them looking like they were already on summer break, two months early.

Delin cleared his throat, thanked the speaker and stepped up to the podium. He smoothed his suitcoat, adjusted his necktie, and began to speak. Slowly at first, then building up in both volume and emotion. The words came forth, spilling out from he didn't know where. Unrehearsed, his speech poured out, accompanied by hand gestures and long pauses. Halfway through, he left the podium to walk before the first row of seats, speaking directly to representatives from New York, Pennsylvania and Georgia, then sending his attention back a couple rows.

And as he spoke, the room quieted down, until barely a clinking glass could be heard. The pipe and cigar smoke had faded away, and everyone in the chamber focused on the blond-haired man eloquently urging the recognition of his home, pointing out the injustices and the inequality, the suffering of people who desperately wanted to belong. People who epitomized the meaning of 'Americans', who had expanded bravely into the wilds where other nations had feared to tread. People who endured, struggled and survived in the harshest of elements—and not only that, they created towns and roads, brought in commerce and even tamed the wilderness.

All this and so much more had been accomplished by *Americans*, by their indomitable spirit—the same spirit that led those initial colonies to revolt and break away from the bonds of servitude. That same noble spirit that even now called out for honor, justice, equality, and at last—recognition.

Delin said all this, and with that final point, bowed his head and returned to the podium.

Several chairs were pushed back, and Delin tried to see who had stood. Several men on their feet, preparing to clap...

But just then a voice cut through the thick anticipation. Someone from the top row, up there in the murky shadows. "Mr. Speaker? A question of the guest."

The Speaker gained his feet, circled his desk and stood beside Delin. "Yes, the floor recognizes the Senator from Nevada. You may proceed."

"Thank you," said the gravelly voice—crumbling down from where a thin haze stubbornly clung to the air, and faces were clothed in shadow. "I believe our guest here has not had the privilege of hearing our opening remarks, which of course, were led by a prayer. So, not wishing to leave him with an impression of heathen lawmakers, I would like to recite a short Biblical passage."

The Speaker sighed. "Here we go again," he whispered to Delin. "Very well, proceed. But be quick about it and then ask your question. We do have other business to attend to."

"Fine," said the Nevada Senator. "Then, if we all bow our heads..."

"Sorry," the Speaker whispered, as he jabbed Delin in the side and lowered his head.

And the Senator began: "The words of the wise are as goads, and as nails fastened by the masters of assemblies, which are given from one shepherd. Let us hear the conclusion of the whole matter: Fear God, and keep his commandments: for this is the whole duty of man." The sound of book thudding against wood echoed in the chamber, and the voice called out again, somberly. "Ecclesiastes, twelve, eleven through thirteen."

Delin's blood froze. His skin erupted in a fevered chill, and he took a step back.

"Now," said the Senator, "I would ask our anonymous guest why, if this land of his is truly so noble, why then—what are you doing? Are you listening?"

Delin glanced up, again trying to pierce the shadows above. "I was asking the Speaker your name, Senator."

"Oh? And why is that? Sounds like a strange request coming from one who insists on remaining nameless himself."

Delin's hands clenched into fists. His blood was seething, his vision clouding. "My name," he hissed, then shouted to the chamber ceiling, "is Delin! Delin Wetherwax. My father was Joshua Wetherwax." He took three huge strides forward. "Does that name mean anything to you, Senator from Nevada?"

The room fell into a hush, with muted whispers breaking out. Six rows up, a chair was knocked over as the Senator lurched to his feet. "It can't be..."

Delin barely heard him. "Tell me!" he shouted, then pointed. "Did you ever shoot a man in the back? In cold blood, then kick his body off a mountain? Were you at the Comstock, Jericho Quitch, hiding in that car? How many Commandments have you defied in your life?"

"No..." Far above, the Senator leaned across the desk, his face straining against the pull of shadow until finally peeling it away like a mask and emerging into the light. "Only the Devil could have brought you back. Your father was a pestilence, and you..."

But that was as far as he got. Delin launched himself, scrambling over the first two levels in a heartbeat, then leaping and climbing. He pushed past astonished representatives, kicked over glasses and papers and chairs, then leapt to the final level and threw himself onto Jericho.

The Senator, unprepared for his assailant's strength or weight, flew backwards and slammed into the floor, with Delin atop him. Two hammer blows landed on Jericho's face, and Delin's fist came away bloodied. He prepared for a third strike—when a sea of blue tackled him. Uniformed guards hauled him off the Senator, even as more came streaming in through the eastern doorway.

Delin screamed and thrashed, kicked out behind him and tossed two guards off and into the path of newly arriving help. He spun, glared at the dazed Jericho trying to get to his feet, then quickly assayed the situation.

He muttered a curse, then vaulted over a railing and raced past two old Senators to the aisle where he dropped to the ground floor. He hit the wooden boards with a resounding pop that echoed off the domed ceiling like a thunderclap.

Amid the cries of "Catch him!" and "Block the exits!" came another voice, a vaunted, strangled cry that overshadowed everything else and stung in Delin's ears.

"You see?" shouted Jericho Quitch. "This is what the Alaskans are like! Savages! Barbarians with no sense of decency. These people deserve nothing from us, not one cent, and certainly not one scrap of independence!"

Delin's scream of frustration burst from his lungs as he pounded his way through three guards who had appeared at the exit. He roared through them, then flew out into the lobby, past frightened lawmakers and clerks, then out into the cold afternoon air, where dark clouds had massed overhead and sprinkles of rain were pattering against the walkways.

Hearing the footsteps behind him, Delin ran. He vaulted another stairway and dropped to the muddy lawn below, where he hit the ground running and sped off toward the nearby road, hoping to lose himself in the crowds.

And with every step, his anger intensified and his heart broke again and again, shattering in a release of pent-up rage. Rage that he had tried to suppress for so long.

I'm sorry, Papa. Sorry... I had him! Again I had him, and couldn't do anything. Couldn't save you then, and I now I've failed again...

For the next three hours he waited around the corner from Eloise's apartment. Standing in the rain, drenched, he stood as the sprinkles turned to a lasting downpour. Her door was locked, and no one answered. So he waited, and watched. Buggies drove by, and the occasional car—a marvel that went unappreciated as he choked back the shivers and wrestled with his rage.

He had to leave, he knew. They would be looking for him after that assault. He berated himself for losing control, for acting so rashly when he should have taken the nobler path. But the chance was gone, the opportunity to demonstrate his honor. He had ruined not only his own chance for happiness here, but had certainly set back the fate of Alaska for decades.

He hung his head, and just watched the water stream from his face and his soaked hair. The trotting of horses caught his attention, and when he looked up, a coach had arrived beside the apartment building, and out came Eloise and a taller man. She clung to his arm as he walked her to the door.

Delin started to rush forward, then held back, suddenly helpless in the face of a rising emotion he had never known. He watched her hug the man, squeeze him tight and kiss his cheek—and inwardly, Delin's heart broke even more—the last hopeful shards splintering.

He leaned against the side of the building and let his shoulders fall. He watched sullenly as the man returned to the coach and it drove away, and then he splashed through deep puddles over the cobblestones to her door. He turned the handle and pushed inside, stumbling into the hallway. A meager electric light fizzled in fright at his approach.

When he reached her door and prepared to knock—it flew open, and Eloise was there, looking up at him with a face as ashen and grim as he had ever seen. But only for a moment—and then it was as if seeing him transformed her. Blood rushed to her cheeks, and her lips cracked into a wide smile and her eyes glowed like starlight through a mist.

"You're back!" she cried and fell into his arms. "And wet!" she added, pulling away slowly.

"Who was that?" Delin asked, still shaking.

Eloise glanced to the door, then looked away, folding her hands. She walked to the kitchen and sat with a heavy sigh. "My uncle."

Delin blinked. "Uncle?" *Of course*, how could he have forgotten? Her uncle had raised her after her parents' deaths, and surely she'd want to see him after so long away.

"We just came from the doctor's," Eloise said, slowly. Her eyes, red from crying, were downcast, and she rubbed her hands in her lap.

"Oh, I'm sorry," Delin said, pulling off his soaked boots and coming to her side. He didn't realize her uncle was sick, and he could only imagine what Eloise must be going through.

Eloise took his hands in hers. She seemed to be wrestling with something, desperately trying to find the words. She sobbed and shook her head. "Delin, I..."

"No," he said. "I'm sorry. I assumed the worst. After the day I had!"

She blinked at him, her tears breaking apart. "Oh no—what happened at Congress?"

Delin's voice hardened. "There was... an incident."

"A what?"

"Did you know who would be there?"

"What do you mean?"

"Eloise, who's the Senator from Nevada?"

She shrugged. "Couldn't tell you. I doubt I could name more than two members of Congress. Sorry, I guess it never mattered that much to me."

"It's Quitch," Delin said, closing his eyes and picturing that bloodied face beneath him.

"Oh my God!" Eloise gripped his hands and forced him to look into her eyes. "Did you...?"

"Punch him? Yes. Kill him, no. Embarrass myself and Governor Hoggatt? Definitely."

"Oh dear."

"Yes, and I must apologize to you again, for this. I believe they will be looking for me. I have to leave."

All the energy seemed to flee Eloise at once; her body deflated and she hung on the chair like a flimsy gown.

"You can come back with me," Delin voiced. "We'll hide

together in the wild; it'll be just like when we met, and..."

"I can't go," Eloise whispered, her eyes never leaving his. "Not now. Not... for some time."

Delin opened his mouth, then shut it. He understood—or thought he did. Her uncle. He needed her here. Plus, she had just returned, and probably had so much work to get back to, and her career to think about.

"You don't understand," Eloise said, and again seemed to struggle with something beyond her ability to explain.

"I do," Delin whispered, and leaned close to kiss her lips. "I'll wait for you," he said. "Whenever you can get away again, telegram me at Juneau, or send me a letter by post."

Eloise nodded, choking on fresh tears. She held him fiercely, digging her nails into his flesh. "But don't go yet. Get out of those wet clothes." She kissed him back and looked pleadingly into his eyes.

"Stay with me. One more night."

In the silvery moonlight dappling through her nightshade, Delin held Eloise close as she nestled on his chest and ran her fingers through his soft blond curls. Their bodies were wrapped as tight as possible, her legs securing his, her arms around his shoulders, and her lips pressing against his cheek.

"It will be dawn soon," she whispered.

"Don't rush it," he replied. And a lump formed in his throat and his emotions cracked. He wanted to break down, to beg her to come with him. To take her uncle, even—maybe the pure air up there could cure whatever ailed him.

"You're right. I won't rush anything," she said. "And I'll never lose this moment. Right here, lying with you in the silence of this night."

He kissed her forehead.

"Tell me something," she whispered. "Tell me... a story."

Delin smiled. "I think you know them all, my dear. I've told you my whole life, and..."

"No, not your past. Tell me... our future."

Delin stopped moving. He felt another tear fall on his chest, and felt her sob as quietly as she could. "Tell me," she insisted, "what it will be like when I find you again. Up in those mountains, surrounded by all that ice. When your dogs bark out their greeting and smother me with kisses. Tell me..."

Delin began, in a cracked voice. "...of how we'll be married by a passing missionary beside the great river, and how we'll build a new cabin—a great, multi-leveled log home, with plenty of room for the dogs... and for our children."

"Yes," Eloise urged, snuggling closer. "Tell me of them. What are their names?"

Delin choked back a surge of emotion. "Ah, their names. Well, names are powerful, potent things, and not to be granted lightly. For our first child, the boy—ah, we spent months and months trying to find the most perfect name."

"And did we? What was it—what did we name our son?"

"Oh, it was beautiful. In fact, *you* picked it out, frustrated when I couldn't choose between several dozen promising Classical names, all with multiple meanings and appropriate connotations."

"Yes...?"

"It..." Delin sighed, looking out through the curtain, backlit by the glowing moon. "It was something so perfect that it made me weep. And I loved you even more than I do now."

Eloise hugged him, sniffled and lifted her face. She gave him a deep kiss, and then whispered to his lips. "And this boy, this perfect son, grows up in your love, doesn't he? And you teach him to experience the world, to bear its cruelties and revel in its joys."

"Yes," Delin said, his lips brushing against hers. "I do. We do, and we live out our days with our beautiful family, prospecting and exploring, celebrating Christmases with licorice and chocolate, toys and books, and..."

Eloise sobbed again and gave him one last, intense kiss before rising. In the weak moonlight she looked frail and trembling, sitting up in bed. Her eyes were haunted and her fingers trembled when she reached out to grasp his hand.

"It's time," she said. "I'll take you to the station and see you off."

Delin nodded and rubbed her cold fingers. "And then my sadness will start—and I won't stop missing you until you appear on that steamship, and I'm waiting there for you on the docks, with a dozen roses and eight very happy dogs."

Chapter 26: Nome—Candle - May 1908

REMATCH WITH THE MOON

ON THE SECOND DAY OF May, Delin returned to Juneau. He had booked passage on the season's first departure with the Alaska Steamship Company.

Upon arrival, having eased past a ferry full of miners shuttling back from Douglas Island, and after docking carefully at the main wharf, Delin stood on the observation deck. He waited as the tourists and merchants crowded the gangplanks. He stood and breathed in the cool air, filtering out the fumes from Treadwell's smokestacks, the halibut canneries on the eastern docks and the rendering plant to the south. It was difficult, but he could still detect the purity of the Arctic breezes blowing off the stately white peaks of Mount Roberts; and the fragrance of wildflowers calmed his thoughts.

The prospect of fleeing through the town, gathering his dogs and rushing home in shame was a mere shadow in his mind. No, he had already decided to face the music. He would march straight to Wilford Hoggatt's residence and personally account for his behavior, apologize as best he could, and beg the governor's forgiveness.

As he slowly marched off the steamship, lugging a heavy pack, he thought despondently on the future. It had been only a month since he had left Eloise, but the gulf between them now seemed as unpassable as the Chilkoot in a blizzard. And something about their farewell stung at his heart with every passing hour. Dread hung about his dreams, which were stale and hollow—just the shadowplay of vague marionettes.

With each step taken, every street crossed, he forced his thoughts to turn to happier times, to the days spent prospecting with his favorite pupil, reminiscing on how love had crept upon him so innocently, so unavoidably.

At last, he stood before the Governor's house, a pillared two-story brick home that was the simplest yet most elegant Delin had ever seen. A well-dressed bald man escorted him inside and directed him to wait in the nearest room—where a large dining table sprawled, flanked by wall-length native tapestries.

"Mr. Wetherwax!"

Delin turned to the voice, and greeted Governor Hoggatt as he emerged through a side door. He wore a thick embroidered robe and seemed to be preparing to turn in.

"You must forgive my attire," he said. "Wasn't prepared to take in visitors. Nasty spot of head-cold lately. Just trying to sleep it off and kill it with a little brandy!"

"Good for what ails you," Delin admitted, then dug inside his coat pocket. "But, may I suggest some licorice?"

"Ah, does it help? Excellent, then." He took the candy and crunched into an inch of it. "So, you're back—and I daresay I admire your spirit. You're a good man to come to me straight-away, but of course I figured as much already."

"Sir?" Delin fidgeted, glancing back at the butler who had retreated to the shadows in the doorway, eavesdropping.

"Oh, I heard all about the scuffle at Congress. Telephone, you know. Even though I wasn't the first to get a line, still—sure beats waiting for those damn telegraphs."

Delin blinked and scratched his nearly-reformed beard. "Then you know I've dishonored you and Alaska. I am deeply..."

Hoggatt took another crunch of licorice. "Stop it. Can't blame you—hell, the bastard killed your father! And besides, I heard it on good sources that up until that incident, your speech had influenced quite a few thick skulls."

"Yes, but after I lost my temper..."

"I said, don't worry about it. You gave it a mighty try, and not even that Casey feller in the poem could have done better. Besides, it's too early, and I was too impatient. Statehood will come, and rights will fall our way—but we have to wait for it. May happen sooner than we think though, the way Teddy Roosevelt's been shaking up the Trusts and slapping big business around—sure woke up a lot of common people."

"But..."

"But nothin', Mr. Wetherwax. You did all I asked of you. However, if you still feel bad about it, there is something you can do to make it up."

"Name it, please, and I'll try to help."

Hoggatt nodded and chuckled to himself as he walked to a liquor cabinet set in the corner; he began pouring out two brandies. "Something's come to my attention. Read about it in the newspaper last year, but it was too late for anything then. Now, however, we can act."

Delin frowned, completely confused, wondering if perhaps the governor intended to send him over to Fairbanks or Tanacross—where Delin had just learned another gold stampede was in the works. "What is it?"

Hoggatt grinned and offered him a swirling glass of orange-colored liquor. "Dogsled race! Up in Nome—second annual All-Alaska Sweepstakes."

"Sweepstakes? I don't follow you. You say it's a race?"

"Three-hundred sixty mile course," Hoggatt said, after taking a sip. "From Nome through ten or eleven mining camps, all the way up to the settlement at Candle, then back. Last year they had twenty teams start it, but only eight finished, the winner completing the course in ninety-eight hours. There's good prize money—ten thousand split between the top three finishers; but the big money's in gambling. This year the race will be carried on the radio and telegraph machines, and betting has already spread throughout California and Texas, and on to Chicago, New York, and down the East Coast."

Delin was stunned—he had never heard of this race. Of course he had spent the last year in blissful solitude with Eloise, but still... "So, last year—who won it?"

"Ah," said Hoggatt. "If all the talk of money hasn't perked your interest, maybe this will. Last year, winning by a good four hours and already promising this time to crush the competition by at least six hours, is the native favorite. A half-breed." Hoggatt grinned and finished his drink. "I believe you know the man."

Delin frowned. His mouth went dry.

"Well," Hogatt continued, "legend has it that a certain young boy delivered this Indian his first and only loss. Happened in this very city. Oh, it must have been twenty-six, twenty-seven—"

"Twenty-eight years ago," Delin said, nearly whispering the words. "*Moon Chaser*."

"Favored ten-to-one, in yesterday's Post-Intelligencer."

Delin's heart was hammering in his chest, and he felt a driving wind prickle at his face. He closed his eyes, hearing the thudding of paws in the snow. "Three hundred and sixty miles," he heard himself say.

"You could do it," Hoggatt assured him. "And think of the press—a rematch between boyhood rivals! Last year's winner, the favorite, challenged again by a ghost from his past. You'd be famous across the country! And don't worry about the hundred dollar entry fee—I'll cover that."

"What about supplies for the dogs?" Delin asked. "For a race that long, they'll need many pairs of moccasins, plus..." he tried to do the math in his head. "A lot of food."

"Covered!" Hoggatt shouted, waving his arms. "All you have to do is enter yourself as Juneau's representative. You can keep the prize money, just put us in the winner's circle!"

Delin scratched at his beard. "I don't know. I've just come from fame—of a different sort. And I was... well, hoping for quiet and solitude. To retreat from the world for a time and wait for..."

"Would it make a difference," Hoggatt asked, "if I told you who Moon Chaser's sponsor is?"

Delin looked at him with half-open eyes. "I doubt it."

"Remember when I mentioned The Alaska Syndicate?"

"Yes. The Guggen-somebodies and J.P. Morgan—"

"—and other financiers, yes. Taking their bites out of Alaska and gorging on our richness. Well, I did some researching after your little experience down in Congress. Seemed to me, that Quitch fellow egged you on before even knowing who you were. Seemed also he might have had something to protect up here, which I found out, he has."

Delin felt his face heating up. A sweat broke out on his scalp.

"He's mining up here, isn't he?"

Hoggatt nodded. "Got several stakes in large operations across the central mining region. Even some at Nome, and a large presence in Fairbanks. Also invested heavily in the emerging canneries. Plus, word has it he's an avid hunter—comes up here once a year to snag some big game. Bear, moose and caribou. And this might just be myth, but word is he always makes his kill using an antique harpoon gun. Can you believe it? Yep, a relic from his whaling days."

Delin leaned against the table and downed his drink in one gulp, washing away the vile taste in his mouth. "So he's sponsoring Moon Chaser?"

"Oh yes," Hoggatt said, smiling as he refilled Delin's glass. "Claims to always back the winners. Care to hit him where it hurts—and pull the rug out from under his ego?"

Delin stood up straight and clinked his glass against the governor's, and his smile held a burning malice that even made the governor flinch.

The trip to Nome took three days longer than he had expected. The governor made good on his promise to assign Delin and his dogs passage on the next northbound revenue cutter, one of the Treasury's finest Arctic-worthy boats, but a spell of cold air sweeping over from Asia had strengthened a swath of ice in their path, and they had to maneuver carefully and slowly.

Finally, they arrived and Delin disembarked, his dogs harnessed close. They seemed to sense the impending competition and struggled and nipped at each other and passers-by. People looked at him and whispered to themselves, giving him a wide berth. He stopped first at the supply station where he cashed in Hoggatt's bank notes for a hundred pounds of salmon, oats and flour, as well as four small bags of cured pork for himself. Then he bought a new sled, some rawhide and three dozen doggy moccasins. And a spare set of harnesses. He was fully aware that the other contestants, Moon Chaser included, were likely to have more dogs—perhaps thirteen or even fifteen, but in this race it wasn't quantity that counted. Besides, every additional dog meant more weight in food and supplies on the sled.

His next stop was the dentist's office.

"Dr. McCloud!" he shouted, barging into the office on the corner of High Street and Crucias Avenue. The dogs yelped and raced inside, scattering chairs and papers in their rush to leap on the frightened little man.

"Dear God!" he shouted, whimpering as he huddled in a corner away from the affectionate animals.

"Good to see you, too," Delin announced. "Glad you don't have patients at the moment. Just stopped in to leave the dogs with you for an hour or so while I go and officially register for this Sweepstakes thing."

McCloud, his white jacket smeared with paw prints, nodded. "Sure, any time. Anything for you."

"How's business?" Delin asked, glancing around admiringly.

"Oh, fine," he answered, pushed into the corner to avoid the jumping dogs. "You know, lots of teeth to pull. Prices going up every day, and people still pay."

Great," Delin said. "All right then, I'll see you soon."

"Going up against Moon Chaser?" McCloud called, just as Delin was almost out.

"Yep." He stopped in the doorway.

"Just thought I'd warn you—man's a nasty cheat. All my patients have been telling me that. In fact, no one around here's been talking of anything else but that silly race."

"So, what's this about cheating?"

"Oh, they tell me he's got a gang of his buddies. Hiding out in some of the mining camps. They call themselves something—oh yes—The Outcasts. Ragtag bunch of bums if you ask me. Anyway, they won't make a move until the return lap, but if anyone's close to catching Moon Chaser, they'll take him out."

"How?"

McCloud shrugged, then patted Cupid on the head as the dog sat and wagged its tail. "Oh, they'll arrange some kind of accident. Maybe shoot one of your dogs, or run out and dig up a hole in the trail before you get there. Although, given that he's got a score to settle with you—I'd be more worried."

Delin tipped his hat to his old partner. "Thanks for the warning."

"Good luck!" McCloud shouted, and sighed as the door closed and the dogs leapt on him again.

After paying the registration fee, and finding he had gotten in just in time, he dodged some reporters and inquisitive gamblers and found his way to where one of the organizers had told him he could find last year's champion.

Moon Chaser sat in the back room of Jekyll's Saloon, across a smoke-filled parlor full of sour-looking Tlingits and Athabascans. Delin walked past the Indians, most of them drunk already. He pushed past two thin-faced men who might have been warriors, a generation ago. One wore a cone-shaped hat, the other had a bleached pony tail. Delin reached into his coat, fumbled around at his belt for the item he had strapped there this morning, and withdrew it.

Several Tlingits saw the weapon, shouted a warning and made to lunge at him—but Delin was faster. He stepped up and hurled the dagger with one fluid throw. It flipped in the air and slammed point-first into the slapboard wall, just inches from Moon Chaser's wild-haired skull.

A half dozen men circled Delin, their knives drawn and pistols aiming at his face. He held up his hands, grinning and trying to peer around the bodies to see Moon Chaser's reaction.

"WAIT!" The men parted and Moon Chaser stood up, slowly pulling the blade out from the wall. He held the dagger up, his mouth open as he stared at the caribou-antler hilt.

His fingers snapped about the handle and his head shot around. He pointed the blade at Delin and his mane of stringy black hair fell over the thick, freshly-cleaned bearskin vest. His face was rugged, aged in the polar wind, and his eyes were even more vicious and dark than Delin remembered.

"I believe that was yours," Delin said. "Must have dropped it the last time we raced."

A crowd of white men had appeared, having followed him from the registration office. Some men were whispering while others had taken out notebooks and were writing fiercely.

Moon Chaser snarled something that was unintelligible to most of the newcomers, but Delin threw his head back and laughed. "That's not how I recall it." He turned and strode through the Indians and into the group of gossip-hunters.

For this race, Delin had chosen to forego the typical tandem configuration and instead tethered the dogs for maximum leverage—in four pairs, with Dunder still at the lead with the longest rope, but just slightly ahead of Blitzen, while their pair was only a foot ahead of the other three pairs. They were ready at sunrise, their feet outfitted and their harnesses secured. They had a huge meal an hour before, and strained at their bits all the way up until the gunshot that set them off.

Fourteen teams launched out of the starting point at ten a.m. on a bright twenty-degree day. Not a cloud in the sky for miles—but a strong westerly wind beat at them from the outset. Delin's team, as the last to register, had been put farthest to the left, on the opposite side from Moon Chaser—which was just fine with him. He could do without any taunting today. Layered up in five thin shirts, three jackets and an outer coat of baby seal fur, he was already hot—but knew that soon, out on the open tundra, he would be grateful.

They sped out, to the roaring of thousands watching from stands, rooftops and streets. Men with radio microphones were scattered along the near sidelines, and with roving reporters, had spent hours trying to interview the mushers and get close to the dogs. Delin had said very little, letting his smile be his answer, and his dogs' growls kept most of them away.

Three hours later, he had pulled ahead of all but Moon Chaser's team and another sled run by a large Swede name Henrik. Moon Chaser and his fourteen dogs had a sizable lead, but nothing to be concerned with yet. Delin purposely held back, conserving strength; he actually had to command the dogs down whenever they passed another team—so eager were they to catch the next. They rode most of the way on a smooth trail that had been flattened out just days before in preparation for the race.

They had crossed through Fort Davis and Hastings, pausing only a few moments at each stop for an official to log their time and to take an accounting of the dogs. When they were closing in on Cape Nome, Delin checked the pocketwatch on his chain—only an hour and half had gone by. Good time, he thought, recalling the stats from last year's race. Up ahead, a dozen cheering men waved them by as they stood in the cold outside their cabins on the hills beside some ramshackle mines. One straggly old man ran out to Delin and offered him a steaming cup of whiskey-loaded coffee.

"Give 'em hell, Delin!" he shouted, raising his fist in the air after the sled had past.

Grinning, Delin sipped at the burning drink and felt his insides tingle. Renewed, he stepped off the runner boards and ran along behind the sled, shouting to Dunder to quicken up as they ascended a short hill. They gained on the Swede, who whipped frantically at his lead huskies until Delin pulled aside and edged past him.

The Swede gave him a sporting nod and shouted something about seeing him on the way back. Delin waved in return, and as they came to a decline, he launched himself back onto the runners and sped the team onward. Nervously, he looked ahead, past the smoke trail above camp Solomon, then over the vast stretch of nothingness that led, ultimately to Candle—ninety-five miles away. In between those two points there was no protection—none, if the weather decided to interrupt their race.

Delin pressed on, running at times, resting occasionally on the boards, then urging the dogs to give their hardest. They seemed to sense the urgency as well, digging in and pulling with every muscle in their bodies, as they were born to do.

And finally, the clouds swallowed up the sky, just as the sun dipped below the horizon. Night fell fast, covering the land in utter darkness. Without stars, without moonlight, or even a sign of fire from the next camp, Delin had to stop.

They had only passed the camp of Solomon an hour ago, and it was another ten miles to Topkok—two more hours. Delin debated letting the dogs run for it, trusting their noses to follow the scent of Moon Chaser's team, but caution held him back. Plus, he was sure the other racers were likewise taking a little rest at least—waiting out the clouds. And he feared an ambush in the dark by Moon Chaser's Outcasts. So he stopped, cooked up some salmon, mixed it with a little flour and oats, and let the dogs gorge themselves. Afterwards, they curled up around each other and slept—and Delin went from dog to dog, changing their booties, massaging their feet and haunches.

After four hours, when he took a short nap himself, with the

Dragoons balanced and ready on his chest, he woke to the sound of growls. He got up in a crouch, the weapons ready. The dogs were looking back the way they had come, and Delin could hear the distant yelps of approaching dogs.

"Let's move," he whispered and re-hitched the lashings to the sled. At just a clucking of his tongue, Dunder took off, and the others followed. Delin took out his compass, cleared away the frost and read it by the faint glow from beyond the clouds. Making modest adjustments every ten minutes, he steered them on toward Topkok.

The blizzard hit the next night. They had raced all day, stopping only twice for short rests, and to eat, and the weather had held off—although the air had chilled to below zero, then the winds kicked in. It had gotten so bad that Delin had to stop and add another series of tethers around the supplies on the sled to keep them in place. The dogs howled and snapped at the wind and shook their defiance, and then Delin had them running off again. But finally, as night fell and they raced through Haven—where Delin stopped long enough to hear that Moon Chaser was about forty minutes ahead of him—the blizzard struck.

Delin considered heading back to Haven, but knew he would have a hard time turning the dogs around—and if he did, he worried they would sense his faltering confidence. So he continued, driving them into the stinging winds and the heavy flurries that grew thicker and thicker. Soon the trail was obliterated and the dogs were slowing, trudging through deeper and deeper snow. Delin knew he would have to run on ahead of them with snowshoes and flatten the trail—but in the darkness, he couldn't see the checkpoints or even gauge their direction.

Finally, with visibility fading to just a few feet ahead so that even the dogs were obscured in the furious storm, he decided to stop. He leapt off the sled, driving it first to a distance off their path where he thought he saw some hilly shelter. He upturned the sled against the wind, pulled out his compact shovel and started piling up snow around the barrier. Even the dogs helped, digging at the snow and finally, as Delin settled in, they dug themselves in, piling up the drifts around themselves and huddling together against the sled.

It was too cold even to eat, much less try to light a match to cook. So they slept, dreamt, and waited.

Sometime, hours later—Delin woke. Or thought he did. Immediately, in the haze of blinding snow, he heard growling. And he thought he saw his eight dogs shaking themselves free of their snowy beds and arranging themselves around him in a semicircle. Their dark forms bristled, and their snarls were as menacing as he had ever heard.

Something was out there. He sensed it—somewhere close. Struggling to rise, but too weak to break free of the compacted snow, he paused and listened. There, above the growls—a high-pitched whistling sound.

Two of them. No—three. Three distinct sounds, almost above audible perception, but clearly within the dogs' capabilities. And then, nearly scattered by the howling wind—a scent of something foul, revolting like disease.

Delin strained to see, but the storm played tricks on his mind, and the swirling eddies of wind and snow kicked up strange shapes—like three amorphous shadows.

With bright red pinpoints for eyes.

The dogs growled, and the storm blew on. The dream closed around him, and sleep tugged him back to its icy realm.

In the morning, the blizzard was gone, and the sky apologetically cleaned up in its wake, leaving only a feathery scattering across the eastern horizon. Delin dug himself out, then righted the sled after clearing it from over four feet of snow. Again the dogs helped, and he rewarded them with a generous portion of salmon while he devoured three sticks of cold pork, washed down with a quart of melted snow.

He made a quick survey of the area and was about to head back to the sled when he saw a set of tracks that froze his blood. Nearly covered with fresh snowfall, they were nonetheless deep enough to prove the heavy weight of those that made them. Just twenty yards from his camp they had come—three distinct sets of enormous footprints, scattered about in a semicircle—and even further in the distance, a mound of deposited spoor, which the dogs warily growled at.

They left me a message, he thought grimly, and suddenly he felt totally vulnerable. He scanned the world all around, and saw nothing but endless packed tundra and bleak, icy expanses leading to blurry mountains. He stomped back, his snowshoes fanning out over the fresh snow and carrying him effortlessly above the drifts. He dug for his supplies and pulled out the rifle, then strapped it to the handlebars for easier access. Next, he checked the Dragoons, worked the chambers and cleared the barrels of snow.

Satisfied, he tethered the dogs, this time in the typical tandem fashion so they could follow in line. He stretched his legs, took several deep breaths, then yelled to them. Called them to follow as he raced on ahead in his wide snowshoes, padding down a trail in the drifts.

They made their way to Candle—where he learned that, miraculously, Moon Chaser had already come through, just two hours earlier—and had turned and passed him last night in the blizzard. Energized, Delin rode through a crowd of several dozen in the icebound settlement, turned around at the markers, and raced back along his own trail, beginning the return trip to Nome.

He raced hard for another hour before tiring. The camp of Gold Run was still twenty miles away—but at least he had found the trail again. He had seen the footsteps of his old nemesis, noted the scraping of his tracks and the dragging of his feet. It had been slow going for Moon Chaser, and Delin was sure he would catch up soon. But first, a short rest, and a lunch.

They started up again and rode hard for the rest of the day, passing six other teams still on their run to Candle. Men and dogs barked their greetings, and Delin asked when they had seen Moon Chaser.

"Three miles ahead," one first-time racer from Vancouver had told him. "Riding those dogs like the devil himself. Although he's down to only ten. I didn't ask what happened to the other five."

Delin thanked him and pressed on, alternating between running and riding, and sometime around midnight he saw a distant firelight. The stars were out, the constellations flashy spectators bathing the track in a soft bluish glow. The dogs stumbled a few more steps, glanced back and whined, and Delin stepped off the sled and called them to rest. And to eat. He eyed the fire up ahead and listened to the stillness of the world, where even the wind had taken respite.

McCloud's warnings came back to him now that he was gaining and they were on the final stretch, and he kept his Dragoons ready, poised for any threatening sound. After a rest, he figured he could reach Council before dawn—then it was only another seventy-five miles to Nome. If they rode hard, he could cross the finish line before dark. It would have taken them three and a half days—almost ninety hours, and not good enough for a lasting record, he guessed—but the storm had set everyone back, and probably ended the race for several teams.

In the early hours of the night, Delin lay awake, propped between Prancer and Cupid, staring up at the aurora which had appeared two hours ago, emerging slowly like a waking bear. He stared longingly into its curtain-like folds and let his imagination tumble with its colorful tides. He spoke to it in whispers, and smiled when it flickered in response.

At last, the aurora retreated into the dark, and Delin roused the dogs and fed them by starlight. He set their harnesses back to the fantail configuration now that they were traveling in the flattened paths of Moon Chaser and the others.

By first light they entered Council, and he had to pound on a few cabin doors to find the administrator and wake him to report in. The man thanked him while grumbling, saying he had just gotten to bed an hour ago after Moon Chaser had ridden through. He also added that what he had heard over the short wave radio was that America was glued to the news, eagerly snapping up details of their check-ins. Wagering was intense, now focused solely on Delin and Moon Chaser, and odds were changing every hour.

"We're pulling for you, youngster," the man said as he picked his teeth. "But mind the river bank near Solomon. If he hears you comin', that's where he'll try to ride you down."

Delin thanked him and pressed on. After lunching outside of Topkok, he finally let the dogs act on their instincts. They had gotten the fresh scent of Moon Chaser's team, and now there was no slowing down, no pausing for rest. Dunder strained on his haunches, and Blitzen barked orders back to the rest of the team, and Delin could only imagine the fire in their hearts.

He ran behind them more and more, only riding along when his legs were exhausted, or they were on a longer downward slope. The temperature actually crept up into the teens and Delin almost prayed for a cooler breeze, or else he'd have to lose his jacket and hat—but in the late afternoon the thermometer fell and the wind picked up as they approached Solomon. And after clearing a slowly-rising ridge, the dogs yelped and pulled harder—and Delin saw the smoke curling up from the fires at the small settlement, and the smoothness of the icy Fish River sent back glaring reflections.

They continued through the town, barely slowing as the official ran beside the sled, taking down figures and shouting "Good Luck! Moon Chaser's just a half-mile ahead!"

Refreshed as if they had just slept for a week, the dogs kicked up snow at the departing mining camp, and pressed ahead in lunging strides. After another half hour without incident, Delin noticed a sled trail veering off to the right—toward a small copse of trees, and to a spot where the river widened. Dunder automatically headed that way too, following the scent of the other dogs. Delin was about to pull him back, thinking to resist what must be a trap.

But why would Moon Chaser get off the path and let him sail by, in the lead? Unless his Outcasts were waiting ahead, over that next ridge. Delin cursed and pulled back slightly on the gangline, shouting to slow. Dunder whined and only slightly decreased his speed. The sled crunched through the freshly-pressed snow, glided over bumps and gullies, and skirted a small forest of pines before dropping down a slick trail to the riverbank—

—where Moon Chaser and his sled waited. Not more than a hundred yards away, he had stopped and was facing him. Alone, fortunately, although... Delin glanced back to the forest. The shadows were thick in there and he thought there was movement in the trees. Snow falling irregularly.

He withdrew one Dragoon and cocked the trigger. The sled continued as the dogs, furious now that they could see the competition, dragged it ahead, to the riverbank and onto the ice. A bitter wind scaled through the forest and kicked up swirls in its wake.

Delin kept an eye on the trees while he approached the half-breed, who stood in front of his snarling dogs. Delin shouted out the command to stop, and suddenly felt like the tables had been turned, and he had walked into a perfect trap.

If it's meant to be, I'm not going alone, Delin thought. Moon Chaser saw him smile, and glowered; but then he pulled his hands out from his back, to reveal a lone stick of dynamite—and a flare in his other hand.

Delin looked down—and swore. The ice was thick, but probably not more than a couple inches, and already he could feel the currents under his boots, warming the water below the ice. The dynamite, thrown from twenty yards, away would blow a huge hole clear through and drag him down with his dogs.

Moon Chaser's teeth—those that he had left, some of them gold, the others silver—sparkled in the sun's reflections off the ice. He lit the flare, preparing to ignite the wick.

Delin raised the gun and pointed, but then both men looked to the forest, where a blood-curdling scream split the silence. A high-pitched whistling arose as the trees shook and wood splintered. Men screamed, and gunshots echoed.

More screams, and then two men came rushing out, scrambling backwards, firing their rifles at something in the woods. Moon Chaser and Delin stood, open-mouthed as they watched the huge, white shape pull itself from the shadows.

It rocked back with an impact, but kept coming. Someone else screamed in the forest, and then a body came tumbling out, flopping like a tattered doll.

And two more Sesquats emerged, their claws and fangs streaked with red, matching their burning eyes. They snapped their heads toward the two fleeing gang members, and pounced on each one before they could fire again.

Delin drew the other revolver as he dispassionately watched the creatures shred the two men into a scattering of bones and tissue. All three creatures suddenly looked up from their grisly work, and froze the two racers and their dogs with those unrelenting eyes.

The dogs growled and turned their attention to the approaching beasts that were fanning out in a flanking attack. Delin pulled back on the gangline and tried to turn the sled. Moon Chaser glanced back at him and shook his head, and said, "Mangl'actuck!"—Cursed One—and then he brought the flame to the short dynamite wick.

In that moment, Delin knew his opponent meant to continue with his first intention, maybe hoping that killing the one with the curse would free him from the creatures' wrath. Might be true, Delin thought as he spread his arms wide and lined up two targets.

The Sesquats hesitantly set foot on the river, tested its strength, then roared their challenge and raced toward him.

The guns recoiled, and thick smoke blasted out in opposite directions. Moon Chaser's chest exploded in a burst of red; he spun and dropped the lit dynamite—just as the other shell struck the largest Sesquat in the chest, leaving a spot of red beside a flank of scarred flesh.

That's the one! Delin saw, a second before his eardrums roared in agony and he flew backward, blown off the sled, which rocked to its side. Ice shards flew in every direction, and a geyser of riverwater, blood and bits of flesh sprayed forty feet into the air. Delin rolled and got to his knees, and saw the massive hole in the ice, spreading out in concentric rings, like some invisible sea monster chomped at the frozen covering from all angles. Moon Chaser's dogs disappeared at once, dragged down with the weight of the sled, and Moon Chaser himself—what was left of him, bobbed on the surface for an instant, then plunged out of view.

Something howled in frustration, then turned to cries of mortal terror. And just as Dunder scrambled to his paws, dug in and turned the team around to race away from the expanding cracks—Delin saw two of the massive Sesquats floundering in the icy water. They slapped at the ice, smashing more of it in their attempts to escape. They screeched and their heads disappeared below, then re-emerged with flailing arms. Every purchase seemed only to crack and split the ice even more, and left them holding great shards and spinning in frothy waves.

Delin struggled to his feet, staggered to the sled and righted it, shouting to the dogs and hoping they could hear his commands even while he could not—as nothing broke through the ringing in his ears and the wailing of the drowning Sesquats. He pushed the sled and ran several yards ahead of the advancing cracks and the collapsing ice. One glance back almost spelled his end—as he slipped and banged his knee on the ice, barely holding on to the uprights as the dogs lurched ahead. The ice below his feet fell away and his legs plunged into a cold so fierce he nearly blacked out—despite the layers of near-watertight sealskin. He gripped the wooden rail with all his strength and let the sled pull him out and drag him free—back up the side of the riverbed and onto the trail. He hauled himself onto the sled, over the bags of supplies, and he bit back a scream as he reached for his boots.

Have to get them off, he thought, then looked back—and the rest of his blood chilled.

One Sesquat remained, pulling itself onto the far bank. Somehow it had gained a handhold by pure luck or damned tenacity, and it hauled itself from the water's frozen clutches. It rolled to its side, then stood and roared up at the sky before spinning around and glaring across the crumbled ice.

Delin shook his head, and a begrudging smile emerged. "There you are," he said with a mindless giggle, pointing. "Won't quit, will you?" He worked at his boots, and all the while, as the dogs struggled to pull the added weight up the hill and back to the trail, Delin stared at the distant shape, locking eyes with the ancient killer, sensing its wrath and hoping it sensed his. The blackened flesh on its side—Delin hoped it still hurt, and that it plagued the creature all these years, even as the memory of Mama's death burned his own heart.

"Soon," Delin whispered to the beast. "Soon..."

He managed to wrap his frozen feet in some dry burlap ripped from the supply bags. Then he tossed out the rest of the supplies—everything, including the rifle—to lighten the load. And, sprawled out on the flat planks of the sled, he called out his commands. To run, run as they'd never run before. To take their master home. To safety.

At some point, he blacked out. Later, the officials from Nome would tell him that he had passed through the camps at Safety and Nome River without personally checking in—although the attendants there had logged his time and assumed he had been asleep. And they marveled at the skill of his trained dogs that they could follow his orders even while he lay unconscious.

And his legend spread, and by the time he crossed the finish line and the dogs collapsed in a heap, the crowds were roaring in thrilled excitement. And when he awoke, he limped on burlap slippers, fighting a brutal fever and near-delirium; but he shuffled through the throng of zealous fans, accepted the trophy, donated his five thousand to the local Indian schools, then collapsed at the feet of Dr. McCloud.

Four months later, he was pronounced well enough to leave, but by then winter had come again, and the seas and rivers were unpassable. McCloud had cared for him, letting him recover in a room upstairs at his office, and he had provided for the dogs—which were, of course, instant celebrities, and had spent the four months feasting and being pampered by fans, tourists and reporters. No one knew what exactly had happened out there past Solomon, but the rumor was that some ferocious bears attacked members of Moon Chaser's gang, and he had perhaps unwisely fled onto the frozen river and drowned, along with his team. A tragic end—one that stoked the ire of gamblers across the country and invoked all sorts of legal wrangling as to the race's outcome.

But Delin was declared the uncontested winner. It made an epic conclusion, and the race would be talked about for years, and the story retold during every annual race to come.

When he had fully recovered, Delin proclaimed regrettably that he would not be racing again—he had done what he intended, had won the prize for Juneau, and had otherwise raced for personal reasons, which he claimed only one other man would appreciate.

With that, Delin took his leave of Dr. McCloud, and insisted that he had to head back to Juneau, then to return to his cabin in the wilds, and await word from Eloise. Already he feared he had been out too long—nearly a year apart. He had tried several telegrams but nothing came back. So, determined, he waited out the ice, and after another four months, he set off for home.

Chapter 27: Alaska - May, 1909

TWO LETTERS

WHEN HE FINALLY REACHED HIS cabin, the ice was beginning to melt. Flocks of geese were soaring listlessly overhead, and foxes, bear cubs and squirrels were emerging in the forest, watching the passing of the dogsled.

At last, exhausted from climbing behind the sled loaded with supplies for the season, Delin dug the melting snow away from his cabin door, entered and prepared to set a fire and warm the interior—when he noticed the two envelopes placed on the table, delivered some time ago, probably before the snowfalls.

His heart lurched and he stumbled to the table. He seemed to move at half-speed, barely able to lift his arms. And with every tear of the envelope his hopes crumbled. *Eloise...*

I have been away too long, he thought. And as he brought the paper to the light, he sensed something heavy and black settling on his shoulders, impatient for him to read on...

July 2nd, 1908

Delin, my dearest love,

Only three months have passed since I saw you off, and yet it feels like a lifetime. Words cannot describe the depth of my attachment to you, how your soul and mine merged up that northern world of yours, and how you melted the ice of my fears.

But you must forgive me, my love, as this letter does not contain good news. May God grant that I can write again soon and leave you in better spirits, and may He also forgive me for keeping something from you.

But I will get to that. First, let me tell you of the stir you caused here in the Capitol. Jericho Quitch has been removed from office! It's true. Reporters from the Post were in the audience that day, and afterwards they did some research. Found out some things about Comstock—like how he and his father ran their mines, and uncovered a host of deaths that happened there due to callous indifference. And yes, they did find a record of an unexplained murder—the body of an unidentified man, not far from where Benjamin Quitch and Caroline had fallen.

So Jericho is gone, but not punished. It's doubtful they could prove anything, but it was a cloud over his head, and his colleagues and constituents would not tolerate it. So he has fled—back into private business. And here is where I must warn you. I found out he has interests in Alaska and the Yukon. His fingers are in many pots—salmon, canneries, hunting, and yes—mining. Moving on from gold to copper now.

Look out for him, Delin. He'll be after you, I know it—determined to kill you for the disgrace you caused him. So I beg you, as morally callous as this sounds, if you are ever given the chance—if you have Jericho in your sights once more like you did on that beach long ago—do not hesitate. This time, just shoot. Kill him before he can kill you, for there is no other way with men like that.

Trust me, my love. You have more to live for now—and I desperately want you to live, to endure.

Even though for you, the pain of what I say next may make that seem meaningless. But you have to trust me, there is much for you left in this world—in fact, there is one final gift I am creating. One beautiful surprise. But you must be patient, and you must trust me. It will be waiting here for you, and should fate be kind, you will see it—and on that day you will finally understand the strength of my love.

But now I must tell you the truth, I must... There is so little time. You granted me more of that precious gift than I had coming; you gave me an unexpected reprieve. More than the doctors would have predicted. Your joyous optimism and boundless energy kept me going, rejuvenated my heart and soul. But some things can only be delayed.

My love, it is not my uncle who is sick. I tried so many times to tell you, but my fears held me back. And I did not, could not, spoil our bliss together. Maybe I thought that if I didn't give voice to it, we would never have to face this moment. But I was wrong. My body grows weaker, but my spirit is driving me on. I have much to do before the end.

Do not come for me, do not even try to respond. There is nothing you can do. They say this disease can waste you away in months—or it could take several years. I believe with all my heart that it will be the latter. Your love has given me reason to cling to every spark of life as long as I can.

I have so much to prepare. Your gift... you see, it's all that's motivating me. I am looking ahead, years and years after I am gone—for that is how long it will take to finish. After I have passed, the instructions I will leave behind, the notes, the words I write—they will finish the molding of your gift.

Oh, I wish I could see your face when you find it—or it finds you. I am smiling, smiling so hard, right now my love. For I do see your face, your straggly beard and shining eyes. I see you on that day, weeping with joy, and I am there with you—on that beautiful day in the future. I am there.

Goodbye, my love.

Look for me, late at night. Soon. I'll be in the aurora, shimmering behind the shields of countless spirits, side by side with your mother, with Joshua and all your dreams.

Look for me in those Northern Lights. As I will be looking for you.

Yours, Eloise of the Sun.

Delin had crumbled to his knees, sobbing by the time he reached the end. Outside, Prancer and Vixen were whining, scratching at the door, sensing their master's pain. He put his head on the cold wooden floor and read the letter again with shaking hands, desperately hoping it would be different this time—as if some nightmare pen had crafted the last one as a cruel joke and, having had its fun, the ink would rearrange itself into the proper words.

At the end, he threw the letter aside and got to his feet. How long? When did this letter come? He tore at the envelope, and saw the markings—last July. A full year her words had been here, waiting for him.

Oh God—was it too late? He could have gone to her! If not for that race, if not for his stupid idea of revenge—and the misfortune of illness. His blood boiling, he started to dash around the cabin, readying supplies, but then he remembered the second envelope.

With wobbling legs, he walked to the table and reluctantly lifted the parcel. It was stamped, THE SMITHSONIAN INSTITUTION, WASHINGTON, D.C. March 1909.

Two months ago, Delin thought, as he slowly worked open the flap. He pulled out the crisp parchment inside, then smoothed out the folds. He closed his eyes, praying intensely, but it was a prayer he never finished. As soon as he began, he sensed an emptiness waiting with those words—a cold silence as profound and lifeless as the arctic tundra.

Numb, he opened his eyes and read.

Dear Mr. Wetherwax,

It is with great sorrow that we write to you, according to the wishes of the late Eloise Griffith, spelled out in her last testament. She has passed from a long illness, 8 February 1909. Part of her estate has been willed to our Institution. As you are no doubt aware, she was in our employ for many years. It was her wish that we give credit to one who made possible her great contributions to our research.

It is not only for the wealth of notes, photographs and documents she has left to us, but also for the great amount of gold she has donated. This gold, she maintains, was a gift from yourself to her to do with as she saw fit. She instructed us to inform you that she—quote—"found where you secretly hid those two sacks in her apartment, and could she do so herself, she would have scolded you fiercely."

In any case, Mr. Wetherwax, on behalf of this Institution and its trustees, we offer you our greatest thanks for such a sizable donation. You are welcome here at any time—although, again, Ms. Griffith has asked that you do not return here until you—and again we quote, here—"know the time is right." While this is cryptic to us, we fully appreciate that you and Ms. Griffith understood one another.

With that said, we again humbly thank you, sir, and wish you well in all your endeavors.

Sincerely, The Smithsonian Institute.

The letter tumbled from his listless hand, and he sat, mouth open as his heart encased itself in a shield of ice.

He sat and stared, ignoring the crying of the dogs and the urgent scratching at the door. Ignored everything for the rest of the day, and far into the night, when at last, he rose, shuffled to the door and stepped outside.

He walked through the whining dogs, and as he crunched through the frosty snow, they followed, hanging their heads when they sensed his somber mood. They held back, following protectively at a distance, until he reached the edge of the cliff, and in the silver radiance of the valley and the moon-speckled ridges on all sides, he dropped to his knees.

And he looked up.

And he waited. And waited.

Finally, it came as if called. A faint glowing that started in the north, then shimmered across to the west, and left ripples in its wake. Green and blue and red, with twinkling afterglows it came, pulsing and twisting, unraveling in majestic waves.

Delin spread his arms, opened his mouth, and cried into the night, sending his sorrow up to the aurora, which seemed to tremble and flutter in response.

Chapter 28: Alaska - October, 1912

SHOWDOWN AT JADE MOUNTAIN

THREE DAYS AFTER HE HAD set out to stockpile some kindling and to fish in Beaver Creek before it froze, Delin returned to his cabin, ascending the path just as the first crisp snowflakes of the season poured down from the hazy afternoon sky. He almost reached the top before the dogs' growls caught his attention, snapping his thoughts from their mired despair.

And when he finally stopped short, just at the edge of the trees, with a sack of salted fish over his shoulder and some sticks under his arm, he cursed his carelessness. Maybe it's a deathwish, he thought, staring down at the fresh sets of bootprints leading up the path to his cabin.

"Back!" Delin called the dogs to his side as he dropped to a crouch. He lowered the wood and the fish, and as the wind blew in from the clearing and snowflakes patted his face, he slowly crawled to the cabin. For once, he was thankful he never put in glass-bottle windows of the kind other miners had used; no one inside would see him approach. The tracks led into his cabin, and already Delin could hear the men knocking things over, kicking at his supplies and possessions.

Blitzen growled, and his eyes—one yellow and one green—looked up at Delin, pleading to be released. The others all crept along behind, advancing like a gray-black tide upon unsuspecting ships. Keeping the dogs in place with a hand gesture, Delin made it to the side of the door. He took a deep breath and leaned against the wall, while he hefted a mining pick from where it lay on the ground.

He listened to the men, hearing their laughter as they rifled through his supplies, and he thought back on the past three years and almost relished a chance to actually meet some other people—even if they were enemies. He had endured out here alone since his return from Juneau, since opening those letters. Venturing out only to fish, and to make sure the dogs stayed alive. He lost weight, and his beard grew. Flecks of gray spotted his mustache and chin, and he avoided clear surfaces in the rivers, lest he catch a glimpse of himself.

Three years had passed, and nothing had changed. Every night he stumbled out to the cliffside. During the first year, he brought with him a bottle of whiskey or moonshine. When the supply ran out, and after it failed to help deaden the pain, he gave up trying to drink away the sadness; but still, every night he walked to the edge, sat and stared up at the sky. Whether it was cloudy or clear, and not just on nights the aurora announced itself. Even the dogs knew the ritual—after dinner and a nap, they would sit at the door and scratch and nervously patter about as he prepared for his nightly pilgrimage.

Now, Delin glanced over to the promontory, to the wooden chair he had erected for himself last fall. The thought that someone had decided to trespass here, to invade his sanctuary and callously root through his supplies, ignoring the miner's creed of keeping fellow cabins sacrosanct—burned at his soul. But for the first time in three years he actually felt a pulse, the semblance of life beating in his breast.

He risked a quick peek around the door frame—and saw the three men gathered around the main table, all staring at the open wooden box and the glittering revolvers resting inside. Why did I leave them behind? Delin asked himself, but he knew the answer—he didn't care. He had been tempting fate these past three years, and he was well aware of it. Let the Sesquat he knew was out there have its revenge. It had earned it, surviving those many attacks, enduring when all its brethren had perished. Who was Delin to deny that noble beast its due?

And more importantly, what did Delin have to live for? Oh, in the darkest of fits, he would recall Eloise's words... her plea for him to hold on, to survive and see whatever gift she had waiting for him. But sometimes, in the arctic desolation, when all life had seemingly ceased and nothing could be heard for endless miles, he would despair and just think about sliding off that cliff—the same edge that precipitously ringed the canyon and led trees hopelessly to its edge.

But somehow—always, when he was at the lowest depths of loneliness and sorrow, the shining Northern Lights would appear, gleefully sparkling above and filling his heart with an unrestrained joy. And the dogs would whine and come over and nuzzle at his hands and face, and he would wrestle them down and forget for a time.

But now, ducking back out of sight, he listened in.

"I told you this was his place," said a deep-set voice. "Just like Q said we'd find it."

"Jake, we're s'posed to be on the hunt for that thing."

"The snowcreature? Just a myth, my friend. You'll see, Q will get us all froze up here half the winter lookin' for it. You wasn't here last spring! We searched around the west face of Jade Mountain for six days in the ice."

"I heard," said a third man. "Still, if it does exist, Q will be the one to spear it."

"You mean, harpoon it—my God, can you believe he carries that twenty-pound gun everywhere?"

"Just clam up already. We found this place—and these guns prove it belongs to the other one we've been looking for."

"Q's been huntin' this guy longer than that snow demon."

"Well, at least he's for real. Come on, let's burn the place and wait for him to come back, and then shoot him dead, just as Q—"

But that was as far as he got. Delin shouted out, "*Ugiarpok!*" then spun into the doorway and hurled the pick with both hands. He then dodged out of the way as the dogs roared inside.

He saw the pick blade strike one of the bewildered men between his eyes an instant before four dogs pounced on the two others. Amidst the vicious snapping, snarls and screams, Delin leaned back against the log wall and turned his face up to the cold descent of snowflakes.

It took more than a minute for the growls and cries to stop, but finally Cupid and Dancer emerged, backing out of the cabin, dragging a still-twitching man with shredded clothing and great bloodied gashes in his face and throat.

Delin stepped over him and around the other two dead men. He picked up the Dragoons from their case, slid them into their holsters, then wrapped the gunbelt around his waist. As the dogs continued dragging the bodies out from the cabin, Delin tidied up, then went to the far wall and turned over the mirror he had reversed three years ago. After a long couple minutes staring down at the man looking back at him, he took a pair of scissors and started trimming his beard, and then moved on to his mustache and up to his hair. Satisfied, he stepped outside.

Delin glanced toward the distant peak across the valley, and with the noon sun he could make out the smoke curls that were usually visible, streaming from the Kendall Mills where they had been mining copper since 1910. "Jade Mountain", they called it, and at first Delin had feared for his privacy, but the miners so far had only worked the eastern mountain range, hauling down trees for their mine supports and fires. He knew they might venture out here one day, but Delin never thought the one to find him would be Jericho Quitch himself.

But now he knew who owned Kendall—or at least a significant share in it. Delin knelt in the snow, patting the dogs' heads as he gazed out over the distant peaks. He had tried to stay out of it, tried to be just who he was—a loner. A solitary nobody content to live off the land and to just exist until passing away like the ancient rivers. But knowing he was out there—so close. And hunting the Sesquat... could it be anything but Fate? Both of his old enemies together?

Delin stood. He took a rifle from one of the dead men and hooked the strap around his back. Then he set out toward the forest. Halfway there, he turned and held out his hands to the eight dogs following in his wake. "Stay!" he told them. "You can't go where I'm heading. Stay and guard the cabin."

He turned and continued walking, though he cringed when he heard their pitiful whines. Glancing back once, he saw that Dunder was on his belly, scooting forward and sniffing the air. Delin stopped and sternly held out a hand. "Stay!"

With that, they quieted down and stayed put. "I would spare you this fight, my friends," Delin said quietly as he entered the forest. "And I may not return..."

He found the hunters' tracks just as the hazy light behind the clouds began its approach toward the mountainous horizon. Walking briskly, eyes to the ground, gliding across the freshly fallen snow, he saw the distinct boot prints—ten, twelve pairs coming from the west. Joining up with six pairs from the south, heading up the ridge together. Delin climbed slowly, then sped up as he heard distant gun shots. He crawled up the final few feet to a large, knotty trunk of a spruce tree.

Just before he reached it, something scampered toward him; he dodged out of the way—just in time as two elegant reindeer bounded over the ridge. A beautiful doe and a stag with great wide antlers. They paused and regarded him solemnly, then snorted, pawed at the ground and ran off, hurriedly putting distance between themselves and the hunters. Delin let himself smile—he had been seeing more and more of these reindeer over the years, as Jackson's vision finally took hold. Eskimos were raising great herds, and some estimates even had them at over three hundred thousand strong.

Peering around the side, he looked down the tree-strewn series of hills, ridges and flatlands. Another gunshot echoed, and far ahead Delin made out the small forms scattered through the forest, all converging on one area.

Herding, Delin realized—they were herding their prey. Forcing it toward the edge of the cliff. He stood and searched for his retractable telescope and pulled it from his pack, leaned against the tree and sighted. Focusing past the thick snowflakes lazily swirling in his sight, he caught a glimpse of a black coat. He held the scope as steady as possible, and swept the view along, stopping briefly at each new hunter.

"Ten, eleven," he counted. "Fifteen... damn. Eighteen." And there—he held his breath. Locked in the circle of his vision: a man in a long fox-fur coat, his dark hair flowing down to his shoulders. An enormous gun rested in both hands—with a toggle-headed harpoon projecting from its muzzle.

"Quitch," Delin hissed, and the man seemed to pause in mid-stride; he glanced over his shoulder, then up to the sky as if a ghost had passed through his marrow. Then he lowered the gun, and pointed ahead, shouting something.

Delin followed his indication, sweeping the scope to the right. He passed it first, then drew back. And passed it again, only to nudge the scope slightly—and there it was. Almost blending in against the cloudy backdrop and merging with the snow along the hill. He saw the telltale scarring on its side: the blackened skin, the hairless flesh. And then he saw the red eyes, seething behind the swirl of snowflakes.

And another shot rang out, followed by two more. A section of the closest tree burst in an explosion of bark and sap, and the Sesquat ducked and snarled—just as something red burst from its shoulder and rocked it backward.

The hunters surged, all nineteen of them—hardly sporting, even for Quitch. Delin looked at his rifle, then thought about the Dragoons. He hadn't brought any extra shells. Twelve shots in the revolvers—and it looked like only three in the rifle. Fifteen he could take out—if he had perfect marksmanship.

Delin sighed. He was going to need some help from an old enemy.

He looked up ahead and decided on a suitable tree about halfway to the cliff's edge; he scampered to it unnoticed and began to climb. Pulling himself up branch after branch until he was about thirty feet high, he settled at an appealing forked limb that overlooked the land.

Four more shots rang out, and he could hear the men yelling to each other—and then, distinctly, he noted Jericho Quitch's voice shouting above them all. "Be strong and of good courage! Fear not, for the Lord is with thee!"

Now he's on to Deuteronomy, Delin mused as he lined up the sights in his right eye and closed his left. For an instant, he was back on the rooftop at Tianjin, sizing up his first kill.

Quitch's back was to him—the snow-flecked coat blowing in the wind. He was running, though, and making it difficult. But suddenly, as three more shots shattered the air, Quitch stopped and brought up the harpoon gun. He dug in his feet and aimed as his men circled around and pressed ahead to the cliff's edge—where the Sesquat roared and slapped at the air. One man got too close and as he fired off a wild shot, the creature lunged and tore off his head and part of his shoulder. Then it spun and fell upon another one; it bit down, then hurled the wide-eyed hunter over the cliff.

Delin focused again at Jericho standing there, preparing his kill shot. Delin hesitated, his finger trembling on the trigger. Should he wait, just another moment? Just let Quitch take his shot—let him kill this foul creature that had plagued Delin's life and his dreams since childhood? Mama's murderer.

But then Eloise seemed to be at his side, cupping her hands to his ear and whispering. If ever you have him in your sights...

And that was enough.

He pulled the trigger—just as Quitch tensed for his shot. After the recoil, Delin squinted and his heart surged. Quitch was flat on his stomach, that much he could see; legs twitching, the harpoon gun a short distance away. His men had turned, scanning the area.

Delin lined up a shot at the nearest one, and fired. The man in a black coat and cowboy hat rocked back with a cry and lay still. Then Delin aimed a little to the side at the next target—but cursed as soon as he squeezed the trigger.

"Shucks!" he hissed as the man moved at the last second and saved himself. Delin dropped the gun and was about to start climbing down when he grimaced at what he saw. Quitch was getting up. Moving slowly, but he was moving. Crawling toward his gun. His upper back had a blotch of red staining through the coat—but he was still breathing.

"Sorry, Father," Delin whispered as he dropped from one branch, then made his way down to the next. Men were shouting and gunshots bellowed, bullets ripping through the branches above. He climbed down a smooth section of the tree, then finally leapt to the ground, hitting the snow just as he ripped the Dragoons from their holsters.

Three men rushed at him. Delin crouched, extended both arms and carefully fired off three shots. All three hunters went down without returning fire, and then Delin was off, sprinting to the nearest cover—a section of fallen trees. Two more hunters raced to head him off, and the Dragoons again spit out their fury, and thick clouds of smoke whipped away in the winds. Delin jumped over their bodies and dove behind the trees just as shells flew into the trunks and bit into the snow.

Another horrible scream erupted back by the cliff's edge, and Delin used the distraction to peer around the cover and get off two more rounds while his nearest attackers were lost in fright—terrified of the beast at their backs as well as the unknown marauder in their midst. Eight down, he thought—plus the three at least that the Sesquat had killed. That left seven, plus Quitch.

He ran straight for the next set of frosted tree trunks, and wove his way between them, edging closer to the cliff. Somewhere ahead, gunshots blasted, men screamed, and Quitch's voice howled. "Depart from me, ye who are cursed! Into the eternal fire prepared for the devil and his angels!"

Delin swung around and ducked beneath a heavy-hanging branch. Ahead stood two men with their backs to him, rifles pointed ahead at the blurry mass of white fur. Delin stopped for a moment to admire the grace of the creature—how it moved and pounced from tree to tree, snapping at the hunters and swiping any within reach. Then he tiptoed ahead and stood with his arms spread wide, the Dragoons aiming at the back of each man's skull. He fired, and held steady as both weapons recoiled, and the men dropped without crying out.

He calmly walked through the smoke, and aimed again as a man ran wildly away from the cliff, his coat torn by long vertical scratches, and his chest a mass of blood. The man tripped and fell, and Delin looked away when he saw the body twitching. When he looked up, the Sesquat had another hunter in its grasp—slowly crushing the man's ribcage—but its ferocity seemed to be subdued. It stood only twenty feet away, and it had locked eyes on Delin.

The dying man gasped and then stiffened—and slid from the Sesquat's grasp as it bared its fangs and took a ponderous step toward Delin. The trees shook and a heavy dusting of snow descended between them. Delin glanced around—two men were approaching from the creature's side, and behind them, Jericho was struggling to rise, using the harpoon gun as a crutch.

With one Dragoon trained on the creature, he moved his other hand to aim to the right, firing once, just as the two hunters squeezed off shots. He heard a grunt of pain, and it took a few seconds to realize it came from his own mouth. He sensed a numbness spreading from his side, and looked down to see the hole in his coat—and the blood steaming out from his hip. Grimacing, he staggered back, and fired at the lone hunter who was stepping over his dead companion.

The Dragoon clicked on an empty chamber.

The Sesquat snarled and took another step. But Delin reacted instinctively, aiming with the other Dragoon—calculating that it had only two shots left. He fired, dropping the hunter just before he could shoot. The man rocked back and rolled down the hill, and Delin returned his aim to the approaching Sesquat.

Fierce red eyes burned into his soul and held him in near-shock, as the pain from his shattered hip spread. His hand trembled, the Dragoon wobbling as it leveled at the enormous hairy skull fifteen feet above the ground. Its fur pockmarked with bullet holes, blood streaming down its chest, the Sesquat snarled, and a foulness wafted over Delin and nearly made him retch. The thing's teeth sparkled in the cold, and a low grumbling vibrated from its chest and echoed from every tree.

And suddenly, its eyes narrowed, its nose crunched up—and it spun around to face the last hunter. Quitch stood unevenly on a slight ridge, balancing himself against a tree as he lined up his shot. Blood leaked from his nose and mouth, but his eyes were wildly luminescent. "Be sober, be vigilant; because your adversary the Devil walketh about, seeking whom he may devour..."

The Sesquat roared, tensed—and leapt.

Delin couldn't be sure, but he thought Quitch laughed as he rocked back with the recoil of the enormous gun. And the vicious spear designed to pierce the toughest, thickest whale blubber ripped into the monster, caught fast, and hurled it backwards. It was a blur in Delin's vision—a mass of fur, arms and legs, and a howling that shook the forest. Then a cruel thud and a piercing cry of pain and frustration.

There, pinned against a thick, ancient alpine, writhed the Sesquat. Caught on the six-foot spear, it thrashed and batted at the long iron pole protruding from its chest and fastened securely into the tree.

Keeping the gun trained on the Sesquat, Delin staggered toward Quitch—who had started to crawl toward his nearest fallen comrade. "Stop!"

Quitch paused, reaching for the dropped rifle only two feet away. The cliff's edge was just ahead—another ten feet, and dusk was spreading over the valley. Far away, on the other side of the ravine, stood Delin's cabin, a mere dot against the twilight-masked landscape.

The monster howled again and Delin glanced at it warily. The entire tree was shaking, grumbling with the Sesquat's efforts to free itself.

"Kill it," Quitch said, pointing as Delin stepped closer and put a boot down on the rifle. Holding his side with his free hand, Delin took another heavy step, as Quitch backed away, crawling closer to the edge. Breathing deeply, Delin's vision clouded, then cleared again. In his left hand, the Dragoon felt heavy, but still warm... and ready. It dangled, pointing at the ground halfway between Quitch and the Sesquat.

"Kill it, you idiot," Jericho said again, as he stopped on all-fours. Blood dripped from his mouth onto the snow.

Delin trembled. Somehow, above the screaming creature and the wind howling through the branches, he thought he heard the barking of dogs. He managed a smile, and tried to focus.

"Sorry," he said, looking at the glittering Dragoon. "Only one bullet left."

"Then use it!" Quitch shouted. "Put it into that monster's brain—or do you want us both to die by its jaws?"

Delin sighed, waving his arm in small arcs back and forth. On the tree, the Sesquat screeched and bent its head down and chomped onto the metal spike, then madly twisted its head back and forth until a metallic pop sounded just as half the harpoon broke away in its mouth.

"NOW!" Quitch shouted, as he reached a tree that angled over the cliff's edge. He tried to pull himself up, but only managed to turn back around and lean against it, facing Delin.

His attention still divided between the two threats, Delin wavered. The Sesquat, with an anguished, moaning sound, slid off the iron harpoon; after a weak cry, it freed itself, staggered to its knees, then tried to rise in a dizzy effort.

"Poison," Quitch said. "Enough to kill a whale, but it's barely touching that devil! Now do you see? Do the right thing, Wetherwax! Kill it now!"

Delin's hand trembled, and he moved the gun toward the creature.

"Yes," Quitch urged. "Do it!"

The snow whipped at his eyes, and the warmth of blood seeping down his leg seemed to soothe his thoughts. His arm wavered, and the gun aimed away again.

"Damn you, Wetherwax! You're living up to your reputation, always making the wrong choices." Quitch pulled himself up a little farther, unsteadily using the tree for support. "You're just like your father!"

The trembling of Delin's gun suddenly calmed, and the wind died—just as the sound of distant barking rolled over the hills. And Delin smiled as he tightened his grip on the Dragoon. He pulled it away from the shambling creature.

—and aimed it squarely at the chest of Jericho Quitch. In a cracking voice that spoke from his heart and vibrated through his soul, in words that beat back the numbness and pain and washed over years of aching regret, he said: "I only hope he thinks so."

"No!" Quitch shouted, and reached into his coat to pull out a glinting knife—

But a thick cloud of smoke blew into his eyes, and he slammed back into the tree as a force like a locomotive struck his chest.

Delin lowered the empty gun and dropped it, and stared impassively as the crimson stain spread across Jericho's sweater. His father's murderer fell to his knees, looking up at Delin in shock. Both his hands came away from his chest bloody, and he slid backwards, teetering on the edge of the cliff, his boots weakly scrambling for purchase.

"I..." he stammered. Took a sharp breath, and focused his eyes. "I... have fought the good fight. I have finished the..."

"Shut up." Delin stepped right up to him and, with a pained effort, lifted his boot and set it on Quitch's chest. "You are dust..."

"No," Jericho whispered through his golden teeth.

"Return to it," Delin said, and pushed. He closed his eyes, and just listened to the scraping, scrambling sounds, and then a sickening thump as Jericho bounced off an icy incline just below, and finally—the dwindling scream that went on and on until the wind gleefully took it up and sent it scattering about the valley.

With a deep breath, Delin dropped to his knees. He grimaced slightly with the pain, but it didn't seem too bad for some reason—hopefully the bullet had passed through his hip. He didn't know. He didn't care.

It didn't matter.

The ground shook. The trees trembled. And that fetid stench enveloped him. Hot breath at his back. A heavy shadow, blacker than the descending night, covered him like a shroud.

It comes to this, Delin thought, bowing his head. The back of his neck prickled in the heat from the Sesquat's breath, and the clattering of its teeth drummed in his ears. He took a deep inhalation, and closed his eyes.

Once again, he felt a sudden and deep connection with this creature; in a flash he was looking through its eyes, out through a sea of red, staring down at his own body kneeling there helplessly. The wind circled around beast and man, kicking up swirling vortexes of white, and masking for a moment the sound of the approaching animals.

The Sesquat cocked its head, and now it sensed them as well—those cursed creatures. Eight of them. Racing down the hill. Making those horrible noises. Coming to this one's rescue.

The connection broke and a grin settled under Delin's snow-patted mustache. He felt his body weakening, the numbness spreading, but he also heard them coming. On, Dunder, he thought giddily. On, Blitzen!

He rocked forward in the wind, precariously close to falling, then held on and righted himself, just as the shadow lifted and something snarled. He waited, expecting the brutal clubbing fist, the talons raking him in two, but they never came. Instead, he heard a scrambling, a desperate attempt to gain footing—then a cacophony of ferocious barking.

Delin looked to his right and tried to make sense of the blurry shapes—the great white figure in the snow, battling the darker, smaller forms that burst up from the ground and snapped at legs and arms, spun and launched again and again. Pushing the creature back, back—

Until, howling and flailing at empty air, dizzily trying to connect with the aggressive pack of attackers, it slipped and scrambled for purchase, reaching for anything but finding only ice and flimsy tree trunks.

With a final, desperate cry, its red eyes locked on Delin's—then it tumbled back and disappeared as the pack of yelping dogs made one last advance.

The snow circled around and around and caressed Delin's cheeks; the wind rippled through his hair, and then the dogs surrounded him, licking at his face, rubbing their cold noses against his skin, nipping at his clothes.

"Okay, okay," he said, after being dragged back from the edge. He fumbled around and found the Dragoon he had dropped, and with the dogs circling him, he stood and looked up the shadowy hill. Five miles back to the cabin.

Only five miles.

On a shattered hip.

He sat back down, and the dogs nudged close. "Just a little rest," he told them. "Wake me soon, unless you want to go get help from the mines."

Dunder barked. And Delin almost believed the dog might just do that. In either case, he wasn't going anywhere. Not just yet. He closed his eyes, and set his head against the warm fur of one of his dogs, as the others climbed up and over him and settled down to protect him from the wind.

His hand touched something sharp. He lifted the object and held it up, and a smile returned to his face. A tooth. One big, sharp Sesquat's tooth—broken off as it had bitten into the harpoon. Delin grinned and tucked it deep into a pocket. *If I live through this nigh*t, he thought, *I'll mail it to Dr. McCloud—he'll appreciate it, I'm sure.*

Then he settled down against the dogs. And he slept. And dreamed of a time long ago, of a night under heavy fur blankets, with Mama and Papa in the cot next to him, and the wind battling the roof of the Long House, and the fire slowly dying. And he vainly struggled against the pull of sleep, waiting, listening for the reindeer to come, and the gifts to be left behind.

He smiled, and drifted deeper into sleep.

BOOK FOUR

"I'm sick to death of your well-groomed gods,
your make-believe and your show
I long for a whiff of bacon and beans,
a snug shakedown in the snow
A trail to break, and a life at stake,
and another bout with the foe."

—The Heart of the Sourdough,
Robert Service (1874-1958)

Chapter 29: September, 1929

RETURN TO THE SMITHSONIAN

DELIN SAT AT HIS POST on the promontory, watching the scene far below, admiring the graceful descent and the picture-perfect skipping on the water's surface before the single-propeller plane turned and glided to a stop on the nearest beach. He had seen a few of these flying machines before—not many out here, but enough to be impressed again by man's ingenuity, conquering one last facet of nature.

Would that those things were around in the old exploration days, he mused. Could have made map-making child's play. He sat and rubbed the head of old Dunder—the fourth husky he'd given that name, and a collection of furry faces came to his mind, bringing a smile. This one was going on ten years old now—and might only have a few more good years left.

Know how that feels, Delin thought to himself, scratching at his beard—nearly all gray now—and rubbing his leathered, wrinkled face. He glanced over his shoulder and saw Cupid and Blitzen hanging back near the cabin, sniffing around the brush for field mice or other vermin. Three dogs—that was all he had left—but it was enough. No need to go sledding across the world every season. He just required some trusted companionship and help with hunting and fishing.

He sighed again, pulled out a thin licorice stick from his pocket and held it up to the sky, frowning. Couple years back they had started making these in different colors and a variety of shapes, probably trying to jazz up their image—as if licorice needed any help! He shrugged and put the tip in his mouth, licked it and chewed slowly. Same wonderful taste...

He waited for the men to make their way up the trail. Waited solemnly, enjoying the fleeting warmth of the summer sun, and staring as if hypnotized by the sparkling Yukon River as it tumbled its way north.

When at last the three men appeared, two of them wheezing and holding their sides as they cleared the forest trail, Dunder ran to meet them with his fur bristling and a deep growl in his throat. Cupid and Blitzen tore across the ground moments later, and finally Delin rose, his bones cracking as he stretched.

He smiled, expecting the men to run screaming from the vicious-looking animals—but a strange thing happened. The three dogs dug in their feet and came to a quick stop, sniffing at the young, red-haired pilot. They wagged their tails suddenly and leapt on him—to his utter surprise, and he tried unsuccessfully to fend them off before petting them.

Delin headed in their direction, shouting to his dogs, at last concerned about the visitors' welfare. "They don't take to strangers!" he yelled, but frowned unexpectedly when he saw their strange behavior. "At least, normally they don't. Must be the unusually warm weather today."

"Maybe," said the pilot, grinning as the huskies snapped affectionately at his face and playfully chewed at his hands.

Still frowning, Delin sized up the other two men: bookish and pale, their hands smooth and obviously unused to any manual labor. Their eyes darted nervously about, as if expecting some great prehistoric bird to swoop from the skies at any moment and carry them off to its mountaintop nest.

"Let me guess," Delin said. "You're looking for a guide, and you're from..."

"The Smithsonian!" proclaimed the heavier man, stepping forward and offering his hand. "Professor McPearson, at your service."

"How did I know?" Delin said, ignoring the hand. "What is it this time? Lose a housecat up in these woods somewhere?"

"Actually," said the taller man, "we're out here for you. Tried for nearly a year to send this invitation by post, but it seems..."

"I canceled that service," Delin muttered, "after receiving some bad news years ago. Best if no one can find me."

"It's been difficult," said the taller one, shrinking away from the wagging tails by his knees, "but with the help of our skilled pilot here, we managed to find your cabin."

"Thought it best to deliver this invitation personally," said the professor.

Delin narrowed his eyes. "Invitation?" Something tugged at his memory, a promise echoing through the halls of the past.

"Yes. There's an exhibit back at our Museum that you may want to see."

"No thanks," Delin said, biting into the last bite of licorice.

Hearing the crunching, the pilot looked up, then stood and reached into his pocket. He pulled out a black twisting strip of candy. "Here," he said. "Have another one. They're coming out with these in a braided shape now. Quite popular."

"No kidding?" Delin snatched it up, and yanked it away of the snapping jaws of Cupid and Blitzen. "Thanks!"

"You're welcome," the pilot said, and Delin tried to peer through the reflective sunglasses on the young man's face. Another good invention, he thought—sure beats wooden ice-goggles.

"So," Professor McPearson said, nervously looking about. "Can you accompany us? We have instructions to bring you back to Juneau, then we'll travel by train to Seattle where we can take the train back to D.C."

"I don't think so," Delin said, nibbling on the licorice. "I don't go out much anymore, and I'm done with Washington. Had a bad experience there last time."

The pilot choked on a laugh, and the others gave him a sharp look. "Yes," said the professor, "but this is really something you need to see. It concerns you, and we have strict instructions not to return alone. And we've come all this way..."

"Oh?" Delin asked. Turning and walking with a limp, he headed back to his cabin. "All that way? What did it take you in that flying machine? A couple hours? I'd have been impressed if you hiked even a fraction of the trail from Dyea. No. Again, I think I'll stay put."

"Sir!" the pilot spoke, taking off his sunglasses. His bright blue eyes sparkled with emotion and an excitement that his passengers lacked. "This exhibit they're talking about? You really should see it. It's something of a... gift for you."

Delin froze; he turned slowly, and the dogs lowered their heads and sat, looking between him and the young pilot. "A gift, you say?"

"Yes. She said you should be told about it, and that you'd come, if you were still able."

Professor McPearson nodded. "Mr. Wetherwax, we apologize that it's taken our Museum so long to accede to the late Ms. Griffith's plans, but the War, and restricted funding and all..."

"But it's done now," said the taller man, folding his hands as if pleading. "And the grand opening is next month. All we need is your approval."

"Mine?" Delin frowned. His head hurt, his mind was spinning, and the sun stung at his eyes. "Why?"

The pilot stepped in close. "You'll see."

Delin looked down at his boots, thinking. Remembering, wistfully, a time long ago. Finally, he looked up and sighed. "Do we have to fly?"

McPearson laughed.

The pilot nodded. "Too bad it's not winter, then we could sled to Juneau, I'm sure. But no, we need to fly, and you can trust me. I'm good at this."

Delin nodded. "I know. Saw your maneuvers." He glanced up to the sky, and followed the lazy spirals of the licorice-shaped clouds. "Someone will have to watch the dogs."

"Can we take them to Juneau?" asked McPearson.

Delin nodded. "If there's room in the plane, they'll follow me anywhere."

"There is," said the pilot, reaching down and scratching Blitzen behind the ears.

Delin sighed, a deep exhalation as he glanced around at his home, then stared out over the valley. "Very well. I always did want to see this land from the heavens."

At the dinosaur exhibit six days later, Delin made the professor and his colleague wait while he stood, leaning on the cane that he had carved out of a caribou antler several years ago. He stared into the hollow eyesockets of the great fossilized monstrosity, the childhood symbol forever associated with the end of his innocence. Delin narrowed his eyes and stared it down, relishing in the feeling that it no longer had any power over him in his old age.

Again he thought back to that bright day on the river, watching the mudbanks slip away, and he felt a notion of sadness for this creature, having been forced into the public's eye after so many millions of years in peaceful slumber.

"Mr. Wetherwax? This way please." Professor McPearson led him along, and slowly he followed around the central staircase and across polished marble floors, through the strangely unpopulated chambers. Their footsteps echoed somberly like Gregorian church bells, broken by the clicking of his cane.

At last, they came to a door set back and enclosed within an authentic-looking timber frame, shaped in a Deidesheimer square-set design. "Cute," Delin said, admiring the work as they passed through the appearance of a mine shaft entrance. Inside, they continued along a claustrophobic twenty-foot hallway with walls apparently carved out of solid rock. Delin noted streaks of imitation quartz spread about the walls.

Halfway to the soft amber glow at the end of the hall, Delin realized the drumbeats he heard were actually the thudding echoes of his heart. And when he finally emerged into a chamber of uncertain dimensions, he nearly fell over, supported only by the cane with both hands. There before him lay a pile of gold. Some of it in perfect bars, others in nuggets, and still more in heaps of dust and flakes. All of it glowing from some internal light source and bathing the room in flickering patterns.

Slowly, as the men tiptoed close to him on either side, his gaze swept around the room—or at least, the first room in what looked to be a series of chambers set apart by only half-erected walls, leading to other areas and other exhibits—all apparently related, and linked by the title above the pile of shining minerals—"SILVER & GOLD: THE STORY OF A NATION'S EXPANSION, AND ONE MAN'S CHRONICLE THROUGH HISTORY."

Stumbling forward, around the gold, he came upon a wall-length map of the West coast of America, showing the coastline and interior from Alaska down to Mexico, and across to a portion of Siberia and down the coastline of China. And across this three-dimensional map, detailed down to snow-capped mountains and crystal blue lakes, a series of red and blue lines were painted, carefully plotting a course from Mexico to San Francisco, on to Nevada, then up to Alaska, where the red line merged with a blue one, and traveled around the interior of Alaska and down to Juneau, then back to Nevada and on to Washington State to a snow-capped Mt. Shasta. Then back to Alaska, to the coast...

Delin choked back a cry, seeing the details of his travels laid out before him in a God's eye view. Too impatient to linger, he stepped around the wall and scuttled through a side entrance to a room where the first gold rush sprawled out before him in a series of exhibits—wax figures panning in a stream at one corner, surrounded by authentic rockers and sluice drains. In the other corner housed a reproduction of an early San Francisco cityscape. Authentic newspaper captions and photographs were mounted in glass frames on the walls, headlining everything from the first discovery at Sutter's Mill to the fiery blazes that nearly destroyed San Francisco. In the west corner a silent movie was playing against a white wall—and grungy actors stumbled about a series of creeks, working the earth and piling up their diggings.

Moving on, quickly observing the various realistic tools hanging on the walls—from long-handled picks to shovels, knives, spoons and pans—he then noted the large daguerreotype reproductions showing every facet of the Argonauts' journey. Next, he came to a section covering other rushes happening simultaneously—Australia, Oregon and Colorado. Here was a diversion on the methods of blasting and drilling, the development of dynamite and nitroglycerin, a view of a cave-in and statistics on miners' deaths throughout the decades.

Wordlessly, he continued on. In the next room stood a twenty-foot diorama of the Comstock seen from above, with miniature rail lines, boats transporting timber, and a scattering of stamp mills on the clay-molded mountains. Beside this structure stood the red-haired pilot—the young man Delin hadn't seen since they had deplaned in Seattle.

McPearson leaned over Delin's shoulder. "In addition to acting as our pilot to fly our naturalists about, young Joshua here has had a hand in several of the exhibits. He's got a keen eye for detail, and has been a great asset to our museum."

"Yes, yes," Delin said, oblivious as he stared in wonder, and continued walking. The next room was filled with nostalgic items from Juneau and early Alaskan history: replica quayaqs; a scaled-down molding of an intricately decorated Long House with an open cross-section; a trio of Raven-headed totem poles. On the next wall hung images of the whaling trade—harpoons and knives, miniature boats, and again—newspaper headlines and photographs as well as manifests and cargo lists. Next was a group of stuffed reindeer grazing along the tundra while a tiny missionary stood on a rocky outcrop above them, waving a Bible.

Delin barely noticed that the three men were following, silently observing him, and he only casually glanced at the heavy-set, well-dressed man in the next room. The man stood beside a life-sized reproduction of a dog team, complete with a true-to-life sled, with the animals posed in straining positions as a bundled-up driver urged them across a painted snowscape.

The well-dressed man came up to him and grasped his hand, shaking it vigorously. "Good to see you again, Wetherwax!"

Delin glanced into his eyes, frowning, and then tried to look around the man's head—to see the depiction of Nome and the photographic images of hordes of men depicted on the wall itself, over a realistic sandy beach. To the right hung a banner for the All-Alaska Sweepstakes, and headlines from seven major papers announced Delin's thrilling victory over the previous champion. His eye was pulled away—and there in the middle of the room stood an enormous replica of the treacherous Chilkoot Pass, with a long line of tiny climbers.

"Delin?" said McPearson, "do you know who this man is?"

Shaking his head, Delin took another look, realizing his hand was still in a tight grip with this stranger. "No... wait!" He bowed his head. "Oh my, I'm sorry, Mr. President."

"It's been a long time, my friend!" Herbert Hoover grinned and slapped him on the shoulder. He pointed over his shoulder to a series of stereographs on the side wall, beside a painted fresco depicting the fall of Tianjin and the Boxer Rebellion. "Good of you to come, seeing as how this was all for you!"

Delin stared around, open-mouthed, and peered toward the final set of timber-frames leading to one last exhibit. "But..."

"Lou will be here for the official Grand Opening," Hoover

said, "but as an advisor and contributor, I got the first peek. What do you think?"

"Astounding!" Delin said, still wide-eyed. "Who...?"

"But there's more," Hoover said, and held out his hand toward the direction they had just come. Delin looked—and a smartly dressed, middle-aged Oriental woman gracefully walked through the Smithsonian men. Head bowed, she tiptoed up to Delin, pressed her hands together, then bowed. She looked up into his eyes, then pulled something from around her neck.

Delin nearly fell to his knees, supported at the last second by Hoover, who lifted him, patting his back. "When you last saw this woman, she only came up to your waist. This is Hashi Lee, granddaughter of Matsei Xien."

"One of twenty-four," Hashi said, bowing again. The gold cross around her neck dazzled like a swarm of fireflies in Delin's sight.

"She immigrated here with her husband and four children, just last year. Naturalized citizens as of this week!" Hoover beamed at her and nodded, and she stepped forward and threw her arms around Delin's neck.

"Thank you," she whispered, then backed up and touched the cross. "I will always cherish this."

Shaking now, his hands trembling, Delin turned away, led on by Hoover toward the imitation mine entrance. "Come on, you're not done yet. And don't worry, being President has its perks, like some free time. The country's practically running itself. Economy's good—people are working. Things are looking good for my re-election!"

The mention of the presidency returned Delin's attention to his situation, and he thought of something to say. "My thanks, Mr. President, for what you did as Secretary of Commerce. Setting up those national parks and wildlife preserves were good first steps. Although... we're still waiting for statehood."

"In good time, my friend. In good time—heck, if things remain quiet around here I might be able to bring up the debate again at the next session of Congress."

They walked past exhibits depicting the boat-building at Lake Bennett, stepped through a reproduction of the Mounted Police Claim Office at Dawson, and passed a model depicting life at the Treadwell Mills on Douglas Island.

Then they stepped into the mineshaft and Delin took the lead, moving without even using the cane, hardly aware of the muted footsteps from the crowd following at his heels. And then he was out, and he faced a wall of tributes, personal and deeply touching, and again he nearly lost his strength. Already his eyes stung with threatening tears, and his throat locked up. Looking at him from across the room, in the softly-flickering candlelight from the log-shaped walls of what looked to be his own cabin—was an enlarged photograph, a familiar one. He and Eloise, surrounded by the dogs, posing at the Harris farm in Juneau, taken just before they had left for Washington—the one he had given her for Christmas.

And around the picture hung notes and aged letters, scrawled in Eloise's perfect penmanship and protected behind polished glass. And there—a replica set of the gold and silver Dragoons, hanging on the wall beside a picture of Samuel Colt. And here, on the bookshelf—a veritable library of classic literature, while on a nearby stand, a box of licorice.

But the thing that finally caught his attention and sent him staggering forward, was the glass case beside the exit sign, and the huge, white-haired, hunched creature inside. Posed in a bent stance, snarling with its great arms spread for an attack. Delin stumbled forward, his cane scraping along the floor as he made it to the glass and looked up into the Sesquat's frozen eyes. He took a moment to admire the detail—every hair and nail perfectly crafted and set. And then he stared into its red eyes, and was somehow not surprised to see his own reflection in the glass, superimposed on the beast's visage. His own haunted eyes looked back at him, his face merging with the creature's; and again he shared its mind and looked out at the world, this time through a glass cage—a noble oddity encased for all time.

Then he noticed the tooth hanging on the glass at eye-level, beside the sign describing the Sesquat—its different characteristics and the legends from around the world. The notes lamented the fact that no one had ever actually recovered one, living or dead—despite great effort. This tooth was all that could be found—and it was up to personal subjectivity as to its validity.

"How…?" he started to ask, when a shuffling sound and a light treading of feet made him turn.

"I donated that!" said the short, balding man in a yellow suit. Beaming, he folded his arms and looked up at Delin.

"Dr. McCloud!" Delin shouted and embraced the little man. He hadn't seen or heard from him since the race at Nome.

"Good to see you, old friend!" McCloud took a step back and peeked upward, trying to get a glimpse of Delin's teeth. "Looks like they held up okay, after all. I guess you were right about licorice!"

Delin laughed and wiped away a tear, even as new ones were forming. "What are you doing here?"

"Fortunate coincidence!" he announced. "Came in last month from Portland—where I'm practicing now, by the way. Big annual conference here for the NDA—National Dentist's Association. We're trying to agree on dental standards and working to increase our membership. I'm their Vice President, can you believe it?"

Delin chuckled and shook his head. "Now I've heard everything. Good for you!"

McCloud grinned like a thrilled schoolboy. "When I heard from your son about this exhibit, I just had to donate that tooth, and..." He looked at the shocked faces around the room. "What? What did I say?"

Delin blinked, then it suddenly registered. "My... what?"

Hoover slapped Dr. McCloud on the back of the head. "Idiot!"

"I didn't know!" he stammered. "I figured one of you would have told him..."

"No," said the young pilot, stepping around the men and standing before Delin. "I was waiting to see if he'd figure it out. The dogs almost gave away the surprise—they knew right away."

"My dogs..." Delin's skin broke out in a sweat and he stared open-mouthed as his emotions boiled over, and he finally registered the conversation from earlier, about this young man. "All this... you did this?"

"Well," he scratched at the back of his neck and then pushed red curls from his face. "It was a long time in coming—and I had to get it just right. When Mom died I was too young to remember her. Her uncle raised me, and every night he would read to me from her diaries and notes, and when I was old enough—he gave me her letters and finally, her instructions."

"Her... gift?" Delin whispered. And in his mind he had returned to that last night, where the moonlight filtered through her apartment windows and she whispered, Tell me a story...

The men around the room had stepped away, and everything else seemed out of focus, shimmering hazily, except this young man, his shining eyes—so much like hers, the breadth of his shoulders and the line of his jaw so much like... Papa's.

Delin gasped and felt faint; his mind replayed the conversation from that night, with her tears drying on his chest as she prodded him to tell her what name he would give to their child, and he had turned it around, saying she would make the perfect choice.

He choked on rising emotions that threatened to explode, and his tears fell uncontrollably. "She named you Joshua."

"Yes," he said, biting his lip and trying to hold his own emotions in check.

"She named you Joshua," Delin whispered, again. It is perfect. Oh, Eloise...

"I've missed you," Joshua said, and at last Delin moved, lunged forward and grasped his son and hugged him fiercely.

"I'm sorry," Delin said, struggling with the words. "I didn't know. I would have—"

"It was her plan," Joshua choked. "The final gift—and it was so hard to keep from looking for you. I'm sorry for not seeking you out earlier, but I had to make sure everything was perfect. Such strict instructions, and I had only the pictures, and my research..."

Delin looked around again, with wet eyes, even as his sobs and heavy breaths became deeper and deeper, even as his cries turned to laughter. And he embraced his son once more. "It's so perfect..."

They held each other for a long time, alone as the others gave them a chance to catch up. And then, invigorated, Delin brought them back in, and took the whole group on an enthusiastic odyssey of the exhibit, recounting story after story and adding personal touches and revelations that had been overlooked. He filled in the gaps of history, regaled them with the untold story of the Nome race and the showdown with Jericho, and then he and Joshua sat alone in the replicated cabin, under the photo of Eloise, and over a specially delivered bottle of brandy, the two of them talked long into the night and on into the next morning.

Chapter 30: Juneau - May, 1933

TEACHING THE TRADE

THE SLED CAME TO A gradual stop, kicking up crisp snow. The dogs whined and looked back to where Delin sat, strapped in on the flatbed. He clicked his stopwatch and lifted his goggles.

"Not bad!" Accepting a hand, he struggled to his feet and stepped off the sled, leaning on his cane as he turned and grinned at his son. "An hour and seventeen minutes flat. You're a natural! Especially since these aren't even your dogs!" He looked over to farmer Willis, who waved from the ranch. Beyond, the city of Juneau basked in the spring mists.

Joshua, panting, bent over and caught his breath. "We hit a good patch of slick ice back there—helped out a bit."

"Nonsense," Delin said. "I have to admit—you could be great. Better than your old man, even."

"Come on," Joshua said. "You know that flattery isn't going to work—I've got to get back to Washington."

"Oh, I know that," Delin said, waving off the idea as he turned and held out his arms for Dunder, who came limping over from the nearby shed; the old dog had been watching the race jealously and wistfully, recalling fonder, younger days.

Joshua looked on, and his eyes misted over, watching the old, limping dog and his father. Dunder's tail perked up, and its ears lifted as Delin stroked its muzzle. "You know," Joshua said. "You could come back with me for a time, and..."

"Nah," said Delin. "Washington's in the midst of all that turmoil. Great Depression, they're calling it now? Poor Hoover, got the brunt of bad luck."

"Yes, but the new guy—Roosevelt—he's going to pull us out of it, don't worry."

Delin shot him a sideways glance. "From what I hear, he wants to stop the minting of gold. Make it illegal, even, for citizens to hold it."

Joshua swallowed hard. He had hoped his father would have been so isolated out here that he might not have heard that bit of recent news. "Just a temporary measure. People are too worried—they're all hoarding their gold, not spending it, and it's killing the economy. The government—"

"Bah!" Delin turned away, grumbling. "Let 'em try to get me to give it up! Alaska's not even a state yet. Damn them if they think they can impose their laws on me!"

Joshua shook his head, smiling. "You'll never change."

Delin sighed, then turned to face him. "Listen, you go on and get home. Don't worry about me. You don't have to come visiting twice a year, you know. You've got your own life."

"Dad..."

"No—what about that girl you were telling me about? Sarah, was it?"

"Yes, Sarah, she..."

"Good name. Means 'Princess' in Hebrew. You love her, I can tell."

"Yes, but we have time, and..."

"No!" Delin fixed him with a strong look. "Never think that. Never count on time being there for you. Go to her, and live, just..."

"Dad," Joshua whispered, and went to him. Hugged him close as Delin shook his head of gray hair against his son's shoulder. "Maybe," Joshua said, "I'll bring her up next year. We can have an outdoor wedding."

"I'd like that," Delin said. And Dunder woofed.

Together, they walked back to town.

On the way to the wharf and the waiting steamship, they passed through a crowded Front Street and a busy marketplace that was surging in the first week of true spring. Shops of every kind had their goods out in the sun, and people everywhere were shoveling snow from the streets so cars could pass and trucks could get in and make deliveries.

"Hey!" said Joshua, pointing to a colorful stand with painted Zodiac emblems on its banner. Delin looked, and frowned at the old woman sitting there alone without any customers, just shuffling a deck of large cards and smiling a toothless smile at them.

"They've got some of these fortune tellers in the fairs in Washington. What do you say, dad? Want to know what's in the cards?"

Delin snorted and pulled him ahead.

"Sorry, my boy, but I just don't think destiny has anything left in store for me. And I wouldn't have it any other way." He hugged him again and pointed his cane at the enormous steamship waiting ahead. "You, on the other hand, have exciting things ahead of you."

"Dad, I...

"Wait until you sail off, then open this." He handed Joshua a heavy item wrapped in brown paper and tied with twine.

"What is it?" Joshua hefted it. "Feels like about ten pounds..."

Delin smiled. "Something... a pair of things, actually... that belong in our family always. I hope, for you, that you never have to use them as much as I have. Keep them for show—and for impressing that lovely Sarah girl of yours."

Joshua blinked away some forming tears. "Every noble gift..."

"Yes, yes," Delin said, and then held out another bag, pulled from inside his coat.

"This one," Joshua said with a frown, lifting the bag, "seems more like twenty pounds."

Delin nodded. "Whatever you do, keep that away from Mr. Roosevelt's clutches."

"Dad, I can't."

"You can, and you will. Take good care of yourself. Start a family, and live your life."

Joshua squinted in the sun dazzling off the glittering water. "You know, you're wrong about what you said back there. About destiny being done with you."

"No, I'm not."

"Yes. You see, that exhibit back in Washington—it's inspired a lot of people. You're famous now, more than even after that race.

Almost a household word."

Delin grumbled something and stroked Dunder's snout.

"Dad, you're famous—and your name will live on, through stories, legends."

"Nonsense," Delin mused, absently waving him away. "Now get going, I've got a long walk back to the cabin."

"For God's sake, Dad. Take the train at least up through Eagle, and..."

"Goodbye, son," Delin said with a final smile, and turned and limped back down the street, with Dunder following slowly at his side.

Epilogue - December 24, 1933

THE HUSKY PADDED SOFTLY IN the crisp snow, approaching the promontory where the Master sat in the night, like always. The dog limped, treading gingerly on its bad leg, sniffing at the ground while above, the brilliant constellations twinkled at its approach. It paused, sensing the cosmic wonder that twisted and unfurled in the midst of all those infinite stars, undulating in greens and blues and reds, a silent kaleidoscope of such intensity as rarely graced even this bountiful arctic sky.

Nonplussed, the dog continued walking, eager to reach its master. It hadn't been fed yet today, and its stomach grumbled. The routine hadn't been followed. Maybe it had been forgotten, but that never happened. So the dog approached, cautiously sniffing. The Master sat in the chair, staring skyward.

Dunder's tail wagged as it neared, and its nose sniffed at the air wafting over the man from the cliff's edge. Finally, the old dog stopped by the chair and its tongue licked the hand that dangled from the armrest.

The breeze stopped, and the air hung still and cold. Crisp and pure, almost sparkling with anticipation.

The dog licked the cold fingers. Nudged the icy flesh that had turned a sparkling blue, matching the frostings on the man's beard and the icicles which perched on his nose and clung to his eyes—which were wide open and flickering with the wondrous pulsing of the aurora.

Dunder whined and hung its head. It turned in a small circle, then curled up by the side of the chair, where it sighed, and whined again, and looked up at the shimmering magnificence in the heavens.

"There's gold, and it's haunting and haunting;
It's luring me on as of old;
Yet it isn't the gold that I'm wanting
So much as just finding the gold.
It's the great, big, broad land 'way up yonder,
It's the forests where silence has lease;
It's the beauty that thrills me with wonder,
It's the stillness that fills me with peace."

—*The Spell of the Yukon*, Robert Service (1874-1958)

END

Author's Note:

In this novel, I have tried to be as faithful to historical facts as possible. For the most part, the historical figures were in the places and times I've described. For example, Herbert Hoover spent several years in China as a geologist for the British consulate, and he and his wife were caught up in the Boxer Rebellion (where the American military actually did stumble upon a vast hoard of silver); the missionary Sheldon Jackson made it his personal quest to bring reindeer herds to the Alaskan wilds; and Jack London ferried gold rushers to the Klondike. I took liberties only with Samuel Colt (not knowing for sure if he ever made it to San Francisco in the early 1850's); however, his creation of a unique set of Dragoon revolvers is fact—one of a pair is on display at the New York Metropolitan Museum of Art.

And there really was a terrible avalanche on the Chilkoot Trail on the date I've presented here, where over sixty men lost their lives. I embellished only on its cause.

There is only one other point where I would beg historians' forgiveness: the Whaling Fleet disaster, such an integral part of Alaska's history, actually occurred some twenty years earlier than I have presented it. To fit Delin's timeline I had to again take a small, hopefully understandable, liberty.

Made in the USA